The Medicine Woman

by

Deidra Whitt Lovegren

ISBN: 978-1-962187-00-8 (Paperback)
ISBN: 978-1-962187-01-5 (eBook)

Any references to historical events, real people, or real places are used fictitiously. Names, characters, and places are products of the author's imagination.

Book design by Blue Marble Publishing
Illustrations by Russell Norman

First printed edition 2023.
Blue Marble Publishing

deidrawhittlovegren.com
bmpublish.com

Dedicated to my students and bored high school students everywhere

The Medicine Woman

Chapter 1

Lincolnshire, The Free State of Florida

With her sharp machete, the Medicine Woman hacked dry palmwood into kindling for another funeral pyre.

"Take this stack to the longhouse," she ordered one of the younger boys—one who normally jumped at her commands. Seeing him move lethargically, she strode over to him and felt his forehead with her forearm.

He was burning up.

She looked at the boy, her one gray eye missing nothing. Covered by a brown leather patch, her other eye socket remained empty, the remnant of her father's final abuse.

"My head hurts," the boy muttered, picking up the palmwood as best he could. His slurred speech was hard to understand.

"Stick out your tongue," the Medicine Woman commanded.

The boy complied, showing her his swollen tongue, covered in tiny red dots. Soon, the dots would grow much larger before bursting into raw open sores. The sores would spread all over his body, painfully, as the virus in him raged.

"Is it the pox?"

She nodded. The boy frowned, resigned to his misfortune. He'd seen so many others die of the disease already. Yet, he'd watched lucky ones—like the Medicine Woman—go about their days unharmed. Some of the children whispered that the Medicine Woman had sold her soul to the devils for her continuing good health. They said the devils had taken her eye for payment.

The boy didn't believe them.

"Should I go to the longhouse?" he asked.

The Medicine Woman nodded again.

"Should I take the wood with me?" he asked, desiring to be useful, even in his weakened condition. Useless things did not fare well in

Lincolnshire.

"Take half of the wood. I'll take the other. We'll walk together," the Medicine Woman answered, more softly than she had before. She placed one of her callused hands on his thin shoulder.

He'd be dead in a week.

Ten years.

It had been a decade since the fall of the United Authority, the death of her father, the loss of her eye. It had taken time to acclimate to her new perspective. The Medicine Woman had to relearn how to track objects, judge distances, and perceive depth, but no one heard her complain.

When frustrated by her limitations, she could be found behind the apothecary, throwing her knives at a target. *Thwack. Thwack. Thwack.* In moments when self-pity threatened to undermine her judgment, she took Patches out on a long ride through the southern end of the plantation, soothed by the red clay and rolling hills.

Unbidden memories of her father replayed in her mind as she threw her knives. The Warlord of Tallahassee had been a wicked man—a liar, a thief, a murderer. The thought of her mother's torture at his hands made the Medicine Woman want to kill him again, albeit more slowly.

It was a shame to kill some people only once.

The man had been delusional right up until the end. *I am your father. I am your father,* the warlord had pleaded for mercy before he died. *You and I can rule this colony together. You and I. Together.* He had held out his arms to his daughter, offering her a rare smile, one that showed his rotted and missing teeth.

"Declare your allegiance to no one!" The Medicine Woman had thrown her father's words back at him before impaling his skull. *In retrospect, she thought, that particular piece of advice was the only thing of value the Warlord of Tallahassee had ever given her.*

Her stepfather, Lincoln, and his commander, Fortinbras, had purged the Illuminati Pagans from Tallahassee, establishing a utilitarian society that functioned as well as it could after the end of electricity.

Lincolnshire's citizenry thrived under Lincoln's stewardship, his fairness notable among the warlords in the South. The community had been spared the worst after the collapse of the United Authority. The resultant power vacuum had been filled by Darius and his consolidation of unaligned MilitiaMen, ushering in a dark age not seen since the Second Reconstruction.

Occasionally refugees would make it across the borderlands, having heard Lincolnshire was a fair and tolerable place to live for those who were willing to work. Lincoln listened to their stories of the Pagan brutality, chilling testimonies from hopeful NewComers. Any of their tales of Darius' exploits would have engendered compassion, even in the most hardened of hearts.

Ensuring the continuity of the community's safety, though, had never been easy, as rogue Floridian chieftains attempted to regain control of the region. Fortinbras faced incursions from the North, too, his seasoned troops proving more than a match for ragtag bands.

The young men of Lincolnshire were required to serve with Fortinbras for civil defense training; the young women were taught civil subterfuge and military psychological operations. Fortinbras found teenage girls particularly good at both.

All were required to learn the healing arts from the Medicine Woman, as well as what berries, fungi, and venom could kill a man or even a squad of soldiers.

On occasion, Darius sent spies deep into the former penal colony, but few returned to him with the ability to walk. Fortinbras reserved Lincolnshire's harshest punishments for captured spies, often flaying them alive, staking their semi-conscious bodies along the borderlands crossing—a stark reminder to others that Lincolnshire was an autonomous region.

On the whole, Lincolnshire had been left in peace. *Pax Lincoln*, the citizenry called it; it was welcomed after the last wars. Craftsmen and tradespeople arrived, ready to work, ready to live in a relatively safe and secure community.

The Illuminati Pagans had more pressing concerns than Lincolnshire. Even Darius quit wondering where the Medicine Girl had gone, becoming less concerned over time that she would show up unannounced in his chambers holding his own jeweled dagger to his throat. He was more preoccupied about his tenuous grip on power.

Consumed with empire-building after easy victories across the South, Darius assumed most of the country would fall in a similar fashion as the southern townships had. But lawlessness had exacerbated social ills, and Southerners were ready to give up whatever liberties existed for a modicum of security—especially when liberty brought rampant starvation and invasive LandPirates. Almost everything west of the Mississippi Arroyo proved ungovernable, with chaotic mobocracies led by unstable personality cults.

The North was another matter, he thought.

Until more propitious times arrived, Darius felt content in his efforts to solidify the South. Hand-lettered placards posted outside most southern communities declared their allegiance to Darius and their operation under the aegis of the Illuminati Pagans. The signs were more than enough to make scofflaws and PadFoots think twice, the high taxes paid into Darius' coffers providing a provisional peace.

After overtaking the remnants of the United Authority, Darius felt the North looked ripe for conquering, too, but he was wary of expanding too quickly. Consolidating his power and fortifying his particular unique style of government, slowly and carefully, would pay off better in the long run for the Illuminati Pagans—and himself. He'd long served men who moved too rapidly and trusted too much.

Darius vowed to do neither.

Sometimes at night, Darius left his empty bed and paced, looking at the wide leather wall map he had artisans hang in his bedchamber after the fall of the United Authority. He ran his fingers over the western lands, the far coastline jagged with approximations, as cartographers were at a loss where the boundaries lay after California had fallen into the sea.

Moving east, he reached his fingertips as high as they could go, a place where the snows still fell regularly.

Before the last wars, the United Authority had conquered Canada, proclaiming it New Virginia, a bountiful land rich with wildlife and game. After the invasion, Canadian insurgents triggered core meltdowns of the former nation's nuclear power plants. The resulting sightings of two-headed, hairless beavers, and beakless Canada geese made hunting unpalatable, no matter how much hunger raged. Aquatic life had ceased as radionuclides settled into the sediments.

Darius moved his hands still further, as if in a trance, feeling the topographical marks of the lands north of the ruins of Richmond. Rumors of the prosperous villages had reached his ears. *Maybe his advisors were right.*

Maybe it was time to move to the North.

"I need more purple pitcher plant," the Medicine Woman muttered, using the last of her supply to make a steam distillation. There was precious little left in her gardens and more was needed as Lincolnshire grew sicker every day. She was tired of burning corpses. "Purple pitcher plant, Megs. Bring me some!"

Her assistant, Megs, mollified her. "We're out, Meddy. The boys have been out looking for it all day—"

"Megs!" the Medicine Woman shouted, filled with unchecked rage. "Tell those boys to look sharp and not get sidetracked, poking frogs or eating blueberries. Send the girls, too. Send anyone who can wade in the bogs. Tell them to dig in ditches or any place with standing water. If I don't have more of it, the pox will spread. It's the only thing that seems to help—"

"Who else can help?" Megs asked.

"Check the WaterCenters. Talk to Mamacita in the main kitchen. Everyone isn't bedridden, Megs. Not yet, anyway."

"What should I do first?"

The Medicine Woman looked at her assistant in utter disgust, biting her lower lip like General Chapman used to do.

"Do *something*, Megs. Just do something..." The Medicine Woman walked away, cursing under her breath. "And don't come back here without an armful of purple pitcher plant or the pox will be the least of your worries."

Megs stormed out of the apothecary, the little shop where the Medicine Woman spent the majority of her days, alone, mumbling to herself.

Few could handle the Medicine Woman's dark moods like Megs.

It was said when the Medicine Woman's mother Mika died, the Medicine Woman's remaining eye became a darker shade of gray. After years of abuse, broken and burnt by the Warlord of Tallahassee, Mika passed away in her daughter's arms.

After her mother's passing, no one called Mika's daughter "the Medicine Girl" anymore. Soon, the Medicine Woman became the most feared person in Lincolnshire. Often short-tempered and cross, she only listened to Jasper or Lincoln—and rarely even then.

From Lincoln, the Medicine Woman had wrestled the power to exile members from the community for infractions she deemed unacceptable, primarily those who impeded public health. From Jasper, she would reluctantly take advice on how to be more diplomatic, but only if that were the most efficacious way to get what she wanted. She was loyal to both men, as no one loved her more than they did.

The longhouse was built for those in the community whom she felt should be quarantined, whether it was a case of cholera, head lice, or the sniffles. Anyone determined contagious was housed until the Medicine Woman deemed them fit enough to return to service in the community at large.

In the hospital at the longhouse, she trained attendants who labored under the Medicine Woman's demanding tutelage. They learned her methods quickly, as she did not tolerate fools or laggards. Twelve colony-hour days were common. Sleep was often a luxury.

With clean water and improved medical care, the community burgeoned under Lincoln's steady governance and the Medicine Woman's watchful eye. Over time, there were fewer stillbirths and infections, less pain, and easier deaths. Yet the Medicine Woman rarely rested on her accomplishments, often aggravating others in her relentless quest to do what her mother had taught her: alleviate suffering.

As the years passed, the Medicine Woman became obsessed with sanitation, pestering Lincoln to build outhouses further out than he had planned. She demanded trash burns three times a week and Fortinbras' troops to dig wells and drainage ditches.

Sometimes when Lincoln saw her marching across the green to his office, he snuck out the back. The Medicine Woman and Fortinbras had so many run-ins that Lincoln forbade them to be in the same room together. Fortinbras kept to his domain of security, leaving a wide berth between himself and the Medicine Woman.

Even Jasper knew when to let her be.

Megs scurried off to the WaterCenters, waving down the head attendant. The Medicine Woman had been instrumental in reviving the potable water trade that her father had begun in the former penal colony. She had expanded his meager efforts on a wider scale by supplementing the evaporation process with other techniques, such as sand and soil filtration.

Megs understood precious little about her efforts, preferring to hunt and gather whatever bark, berry, or blossom the Medicine Woman needed for her potions. Her curiosity did not extend beyond ensuring she was chastised as little as possible.

Megs walked into the BoilingRoom where large vats of swamp water were being processed to provide a steady supply of clean drinking water for the community. Although boiling water was a laborious process, it proved to be the most reliable and consistent method.

There weren't many workers on the main floor, as so many had fallen ill. Those who managed to recover from the pox returned to the vats, scarred and spent. It would be months before the afflicted would return to full strength.

To the chief attendants, Megs repeated the Medicine Woman's edict.

Everyone who could be spared needed to gather purple pitcher plant. Within moments, several of the WaterWorkers left their positions to head into the woods and swampland, empty buckets in hand.

Megs encouraged them to hurry.

The Medicine Woman hated to be kept waiting.

"Your fever is down. When was the last time you vomited?" the Medicine Woman asked her latest patient.

"The last time you made your possum and leek goulash," Jasper replied, attempting to laugh before she swatted him.

"You are an awful man and I hate you." She kissed the top of his head, then pulled over a stool to sit by his bedside.

"You hate me for getting sick. You despise weakness."

She opened her mouth, then shut it. *He wasn't wrong.*

After the death of Mika, the Medicine Woman had taken to living with Jasper, hoping for a child of her own—maybe one with gray eyes. She delivered most of the community's babies, training her attendants to do so in her stead, but she yearned to hold her own child, one who looked like the man she lay next to each night, the only person who could silence her with a smile.

"Open your mouth," she demanded.

"Say please." Jasper teased her.

"Jasper, please, I'm tired," she wearily confessed. "I need to see if you have ulcers in your mouth. Don't aggravate me—that's what Megs is for."

"You torment that poor girl."

"Megs is stupid."

"Megs is not stupid. She tolerates your temper, which is more than most people do."

"Jasper, only half the community is in any shape to do anything, and the remaining half are demoralized and exhausted. We're sick and tired of being sick and tired. We're afraid of catching the pox, and we're weary of burying the dead."

"Sounds like you have a case of compassion fatigue," he replied, holding her hand. "Which magical plant can cure that?"

"I do not have compassion fatigue—I have regular fatigue. Now, dammit, open your mouth."

"I'm sorry," he apologized, his handsome face flushed red with fever. "I'll open wide. Ahh."

The Medicine Woman looked down her partner's throat, shaking her head. She pulled out an old plastic thermos, a quarter full of tonic, and placed it in Jasper's icy hands.

"Sip this every 15 minutes, even if you don't want to. Even if your throat burns. I'll wipe oil on your skin to prevent scarring once the blisters fully form."

"Is this from the purple pitcher plant?"

"Yes, the extract is in both," she explained. "And to answer your next question—no, we don't have much left in the apothecary. It seems to be the only thing—"

Jasper put a hand on her knee.

"You need rest," he advised.

"Rest? There's no resting now—"

"If you don't take care of yourself, then you can't take care of the community," Jasper said measuredly. "And if you get sick, you can't take care of me. I need you to take care of me. I always have."

She smoothed his blonde hair, thinking of the day she met him on the scrapping field, needing his badly injured leg amputated. She frowned at the heat that radiated from his forehead.

"Jasper," she murmured, her head low. "Lincoln's recovery is taking longer than I expected. His face is scarred—so badly scarred. His fever isn't breaking, and I'm—I'm afraid he may relapse. He's riddled with pox from head to toe..."

The Medicine Woman slumped against the wall near Jasper's bed. They both remained silent for a time.

"So, is that what comes next—after the rash?" Jasper slowly pulled up his sodden shirt. She looked over to see his chest blistered, covered in fluid-filled pustules with small indentations in the center.

"That is how the disease progresses, Jasper. Those sores will scab over and leave scars. Use the oil. You don't have too many on your face and neck."

"If I come out of this looking ugly and pockmarked, will you still love me?"

"You're ugly enough now," she replied, affectionately patting his arm. She took a clean cloth and wet it from a basin. She squeezed the excess water out, folding the cool damp compress and laying it across his forehead.

"I'll monitor your recovery myself."

Jasper weakly reached out for her wrist, holding it as tightly as he could.

She looked down. His eyes were kind as always, showing neither fear nor regret.

"Am I going to die?"

His question made her throat constrict.

"You aren't going to get away from me that easily," the Medicine Woman griped, rearranging his bed covers. "And if you think you can run away from me, I'll cut off your other leg."

She held out the thermos to him, tacitly ordering him to drink. Like most of Lincolnshire, Jasper obeyed her without much complaint.

The Sylvanians prided themselves on being independent, overthrowing the New Yorkers after so many of them fled west when Manhattan burned. During the last wars, scores of dirty bombs rendered many of the eastern port cities uninhabitable. There weren't enough potassium iodide tablets to prevent the initial die-off. Those who could move to the West did, causing friction with the local populations, especially in the Sylvanian capital.

Since then, the Sylvanians kept to themselves, well aware of the

Southern MilitiaMen and their atrocities. A figure they couldn't take seriously, Darius, seemed merely to be an opportunist, cobbling together the remnants of what passed for civility south of the Mason-Dixon Line.

The Sylvanians were orderly and relatively prosperous compared to the South. They traded with inhabitants all the way to New Virginia, keeping their borders secure, their people fed. But as the New Yorkers had brought their diseases from the East, now refugees did likewise, fleeing the Illuminati Pagans in the South.

A few humanitarian groups took in whomever they could, but soon blackened and blistered corpses lined the Five Seven Nine, the main walkway through the heart of Sylvania. The medical care they had was rudimentary, ineffective against the pox.

"What do you think?"

Papa Jack, a beast of a man, stared out of the Westin Hotel's paneless window, overlooking the Allegheny River.

"What do I think about what," Papa Jack grumbled.

"What do you think about using our reserves? We need to stop the endless stream of pox refugees." Sounder indicated the entry points on a hand drawn map placed before him. Voices murmured their varying concerns.

"How many arrived today?" Papa Jack asked, silencing the side chatter.

"Maybe a dozen," Sounder replied.

"Are they all sick?"

"Hard to say."

Papa Jack looked at the CouncilMembers, all lifelong friends who sat with somber countenances.

"Thoughts?" he asked.

The CouncilMembers were not sycophants, but trusted colleagues and partners-in-arms. Each represented a section of Sylvania, between the Seven Six to the Seven Nine. All had an equal voice. But Papa Jack made the final decision.

"Send the MilitiaMen down to the immigrant camps," one man advised. "We can scarcely feed ourselves, and there isn't any work for immigrants to do—even if they are healthy. It's too big of a risk."

"We have enough to share. Perhaps we should be merciful? We could use day laborers in the fields. Perhaps we can offer them an indentured servitude?"

"The Southerners are filthy, diseased, and depraved. They aren't redeemable. I say we butcher them for the hogs."

"Our wives and daughters won't be safe."

"They're families fleeing to safety, not bands of criminals. How can you paint them all with such a broad brush?"

"How can you be so idiotic and trusting?"

The CouncilMembers's discussion continued, loudly, unabated.

"Enough." Papa Jack raised one of his meaty palms. The room returned to order.

"Sounder, you had an idea about keeping the pox out of Sylvania?"

"I do." Sounder rejoined the circle. "Hear me out. I know a Temporary Wife Keeper who's never had a problem with disease, venereal or otherwise. It's one of your assets, Papa Jack. The Black CatHouse II."

"Yeah, I know it. Run by two women," chimed another. "Mama Mitzi and Jalen."

"That's the house. I asked the Keepers how they did it, and she told me there was a Southern girl who knows how to use leaves and flowers and twigs to keep lady parts healthy. She'd taught them how to prevent pregnancy. She knows how to cure sores and lesions."

"How does that help us, Sounder?" Papa Jack asked. "How does that help us fight the pox?"

"The girl knows how to cure all sorts of diseases. Apparently she taught the United Authority's MedicMen before Richmond fell."

"Didn't help them much," a voice called out from the back. The men laughed. Again, Papa Jack held up a hand.

"Explain, Sounder."

"I say we go get the girl. She can teach our MedicMen all she knows. When she's done training them, we can set her free to return home or we can keep her on. Either way, we need to know what she knows. If not for this pox, then how to prepare for the next one."

The men silently considered what Sounder had proposed. Like war, plagues often made their unwelcomed rounds, especially in winter.

"Gentleman?" Papa Jack inquired. "How do you feel about this proposal?"

"Aye," came several voices from the back. They were soon joined by the others affirming Sounder's plan.

"With no objections, I would like you to handle this matter, Sounder. Let me know when the girl arrives."

"One question," one of the men asked. Papa Jack nodded for him to speak. "Where is this girl who knows so much?"

"In the panhandle of the former Florida Penal Colony," Sounder replied. "The place they used to call Tallahassee."

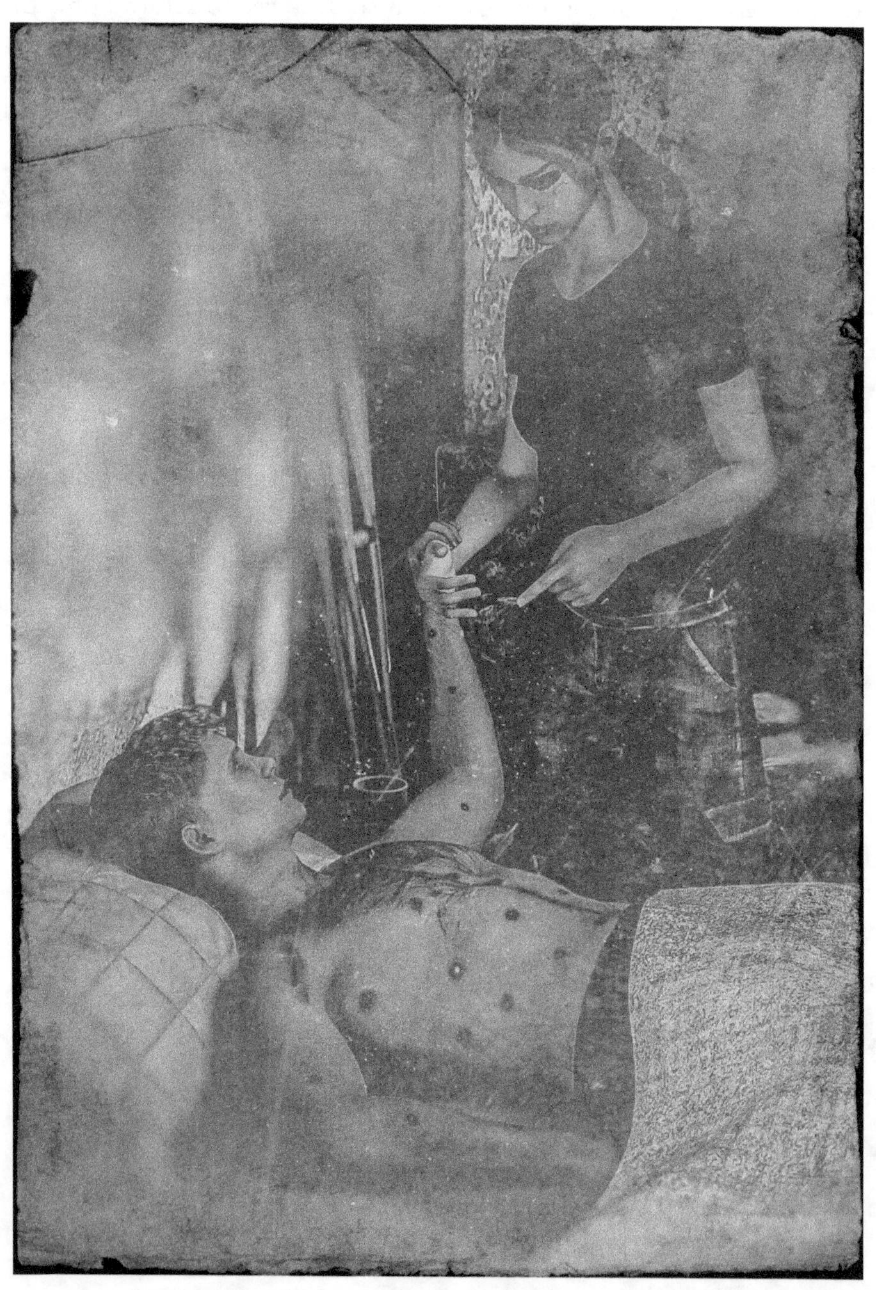

"And if you think you can run away from me, I'll cut off your other leg."

18

Chapter 2

Silver Lake, The Free State of Florida

It took two colony-hours to ride to Silver Lake, the place where Lincoln had asked to be interred. Ringed by tall trees, Silver Lake's white sandy beaches were warmed by the spring sun. The few bald eagles left in the region reigned from their nests, looming large over the smattering of songbirds who fled in their wake.

Lincoln had loved taking Mika to Silver Lake before she passed. The two of them would ride double on his favorite steed, a tawny Belgian draft horse. He had loved feeling his wife's arms wrapped around his torso while galloping through cypress, oak, and tupelo trees. He would cover her strong brown hands with his larger black ones, protecting her as he should have from the Warlord of Tallahassee.

Had he known the extent of Mika's abuse, he would have saved the Medicine Woman the trouble of killing her father. Despite his strength and stature, Lincoln succumbed to the pox, blinded by corneal ulcers, weakened by fever. His last few days were dark and painful. The Medicine Woman had sat by his side, using every ointment, unguent, and elixir from the cupboards of her apothecary to give her stepfather any modicum of relief.

Alleviate suffering, her mother had taught her throughout her life. In this case, she felt the directive keenly. The Medicine Woman had pots of steaming water close to Lincoln's bed to help him breathe. She made turmeric tinctures. She used the remaining purple pitcher plant extract—all in vain.

"It's hard to breathe," Lincoln whispered to her.

"You have pneumonia," she explained. "I was hoping for a simple case of bronchitis."

"Neither one of those sounds good." He offered her a wry smile. His handsome face was marred with weeping sores.

"It's *not* good, Lincoln. Now breathe deeply for a count of ten. If you cough, that's a good thing. Cough up as much fluid as you can."

She watched him drift in and out of a restless sleep.

"Mika?" he called out, weakly, in a delirium. He reached out to touch the Medicine Woman's hair.

As the years went by, the Medicine Woman had grown to look like her mother. Lincoln squinted to see her face, most of it in shadow, her stoic expression belying the gravity of his illness.

"Mika?" Lincoln's hand reached out to touch her forearm.

"No, Lincoln. I am not Mika, but she will come for you. When she does, go with her. There is nothing more that you need to do here. You can go."

Lincoln nodded, grateful for her words, relief spreading across his face. After establishing plantations and overseeing the health and welfare of his people, the idea of being finished brought him great peace.

Having attended many deathbeds, the Medicine Woman understood that assuring people that their work was done made letting go easier. Ideally, a child or spouse offered comforting words to the dying. Most seemed to pass more peacefully when they felt their duty to the mortal realm was complete.

On the last day of his life, Lincoln lay prone, quiet, still. He offered no movement or sound as the Medicine Woman rubbed warmed lavender oil on his pockmarked skin. She never knew whether it helped him or not, as Lincoln lay motionless with a tight grimace on his face.

When his breathing slowed and became labored—when the death rattle came, the Medicine Woman took her stepfather's ravaged body into her arms. She cried for the good man who loved her mother, who made Mika's last years joyous though her mind and body were broken. She wept for Lincoln's children who'd been murdered at the Warlord of Tallahassee's command, during his thuggish raid on a peaceful people.

Yet even as the Medicine Woman felt grief wash over her in waves, her heart hardened. The vagaries of life threatened to undo her; the inability to control any aspect of mortality made rage build up inside her.

In her anger, she'd run through the swamps late at night with her small machete and slashed at things that moved. In the morning, she'd bandage her gashes and bruises, avoiding Jasper's worried looks.

After lashing out, her final response to Lincoln's death was one which had served her well: she chose not to feel anything. The feeling of being useless sowed bitter seeds in her gut, causing her to grind her teeth at the futility of all things.

After Lincoln breathed his last, she walked out of his sickroom without another word. At her brusque departure, Lincoln's attendants covered his body in fresh linen, tying the ends securely, offering up prayers of gratitude for the good man's life.

The following morning, a small retinue followed the Medicine Woman to Silver Lake. She rode on Patches, leading the Belgian draft horse, Lincoln's body strapped across its back. Behind them rode Fortinbras, Mamacita, and a cadre of loyal retainers who were well enough to journey west.

They traveled in the fresh spring morning to bear witness to a rare leader who prospered during difficult days, an unusual warlord beloved by his people.

The Medicine Woman scanned the horizon, wary of what lurked at the edges of the swamp. As nature reclaimed more of the land, animals could be seen foraging in the sandy soil—turtles, alligators, turkeys, armadillos.

A few of Fortinbras' Scouts had spotted a bear. One of his men made the suggestion that they use the bear in dispatching a few of Darius' spies, regularly found lurking on the perimeter of Lincolnshire.

The Medicine Woman scowled at them. There would be other times to talk about torture and death.

Stopping at a shady grove by the lake, the Medicine Woman dismounted. The others followed suit.

"Over there by the oak," Fortinbras called out to his men, shovels in hand, preparing to dig Lincoln's grave. "Make it deep," he ordered. The idea of animals mauling Lincoln's body distressed him, as Fortinbras had seen too many battlefield corpses exposed to the natural elements.

He walked towards the Medicine Woman; both watched the men labor.

"It would have been easier to burn his body," she remarked in her matter-of-fact way.

"I think Lincoln had enough of fire in his life," Fortinbras muttered. "This is a more fitting end. A peaceful end."

"An end is an end. There isn't much difference."

Fortinbras wanted to object, but he found talking to the Medicine Woman frustrating and pointless. Regrettably, he had weightier matters to discuss with her. He'd considered softening what he had to say, but if anything, the Medicine Woman appreciated his bluntness.

"Lincoln asked me to assume the leadership of Lincolnshire. He'd dictated his final—"

"Good," she said.

"Good?" Fortinbras was gobsmacked by her indifference. He'd been prepared for a fight.

"Be the Warlord of Lincolnshire. You'll continue Lincoln's legacy in good faith. Let me do what I need to do and stay out of my way."

His jaw dropped. *Did she think he needed her permission?* Fortinbras wanted to respond but thought better of it. He gave her a curt nod, a gesture to make the mutually agreed upon transfer of power complete.

With Lincoln's grave dug, two attendants removed Lincoln's tightly shrouded corpse from the back of the Belgian draft horse, reverently carrying it to the pit. The Medicine Woman walked over to watch her stepfather interred, his large frame emaciated after weeks of illness.

Fortinbras took out a flask, nipping a bit for himself before pouring a good measure onto the ground. "To Lincoln, a fair leader in a terrible world. May the gods reunite you with Mika in the heaven of your choice."

"Amen," called out a few of his men.

"Would you like to say something about your stepfather?" Fortinbras asked the Medicine Woman.

"No," she replied. "There is nothing to say that will change the fact that Lincoln is dead."

She turned from the group, mounted Patches, and rode alone along the lesser trails.

She returned to Lincolnshire late into the night.

The door to the apothecary slammed open, awakening Megs who had dozed off in the middle of the morning.

"Oh!" Megs cried.

"*What?*" the Medicine Woman said, instantly irritated at the startled girl who looked at her like a demon.

"N-nothing," Megs muttered, cowed into silence.

The Medicine Woman was an imposing figure, almost six colony-feet tall, broad shouldered, thin as a rake. Her hair hung down her back like a curtain of black satin, pulled off her angular face by a bit of twine. Her one gray eye blazed, missing nothing. Her leather eyepatch gave her a menacing look when she frowned, head often tilted to improve her peripheral vision.

On her person at all times were her knives, some visible, others not. Megs had seen her slay spiders and vermin without turning her head, her knife splitting their frames neatly in two.

"Nothing? Nothing happened while I was gone?" the Medicine Woman asked, incredulously. "I left you with a half dozen things to do."

Megs amended her remark. "Actually, not nothing. While you were gone there was something. A lot of something. In fact, a lot of everything."

The Medicine Woman pursed her lips. "Megs. Breathe. Start at the beginning. I have no idea what you are talking about."

"Okay." Megs looked at the floor, taking her time to gather her thoughts.

"Now tell me what happened while I was gone."

"Purple pitcher plant!" Megs cried, her arms wide. "Some of the boys found a huge cluster by the cesspit." Megs opened a wicker basket to show her.

The Medicine Woman walked over to feel the verdant stems. Each stalk had a solitary flower at the top, dark with maroon petals. She inspected the hollow gibbous leaves that acted as a pitcher, collecting rainwater, trapping insects at the base where they were digested by the carnivorous plant.

She offered Megs a thin smile as she ran her fingers over the stiff, downward pointing hairs that prevented insects from leaving, once they were enticed by the goodies at the bottom of the pitcher.

She remembered boobytrapping a staircase once using exactly the same method with a satisfying effect.

Clever plant.

Sounder wasn't stupid. He'd been Papa Jack's faithful friend since their fathers established Sylvania in the ruins of Pittsburgh after the Second Civil War.

As little boys, he and Papa Jack had watched as the descendents of Eastern Europeans united against external forces, beating back both the New Yorkers and the United Authority, forming an independent colony—much like the Sovereign State of Texas. For the most part, other groups had left the Sylvanians alone, letting them entrench in the Alleghenies.

Broadbacked and wiry, Papa Jack only trusted his CouncilMembers, consisting of men who'd been boys together in the darkest of days. They'd seen neighbors strip bark off of trees to eat. They'd seen children disappear.

Older, bald-headed, and stout, Papa Jack's mouth was perpetually set in a thin line, whether he was pleased or disappointed. Under his rule, food had become abundant in all seasons, shared among those in the tight-knit community.

Against man's natural inclination to stratify, Papa Jack carried on the legacy of his fathers by ensuring his people equitably received according to their need. Though Sylvanians numbered only a few thousand, the Northerners marked them for their resilience, their allegiance to one another, and their indefatigable work ethic.

Even in the winters where tales of ManEaters trickled down from Classical Massachusetts, the Sylvanians found ways to survive without giving into sheer barbarity. They knew how to survive—even thrive in the good years, as Sylvanians were mostly hearty sons and daughters of old coal miners.

Sylvanians still labored in the defunct mines to dig for fuel, although the anthracite coal near Philadelphia burned better. However, Philadelphians were an anathema to the Sylvanians, who regarded their eastern cousins as having all the worst qualities attributed to the NorthMen. The two camps had long decided to ignore one another.

"How many Scouts should we send South?" one of Sounder's councilors asked.

Sounder calculated how long it would take to ride from Pittsburgh to the panhandle of the former penal colony. He also added up how much it would cost in tribute to pass through the different territories and regions. *Getting the girl would be expensive, but Sylvanian medical knowledge was far too limited,* he thought, *and she would more than make up for the initial expense.*

There had been a failure to transmit medical knowledge as the OldOnes died off. Of course, when one's entire day solely consisted of keeping the populace fed, the niceties of medical care and education went by the wayside. Yet now, Sounder used his political clout to advance the cause of general welfare. He was tired of seeing Sylvanians needlessly die.

"How many, sir?"

"Three. I need three Scouts who travel well together on horseback. It'll take them five colony-weeks to make it that far South—assuming the weather holds. Hurricanes seem to brew year round in the gulf."

Sounder's people had been displaced Cajuns from Louisiana, run out before the entire state had been declared environmentally unsound. In his nightmares, he remembered his aunties with goiters the size of melons and his uncles with cancerous skin lesions that peeled off in chunks. They'd continued to fish in the toxic bayous even after the Second Civil War.

"I'll bring in a team. Would you like to select three Scouts yourself?"

"Of course," Sounder snapped, irritated at the attendant's question.

How was that even a question?

❖ ❖ ❖

Jasper's lungs were weak.

"I don't want to do this," he complained, but the Medicine Woman was never easy on anyone—especially Jasper.

"I don't care what you want to do. I'm telling you exactly what you will do. Now, lie down."

"Okay. Are we done now?"

"No. Put one hand on your belly and one on your chest."

"There. Are we done now?"

She frowned at him. "If you are going to act like a child, I will treat you like one." She rolled him over and slapped him on his backside.

Jasper wheeled around, grabbing her about the waist, pulling her towards him. He kissed her frown until she relented and kissed him, too.

She pulled back and looked at him.

"Practice deep abdominal breathing. Now."

Jasper nodded.

"Breathe in, hold it. A little more, hold it. Breathe out through your lips while I apply pressure here."

He started to cough while she used her strong hands on his stomach. The cough was still worrisome, but incrementally better.

Jasper grabbed her hand and kissed it.

"Megs is coming over with some eucalyptus leaves that I want to steep for you." She combed his hair back off his face with her fingertips. "But she won't stay long," the Medicine Woman whispered in a low voice, kissing Jasper full on the mouth.

He grinned.

"Now breathe," she ordered.

As usual, Jasper complied.

❖ ❖ ❖

"Since the worst of the pox is over, Fortinbras ordered the CatHouser's to move towards the western part of Lincolnshire. He wants the main property for families. This did not go over well with the CatHousers since—"

"Megs?" interrupted the Medicine Woman.

"Yes?"

"I think Jasper needs to rest. I'm sure he appreciates you catching him up on all the town gossip while he's been recuperating."

"Oh," Megs apologized. "I've stayed too long. I'm sorry."

"Thanks, Megs." Jasper grinned. "It's good to know that the more things change, the more they stay the same. Sounds like Fortinbras has the exact problems that Lincoln did."

"But they respected Lincoln," the Medicine Woman added.

"They respect Fortinbras, too," Megs said.

"He gets respect because he leads the MilitiaMen. They respected Lincoln because he cared for them."

"I think you are being a bit unfair. Fortinbras authentically wants the best for his people," Jasper suggested, knowing how the Medicine Woman hated to be corrected, especially in front of Megs.

The Medicine Woman gathered up the peas she was shelling and walked out the back door of the apothecary. *How easily people moved on,* she thought.

She caught movement out of the corner of her eye, on the edge of her peripheral vision.

No one with good intentions moved that fast or silently.

She felt for the knife strapped to her ankle while moving in the opposite direction from where she felt the danger was, circling around the house.

Jasper was still bedridden. And Megs. *Megs.* Through the open windows, Megs could be heard gossiping away, yammering on to Jasper about the most mundane things.

As the Medicine Woman peered around the corner of the apothecary, she spied a nondescript white woman about her age approaching the front door, thick cudgel in hand.

It made no sense. A cudgel? *Was the woman planning to beat her to death?*

The Medicine Woman had learned to heal from her mother, but she learned to kill from her father, watching the Warlord of Tallahassee's grim brutality ever since she was young.

She had little time to react. *Was the Scout's purpose to observe, injure, or kill?*

Obviously the Scout had staked out her home. She appeared to move too confidently about the area.

For a moment, she almost called out, scaring the young woman away. *But then again, if the Scout had been a man—would she have hesitated to dispatch him, especially if he were armed with a deadly weapon?*

The Medicine Woman lunged low, using her small machete to cut deeply across the back of the Scout's right knee. The Scout gave an anguished cry before collapsing into a heap.

"Four minutes," the Medicine Woman muttered, standing over the Scout. "I've severed your popliteal artery. You have four minutes before you bleed out. Who are you and why have you been sent to kill me?"

The Scout rolled over into the fetal position as gouts of blood spurted from her leg. She tried in vain to hold the nearly severed limb back into place.

"Eve?" Jasper called out, using the nickname Jalen had given her.

Megs threw open the front door and shrieked to see the Medicine Woman covered in a spray of blood, her steely gray eye glaring at a gory body. She nudged the body with her foot.

"Tell me why you are here," the Medicine Woman demanded, kicking the dying Scout in frustration.

"Should I get a tourniquet?" Megs asked, teary-eyed, frantic.

"Nope," the Medicine Woman replied, kicking the corpse to the side of the road. She entered the apothecary and began boiling water in a large kettle.

She had grown to dislike bathing in cold water.

The second Scout waited until the Medicine Woman was knee deep in the swamp, on a perpetual hunt for purple pitcher plant. The apothecary's cupboards were bare, and although the pox had moved North, she had found the tinctures she made from the purple pitcher plant were good for other ailments. A diuretic, hepatic, laxative, stomachic, tonic—the purple picture plant was becoming her favorite cure-all.

She bent down to pick a plant before feeling the hairs prickle on the back of her neck. As usual, she acted instinctively, pulling out a knife strapped under her arm, slashing back in a tight arc.

This time, she managed to cleanly cut the spinal cord at the base of another young woman's skull. She, too, carried the same type of cudgel.

"Another one," the Medicine Woman exclaimed, entering the apothecary. She tossed the Scout's weapon to Jasper who studied it closely.

"Much like the first," Jasper remarked. "These are both made of Norway Spruce." He held up the finely crafted weapons, made of hard, creamy white wood with a hint of yellow to the fine, even textured grain.

"Well?" the Medicine Woman asked.

"Your friends are from the North." He looked gravely concerned.

"There is no one I know from the North."

Jasper walked over to comfort her, but she waved him off.

She could take care of herself.

Jasper felt well enough to tend to the smaller animals, feeling more at home with the chickens and rabbits than the larger livestock. He managed well enough on his wooden leg, only using a crutch now and again for the more uneven topography around Lincolnshire.

The Medicine Woman grinned, as he made his way down to the main village, glad to see him upright after being bedridden for so long. When his vital signs stabilized, she allowed him to resume limited chores.

She couldn't lose Jasper, too.

As he walked away, Megs appeared, smiling, in fine spirits.

"Good morning!" she called out, sailing into the apothecary a bit later than expected. She munched on a large nutty cinnamon roll, fresh from the corner bakery. It was the size of her hand.

"That's quite a feast," the Medicine Woman remarked, wondering if the handful of berries she ate at dawn would last her through the morning.

Megs gave her a funny smile, giggling with pleasure. "I brought you one, too."

The Medicine Woman paused. *Thoughtful of her*, she mused.

Gleefully, Megs presented another pastry wrapped in a clean cloth. The two sat in the apothecary's back kitchen table on two rickety stools.

"Thanks, Megs." *The first bite was delicious.* The Medicine Woman groaned with pleasure. The pastry was buttery, sugary, rich, decadent.

"Of course," Megs replied, enjoying a quiet moment with the Medicine Woman that didn't involve her being reprimanded.

"Look, I know it's been tense these past months," the Medicine Woman admitted. "With the pox. With Jasper being ill. With Lincoln—"

"It's okay," Megs said, touching her arm. Megs giggled, uncontrollably.

The Medicine Woman looked down at her own arm. *It wavered.* When she went to touch it, her hand trailed slowly, leaving iterations of itself behind.

"Don't eat—" the Medicine Woman started to speak, dropping the nearly finished roll from her hand. Megs stared at her, eyes unfocused.

A young woman with blonde dreadlocks walked in the front door of the apothecary, as if waiting for the appropriate time to make her entrance.

The Medicine Woman, incapacitated, felt a cold wave of fear run through her. *She could not move.*

Dreadlocks noticed the panic behind the Medicine Woman's one good eye.

"If I wanted you dead, you'd be dead."

"Who—" The Medicine Woman couldn't finish her sentence. She

also couldn't place the woman's accent.

"It doesn't matter who I am."

"Who—" She tried to speak again, looking over at Megs, who had passed out on the table. The Medicine Woman's eyes teared up.

"You aren't dying," Dreadlocks assured her. "Your breakfast pastries contain henbane seeds, not hazelnuts. You'll probably sleep for a day or two. We'll talk then."

"I need—" *What did she need?* Her mind was shutting down. She struggled with maintaining rational thought. Her mind was ablaze with questions.

How much did I ingest of this narcotic? Could she reach an emetic and warm water and powdered charcoal? Will I wake up? Will I see Jasper again?

Jasper. Her final thought was of the only man she had ever loved—the only man whom she trusted—right before a black, inky sleep enveloped her.

"You'll probably sleep for a day or two. We'll talk then."

Chapter 3

Rockdale County, The Kingdom of Georgia

Dreadlocks drove her team of horses up the Three One Nine, pulling off the main thoroughfare as night fell. Before she dismounted, she checked the covered wagon, noting what moved in the dusk.

Her companions had been silent most of the way. *Smart*, she thought. *Reserve your strength for when you find a more opportune time to attack.* That's what she would have done, too.

Dreadlocks let the Shetland ponies feed in the rich clover, abundant after the spring rains. She stopped to refresh herself as well, drinking from a large plastic tumbler, a container proven indestructible over the years. It had been handed down from her grandfather, who still lamented the end of the Steelers GamePlayers.

She stretched, leaned against a utility pole, surveyed the landscape, haunting and bleak in the sunset. The long journey back to Sylvania had proven uneventful so far with only a few highway stragglers on foot, staring enviously at her horses. One passerby looked as if he were calculating the odds of waylaying her, but Dreadlocks shook her head slowly while they passed. The look on her face was so unsettling that he melted into the brambles.

As in most parts of the country, the terrain was littered with assorted refuse, useless hunks of plastic, scrap metal. Rusted hulks of cars lined the highways. Plastic debris choked waterways and vacant lots. Farms were wild, overgrown, untended, reclaimed by the elements. Former homes were charred and caved in. Portions of land were either flooded or drought-stricken. Rib cages, skulls, and long bones lay scattered across numerous scrapping fields.

After the fall of the United Authority, the land looked as exhausted as its people. Though large scale battles had ceased for the most part, skirmishes often broke out between regions, clans, and individuals. She'd passed by gods knew how many recent horrors, the stench of the dead and dying hitting her long before the grotesque tableau of butchery.

Skittish gleaners scattered whenever she rode too close to them. Before Richmond fell, scavenging from the dead merited a death sentence. In the aftermath of anarchy, it was well worth the risk when no MilitiaMen were near.

Dreadlocks decided she hated the South and couldn't wait to return to the comforting embrace of the Allegheny Mountains. There was no Papa Jack here to ensure order.

That was the main thing that bothered her about the South: its lawlessness. NorthMen had their faults, but their ClansMen united in a common cause. True, internecine conflicts occurred as resources were limited, but on the whole, she'd trust a NorthMan over a feckless Southerner any day.

Dreadlocks pulled out her sack of provisions. Pork jerky. Dried apple slices. A few handfuls of shelled nuts. Before she left the apothecary in Lincolnshire, she'd taken all the foodstuffs along with the Medicine Woman and Megs. She cut pieces of goat cheese, popping them into her mouth, one after another.

After eating her fill, Dreadlocks wandered over to the wagon. Her two companions appeared stiff as cordwood in the bed of the wagon, breathing deeply, moving little.

Getting them into the wagon had been hard enough. She had awkwardly hoisted them, one at a time, over the side rails of the wagon. They fell in like sacks of sweet potatoes. The indigenous one was tall, attractive, but mostly all knees and elbows. She was especially hard to maneuver until Dreadlocks trussed her limbs together.

The younger girl, Megs, was pliable as taffy. Dreadlocks threw her over her shoulder, deciding to take her along in case Papa Jack needed an attendant for his medical director. If he didn't want Megs, Dreadlocks would drop her off at a Sylvanian CatHouse or off a bridge.

As the two females had ingested an enormous amount of henbane, Dreadlocks frequently stopped during their departure from Lincolnshire to check on their vital signs. Eventually, their heartbeats quit racing as the toxins began to work themselves through their systems. Bathed in sweat in the cool evening, Dreadlocks cleaned up the women's urine, excrement, and vomit, placing both Megs and the Medicine Woman on their sides to avoid choking. Papa Jack would never forgive her if they died in the most idiotic way possible.

She hoped they wouldn't experience any more hallucinations. The cries of the younger one had been shrill and unnerving. Dreadlocks had little patience for people out of their right minds, even if she had caused the distress herself. Regardless, she wasn't entirely sure Megs would make it to Pittsburgh, having annoyed Dreadlocks to no end with her moaning and whimpering. Out of frustration at the last stop, Dreadlocks repeatedly kicked Megs in the side until the young girl covered her head and wept quietly.

The Medicine Woman occasionally moved, restless in her ropes. Dreadlocks thought about loosening her restraints, but decided against it. *The tall bitch killed two friends*, she thought, gritting her teeth. If it were up to Dreadlocks, she'd return the favor in a more creative fashion.

But Papa Jack and Sounder waited for her return, and there wasn't anyone she feared disappointing more than Sounder—even Papa Jack. Although both were exacting in their commands, Sounder's hazel eyes were unflinching, hard to read.

As for Papa Jack? He was particularly fond of Dreadlocks, treating her like the daughter he never had. For the two colony-decades she'd been alive, Papa Jack proved himself to be the only man she ever could trust.

Sounder was most like herself. Headstrong. Calculating. Feral. How Papa Jack tolerated them was beyond her reasoning. She'd seen how he'd forgiven CouncilMembers' mistakes, an attribute she falsely believed at one time showed weakness. However, immediately after being forgiven, Dreadlocks saw an increased level of performance and unflagging loyalty from the offending parties. The lesson was not lost on her.

Like the Shetlands heeded her, the CouncilMembers obeyed Papa Jack without question. His hold on the Council was absolute. Not for the first time, she wondered where her place was in the Council. Was there a place for her in the leadership? Would Papa Jack give her a territory to rule? It wasn't the first time she ruminated on that particular thought, running various scenarios in her mind.

Dreadlocks pondered her predicament while she harnessed the horses to the wagon. Returning to the perch, she lightly flicked the horses with her crop, nudging them North. The horses obeyed her commands, dutifully and without complaint.

"W-water," mumbled the Medicine Woman. A thin hand reached up from the wagon bed.

Dreadlocks frowned. *Always something with those two.* She threw a plastic container over her shoulder without looking, malevolently smiling when she heard it hit flesh.

"Ow!" Megs howled.

"Shut up," Dreadlocks snapped.

Silence.

Good. Now I will reward you, Dreadlocks thought.

She threw back stale bread, then a bit of the cheese for good measure. She heard the two whispering in low voices, but Dreadlocks had them firmly secured and ceased to care. She'd learn to tie secure knots before she could walk.

It would be easier to travel if the two in the back slept most of the way. If either of them became problematic, Dreadlocks had no problem drugging them again. She had no problem rendering them unconscious by physical means, either. A couple of concussions would make the weeks on the road to Sylvania all the more peaceful.

Instinctively, Dreadlocks felt for the ever present cudgel in her right pocket. *It's a blackjack,* Papa Jack had explained when he gave it to her. *It's what we used in the old days to keep people in line. Unlike most things, Little Dready, blackjacks have stood the test of time.*

Dreadlocks, as usual, discovered Papa Jack was right about most things. Cudgels, too.

"So girls, is there anything we haven't addressed yet? Any concerns before your temporary spouses arrive?"

Silence.

"I know a lot of you are new. You are safe here. Ask me any question you want." Mama Mitzi looked around, seeing a small glimmer of hope in a few of the new girls' eyes. *A safe place,* they thought wistfully. *What does that feel like?*

Mama Mitzi had learned the art of waiting for new temporary wives to find their voices. She and Jalen had long run Comfort Stations before the fall of the United Authority. After Richmond burned, the sex trade returned to the private sector, offering opportunities for entrepreneurs and cautionary tales for fools.

"Um, when do we eat?" Tammy asked in a small voice. She was a scrawny slip of a girl with a lazy eye. Mama Mitzi had tried to scrub the docks off her, but Tammy looked as grimy as ever, even after two hot water baths. *There would need to be a third,* Mama Mitzi thought.

Indeed, Tammy smelled of rotted fish and river water; the whites of her eyes were as yellow as the sun. Mama Mitzi had rescued Tammy from a savage beating earlier in the day, appropriating her from a FishMonger who didn't seem too reluctant to let her go. Mama Mitzi planned to place Tammy in one of the interior rooms so the men couldn't see the signs of her liver disease or the sores around her mouth.

"Tammy, the Black CatHouse serves breakfast at ten. You are on duty from noon to midnight."

"I'm only on for 12 hours?" Tammy smiled in disbelief. "What are the other chores?"

"There are no other duties. The other half of the day is yours entirely."

"Oh, that's lovely," Tammy gushed. She gleefully looked around, then down at her callused hands and cracked fingernails, humbled by her good fortune.

"Dinner is at seven. When the last temporary spouse leaves, we all meet in the front parlor to discuss the day. Then we'll have dessert!"

Tammy's eyes grew wider. "You eat twice a day? You have dessert?" She looked at Mama Mitzi like Christmas morning.

"Dessert is my favorite part," Pomona stage-whispered to her. "Cook makes maple syrup cookies, served hot, right out of the brick oven!" The young teenage girls gleefully giggled together.

Mama Mitzi grinned, glad for a grove of sugar maples on the property. It was a good place to be, this part of Sylvania. Papa Jack had been generous with his lease, allowing both she and Jalen to run a brothel so close to the Sylvanian Stadium. Between the athletic competitions, sporting events, and public executions, being near a popular destination all but ensured sufficient clientele.

After leaving Lincolnshire, Jalen and Mitzi forged a thriving business among the NorthMen. Rumors of the NorthMen's preference for children proved mostly ill-founded, as the Black CatHouse II operated at full capacity. The only trouble was finding enough girls to fill the beds.

Papa Jack owned the former 24-unit condominium building, still in passable shape. As with most Sylvanian homes, there was no running water. Papa Jack had attempted to remedy that concern as well as the sewage situation, but for the present, boiling river water and building outhouses was the best they could do.

The orderly nature of Papa Jack's Sylvanians allowed other occupations to thrive in the community. WaterSellers delivered barrels early in the morning alongside the DairyMen who brought in milk, eggs, and cheese.

Sylvania food markets boasted a steady supply of goods, ever since the local farms had united under the protection of Papa Jack. With his hefty tribute, Papa Jack paid for former United Authority mercenaries, the most feared in the region, for protection. His men were notably armed with the blackjacks and cudgels that Papa Jack found endearing. Yet, still, hunger drove MidWesterners east on bloody raids, often ending badly for the invaders as Sylvanians were as fearless as they were intelligent and organized.

"Are there any more questions before we get on with the day?" Mama Mitzi asked.

Tammy raised a small hand.

"Yes, Tammy?"

"Um, what's for supper tonight?" Tammy immediately blushed red when the other girls started to laugh. "I-I wanted to think about food until then," she added lamely.

Mama Mitzi quieted the other temporary wives with a stern look. "Jalen dear, do you want to answer Miss Tammy?"

"Of course," Jalen stood up from the desk and smiled. Her long blonde hair had been braided into a single plait that hung down her back. Her black dress was a tight fitting relic from decades prior, cut low in the front and back. Her eyes were rimmed in green-tinted cosmetics, her lips full and red.

"Tonight we're having parsnips and greens, fry bread with honey, and rissoles of walleye pulled out of the Allegheny this morning."

Tammy almost swooned at the menu. *Never such luxury!*

For years, Mama Mitzi and Jalen's partnership, both professional and personal, thrived in Sylvania. Mama Mitzi took care of administrative functions, Papa Jack's tributes, and personnel recruitment, while Jalen oversaw the day-to-day operations, the kitchen, and dispensary. Jalen took personal pride in the meals they served for their ravenous girls, remembering the times she worked the beds with little to eat.

Jalen knew how poorly most establishments were run. From the Medicine Woman, she'd learned how to care for the basic health needs of temporary wives. Jalen knew how to abort fetuses, deliver babies, sew stitches, distill ointments, and diagnose a host of diseases. Before she and Mitzi left Lincolnshire, Jalen watched the Medicine Woman dilute vinegar for pubic lice, use colloidal silver and honey for gonorrhea, and make salves from goldenseal roots for trichomoniasis.

Although Jalen had become proficient at alleviating suffering, she often missed the companionship of her friend and teacher. She and the Medicine Woman had wept when they parted, but Jalen wasn't one to stay in one place for very long. And wherever Jalen went, Mama Mitzi followed.

After a few spectacular failures, the Black CatHouse II was founded in Sylvania and rarely lost a girl to abuse or disease. Occasionally a MilitiaMan or ClansMan brought in a strain of Temporary Wife Disease that dispatched a girl or two, but most afflicted women took matters into their own hands and jumped into one of the three rivers, the Allegheny, Monongahela, or Ohio. It was the best way to avoid tertiary syphilis.

Jalen trained the temporary wives' attendants well, as linens and towels were washed after each use in boiled water and bleach.

During outbreaks of respiratory illnesses, the Medicine Woman had been adamant about handwashing and face coverings. Mitzi had the idea of making face coverings part of the Black CatHouse II's fun: *a masquerade every night!* Although the patrons may have missed kissing temporary wives' on the lips, the transmission rate of herpes dropped considerably—along with other viral illnesses.

"We need to order more lambskins," Pomona noted, as Mama Mitzi made a notation for the SheepKeepers. "I ran through two dozen myself after dinner last night."

"It's on my list. Anyone else?"

"Could I get a new pillow? I don't like goose down. It makes me sneeze," asked Katerina, a short stocky brunette.

Mama Mitzi wondered if they coddled the girls too much.

"I'll see what I can do."

"And I'm out of lambskins, too."

"Katerina! You have to let me know earlier."

"I'm sorry," Katerina cried, crocodile tears rolling down her face.

"Ugh, save the theatrics for your temporary spouses. I'll send word to the SheepKeepers."

Pittsburghian SheepKeepers made condoms especially for the Black Cathouse II, using intestinal membranes from slaughtered lambs. Providing condoms was another layer of protection for both the patrons and the girls, a luxury that other houses did not provide. This further differentiated Jalen and Mitzi's CatHouse, which was why their girls went for a premium, triple what DockWomen went for.

The Black Cathouse II's commitment to providing quality temporary wives and maintaining public health was a primary reason Papa Jack supported their business—a reason second only to the substantial tributes they paid him.

As the Black CatHouse became more prosperous, Papa Jack took more of an interest in their affairs, discussing with Mama Mitzi the possibility of expanding.

A low knock came from the side door. Her mouth a thin line, Mama Mitzi looked at Jalen.

"Sounder is early," Jalen said. "Pomona, answer the door and show Mr. Sounder to my room."

Mama Mitzi's face became an expressionless mask. "I put the tribute script on your nightstand."

Jalen nodded at her partner who abruptly left. She ignored Mama Mitzi's jealousy, focusing instead on what needed to be done. She dismissed the girls to their rooms, then prepared herself for Sounder.

Rarely did Jalen take to the beds, but she found being with Sounder inordinately thrilling. From the first time he came to inspect Papa Jack's new venture, she was drawn to him—much to Mama Mitzi's dismay.

They'd slept in separate bedrooms since.

The sudden sunlight blinded the Medicine Woman, who squinted at the tarp's opening.

"Get up," Dreadlocks ordered.

"Untie me."

"Your bonds are loose enough."

The Medicine Woman grimaced as she sat up, knees bent, arms tied behind her back. She noted the ropes had chafed her wrists raw. *If the abrasions were not treated soon, the sores would fester.* Infections were highly problematic since her supply of Neo had been depleted a lifetime ago. As her eye adjusted to the light, she scanned the terrain to ascertain what remedy she could use.

And where was Megs? It took her a moment, but the Medicine Woman registered her blithely snoring, tucked in the farthest corner of the wagon bed.

Suddenly, the Medicine Woman began violently rocking the wagon, back and forth. The horses whinnied their disapproval.

"What are you doing?" Dreadlocks yelled.

The Medicine Woman didn't respond, and neither did Megs.

"Holy shit, you are pure chaos..." Dreadlocks leaned into the wagon bed and punched her sharply in the chest, knocking the wind out of her.

The Medicine Woman gasped for air, sputtering while Dreadlocks waited for her to calm down.

"Who are you?" the Medicine Woman demanded, standing up on her aching knees, stretching as far as her bonds would allow.

"I'm your transporter."

"Transporter? Hah! Where are you transporting us to? Which warlord do you serve, you low-level lacky?"

"I'm your transporter, but accidents happen along the way. Don't make me kill you."

"Come into the wagon, tough girl."

Dreadlocks frowned. "Look, you aren't special, Witch Doctor. And I don't feel like killing you. Yet. So quit asking me questions. We'll get there when we get there. Besides, you are merely a curiosity for my warlord."

"You are *expendable* to your warlord. He doesn't care if you live or die attempting to kidnap someone like me. Do you know what I'm capable of?"

"The only thing I know about you is that you are easily abducted." Dreadlocks grinned, her hair wild, her eyes stone. The Medicine Woman returned her sullen look, her steely gray eye boring holes into the other woman's skull.

A heavy silence punctuated their impasse.

"I see some diplomacy is in order. So, let's start over," Dreadlocks began, hands on her hips. "I'm Dreadlocks. The Sylvanians are in need of your expertise."

"I have been poisoned, beaten, and abducted," the Medicine Woman flatly stated. "Sylvanians can go straight to hell."

Dreadlocks collected herself before responding. "We are in need of medical training to prepare for the pox. We need you to help us stop it."

"The pox is heading North. There is no way to stop it. I hope it kills your warlord and scars his children. I hope it maims your parents, and I hope you die last, alone and in pain."

Dreadlocks shook her head. *This wasn't going to be easy. Papa Jack would have to pay her double for this mission.* "Yes, we know the pox is coming North. We are making contingency plans."

"And *we* are injured," the Medicine Woman said. "I am going to need a colony-gallon of boiled water, two changes of clean clothes, several cloves of garlic, powdered turmeric, and—"

"I am going to need you to shut up."

"Why don't you come over here and shut me up, Snake-hair?"

Megs stirred.

"Now look at what you've done. You've woken up the annoying one." Dreadlocks sighed.

"Medicine Woman?" Megs croaked, her voice raspy and dry. "I'm very thirsty."

The Medicine Woman leaned over, put her cool cheek on Meg's fiery forehead, then frowned.

"This girl is sick. My wounds are suppurating."

"I am aware of both."

"If you want to kill us, then kill us. We don't have to needlessly suffer..."

"We've made a slight detour. I know some people who will help us."

"I don't believe you. You are going to sell us, aren't you?" The Medicine Woman spat.

"I'm going to untie your leg bindings. If you run, I'll catch you and cut out your other eye, but not before you watch me dismember your friend. So calm down."

The Medicine Woman fell silent.

"Now listen to me. We need a few months of your time and all of your skills. Come to Sylvania with me and teach our MedicMen how to deal with the pox. When we're done? I'll bring you back. All safe and sound. I promise."

"And if I refuse?" the Medicine Woman snapped. "Let me guess. You'll kill me."

"I won't kill you, but I will kill Jasper, and I won't do it quickly."

Hearing the threats on Jasper's life, the Medicine Woman clenched her jaw. She felt for her concealed knives, but was unsurprised they'd been taken.

"I know what you're thinking. You'd like me to be your third kill this week. But, if I don't show up in Sylvania in time, there are many more Scouts far less humane than I am who will ensure Jasper suffers exceedingly. So make your choice."

"It doesn't sound like I have one."

"Well, you do have a choice about your attitude. I'd prefer a more pleasant traveling companion, so let's see if we can make you more comfortable."

Dreadlocks untied the Medicine Woman's legs, then pulled Megs down from the far corner of the wagon bed by her feet.

In a single movement, Dreadlocks lifted Megs up, throwing her over her shoulder.

"Let's go," Dreadlocks ordered, without looking back.

She led the way down a long winding driveway, potholed and broken up from years of neglect.

The Medicine Woman hopped down from the wagon, her legs wobbly, hands still bound, and slowly followed behind.

*She heard the two whispering in low voices, but Dreadlocks had them firmly
secured and ceased to care.*

Chapter 4

Conyers, The Kingdom of Georgia

The moment Jalen's door closed, Sounder's meaty hands fell on her. He grabbed her, held her tight, pressed the small of her back towards him. This time, he'd foregone counting the tribute script first, leaving it on the nightstand where Mama Mitzi had placed it. There would be time for that later.

"I've missed you," he murmured, mouth and chin nuzzling Jalen's neck, his fingers impatiently tugging at her clothing. His grizzled beard raked her white skin as his hands explored the hidden recesses of her body. Wordlessly, he picked her up and took her to bed.

Jalen didn't protest, luxuriating in his guttural grunts, matching them with her own low moans. Their lovemaking was frenzied, desperate. Often when Sounder visited, Jalen's room looked like the aftermath of a barroom brawl.

In the quietude after their coupling, they lay entwined, forehead to forehead, hands quiet, voices low. Sounder didn't lessen his grip on her, clinging to Jalen's body like a man drowning. Her fair skin bruised easily and already showed the marks of his ardor. Later, she would trace each bruise in a silent reverie.

Jalen found Sounder's lust for her intoxicating, especially when he bypassed the younger girls who—if she were honest with herself— were much more alluring. Decades older than she, Sounder proved as vigorous as any MilitiaMan she'd ever lain with. Yet, she felt there was more to their relationship than simply her vanity and his virility.

Sounder confided in her, mid-afternoons or late into the night. He discussed Papa Jack's leadership and the weighty affairs of the Sylvanian state, authentically wanting her thoughts and insights.

She often played devil's advocate, making him look at a problem from an entirely different perspective. This, more than anything, made him more useful to Papa Jack, as the CouncilMembers were nothing more than an echo chamber.

Jalen, that is sound reasoning, he'd tell her, stroking her hair before pushing her head between his thighs.

In all ways, she pleased him.

Increasingly, Sounder found himself stopping by the Black CatHouse to see her, not only for physical release, but to talk. *His unflagging trust, more than anything, was an aphrodisiac,* Jalen mused, standing at the window, waiting to see his familiar form appear.

Mama Mitzi watched their burgeoning love affair from a distance, evanescing back into her office with the files and ledgers. No one saw her expression change or heard her heart break.

As for Jalen and Sounder, in bed they continued to speak in whispers, murmuring terms of endearment. She nestled into his side, her head pillowed on his thick bicep.

"You don't see other men—do you," he murmured. It wasn't a question.

"I'll see who I please," Jalen giggled, teasing him, poking him in the chest. He grabbed her by the wrist.

"I will hunt down anyone who's ever touched you," he promised. "From this point on, Jalen, you belong to me."

Jalen looked at his face, dark brown eyes placid and content. The menace in his monotone voice thrilled her.

"I am not yours." She attempted to roll out of his embrace. "I am not yours, but I choose to be with you. For now."

He merely tucked her back under his armpit.

"You are mine."

Jalen failed to suppress a smile. He kissed her again, this time harder, his urgency building as he pulled her on top of him for a second time. There would be a third time before he left at dawn.

Jalen watched Sounder obsessively, every ripple of muscle and every blink of his eye, while she undulated on top of him. *I love you,* she almost blurted out, surprising herself at the thought. Still, it was true. It seemed so natural to say that to this beast of a man, the one who consumed her thoughts.

She shook her head to clear it. *Falling in love at her age? Ridiculous. No good would come of this.*

Before his arrival, she had spent all day in a churlish mood, yelling at the cook to make a special dish for Sounder, finding a dress she hoped would please him.

"I want you to live with me," Sounder said.

"I can't," Jalen replied. "My home is here, with Mitzi and the girls. I can't abandon them. I can't leave."

"You can leave them. Easily."

"Sounder, I—"

"I will take care of you. There's nothing here you will miss."

"You don't understand. I *like* running the Black CatHouse. I *like* working in the kitchens. What would I do at your place besides wait for you to come home and pay attention to me?" She laughed, hollow and thin.

Sounder lay in silence, a finger outlining the curves of her body. He particularly liked her spine, running one of his hands over the knotty bones underneath her cool skin.

"You will live with me," he repeated.

She turned from him, rolling over in the bed, giving herself a chance to think, but Sounder clouded her thoughts entirely.

Jalen understood quite well what men wanted: novelty. *How soon Sounder would tire of her once she was his!* It was much better to remain an occasional treat.

"You will be happy with me," he promised.

"For a time."

"I'll sing you songs, wash your hair, rub your feet..." He kissed each one of her toes.

"You will send me packing after three months."

He brooded, which Jalen took as proof she was right.

"Sounder, I'm not a young woman. What we have is wonderful. But it's temporary."

"You are mine," he said, more firmly. He tucked a strand of her hair behind her ear.

"Both you and I have been around long enough to not give our emotions much credence. Let's spend time together and enjoy one another's bodies for a season, all right?"

He slapped her.

Jalen's eyes watered; the hairs on the back of her neck stood up straight. Her heart pounded in her chest.

"You are mine," he repeated, voice thick with emotion. "And you will be my wife."

"They say you already have a wife."

He looked at her again, eyes narrowing at her brazen words.

"Jalen, you will leave this place at the end of the month. My attendants will come for you and your things. You and I will live together until our deaths."

"Sounder, I—"

"You will no longer work here. *I* will be your work."

A cold sickness washed down Jalen's throat, nauseating her, but she slowly nodded.

What else could she do?

Dreadlocks carried Megs over her shoulder from the horse cart to the main gate of the monastery. Stained glass windows reflected the midday sun in a kaleidoscope of colors.

The Medicine Woman shuffled, legs stiff, hands useless behind her. She watched as Dreadlocks banged the iron knocker on the side entrance of the sanctuary.

Dreadlocks unloaded Megs onto a pile of soft loam, then straightened her hair and clothing, cleared her throat, and squared her shoulders.

In time, a short, thin man in a cassock opened the creaky oak door.

"Lillibet!" the priest cried out, arms embracing Dreadlocks. He patted her enthusiastically on the back, kissing her on the forehead. "Oh,

Lillibet! It's been so long. I haven't seen you since your grandmother—"

"*Lillibet?*" the Medicine Woman snorted in derision, muttering under her breath. "Lillibet's a stupid name."

Dreadlocks shot her a murderous look.

"Father Seamus," she greeted him, respectfully, taking both his hands and kneeling in deference to the man.

"You don't need to bow to me, child. Come in! Come in! Welcome to the Monastery of the Sky Father. Bring your friends!" The priest tottered off into the recesses of the sprawling building.

"*Friends?*" the Medicine Woman replied with an eyebrow raised. Clearly she and Megs were restrained, bruised, and battered. *Was the priest blind?*

Dreadlocks put an arm around the Medicine Woman's shoulder and pinched the soft flesh under her arm.

"Stop it, Lilli-bitch." The Medicine Woman elbowed her. "That hurts."

Dreadlocks pinched her harder a second time.

Joined at the hip, they walked steadily through the narthex and down the nave.

"What about Megs? She's still outside."

"The brothers will get her."

"That's what I'm afraid of," the Medicine Woman replied.

"Don't be. These men are eunuchs."

The Medicine Woman had a dozen questions on her lips before Dreadlocks pinched her again to be quiet.

"Ladies," Father Seamus said, turning about quickly. "Have you eaten?"

Dreadlocks nodded. The Medicine Woman turned to her, astounded at the lie. Clearly, the man must have heard their stomachs grumbling. They'd eaten nothing for days.

The Medicine Woman started to open her mouth when she grimaced from another well-placed pinch.

"I'm hungry," the Medicine Woman whispered out of the side of her mouth.

"Shut up," Dreadlocks replied. The strange look in her eye puzzled the Medicine Woman more than anything else.

"Are these Catholics?" she asked petulantly.

"No, they're Xenios."

"W-what are—"

Pinch.

"STOP DOING THAT," the Medicine Woman scream-whispered.

"I'll explain later. Eat nothing."

They eventually caught up with Father Seamus.

As they walked, the Medicine Woman saw that the stained glass windows were not depictions of Christ's life. They had been replaced with those of the Greek Gods. Where statues of the twelve apostles once stood, now twelve Olympians lined the aisle into the transept.

The Medicine Woman noted the statue of Athena appeared to watch her, though her peripheral vision was not what it used to be, before her father had gouged out her left eye.

Father Seamus beamed behind the altar. A small boy in stained red robes entered from the side, spoke something into his ear, and then retreated from whence he came.

"Shall we pray?"

Dreadlocks knelt and clasped her hands. The Medicine Woman struggled to kneel with her hands still tied behind her, cursing Dreadlocks all the while.

"You're going to have to free my hands," the Medicine Woman stated.

Dreadlocks thought about it before shrugging and unsheathing her Bowie knife. In one swipe, the bands were cut.

The Medicine Woman almost fainted from relief. She stretched her shoulders and massaged her bloodied wrists, working out the kinks in her joints and ligaments. She flexed each one of her fingers.

"O Zeus, Father of all that is. We receive these strangers in the spirit of Xenia—the giving of hospitality as taught in ancient days. You are our protectorate, Lord Zeus. May these two women be deities in disguise so that we may be blessed by serving them. Peace be unto you."

"And also with you," responded Dreadlocks. She glowered at the Medicine Woman, nodding for her to speak.

"And also with you," the Medicine Woman repeated, still taking in the strange church, still massaging her arms.

"And Zeus, smite Darius and the evil ones who follow him. Let him turn to you to find peace for his malevolent soul. Let him turn to you to care and comfort those who are ill. Let him turn to you to feed the hungry and faithful. Peace be unto you."

"And also with you," both women recited in unison.

"And also with Zeus, to whom we bless our meal."

The boy in red returned with a stew pot. The aroma made the Medicine Woman's mouth water. Father Seamus carefully ladled large heapings into a tarnished silver bowl in front of him.

"Are you sure we cannot serve you?" he asked.

"No, thank you, Father," Dreadlocks replied. "We've filled our bellies earlier. There are others who would rejoice in Zeus's offering."

"The gods have been appeased. To each his own," Father Seamus proclaimed, noisily slurping from the bowl. He took part of an organ from his mouth, holding it up as if he'd won a prize.

The two girls watched, faces silent and reserved.

"He's eating one of Darius' men, isn't he?" the Medicine Woman whispered.

"Yep."

"Are we going into the stewpot?"

"Probably not. I've only been here a few times, but I made the mistake of eating the stew once. I don't recommend it."

"ManEaters," sighed the Medicine Woman. "Why the hell did you bring us here? What are they going to do to us, Dreadlocks?"

"They'll treat our wounds and send us on our way. They'll give us bread and cheese for the road. The Xenios are very generous. All part of their religion. The bread is quite good, and it's definitely not made from humans. I think." She offered a disconcerting smile.

"How do you know these people?"

"Father Seamus? He's my maternal grandfather."

"Of course he is."

"Look, we'll get patched up, rest a bit, and then be on our way. We're tracking late to Sylvania. My warlord will send someone decidedly less cheerful than I am if we delay any further."

"What if I head back to Lincolnshire? Tell your warlord you couldn't find me."

"Then he would kill all of us. Including Jasper."

At the sound of Jasper's name, a brief flicker of concern crossed the Medicine Woman's face. She blinked hard to regain her composure.

"Do you have any idea where Megs is?" the Medicine Woman asked, pivoting while breathing low and deep, as her mother taught her to do to sharpen her thinking.

"In the Infirmary, most likely. We'll go to her next. Trust me, she's in good hands. The Xenios are renowned for taking care of strangers is central to their beliefs. Megs will be fine. They make clean bandages from flax, and they even have yellow tubes!"

"They have Neo? Here?" The Medicine Woman's mind raced.

"It is time to speak to the Oracle," Father Seamus cried aloud, bringing out a green polished sphere from the base of the altar. Three holes had been drilled into the top, the number 12 etched in black above them all. He carefully placed the object onto a stand so it would not roll off the altar.

"There's *more* to this service?"

"Father Seamus is only getting started."

"Hector!" Darius yelled. He was still at his dressing table, dozens of small pots of colored cosmetics laying open before him. He used a thin brush to paint menacing eyebrows, covering up his thinning ones.

"Hector, come here!" he bellowed again. "Go get Hector," he finally muttered to one of his attendants. "He's probably at the sign installation. I'll meet him there after I finish. Prepare an escort for me."

The attendant curtsied and left, passing by guards on both sides of the bedchamber doors.

Darius looked at the business of the day, neatly stacked in reclaimed paper on his desk, all written in Hector's spidery handwriting. He flipped through a half colony-dozen sheets, impatient with trying to figure them out himself. That was the one thing Hector was good at.

Darius' gaudy rings clacked against the laminated table. He tried to focus again, reading and re-reading the memoranda. Finally, he threw the entire stack high in the air in frustration. He couldn't make heads nor tails out of Hector's notes.

Wearing a sequined dress from the amusement park's catacombs, he returned to his mirror and cosmetics. Decades old, the dress had been let out for his stocky frame, fashioned into the tunic-style that he preferred, especially as he grew more portly.

The Romans had it right, he thought. *Togas and sandals, even in the coolest parts of the year.* Although in the mountains of Tennessee, no one had seen snow for years.

Darius had commandeered Dollywood for the Illuminati Pagan headquarters, as it was central to Old Virginia, the Carolinas, the Crimson Republic, the Kingdom of Georgia, and Arkansippi.

Impatiently, he awaited news of an alliance with the Sovereign State of Texas. But even on his most optimistic days, Darius knew what the Texans' answer would be. *Lone wolves in the Lone Star State.* He'd have invaded them already had Louisiana not been a toxic wasteland and had the Texans not been armed to the teeth. From what Darius had heard, every town had more firepower, horses, and weaponry than the United Authority at the height of its glory.

Darius wandered to the wide leather wall map in his bedchamber. The East Coast cities enticed him. *But what was there to gain?* He'd have more citizenry to coddle. As it was, the people under his rule aggrieved him on all sides, all needing something. Water. Food. Safety. Southerners complained incessantly.

North, he thought. *The North was the next place to conquer.*

Darius flinched, hearing rapid footsteps approach his chambers. Instinctively, Darius pulled out a small jeweled dagger from a pocket in his tunic. The Boston Museum would never miss his appropriating it, as the museum no longer existed.

The guards parted as Hector entered.

"Sir! The sign is complete. It has been erected for your BirthFestival."

"Good, good. I will ride down today and see it."

"Sir," replied Hector, wiping sweat from his brow. "You don't have to leave. You can see it from here. Look!"

Hector pushed open the heavy drapes from a vast picture window. Overlooking the ruins of the park loomed large wooden letters, painted to match much older ones.

DariusWood.

The W was in the shape of a large butterfly.

"It is good, Hector." Darius smiled, creasing his eyeliner which had not yet dried.

Hector beamed.

"Now, I need you to contact the AdvanceBrigades. I'm thinking we will move North."

"NorthMen are prosperous, Darius. We could make them more so, by opening up trade with the South. They would do well under the Illuminati Pagan banner. Where are you thinking first?"

"This region. Where the Three Rivers meet."

"Sylvania?"

"Yes."

"Sylvanians are tough. A little too smart for their own good. Resilient. They won't cower like the craven Carolingians. From what I hear, they are territorial fighters. Organized. Fearless."

"Good," replied Darius. "Those are the type of people we need to help us unite the rest of the country."

Joined at the hip, they walked steadily through the narthex and down the nave.

Chapter 5

Scorpion Hollow, The Kingdom of Georgia

Megs looked well. She enthusiastically greeted Dreadlocks and the Medicine Woman when they entered her recovery room, talking nonstop while eating ManEater stew, one spoonful right after another.

The Medicine Woman sat on the straw tick bed, averting her eyes from Meg's meal. After checking her vital signs and general health, the Medicine Woman helped herself to a large wedge of warm brown bread on the girl's plate, smearing a thick pat of butter on top. *Dreadlocks was right. The bread was very good.*

"The priests gave me clean clothes after my bath. See? They smell like sunshine!"

The Medicine Woman looked around the room, determining what she could appropriate for her use. She'd noted loose bricks by the entryway when she first entered. A railing by the stairs could be pried off in a moment's notice and used as a club. The thought of bashing in Dreadlocks' head brought her a moment of contentment.

What the Medicine Woman really wanted to appropriate was hidden away by the priests.

"The brothers said I couldn't go to communion because I wasn't feeling well. They said you and Dreadlocks fully participated in the services. I didn't think you were the type to—"

"Who else is here?" the Medicine Woman interrupted. "Who else have you seen in this place?"

"Several men. I didn't see any female attendants, but apparently there's a village nearby. Acolytes are sent out for provisions, the little ones in red capes. Did you get something to eat?"

"Yes," the Medicine Woman replied, polishing off the rest of the bread.

Megs continued to babble away while the Medicine Woman walked towards the window, determining which direction the village lay, wondering if she should run to it or far from it.

Dreadlocks looked at them both, bored, impatient. She didn't have time for general niceties. Now that Megs was better, they needed to be on their way. Dreadlocks had a deadline to meet.

"And then the attendants bathed my feet and called me Aphrodite. *Aphrodite*! I had fruit and soup and cheese and a hot bath—ooh! I sat in a bathtub large enough for three men." Megs eventually took a breath between talking and eating, looking hopefully at Dreadlocks. "How long are we staying?"

"We are not staying. We're heading to the North as soon as possible."

While Dreadlocks spoke, the Medicine Woman stared at Megs, attempting to communicate her intentions. *We're not staying. We are not heading North. I'm going to kill this snake-haired harpy, then we'll go home to Lincolnshire.* Megs was oblivious.

"You sure we can't rest up for a little while? A couple of days?"

"We'll leave when Father Seamus declares you cured. You will tell the priests you are feeling much better, and then we can go," Dreadlocks replied, a steely undertone punctuating her words. She had long grown tired of Megs and didn't need an extra problem. The girl was proving to be a liability, a distraction. *Perhaps Dreadlocks could smother Megs with a pillow?*

Dreadlocks wandered outside the room, checking for listening ears, looking for watchful eyes.

"Can we stay here for the night?" Megs whined, reaching out for the Medicine Woman's hand. "I hate the wagon. It's so uncomfortable."

"So is getting poisoned, kidnapped, tied up, and beaten, Megs. Finish your—finish your *stew*, and let's get out of here. Stay close to me."

"We're going to leave? Now?"

"As soon as we can. Be ready."

"I'm afraid that's not possible." A deep voice startled both of them.

The Medicine Woman looked up, surprised at how stealthily the fat priest had moved.

"Your friend is dehydrated and badly injured. Aphrodite must be healed. It's our duty to the gods." The priest withdrew a yellow tube from his robes, squeezing out precious little of the ointment, attending their cuts.

Neo. The Medicine Woman's eyes followed the tube, watching where the priest secreted it on his person.

"Megs says you know how to cure the pox," the fat priest said.

Megs and her mouth. The Medicine Woman remained silent.

"You must share your ways with us," he asked, smiling benignly as he stood to leave.

"You'll need purple pitcher plant," Megs added helpfully. "A lot of it. The Medicine Woman can make a distillation that works wonders!"

The Medicine Woman cringed inwardly, angry that one of her few bargaining chips was gone. *She needed Megs to stop talking.*

"I can help!" Megs cheerfully continued. "I know how to find it in the bogs. The ones with the big veins usually are the best—"

"Good, good," the priest murmured, patting Megs on the shoulder. She leaned over and hugged him.

"Thank you for your good care," she smiled, beaming up at him like an angel.

"Good, good." The priest continued to pat Megs like a puppy. "I'll send you out with the acolytes to look for the plant in the morning. Perhaps your friend will show us the most efficacious way to prepare a tonic so that we may serve others?"

"Of course," the Medicine Woman answered. Over his shoulder, she saw Megs tuck something up her sleeve.

"It is time for our evening prayers." The priest sighed, withdrawing towards the hallway. "Dreadlocks will bar the door for you—for your own safety. I'll wake you for the morning meal."

"Safety? The bar is on the outside of the door," the Medicine Woman remarked, skepticism heavy in her voice. "How is that for *our* safety?"

"It isn't appropriate for you to leave until we are done giving you our hospitality." The priest replied, his sincerity as strong as his delusion.

"They are really nice here," Megs reported, holding up the stew.

"Could I have some more?"

Dreadlocks chuckled, giving the Medicine Woman a small smile before following the priest out. The Medicine Woman said nothing, her hands tightly balling into fists as she heard the door barred behind them.

Papa Jack's routine seldom varied.

Long before the Sylvanian sun arose, he met Sounder in the gymnasium on the 4th floor of the former Westin Hotel. An attendant brought them boiled water, apple cider vinegar, and fresh eggs.

Although the decades ravaged much in Western Pennsylvania, the hotel's set of standard weight plates, barbells, and kettlebells remained intact. The Stairmasters and treadmills had been useless since the end of electricity, yet the weights were all they needed.

When Papa Jack's father first appropriated the property for the Sylanvian headquarters, he'd taken Papa Jack and showed him how to properly lift weights, impressing upon him the need to maximize his physical strength.

"You can only be as mentally strong as you are physically strong," his father advised, making his son train twice a day on top of his other chores.

Although his father was shorter than Papa Jack, he had been broad across the back, much like the long line of Irish DockWorkers they'd descended from. He'd seen his father beat a man unconscious only with a few uppercuts.

Papa Jack mourned his father's death at the Battle of Three Rivers, when the New Yorkers threatened Sylvania after New York City had become uninhabitable. Since then, Papa Jack never took an Easterner prisoner, preferring them to beg for their deaths.

Papa Jack and Sounder exercised together in a silent morning ritual. When it was time to bench, Sounder acted as Papa Jack's spotter, as Papa Jack tended to overdo it, adding on more plates for fun. They reminisced about the time Papa Jack had been trapped when Sounder had stepped out of the room. The overweighted bar threatened to crush

Papa Jack's chest, but Sounder deftly lifted it in time. That particular incident solidified their childhood friendship and trust all the more.

Papa Jack counted on Sounder, as ever since the assassination attempts, rarely did Papa Jack leave the Westin during the day. Although there were 26 floors in the old hotel, few of them were suitable for living.

Papa Jack had assigned guest rooms to his CouncilMembers and their families, modifying floors over the years. The top five floors had been converted into a quasi-greenhouse, providing vegetables and fruits year round for a privileged few.

As of late, Papa Jack did not feel content, and it worried him that he was worried. He ticked through his major concerns, trying to identify what bothered him on a subconscious level.

The CouncilMembers were fairly united and ruled justly and fairly in the regions. The borders were as secure as possible, the citizenry were peaceful, and enemy Scouts were routinely caught and summarily punished.

Still, the Irishman in him fretted. The pox was moving to the North, laying waste to old and young alike. The Mason-Dixon Quarantine appeared to be breached, as Marylanders attempted to flee northwest.

In the back of his mind, Papa Jack thought about his wife and daughter, who'd begun frequenting the Boston Dens. For a small fee, Sylvanians could smoke Classical Massachusetts Opium all day, all night. Papa Jack had managed to shut down the Boston Dens on Riverside, but they proliferated—like the large rats his populace fed on.

Papa Jack often returned to his living quarters, finding both his wife and daughter gone. He'd have attendants bring them home in the morning, craving the drug, spiteful and unrepentant.

Maintaining the Sylvanian's respect and the CouncilMember's obedience was difficult enough without having to hunt down what hovel his wife and only child had holed up. So he subsisted, with his family's troubles interrupting his thoughts, unwanted and unbidden.

"Why not find a little happiness in the world, Jack?" His formerly beautiful, hollow-eyed wife had asked him, laying on their bed. She'd grown unnaturally thin from blowing blue plumes of smoke from her opium pipe at the ceiling. She swatted his hand away when Papa Jack came too near, afraid he would take her pipe away.

Oftentimes he wondered whether he should have joined them in their bliss, oblivious to the Sylvanians' endless cries for potable water, warmth in the winter, food for the vagrants, hope for their children. *How much easier would it be to lay on his side, light a pipe, and let others fend for themselves?*

His wife had been too weak for the brutal world she inherited; his green-eyed daughter was like her, pretty but as strong as smoke.

He'd placed attendants to watch over them until they dug their way into the earth, death the only end of their addictions. But for the moment, they were home with their pipes. He worried more when they went looking for something to put into them.

The weights clanged as he dropped them.

Papa Jack picked them up and did a dozen more repetitions, failing to notice the tears streaming down his face.

Sounder didn't notice either, or at least, he pretended not to.

They only got as far as the One Five Five before running into an entire company of Illuminati Pagans. While picking thorns out of her neck and side, the Medicine Woman found herself ruminating on how things had gone so wrong. While she put her head in her hands, angry tears seeped through her fingers.

After being locked in Megs' recovery room, the Medicine Woman immediately held out her hand, demanding what Megs had pickpocketed from the priest.

"What?"

"Hand me the Neo."

"I was going to give it to you later," Megs lied. She pulled out the small yellow tube from her sleeve and placed it into the Medicine Woman's hand. *Almost an entire tube of antibiotic ointment!*

"What were you going to do with this?"

"Sell it," Megs replied.

The Medicine Woman was taken aback. She had no idea that Megs could be that calculating. Both impressed by Megs' sleight-of-hand and concerned about her duplicitousness, for the first time the Medicine Woman wondered about Megs' fidelity. She had always taken her good nature and lack of guile for granted.

"We're not selling it. We're going to keep it and, like the priests, we'll find a way to use it to alleviate suffering."

"Are these good or bad priests?"

"I don't know, Megs. They're weird," she mumbled, distracted by more serious matters. "Now get off the bed. We're going home."

Megs agilely jumped up, evidently more recovered from her ailments than she had let on. Again, the Medicine Woman marveled at her prevarication. Megs appeared so frail before, fooling everyone in the room—*even her.*

Without another thought, the Medicine Woman stripped the straw tick mattress of its flaxen sheets. Tearing long lengths of the fabric, her clever hands braided and knotted the material into a strong, thick rope.

Megs scoured the room for anything useful, finding precious little they could use to defend themselves. She made a rucksack out of some of the remaining fabric and tucked in chunks of the loose brick, a small crocheted blanket, the bowl, and the soup spoon.

Meanwhile, the Medicine Woman secured the loose end of the sheet rope to the bed frame. She tossed the rest of it through the paneless window on the third floor, the end of it hovering over the bramble of wild rose bushes directly underneath. She roughly calculated the drop of five or six colony-feet to the ground. This gave her pause. A bad landing would twist one of their ankles. Then there was the freefall into thorns.

Megs joined her at the window, peering down in the darkness. "Look. We'll climb down. When we get to the bottom of the rope, then we can swing to the sides," Megs suggested.

"That will make the drop higher." The Medicine Woman frowned.

"But we'll clear the bushes!"

"Swinging the rope is not going to work."

"Only one way to find out." Megs threw the rucksack over her shoulder. She swung both her legs over the ledge and made her way down the sheet rope, hand over hand.

The Medicine Woman watched until she came to the end of the rope, feet dangling precariously over the wild roses. The Medicine Woman took the rope in her hands and slowly moved it back and forth, like a pendulum, until the momentum swung it far enough for Megs to clear the bushes.

When Megs was ready, she launched herself, rolled to a stop into the thick grass, then stood up. She gave the Medicine Woman two thumbs up.

"Damn," the Medicine Woman remarked, impressed at her dismount. She thought of herself a decade earlier and wondered if she'd been that nimble. To prepare herself for the drop, the Medicine Woman wrapped her forearms and legs in the bedding remnants.

A foot taller than Megs, she descended the rope more quickly. At the end, she stretched her six foot frame to the tops of the bushes and let go, preparing for the impact.

It hurt far worse than she'd imagined.

Grimacing, she extricated herself from the small grove to where Megs was laughing at her. The Medicine Woman had scratches and gashes on her face, but her wrapped arms and legs were fairly unscathed.

"You should put some Neo on your face," Megs suggested.

"You should shut up and follow me before the priests feed you another bowl of ManEater soup, *Aphrodite*."

"ManEater soup—wait, what?"

The Medicine Woman did not reply. At a steady clip, she took the lead southward, with Megs following closely behind. They silently walked for a long period of time.

In a night black as pitch, they eventually stumbled into a midnight crossing of hundreds of men heading to the North. The Medicine

Woman clamped one of her hands over Megs' mouth before a barrage of questions spewed forth. Wrestling Megs to the ground, the Medicine Woman attempted to find her bearings while making contingency plans in her head.

"Don't move," she hissed.

"I can't move. You're on me."

How could I be so stupid, the Medicine Woman chastised herself. Somehow she had managed to walk them directly into the middle of a midnight troop movement. They were flanked on every side.

She closed her eyes and cursed herself. *Hadn't she smelled the campfires? Hadn't she heard the horses? Didn't she feel the rumblings on the ground?* Her desperate longings for Jasper and Lincolnshire had made her careless.

They would be killed upon discovery. The Kingdom of Georgia had established a dusk curfew long ago. *Perhaps a quick death wouldn't be so bad? The Medicine Woman thought. This life was so tiresome at times.*

Megs busied herself shoving the rucksack under her clothing.

"What are you doing?" the Medicine Woman angrily whispered.

"You! Stop right there," a hard voice called out.

"Help!" Megs plaintively cried. "Help us, please!"

Three men came over, dressed in filthy Illuminati Pagan uniforms. "What the hell is going on?" one demanded.

"Carolingians burned the monastery in Conyers!" Megs screamed, holding her belly. She began to weep, turning to clutch one of the MilitiaMen's pants' legs. "Oh, the child comes! The child comes!"

The men recoiled.

"All I have is my aunt!" Megs cried, flinging out a hand, gesturing to the Medicine Woman. "She is simpleminded and cannot help anyone. Not even herself! See how she's scratched her face!" Megs grabbed at her lower abdomen and shrieked. The men's faces screwed up in distaste.

"You there!" one man yelled, kicking the Medicine Woman. "What happened?"

"She cannot speak. She is mute!" Megs replied.

The Medicine Woman shot her a murderous look.

"Where can we stay the night? Please, help us! There is no one else. We are citizens under Darius' rule." She faked another contraction, writhing on the ground.

"Do you have family in the area?"

"Yes, yes, a few colony-miles west. We need safe passage."

"I can get you a tent for the night. We're breaking camp. Do you need a MedicMan?"

"No, I can deliver the child myself. Like all my other babies! Winnipeg is three years old. Joshua just turned two. He's the cutest tyke with blonde hair and big blue eyes..." Megs faked another contraction, howling in imaginary pain.

Shortly, a tent was set up for the women, far away from the main camp. The Medicine Woman sulked in the corner.

"This is not bad, but the monastery had better mattresses," Megs complained, pulling out the rucksack from her undergarments.

"So I'm simpleminded?"

"Sorry. Look, most men cannot deal with birthing babies or mental illness. I figure we'd give them both reasons to avoid us."

"You could have gotten us killed."

"You threw down a makeshift rope into a patch of thorns and walked us into a Pagan battalion!"

The Medicine Woman lay down, turning away from Megs. In no time, she could hear Megs' light rhythmic snoring. She imagined Megs grinning in her sleep, far off in the black velvety night, oblivious to the terrors all about them.

But the Medicine Woman knew all about what lay outside their tent, and her own eyes would not close.

Megs grabbed at her lower abdomen and shrieked. The men's faces screwed up in distaste.

Chapter 6

Clyde, Carolinas

In the morning, two of the Illuminated Pagans returned, standing respectfully outside the tent.

"Ma'am?"

"Yes?" Megs replied, in a voice heavy with sleep.

"We're breaking camp, heading to the North. We've been ordered to take you both with us."

Inside the tent, the Medicine Woman shook her head.

"We will be fine staying with family," Megs replied, improvising badly.

"Sorry, ma'am. I have orders to take you to DariusWood. Near Pigeon Forge."

"Oh."

"How did the birthing fare?"

"Not well," Megs coughed. "Another stillborn."

"Do you need assistance?"

"No, no. I'm medically trained. I can look after myself."

The Medicine Woman shot her a stern look.

Megs shrugged an apology.

"I'm sorry for your loss. Are you sure you are all right?"

"Yes, the afterbirth came out fully intact. We buried it and the babe deep in the woods. No animal will find her."

"Good. We requisitioned a PullCart for you and your mentally impaired aunt."

The Medicine Woman shook her head emphatically. She mouthed the word *no*.

"Okay. That sounds fine," Megs agreed. The Medicine Woman rolled her eyes.

"Ma'am, we need your medical training. Several of our men are badly injured."

"All right. That sounds fine. Happy to help out the cause." Megs forced a smile, making her voice sound cheery and compliant.

"And ma'am? We need to take the tent down. We'll take you to your transport."

The Medicine Woman put her head in her hands.

She'd had enough of carts for one lifetime.

Sounder had covered the floor of his bedroom in the Westin Hotel with brightly colored flowers. Armloads of azaleas and forsythia and hyacinths scented the air with rich perfume.

He'd hoped that when Jalen walked in, she would be dazzled by the sheer pageantry—a pastiche of yellows, blues, pinks, and reds. He would watch her hold the blooms in her hands, pressing them to her nose, inhaling their fragrance, deep and long.

Sounder's suite of hotel rooms smelled far better than most of Sylvania. Plush couches had been washed, mended, and refurbished in preparation for Jalen's arrival. Coffee tables shone from being polished, sporting lovely objets d'art appropriated by Sounder's attendants. Great swaths of mismatched carpets had been laid in pleasing patterns.

When Jalen finally came to him, seeing the beauty of Sounder's living quarters would melt away any of her guilt. Mama Mitzi had been stoic about Jalen's leaving, even helping her pack. However, clouds of bitterness hung about Mama Mitzi like a dismal fog.

"Oh Mitzi," Jalen sighed, as they folded up the last of Jalen's things. No words followed. *What could she possibly say to make it right?*

Fortunately, Mama Mitzi had business matters well in hand, agreeing to an equitable split. Jalen took her payout in script, as Sounder had forbidden her to work.

Business at The Black CatHouse II had been better than ever, as young refugees showed up at the riverfront, ready to do anything to feed themselves. Mama Mitzi hired an attendant to procure girls since Jalen had scarcely done much of anything of late.

"I get it, Jalen," Mama Mitzi said, resignedly. "Things run their course, and we had many good years together. We founded good CatHouses—"

"Two of them," Jalen agreed.

Mama Mitzi nodded, adding, "I only wish…"

"What?" Jalen asked.

"I wished we had stayed in Lincolnshire."

Jalen was a bit taken aback. They both had agreed to move to the North for many reasons, mainly because of the abundant opportunities for their particular line of work. Lincolnshire had too many constraints. Lincoln himself wasn't particularly fond of CatHousing in general or the remnants of the Family Trading Stations. That had put both Mama Mitzi and Jalen immediately at odds with Lincolnshire's administration, and both women wanted a fresh start.

The North had been spared the worst after the fall of the United Authority. Rumored growth in the mid-Atlantic region spurred both industry and entrepreneurs to relocate, as the South seemed to be perpetually at war with itself, and the West was a law unto itself.

The North had been attractive in its relative stability. There was even talk of steam power in certain areas, but those rumors had yet to be substantiated. At the time, Jalen recalled, moving North appeared to be in their mutual self-interest.

And for almost six years, it was.

Truth be told, Jalen herself would have stayed in Lincolnshire simply to maintain her friendship with Eve, her pet name for the Medicine Girl. She'd often thought of her, wondering if Jasper had managed to tame the wild child into a loving wife and mother.

Carrying down the last of her luggage, Jalen found leaving the Black CatHouse II far easier than she expected. Yes, she still loved Mama Mitzi and cared for the girls and the attendants. She'd miss the kitchen ladies, the laundry workers, the long talks after the temporary husbands left, the bawdy jokes, the endless stream of visitors, and the endless gossip that more than not proved true.

But in all of her years, she'd never loved anyone as deeply or as passionately as Sounder. She remembered how he started to cry when she agreed to move in with him at the Westin. He tenderly kissed her hands, her fingers. She had called him an old man for being so soft, and he agreed, his brown eyes fastened on her like they did whenever she was near.

Before Jalen finally arrived, Sounder waited nervously on the corner of Penn Avenue and 10th, pacing, gritting his teeth. For a moment, he considered she might not come. That idea, though unwarranted, enraged him.

She wasn't going to come, he thought, a surge of panic in his chest. *He was going to be humiliated by a temporary wife*. He'd punched an old telephone pole until his knuckles bled.

He closed his eyes, willed his heart and breathing to regulate. *Of course she'd come*, he thought, relieved when seeing her transport arrive. *Why wouldn't she give up everything for the man she loved?*

While Jalen gingerly exited the PassengerCart, Sounder tipped the two gangly youths who pulled her. They thanked him, departing quickly, covered in the greasy filth of the downtown streets.

Sounder grabbed Jalen about the waist and spun her around, giddy in knowing her porcelain face would be on the goose down pillow next to his for the rest of their lives.

"You're here." He buried his face into her neck, which smelled of fresh soap and lemon. "I'm so glad you're here."

Jalen laughed, especially when Sounder threw her over his meaty shoulder like a sack of laundry. He carried her up a dozen floors until they reached his chambers.

He'd had the hotel walls removed, reconstructed into an open air floor plan. Jalen could see from one end of the Westin to the other, light flooding in from dozens of windows, only a few of them missing panes.

Besides the acreage of flowers Sounder had arranged to be strewn, stacks of pastries and nuts and candied bacon were arranged in serving bowls on low buffet tables, a reminder of better days.

The majority of Jalen's things had been delivered previously, and she inspected her new living quarters, comforted by the sight of her possessions. Her cosmetic jars had been set out on a long, marble vanity counter. An assortment of mirrors were affixed to her dressing room's walls. Her clothing had been carefully arranged in a walk-in closet. Even the yellow teddy bear Sounder gave her—the one she nicknamed "Butter Bear"—was prominently displayed.

Sounder had his private attendants scour salvage stores across Sylvania and into the GermanTowns for costume jewelry and other fripperies that he thought she'd like. An assortment of jewelry boxes lined the walls near her shoes and accessories, overflowing like small treasure chests.

"Ooooo!" she cooed, holding up long strands of black beads and rhinestones. "Where did you find these? They're lovely."

Sounder took the glittery chains and gently placed them around Jalen's neck.

"They're so pretty," Jalen whispered breathlessly, touching the chains, posing in front of a cloudy mirror over the bathroom sink, partly illuminated by the midafternoon sun.

"They need one thing," Sounder remarked, unzipping her dress. "They need your skin."

As her dress fell, Sounder stood behind her, kissing her shoulders.

"Jalen."

"Yes?"

"I want you to be with me when I ask Papa Jack."

"I thought Papa Jack rejected your proposal outright?"

Sounder clenched her waist more tightly. She winced.

"I'm going to ask him again about restructuring the Council, Jalen." He let her go and walked over to a window, one that looked over the Allegheny River.

"You said he was decided on the matter." She gave him a curious look. "Equal ruling even after his death."

"Papa Jack is decided on the matter. I am not."

Jalen did not respond.

"Sylvania is untethered these days," Sounder paced, walking to the windows, peering out into the expanse. "It needs a firmer hand. Papa Jack is getting soft. Do you know he walks the city by himself?"

"Sounder."

"Jalen, don't tell me to tread carefully."

"Tread carefully."

Sounder walked over and picked Jalen up, strands of gaudy jewelry falling from her shoulders. He took her to his main bed, large enough for three or four. He lay her down gently, staring into her eyes. He left her, resuming his pacing like a panther in a cage.

He grabbed a piece of fruit, bit into it, then threw it against a wall. An attendant scurried to clean up the soiled area.

Sounder waved the attendants away.

He returned to Jalen after walking the entire length of his assigned hotel floor. *One day he'd occupy the top floors, the ones under the greenhouses*, he promised himself. *Jalen would be by his side.*

Jalen trembled a bit in the darkened corner of the bed, watching Sounder remove his clothing as if he were angry. His broad chest was covered in salt-and-pepper hair, various scars and bruises over his ropy muscles.

"Sounder," she murmured, low and inviting, hoping her voice would change his mood.

"Jalen."

"What are you planning to do?"

"Right now? I'm going to make love to you. Then I'm going to bathe you."

She curled into him, a dazzling smile unfolding across her face as he drew closer.

"Then next week, we will visit Papa Jack. We'll reason with him about cementing the future leadership of Sylvania. You and I. Together."

"All right, Sounder."

"Of course it is." He gathered up her long blonde hair in both of his hands behind her head. He pulled it down until her mouth rose up to meet his. "Of course it is," he repeated.

He kissed her hard.

"I'm glad you are here," he whispered.

"Me, too," Jalen answered truthfully. "And I will go with you to meet Papa Jack, if that's what you want—"

"It is. But that's not all I want."

He reached for her.

"What is your name?"

Slap.

The Medicine Woman relaxed her jaw, turning her face and shoulders away from the impact, lessening the sting. She'd been directly hit on the cheekbones before, and it wasn't pleasant. It was so much better to turn with the hit.

The GleanerBoy hadn't been properly instructed in how to injure someone with his hands, but she would have been happy to show him how.

Slap.

"Answer me!" he screamed. He did not tolerate the Medicine Woman's silence well. "I see you lost one eye. How about we take the other?" he threatened, pulling out a dull blade. He came at her, waving the knife, a menacing look on his boyish face.

She had watched both he and his stupid companions strip the corpses from the scrapping fields. They were squeamish and wasteful, taking only what they felt was of value. They pocketed trinkets instead of flint, money instead of knives. They ate any food they came across, glutting themselves on the dead's possessions.

"You're gonna talk," he laughed. "I'll make you." From the chaos in his eyes, he appeared to be conflicted, unsure, even as he blustered and threatened her. "Why'd the Illuminati Pagans leave you behind, anyway?"

The Medicine Woman scratched her chin with her shoulder since her hands were bound.

"My brothers took your little friend into the barn. You want to join them?" He motioned to a dilapidated structure with the roof stove-in.

The Medicine Woman did not turn her head, focusing solely on the boy in front of her.

"Get up," he ordered.

Badly beaten, the Medicine Woman struggled to get to her feet, standing up to her full height, looking down at the pasty-skinned boy. He had a few whiskers on his chin. His voice cracked when he spoke as his larynx was not fully developed.

"You should thank us," he tried another tack. "The Illuminati Pagans left you with the dead. With us, you'll live a little while longer."

"Thank you," she said in a benign monotone. Her lips pressed together into a flat line.

"Now, I want—"

The boy's first mistake had been his inability to properly tie a clove hitch. Clove hitches were notorious for coming undone if the object in question rotated to any degree. She'd carefully twisted her bindings as he lorded over her, slapping her face at will.

If she were to bind his hands, she would have used the constrictor knot or a combination of basic knots to form a single-column knot. When she first realized he was tying her up with a clove hitch, it was all she could do not to laugh.

Regardless, her hands were now freed.

The boy's second mistake was turning his back on her. She quickly wrapped her right arm around his neck as she moved directly behind him, placing her elbow under his chin. She squeezed her bicep and forearm on either side of his neck, restricting his airflow. He clawed at her arms in terror.

She then placed her left hand behind his head, pushing his head forward into the vise of her arm. As he started to froth at the mouth, she threaded her right hand inside the fold of her left elbow, wrapping her fingers to lock her right arm into place. She continued to squeeze, pressing on his neck from all sides.

It had been a while, but she'd decided to count to fifty in Latin, like her grandfather had taught her, until the boy's eyes bulged and his loins loosened.

Nihil. Ūnus. Duo. Trēs.

She counted to fifty again to make sure he was dead before snapping his neck.

Then she headed to the barn.

Outside of Franklin, Dreadlocks retrieved a pair of binoculars from a Carolingian MilitiaMan urinating in the woods. He appeared unduly surprised by a wiry blonde wearing an Illuminati Pagan uniform. He'd died before tying up his trousers.

She rummaged through his knapsack, looking for something to eat. Finding several oatcakes, dried peaches, and peanuts, she forced herself to chew slowly, so as not to throw up the first food she'd eaten in days.

She took off the uniform jacket, replacing it with the roughspun tunic of the dead MilitiaMan. She looked at his boots, finding them superior to her own footwear, then began to unlace them. His socks were newly made from thick-spun cotton. She took those as well.

Tracking Megs and the Medicine Woman, Dreadlocks had followed a Pagan platoon up the Seven Five to the Six Four. She took parallel roads, keeping out of sight, moving behind them as they made their way to DariusWood.

In the middle of the night, she had awakened to see local MilitiaMen congregating along the Two Three. Were they really going to stage an unprovoked attack on a platoon? *Carolingians were unpredictable that way.*

As the Pagans continued to the North on the Two Three, they stopped only once to put the Medicine Woman in a NeckCollar, chaining her to the PullCart by her throat. Dreadlocks laughed, watching the confrontation through her binoculars. The Medicine Woman had been a handful, biting and spitting at any who came near her.

As for Megs? The best Dreadlocks could tell was that the girl slept most days or was ill. She rarely saw the girl leave the cart. It was the Medicine Woman who emptied bedpans full of waste over the side.

Whether Megs lived or not was inconsequential, but Sounder had wanted the Medicine Woman alive.

From a hillside off the Seven Four near Clyde, Dreadlocks watched the Caroligian ambush from start to finish, ending with the outnumbered Illuminati Pagans retreating from a surprising number of local MilitiaMen serving an unknown warlord. This puzzled Dreadlocks. *Who knew Darius was so universally hated in this part of the country?*

But truth be told, the Carolingians fought as ruthlessly among their own kind. It was why Dreadlocks avoided traveling through the Carolinas unless necessary, as the utter disregard for life in the South unnerved her.

After the skirmish, gleaners came onto the scrapping field. Dreadlocks broke into a run, seeing that the PullCart had been too much of a curiosity for a few lanky boys.

By the time Dreadlocks reached the barn, the Medicine Woman had exited, covered in gore, carrying Megs' ravaged body in her arms.

"Hold her," the Medicine Woman ordered. Dreadlocks had no choice but to gather the girl into her arms.

Megs' face was unnaturally pale. After the Medicine Woman ensured Megs was secured in Dreadlocks' arms, she fell face forward into the dirt.

A knife blade was lodged in the side of her upper thigh.

Dreadlocks gently lay Megs onto the soft grass, running an expert eye over both women's injuries.

"He missed an artery," Dreadlocks said to the Medicine Woman. "You're lucky."

"Don't pull the knife out."

"I wasn't going to."

"I felt your hands on the hilt."

"I was *looking* at the wound."

"I hate you," the Medicine Woman mumbled, closing her one good eye, feeling dizzy and nauseated.

"Anyone left in the barn?" Dreadlocks asked, pulling out her cudgel.

"Not anyone breathing."

"Any animals?"

"A sheep or two. A donkey."

"Good. The donkey can pull the cart. I'm tired of walking."

Megs suddenly cried out loud, then screamed something that faded into a whimper. The heartbreaking sound silenced them both.

"Dreadlocks?" The Medicine Woman's voice was faint, her breathing fast, shallow.

"Yeah?"

"I'll go to the North with you. I'll train your MedicMen and teach them everything I know on two conditions."

"Name them."

"Help Megs. Take us North on the Four Oh."

"How far up the Four Oh?"

"70 miles or so."

"That's close to DariusWood. Scouts will be all over the place!"

"Dreadlocks," the Medicine Woman's voice quivered.

"No deal. Besides, you'll probably run when you get a chance."

"No, I won't." The Medicine Woman looked plaintively at her. "I need Megs alive. I need to go North on the Four Oh. It's on the way to Sylvania, Dreadlocks. I promise. I give you my word."

Dreadlocks pursed her lips.

"What's so important that's 70 colony-miles away?"

The Medicine Woman's face flushed, tears streaming down her face.

"I said," Dreadlocks repeated, hovering over the Medicine Woman's face, "what is so important that's 70 colony-miles away?"

The Medicine Woman swallowed hard. Her voice was thick.

"Goats."

By the time Dreadlocks reached the barn, the Medicine Woman had exited, covered in gore, carrying Megs' ravaged body in her arms.

Chapter 7

Witt, Tennessee

As was his custom, Darius was dressed in the finest fabrics. Reclaimed silk draped his portly frame.

With little to do but read Hector's depressing memoranda, Darius chewed on sweetcakes and candied nuts, mulling over a myriad of problems. Of late, he ate constantly, food supplanting any other leisure activities he once enjoyed. Hector quit procuring evening consorts for Darius, since he had lost interest in either male or female companionship.

Darius no longer liked walking the grounds or meeting with warlords or other visiting dignitaries. He didn't like to read more than was necessary or to gamble. He didn't like watching enemy Scouts being tortured.

He didn't like much anymore.

Nothing seemed to pique Darius' interest except food and drink. Darius ate slabs of venison, turkey, and ham at every meal, washing the meat down with fermented honey or oakwood whisky. His chefs attempted to outdo one another with rare and expensive dishes, from poached birds' eggs to rich braided breads. Darius polished off fruit pies, buttery biscuits, and maple syrup cakes throughout afternoons and into the night.

The previous evening Hector had found Darius staring at the large leather map in his bedroom while sitting at his cosmetics table, dabbing on facepaint and lotions and creams. Darius cursed at his reflection, toweling off the mess only to start all over again.

A platter of doughnuts, stuffed with berry purée and coated with honey, quickly became depleted.

"I'm getting old, Hector," Darius brooded, speaking with his mouth full. "And I'm getting ugly."

"Untrue, untrue," Hector murmured.

"I'm going to die one day, aren't I?"

"We are all mortal," Hector replied, treading carefully. "But that day is too far away to consider."

"I don't want to die," Darius complained. "Yet it's too dull to live sometimes. Perhaps death is more interesting." Darius picked up his jeweled dagger and considered it closely. He stabbed two doughnuts with it, chewing on the confectionaries while lost in thought.

"Would you like me to arrange a meeting about the Northern incursion?" Hector suggested, trying to improve Darius's mood.

Darius flopped down on his bed like a petulant child.

"Oh, I suppose," he replied. "Aren't we attacking them in the fall? I want to see the battles for myself, but I don't like the cold."

"I think your generals believe autumn is the most auspicious time."

"Well then, I will need some new coats. I want warm ones. Beaver fur. And not from the diseased three-legged ones from New Virginia!"

"I'll see what can be arranged."

"I don't like the fall. Everything dies then. I prefer spring when things are green and lively."

"We can discuss that with your military leaders at the next meeting."

"Hector," Darius said, stopping him from leaving. "Are the necromancers here?"

"They are on their way, Darius."

"I hope the bald fools have something worthwhile to say."

While Darius finished his doughnuts, several barefoot men entered, bowing low. Darius waved the others away.

"And take the guards with you."

"But Darius," Hector objected, motioning to the reports he'd written in his own handwriting. He had spent much of the morning transcribing missives detailing an unsettling spike in rogue MilitiaMen attacks.

"Will you be safe?"

"If I'm not safe here, Hector, then I'm not safe anywhere in the South." Darius walked to the bay window, which offered an unparalleled view of the old amusement park.

Looking at his new headquarters, Darius Wood had been successfully refurbished into an armed compound, one only the most foolhardy would attempt to breach.

"Would you like me to stay?"

"If I wanted you to stay, Hector, I would have asked you to stay. Now leave me alone with these men."

Hector flushed, knowing Darius' darker moods. The other day Darius had a young attendant flogged for mopping the floor too slowly, then again for doing it too quickly. Her horrified cries still pierced Hector's ears. Hector spun on his heel and shooed the attendants and guards out in front of him. As usual, Hector would wait in the corridor in case Darius needed him.

When the door was shut, Darius walked over to the men, eyeing each one carefully. They did not meet his gaze; instead, the old men shifted on their feet, anxious to return to their lair on the fringes of the city. It was a place where small animals were not missed and odd screams could not be heard.

"You wanted to see us, sir?"

The necromancers clumped together closely, the tools of their trade around their necks and in their hands.

"You said I would be successful in our last battle if the Pagans made the proper sacrifices," Darius said.

The necromancers caught the dangerous tone in his voice.

"Sir, you were victorious overall," one man replied lamely.

"I am *not* winning," Darius roared. "Up and down the roadways, my men are suffering from attacks. And not solely from MilitiaMen! CowHerders and beggars and comfort wives are rebelling. Whole townships are balking at paying tribute. You do know what that means?"

The necromancers hung their heads, their impotent guilt causing them to cower into a corner of the room. Darius continued to rage. He grabbed a doughnut and squeezed it in his hands.

"Dissent is spreading. My people think I am weak. They think I am slipping—"

"These are evil times, indeed, sir," one of the magicians replied, attempting to placate him. Quickly, the man untied a burlap bag of animal bones and tossed them on the floor tiles. The others gathered around.

"The pox is coming North," one whispered.

"Any fool knows that." Darius walked over and wiped his hands on the man's cloak. "We're quarantining until the pox passes. I have Scouts set along a two colony-mile perimeter."

Another necromancer dug into his waist-pouch, throwing down a large wriggling snake. It began to eat its own tail.

"Ouroboros!" Several of the men cried aloud, holding up their hands in an ancient gesture to protect themselves.

"There is a pox on your land, but also a pox on your reign!"

Darius walked up to the one who spoke, eyes wide, watering with intensity.

"Who is coming against me? Who threatens the Illuminati Pagans?" he demanded.

The man peered into the chicken bones. He dug into his pockets for multi-sided dice. Hands shaking, the man rolled them several times, looking more and more distraught.

"It's hard to tell, sir."

"Look again," Darius commanded.

"I see a girl!" cried one.

"No, it's a young woman. Three young women," whispered another.

"It's three witches!" shouted the smallest of the necromancers.

"Tell me exactly who they are," Darius requested, remaining calm. "Tell me so I can have these women burned."

The necromancers huddled together, mumbling a chant in an otherworldly tongue. They swayed in unison from side to side.

Darius grew impatient. "Come now! What answers do you have for me!"

The necromancers looked collectively pained.

"The other realm is quiet," one admitted.

"Then invite the gods to speak more clearly," Darius snapped.

The tallest of the necromancers cleared his throat. "It isn't the gods who advise us."

"Then invite the *devils* to speak more clearly."

Fools, Darius thought, watching their fearful expressions. They knew they had disappointed him with their simpering prattle. They were no more magical than he.

He called for Hector.

"Yes, Darius?" Hector replied, always reliable, always at his elbow. Eight large attendants walked behind him.

"The necromancers are leaving. Ensure they do not make it home. It seems the deities require a greater sacrifice to be made. Perhaps another batch of priests will be sufficient in obtaining clearer directives for our cause?"

At their extermination order, each bald-headed man looked up like a meerkat at a watering hole.

"Surely, Darius, you cannot offend the spirits!"

"The only spirit I am going to offend is a bottle of Scotch from my reserve. You are fraudsters and have wasted my time. You haven't given me a shred of meaningful insight since you wormed your way into my city!"

A few of the necromancers fell to their knees, begging for mercy. The tallest of the men stood, raw disgust on his face. He knew there was no mercy in Darius, nor honor, nor fidelity.

"Even among demons there is greater fellowship! Kill us as you please, Darius. But three witches are in the land. One will die at your hands. One will steal your kingdom. The other will take your life."

Darius grabbed a fistful of sharp animal bones from the floor tiles and forced them into the man's face, cutting through skin and tissue. When the man cried out in pain, Darius laughed, wiping his hands on the front of the man's tunic.

"Get them out of my sight," he ordered, motioning to Hector.

He stood, hands on hips, exhausted by their incompetence. *Enough of wizards with their lies and dubious prophecies!*

Even as a boy from the Family Trading Stations, Darius had supposed that the heavens were closed. Apparently the gates of hell were closed, too, keeping whatever truth the devils knew a secret to themselves.

There is no one with any more knowledge than I, Darius thought, catching his reflection in the bay window's glass.

It's always been me.

The Goatman of Witt's favorite time of day was the early morning, just as the rosy dawn peaked over the blue mountains, still hazy in their sleep.

As he tended to his beloved goats, he unconsciously fumbled with the old signet ring he wore around his neck: the vesica piscis bishop's ring, engraved in a double pointed oval.

The ring's memories became more vivid and poignant the longer he lived. He had hoped the tumultuous decades would have faded them a bit, but his recollection of the love of his life proved both comforting and cruel.

Oh, Genevah. Beautiful Genevah. Tears streamed down his face. He dried his eyes on his shirtsleeve.

Genevah, my dearest, how I still love you!

He looked at his hands, gnarled with age, scars from goats' hooves and teeth. He felt his bald head, rubbed his rheumy eyes and gums. The last of his teeth had fallen out the previous summer.

I am old. I should have died long ago.

Genevah. Only on occasion did the Goatman of Witt allow himself to unlock her memories, safely stowed in his heart.

Though Genevah existed a lifetime ago, still, if he tried, the Goatman could feel the silkiness of her skin on his fingertips and the warmth of her soft lips on his. He remembered talking late into the nights with her, her feisty banter, her throaty laugh.

Her memory made thinking of the afterlife a comfort, as he felt sure she would greet him where the two realms joined.

If our love had not been true, then what is true?

"Goatman, you are a fool," he chastised himself aloud, focusing on his chores. His goats bleated good morning to him as he took them out to graze.

"Francis, stop dawdling and keep up!"

Francis butted his legs with his horns, obstinate as usual, annoyed at being singled out.

"Maribel, stay with the group," he called. "You are acting like cows today, and you know how much I hate cows!"

Perceval, his favorite, came to nuzzle, putting two hooves upon his leg, reaching up for a good scratching under his chin. The Goatman obliged him.

It was warm, he thought, wiping his brow.

He walked them to a nearby pasture with a thin stream of spring water. Most of the other bodies of water had been hopelessly polluted, but this particular aquifer had remained crystalline and pure.

In great contentment, he watched the animals drink their fill. He sat on the ground, cross legged, groaning a bit to get situated. He and his aching knees and hips had long forged a truce, but now his back hurt, cracking and popping like a bramblewood fire.

Oh, he was feverish, he complained to himself. Was he truly ill, or perhaps it was his body betraying him again? Recently he'd had roiling fevers and night sweats, awakening him in the middle of the night.

Though most of his aches and pains were old friends by now, the Goatman of Witt found the new ways his body disappointed him disconcerting. So he decided to ignore them.

The morning passed. He closed his eyes, delighted with the sounds of goats munching tall grass and the fluffy white clouds overhead.

When he'd been a child, the church had been full of people seeking answers, desiring forgiveness, needing connection. As a young man, he'd found himself attending to all, teaching college courses, caring for the widows and orphans, keeping his covenants with God, and being a good Jesuit priest.

But when the wars came and brought the end of electricity, it also ushered in the end of his faith. The level of suffering and casual cruelty he witnessed couldn't be explained if there were an omnipotent God. *Hadn't Epicurus warned western civilization long ago about the paradox of evil?*

A ladybug landed on his knee, which charmed him to no end. He was intent on examining it when a tall blonde woman appeared on the horizon, directly in his line of vision. She stumbled a bit, pulling a rickety handcart.

He stood, goats coalescing around him as they sensed strangers in the immediate area. The Goatman raised a hand to the woman in greeting.

Spying the man, the blonde woman hastened her pace, calling out to him. Her lips were blistered, her eyes glazed.

"I need water, I need water."

He reached for his goatskin, walking quickly to meet her. The goats bleated, trailing after him.

When he reached her, she fell to her knees, taking the goatskin with both hands and drinking deeply. She coughed and spluttered, paused, then drank again.

"Easy, my dear. There is more."

"No," she corrected him. "There is not much to drink or eat in many colony-miles. Too many soldiers on the highways. It's a wasteland here!"

"Are the wars back so soon? I haven't traveled much past this paddock, I'm afraid. Come, there's a spring nearby where you can drink your fill. I can offer you goat milk as well."

"Goat Milk? I-I'm here to see the Goatman of Witt," she replied. "Do you know him?"

"My dear, who else could I be? Here I am," he smiled, his face wrinkling in delight. "I am the Goatman of Witt. How do I know you? Remind me."

"You don't know me, but I have brought you someone who does."

Genevah? The Goatman of Witt's hopeful heart conjured up the impossibility of seeing her. *How much he wished this strange woman had brought his great love home to him!*

He followed after her, back to her cart. In the cramped back lay two bodies, one with the hilt of a knife sticking out of her leg, awkwardly bandaged to staunch the bleeding. The other girl appeared less physically injured, but her face was locked in a frozen stare far into the distance. The Goatman touched her face, hoping for a flicker of cognition, but the young girl's brown eyes seemed past feeling.

The Goatman attended to the other, rolling her on her less injured side to see the extent of her maladies.

"Oh sweet Mother of God," he whispered. "My little Medicine Girl!"

The late evenings in Witt were chilly, so the Goatman built a fire in his cedarwood cabin.

"Are they well?" Dreadlocks asked, returning from her bath in a sheet metal trough behind the Goatman's chicken coops.

"They are asleep," the Goatman replied. "I removed the knife and sewed up the Medicine Girl's wounds. She will be on the mend shortly. Nothing appears to be broken."

"And Megs?"

"Ah, the little one," he frowned. "She appears to be in a catatonic state. Was she traumatized?"

Dreadlocks shrugged, helping herself to another bowl of pottage, a hearty stew of chicken and mushrooms. She had dressed in a goatskin robe, feeling a warm contentment wash over her along with a wave of exhaustion.

"Why do you call her the Medicine Girl?" Dreadlocks asked between bites, helping herself to a slab of goat cheese.

"What do you call her?"

"I know her as the Medicine Woman," she replied.

"Oh, she was a little girl when I first met her," the Goatman thought out loud. "Of course she has grown up. Did she manage to locate her mother?"

Dreadlocks shrugged again.

"Where are you three heading?"

"Sylvania. My warlord needs her medical expertise in stopping the pox and the other diseases we are afflicted by," she answered honestly, surprising herself at telling the old man the truth.

"The Medicine Woman was here years ago with a great general from the United Authority, shortly before Richmond fell." While he spoke, he prepared a plate for himself, bowing his head and making the Sign of the Cross.

"Bless us, O Lord, and these, Thy gifts, which we are about to receive from Thy bounty. Through Christ, our Lord. Amen."

Dreadlocks looked around the room.

"Who are you talking to?" she inquired, raising an eyebrow.

"Jesus Christ."

"Who?"

"He's a god."

"Which one?"

"All of them," he replied, smiling before digging into his stew.

After midnight, the Medicine Woman bolted upright in the Goatman's bed. Megs lay next to her, curled alongside her into the fetal position.

With one inhalation of cedarwood, the Medicine Woman knew immediately where she was.

"Goatman?" she called out in the dark.

"Medicine Girl, you are awake!" The Goatman padded across the room, face illuminated by the dying embers in the fireplace. He went directly to the stove and fussed with a teapot.

"Here, drink this." He held out a mug of herbal tea. As he leaned down to hand it to her, she threw her arms around his neck. To avoid falling over, the Goatman sat on the edge of the bed and patted her back while she freely wept.

"It's all right, my dear. Tomorrow you will feed the goats and tell me all your troubles," he assured her. "Finish your tea. Please rest." He tucked her back into the straw tick bed.

"My leg hurts," she whispered.

"It will heal in time. There was a bit of infection, but I've taken care of that," he assured her.

"I have Neo," she offered.

"I found the tube with the knife you keep strapped to your ankle."

"Yes, good. All right, then," she muttered. "You won't have to amputate my leg. I had dreamt it rotted off. I dreamt you had to—to cut it off. Like Jasper's leg. I had to cut off Jasper's leg—"

"Medicine Woman," he said sternly. "You must rest now. In the morning I will have boiled eggs and radishes for you. You can tell me all your stories then, all right?"

"All right..." she agreed.

"Now, rest. Breathe deeply. Let your body mend itself. Tomorrow you will feel much better."

"All right..." she repeated.

The Goatman of Witt started to say something else, but he noticed the Medicine Woman had already sunk into a dreamless sleep.

He smiled and walked back to his rocking chair by the fire, pulling a goat wool blanket around himself.

It was good to have her home.

To avoid falling over, the Goatman sat on the edge of the bed and patted her back while she freely wept.

Chapter 8

Duffield, Old Virginia

The Goatman found her among the chicken coops, collecting eggs like she had done as a young girl. He was pleased to have one less chore to do, but he was more grateful for her companionship.

"You are up early," he noted, sitting gingerly on a tree stump. His knees ached more every day, the dampness of the morning seeping into his joints.

"I should never have left Witt," the Medicine Woman said. "I should have stayed with you. If we hadn't gone to Richmond—"

"But you did go to Richmond."

"A lot of good that did," she pouted.

"Going to Richmond was neither good nor bad," the Goatman replied. "Life just is."

"Life just is *shit*," the Medicine Woman countered, limping on her good leg. She tied up her shirt to carry the colony-dozen eggs or so she'd found underneath the feisty hens.

"Regardless of the outcome, your time in Richmond is over. Onward, yes?"

"Is there another choice?" she asked, almost sincerely, and that made him laugh.

"There is always a choice, little girl. Now tell me about your travels."

The Medicine Woman sighed. "They've been very long."

"I can imagine."

"I will tell you about my mother when there is less work to do. Megs is still in bad shape, and the she-goats need milking. And I noticed two holes in your roof."

"I was planning to get to those before next winter," the Goatman lied, not paying her much mind. The holes would never be repaired, as he grew less and less concerned with maintaining creature comforts. He felt it was easier to put on another blanket than to recover from falling off a ladder.

"I should get Dreadlocks to do some of the work around here. She needs something better to do than whine about how we aren't leaving fast enough."

"Dreadlocks is arranging business with the HorseSellers," the Goatman replied. "Why are you heading to Sylvania, anyway?"

"Don't ask," she mumbled.

"I am asking."

"Fine. I'm preparing them for the pox," the Medicine Woman said as evenly as possible. "Against my will."

"Against your will? Surely that will be a blessing to the Sylvanians. Think of the lives you will impact for good."

She frowned, aggravated with him for the first time in her life. *Priests were always looking for a soul to save.*

"Goatman, Dreadlocks threatened to kill Jasper if I don't go to Sylvania. And as for my impact for good? There is no good in this world. I'm tired of people saying that there is. I find most people are so—so..."

"Disappointing?"

"Yes. People are very disappointing—and annoying."

He patted her shoulder.

"I wish I'd stayed in Witt," she muttered under her breath. "I should have stayed with you and the goats."

"You weren't meant to hide in Witt, and you weren't meant to live your life facing backwards, either. Besides, Chapman is here. You're with us now."

The Medicine Woman turned to look at Goatman, her face incredulous.

"*Chapman?* He's here? Why didn't you tell me!" She quickly left the coops, ducking under the fencing. She placed the eggs in a small crate and wiped her hands on her pants. "Let's go, Goatman! I have missed him!"

"Come. Let's go see him together." The Goatman took her warm brown hand in his small wrinkled white one and walked her over a dale and up an embankment. She towered over him by a colony-foot, pulling him along in earnest.

As they reached the crest, the Goatman shambled over to a long mound, outlined in pretty colored stones.

"Oh no," the Medicine Woman gasped.

The Goatman gave her a wan smile, waiting a length of time before speaking.

"I'm sorry, Medicine Girl. Chapman is here with us in spirit. I talk to him every day."

"Oh, Chapman," she whispered. "No, please, no."

"He died two winters ago. I hadn't expected him to live as long as he did, as he suffered a great deal during the Siege of Richmond."

The Medicine Woman fell to her knees, reverently touching the stones that marked Lieutenant General David Lee Chapman's grave.

"He arrived on horseback one night, alone, a Pagan bounty on his head. Darius was afraid of United Authority leaders returning to power. Most were eventually tracked down," the Goatman explained. "Not Chapman, though. He eluded them at every turn."

"Oh, Chapman..." The Medicine Woman covered her face with her hands.

"I managed to nurse him back to health, but he was broken in ways I couldn't fix. Even so, he never complained," the Goatman mused. "We did have so many good conversations late into the night. He never came to like the goats, but he was very good with rabbits. He was especially fond of the rabbits."

"Goatman!" the Medicine Woman cried out in anger. "The General could have left Richmond before the war! Lincoln could have kept Chapman safe!"

The Goatman sat down by the mound and the weeping woman, patting her on the back again, making shushing sounds.

Since when did tears help anything?

"Chapman loved you like a daughter. He'd never have put your life in danger."

"I should have gone into Richmond. I should have found him," she bitterly cried. "But on the outskirts, I ran into Jasper and—"

"Chapman wasn't yours to save. He was happy to have saved you. He returned you to your mother, as he promised, and that gave him great peace at the end," the Goatman explained. "He said it was the best thing he'd ever done in his entire life."

The Medicine Woman stood in silence as the sun arose, illuminating the pretty hillside, a late spring green boasting sprigs of flowery blooms. Purples, whites, yellows.

Chapman's resting place faced east, a perfect view of the rolling hills and lush greenery. *A peaceful place for a man of war.*

When her tears subsided, the Medicine Woman walked around his grave.

"I loved him," she whispered.

"He loved you, too." The Goatman stood by her. "Stay here as long as you'd like. I will get the eggs and make you a wonderful breakfast."

He toddled off towards the coops while the Medicine Woman offered her private prayers to no one she believed in.

"Now, who is this Dreadlocks person?"

"Ugh," the Medicine Woman groaned. "Some bitch who abducted me and my attendant. Weeks ago."

It was the Goatman's turn to be surprised.

"Why have you stayed with her? I know a bit of your skillset. Even as a young girl, you were formidable."

"If I don't go with Dreadlocks, the Sylvanians will kill Jasper," the Medicine Woman muttered. "And Megs. And probably Fortinbras. Maybe even you and anyone else who has had the misfortune to know me."

"I take it Jasper is your man?" the Goatman asked.

She nodded, and he understood. *What would he have not done to keep Genevah safe?*

Listening to Megs snoring in the one-room cabin, they both helped themselves to radish slices while the Goatman finished preparing a feast for his three guests.

"If I don't go, the Sylvanians will murder everyone I love. And I also gave her my word. Whatever that's worth," the Medicine Woman added ruefully. "I told Dreadlocks I wouldn't run off or kill her in her sleep if she brought us to you. I know you hate outsiders, but I was afraid Megs would die."

"Megs may still die," he cautioned.

The Medicine Woman exhaled in frustration. "I don't know what to do."

"Listen to me," the Goatman counseled. "Leave Megs here until she fully recovers. She won't fare well on the road or in Sylvania."

"You're right." The Medicine Woman agreed, then reached over and hugged him. "I'll collect her on my return to Lincolnshire."

"As for the Sylvanians, train them how to alleviate suffering, like you did with the United Authority. Your mother gave you a gift, and you'll bless her name when you share it with others. There is too much darkness in this world, and we have a duty to lighten it."

"Why isn't someone else *lightening* it? Why does this fall on me?" she protested. "I have my own people to care for. I might as well kill Dreadlocks after breakfast and be done with it." Folding her arms, she was only half kidding.

"God works in mysterious ways," the Goatman smiled.

"God doesn't work at all," the Medicine Woman countered, but the Goatman pretended not to hear her blasphemy.

"You might come to like the Sylvanians. They're an intelligent and resourceful people."

"I want to do my job and go home. I want Jasper to be safe."

"I'm sure you do," he conceded, chopping up fresh parsley and wild onions. "I'll send word to Lincolnshire. I'll find a way to let Jasper know that you are well and will be home in a few months."

"Jasper probably thinks we're dead." The Medicine Woman chewed on her bottom lip, like Chapman used to do when he worried. "Please find a way, Goatman. It would be a great relief for him to know where I am."

"Dreadlocks plans to leave at midday. I'll walk the goats into town and commission a dispatch runner, assuming I can contract with one."

"Thank you, Goatman. Thank you for everything." She leaned over to hug him once more.

"One other thing I should tell you," he added. "I think Dreadlocks can be trusted..."

"*Trusted?* She drugged me!" The Medicine Woman slapped the table. "With my own herbs!"

"Yes, yes. I understand all that. But I watched her dress your wounds and take care of Megs throughout the night."

The Medicine Woman brooded.

"And if I know the Sylvanians, they will appreciate your expertise, learn what you know, then send you back straight to Lincolnshire with a gratuity for your troubles."

"You mean I'm going to get paid for being kidnapped?"

The Goatman gave her a thin smile.

The Medicine Woman rolled her eyes. "You old priests see too much good in people."

"It beats the alternative," he said, shrugging his shoulders.

"I miss Chapman," she sighed. "He'd understand my situation better than you."

"I miss him, too. But he would agree with me," the Goatman grinned. "Chapman's family was Sylvanian."

"You two are still in cahoots—even beyond the grave!"

The Goatman laughed again and loaded her plate with poached eggs and fried chicken livers.

"Chapman and I solved the world's problems, one debate at a time, right there in front of the fireplace. I look forward to continuing our discussions in the next life."

"You seem awfully certain there will be one," she replied.

Carrying her over-ladened plate of food, the Medicine Woman walked to Goatman's bed where Megs lay. Megs' lips were chapped and dark bruises mottled her neck and face. The Medicine Woman put her plate aside to check Megs' vital signs, concerned with her rapid pulse rate, wondering if she should wake her to feed.

At this point, it is best to let her sleep, her mother would have advised. So the Medicine Woman ate her fill, watching her dutiful attendant fitfully sleep.

Before she departed North, the Medicine Woman would awaken Megs, feed her a rich bone broth, and bathe her the best she could. She would explain where she was going and when she would return. She would explain that Megs would be safe with Goatman.

But for now, the Medicine Woman's annoyance grew as Dreadlocks readied their two mounts with provisions. They had a five hundred colony-mile ride ahead of them, and Dreadlocks let her frustrations be known about lingering.

"Has that bitch eaten yet?" the Medicine Woman asked Goatman.

"Yes, Dreadlocks ate earlier. She has quite a robust appetite."

"I could easily kill her, Goatman. Then I could stay here with you until Megs recovers."

"Let's not kill anyone this morning," he replied, reprimanding her. "Do as you promised and then return. In the meantime, I'll ensure Megs returns to health—she'll be hale and hearty when you see her again."

"I cannot thank you enough."

"No need for thanks, little girl." He handed her a piece of honey cake. "But it appears we have little time before Dreadlocks spirits you away. So while I wash the dishes, tell me about your mother and what happened to your eye."

"Classical Massachusetts Opium continues to flood into the city.

Unabated," a member of the Council grumbled.

Papa Jack glowered at him, his dark eyes barely registering a simmering rage. *Rarely did anyone bring up the topic of opium in his presence.*

"Explain," he replied.

"It's not only my jurisdiction, Papa Jack. It's coming in from all points on the three rivers. We've pulled over seven or eight merchant boats this week. Every type of water vessel seems to be transporting Classical Massachusetts Opium. Crates of it! It's coming right out of the Northeast."

"I trust the merchant pirates you've apprehended are no longer able to continue their trade?"

"They were terminated with extreme prejudice, Papa Jack. We put their heads on pikes on the bridges near the wharfs."

"Where they should be. There is no place for opium in Sylvania," Papa Jack stated.

Sounder's face remained stoic as he sat silent, ramrod straight on Papa Jack's right hand.

"What about the opium dens? They spring up like mushrooms," inquired another CouncilMember.

"The dens are hard to track down. Even with the Opium Brigades, we close one down and two more pop up. Even the CatHousers appear to be involved, mainly on the distribution level."

Papa Jack took his time to ruminate.

"Should we punish the users?" a lesser CouncilMember asked. His troubled region was on the outskirts, poorly managed and often in need. "Could we make an example of them?"

Slowly turning his head, Papa Jack took in every man around the table. They had known about the recent deaths of his wife and daughter. *Why were they pressing him on this matter? Certainly there were other more important things to discuss.*

Sounder intervened. "Regarding the punishment of Classical Massachusetts Opium users, I would like to poll the CouncilMembers."

In turn, a smattering of ideas were bandied about. Some were thoughtful, others idiotic. After a few moments, the men began to refute each other's views, championing their own courses of action, grandstanding for Papa Jack.

God, this Council, thought Papa Jack, wearily. *They seemed to bicker more as Sylvianian problems grew more entrenched.*

Papa Jack stood as the room immediately went quiet. His brow furrowed, more out of disappointment rather than anger.

After everything they'd been through, were they failing to work together now?

Sylvania had always been united, but Papa Jack wondered if looming civic problems had frayed their brotherhood. After the fall of the United Authority, they had come together against the Pagan threat. Yet, after the recent economic downturn, the sewage failures, the waves of immigrants, the threat of the pox, and now the opium crisis—the Herculean challenges weighed heavily on their collective shoulders, but most notably, Papa Jack's.

Was there any political will left, or were they simply going to quarrel while things fell apart?

As he stood, Papa Jack appeared to be considering the CouncilMembers's points, but his heart felt sick.

Their weekly meetings seemed pointless and redundant, a regurgitation of the same concerns with few viable solutions.

His citizenry seemed less altruistic, more self-absorbed, increasingly critical of leadership. In the past, under threat of the New Yorkers, and to a lesser extent, the Jerseyites, there'd been a common enemy to rally against.

Now?

The enemy seemed lodged within themselves.

Papa Jack looked out the window of the old Westin Hotel onto the gleaming rivers, sparkling with promise. The late afternoon sun grew heavy in the sky, almost as anxious to go to bed as he was.

He'd go out walking tonight, he decided. He liked to slip away from his attendants and walk the streets of his childhood, when things were much simpler, or made so by the adults who did the worrying for him.

"And I personally think opium users are as guilty as the traffickers! Why shouldn't they suffer the same fate?"

Papa John shot a glance at the CouncilMember in the back of the room who had forgotten himself.

Sounder leaned forward with a gravitas that silenced the room. "The extermination order will stand for traffickers and distributors only. Users will be sent to the Infirmary for withdrawal and education."

Papa Jack nodded. *It was exactly what he would have said.*

Without another word and without caring how it looked to the Council, Papa Jack got up from the long conference room table and walked into his private office. *Sounder could close out the meeting.*

He heard the men curiously mutter as he left. He knew what they were thinking.

Papa Jack is too weak for these times.

Maybe so, Papa Jack thought. *Maybe so.*

He returned to his adjoining office and lay down on an old black leather couch, smooth and cool, cracks in the fabric held together by old duct tape.

He completely exhaled, looking at the cracked ceiling tiles with protruding wires that had connected to something electrical in a previous age. Maybe a light fixture? How odd would it be to bring the day into night? He wondered again how anyone slept soundly before the end of electricity.

But sleep did not elude Papa Jack. It was all he wanted to do of late, besides walk the streets alone at night.

He heard the men on the other side of the door debating the issues brought before the Council. Something about contaminated well water and a cholera outbreak. Something about schools being set up for Sylvanian children. Something about immigrants stealing from the open air markets.

"God," he cried aloud. "God, god, god." But whether it was a prayer or a curse, Papa Jack wasn't sure. He'd had enough of the endless problems, endless shortfalls, endless complaining.

What was the point of it? Why did he spend his days agonizing over a few thousand people, trying to find ways for them to scratch out a wretched existence for another few years or even a decade or two?

Was anyone particularly happy to be a Sylvanian?

Was anyone particularly happy to be alive?

Papa Jack closed his eyes. *He was so tired, so ready to escape into the softest corners of his mind.*

He smiled a bit, remembering his beautiful wife. *Oh, her wit cheered him.* She could mimic every one of the CouncilMembers, lampooning their verbal tics and facial expressions to his great delight.

He held up his own hand and looked at it, remembering how it touched her fair skin—a shoulder, a hip, a calf.

Why not find a little happiness in the world, she had asked him on many occasions.

His smile faded when he looked out the window to see dark, billowing clouds approaching the downtown area. The imminent rains would preclude his only respite, his long solitary walks, the only thing that could untangle his mind and mend his broken heart.

Behind the door, he heard the Council end its meeting, giving the Sylvanian Shout in unison.

Papa Jack sat up at the sound.

There was a small rapid knock at the door. *Sounder's knock.*

Papa Jack cleared his throat. "Come in, Sounder."

He looked up in time to see a startling blonde, beautifully dressed in a tight turquoise dress, the blue matching her eyes.

Sounder immediately appeared beside her, his hand encircling her waist.

"Papa Jack, this is Jalen."

Papa Jack nodded in greeting.

"We have a proposal for you."

The Medicine Woman hadn't spoken a word in two days, balefully glaring at Dreadlocks as they rode astride.

Dreadlocks couldn't have been more pleased at the silence.

As they continued up the Five Eight, they spotted thin plumes of smoke from beyond the bend. Dreadlocks pulled out the Carolingian's binoculars she kept in her knapsack, focusing in on groups of men encamped hundreds of colony-yards up the road.

"Dammit," she muttered.

"What now?" the Medicine Woman spat, bringing her horse to a halt.

"Tents. Not sure whose."

"What do you want to do now, *Lillibet?* I told you we should have gone at night. I told you we should have taken the Two Five from Witt."

"Shut up."

"You shut up."

"Shut up or I'll shut you up," Dreadlocks shot her a menacing glare. "Now, look. We're going to take the Eight Seven One. It's up ahead."

The Medicine Woman shook her head. They were now on a circuitous route, lengthening her servitude, but she kept silent. The horses needed to feed and rest in any event, and the sideroad seemed to lead towards richer pasture.

As they continued along their new course, one heading due east, they passed a large dilapidated sign announcing the *Natural Tunnel State Park.*

It had seen better days. The visitor center, cabins, and yurts were in ruins. A train engine lay upside down, its rusted hull cracked in half. The remnants of a chairlift were downed from their perch, a tangled mass of cables in tatters.

In time, the two women approached a vast tunnel, 850 colony-feet long and 10 stories high, carved through a limestone ridge. Dreadlocks and the Medicine Woman were silenced by the tunnel's quiet grandeur, punctuated by steep stone walls and impressive pinnacles.

Suddenly, their horses whinnied, rearing up before Dreadlocks and the Medicine Woman could calm them.

A gray-haired crone stood directly in the roadway.

Eight other older women stood behind her, all holding large bobcats on thick leather leashes.

"The MilitiaMen are coming," the crone warned in a strong, firm voice. "Come to the caverns with us if you want to live."

As they reached the crest, the Goatman shambled over to a long mound, outlined in pretty colored stones.

Chapter 9

Jenkins, God's Kingdom of Kentucky

Dreadlocks and the Medicine Woman dismounted, wordlessly, cowed by the gravitas of the crone. Their horses chuffed, making their displeasure known, spooked by the proximity of the bobcats.

"The MilitiaMen are convening at the base of the tunnel. They plan on raiding the Pagans at dawn. We will wait out the melee in the caverns. You may shelter with us, but your horses cannot come."

"Can't come? What do you suggest we do with them?" Dreadlocks asked, petulantly.

"Free them. Your horses have a better chance of surviving if they are free rather than being tied up for the soldiers to find. The men will commandeer then brutalize them or eat them. It would be best to let them go."

"But they were expensive! They're broken in. They're tamed," Dreadlocks protested.

"No living thing is too broken to know when freedom is offered," the crone replied.

Before the crone had finished speaking, the Medicine Woman had removed her horses' halter and reins, swatting the stallion on the rump to send him off into the woodlands. Calculating her losses, Dreadlocks reluctantly did the same, although aggrieved at what it would cost her to replace them for the trip North.

The old women continued to walk ahead of them at a lively pace, their bobcat companions padding dutifully at their heels, heads low, sweeping the area for prey.

Rats abounded in caves, the Medicine Woman thought. *The bobcats would be useful there.*

The women stopped before a fissure in the rock, indistinguishable from the others they'd passed. One of the women pulled out a small burlap sack, fished about the bottom for yellow beeswax candles, then disseminated them.

Another woman lit the candles, one by one, with a high carbon steel striker before they entered the cavern's semi-darkness. Yet another helped her colleagues enter the cave, holding hands and arms, ensuring no one fell while navigating the rocky crag.

Each old woman had her purpose, equal and necessary, noted the Medicine Woman. Though the crone spoke for the collective whole, they acted in the same quiet unity.

Dreadlocks and the Medicine Woman dutifully shuffled in behind them into the dark.

Candlelight threw distended shadows on the walls, the arches, the columns, the stone formations. Veins of ancient minerals glittered in the artificial light, illuminating the reds, blues, grays, browns, and sparkling whites, a cascade of colors buried in the underworld.

The crones' pace never faltered in the dank darkness. Each step brought them deeper into the quiet. The Medicine Woman felt chilled in the sunless place, but it was oddly comforting, like a cool black blanket enveloping her entire body.

As they walked on, the Medicine Woman pondered the endless ages of the rock walls, how silently they stood, bearing witness to the inexorable passage of time. She remembered her maternal grandfather telling her about ancient civilizations in Egypt and how Cleopatra had lived closer to the time of electricity than when the first pyramids of Giza were built.

At the time, the Medicine Woman disbelieved her grandfather and his stories, that mankind had gone to the moon or built triangle buildings to appease lion-headed gods. But before the end of electricity, there were allegedly even grander things that no longer mattered. *What good was going to the moon when getting water for the day was problematic enough? Let the moon keep its secrets.*

Dreadlocks stumbled into the Medicine Woman, breaking her concentration, causing them both to fall in a heap.

"Get *off* of me," the Medicine Woman yelled, irritated that she'd skinned both of her knees. She shoved Dreadlocks to the side of the narrow path. Dreadlocks struggled to get to her feet. The Medicine Woman helped her up, steadying her gait.

"Are you all right?" the Medicine Woman asked, taking a glimpse of Dreadlocks' face, pale and sallow in the halflight.

"I'm good," Dreadlocks answered, weaving a bit. "I'm good. I mean, it's not every day you're swallowed up by the earth…"

"You're not fine. You are breathing rapidly and sweat is dripping off your face. Are you claustrophobic? Because—"

Before she could finish, Dreadlocks fainted face first into a stalagmite, turning in time to avoid breaking her nose.

The old women didn't stop their progression, and the Medicine Woman panicked, as their collective candlelight grew smaller as they continued deeper into the cavern.

"Dreadlocks. I can't carry you. Get up," she ordered. She rubbed the woman's sternum and called out her name. She pinched her. Finally Dreadlocks' eyelids fluttered to life. The Medicine Woman put an arm around her, half-dragging her along the cavern floor, sidestepping crevices and rock formations that threatened to impede their way.

Squinting in the dark, the Medicine Woman watched the yellow dots of candlelight tack left. She hurried her pace until she caught up with the old women, who were now visibly relieved to have entered a larger area, comfortably furnished with blankets, wooden chairs, and a few tables.

An underground spring fed a pool near the corner of the open area. At the back were food stores, bins of apples, garlic, onions, potatoes. Barrels of herbs, cornmeal, dried pork, and legumes lay next to glass jars of honey and sunflower oil.

The bobcats were unleashed to find their own dinner, enjoying the freedom to explore the expanse, traveling together in a pack. The Medicine Woman watched the animals depart, as fluid as water, stubby tails alert and wagging with the pleasure of a hunt.

"Have you had the pox?" the gray-haired crone asked.

"No," the Medicine Woman replied. Dreadlocks shook her head as well, while slumping to the ground, her eyes watering.

"Is that one ill?"

"That one," the Medicine Woman nudged Dreadlocks with her foot, "is afraid of being underground."

"Ah, speluncaphobia," the crone said, turning to her peers and chuckling. They laughed with her, good-naturedly. "No matter. She'll fare much better down here than up there with the MilitiaMen."

"Have you eaten?" asked another, beginning to build a small fire in the center of the cave.

"Not today." The Medicine Woman felt ashamed at her response. She felt inadequate around the old women, their eyes sparkling with intelligence, their bearing as regal as queens. It was as if they had divined all that mattered in the world, and now patiently waited to be taken out of it.

"Then you will eat with us," the crone smiled. "The earth is full. There is enough."

Four of the old women busied themselves with food preparations, while the others laid out bedding and organized the camp's necessities. The women were happy in their labors, making idle chatter while their clever hands made cornmeal dumplings, folded bedding, and pared apples.

The crone made her way past the hubbub to Dreadlocks, carrying a long thin plastic straw and a small jar in her hands. She unscrewed the lid from the jar, filled the straw with a powdery substance, tilted Dreadlocks' head back, then blew the contents up her nose.

In her unconscious state, Dreadlocks sneezed.

Two old women helped carry her to a thick quilt, nestling her in, offering her a drink of spring water, giving words of encouragement.

"And now you, my dear."

The crone came towards the Medicine Woman with the straw and jar.

The Medicine Woman put her hands up, eyes wide, feet stepping back a pace.

"I know you mean no harm, but what is that? What do you want me to ingest?"

"Lesion powder," the crone replied matter-of-factly. "It's ground from dried skin pustules of those who survived the pox."

"Will it work?" the Medicine Woman asked, with skepticism in her voice. "Will it prevent illness?"

"Variolation has always worked. For thousands of years."

The Medicine Woman looked at the crone's countenance, otherworldly in the candlelight, the face of a serene deity, beneficent and wise. The wisps of gray hair framed a wizened face.

"Will you tell me how to make this powder so I can alleviate suffering?"

"Of course, my dear." The crone shrugged. "What's the use of knowledge if it isn't shared?"

The Medicine Woman tilted her head back to receive the dose, listening to the warm chatter of the old women in the cozy lair, far under the earth.

Uneasy is the head that wears a crown.

Xerxes had muttered that complaint a hundred times when Darius was his Chief Consul. Xerxes had often quoted the Bard, having immersed himself in one of the last remaining collections of Shakespearean plays. *Xerxes had been a pedantic bastard*, Darius mused. *Always showing off his love of books which eventually proved his undoing. Still, Shakespeare had a point.*

It would have been vastly different if Xerxes had lived. But the little Medicine Girl had changed that by stealing Darius' jeweled dagger and stabbing it into Xerxes' chest, propelling Darius towards his destiny of uniting the states under the Illuminati Pagans. Darius wanted to thank her, if she still lived. She occasionally visited his thoughts, the gutsy little beast.

Knowing himself all too well, Darius felt he'd been destined for greatness despite his upbringing. An accomplished leader in his eyes, his cruelty had a point, serving a higher purpose rather than merely fear and terror. He felt he'd been fair, meting out punishment when it was due.

He had his ways, effective even in their barbarity.

Though this be madness, yet there is method in it, Xerxes would have said.

Darius knew the traps of autocrats, those who believed in their own propaganda, who encircled themselves with sycophants, lickspittals who said what they wanted to hear. For that, he was grateful for the bleak misgivings that came late at night to torment him. *Surely there were ways to prevent an inevitable fall from power?*

He found himself again staring at the map in his bedchamber, running various strategic scenarios through his mind, calculating how other city-states might respond to his incursions or withdrawals. He frowned, remembering his generals getting ambushed on the fringes of Pagan lands.

Ungrateful bastards!

He'd brought order to the lawless and freedom from the strictures of the United Authority. Initially, Darius felt warmly welcomed by the populace as the remnants of the federal government had been corrupted by its Family Trading and Comfort Stations.

Now what concerned Darius most was the widespread but unorganized resistance to his latest edicts, especially the requisite military service of young men between the ages of 17-21. *Was five years too much to devote to public service?* The conscription was enacted charitably, in lieu of raising tributes as paying taxes riled his citizenry all the more.

Perhaps he should divest his power, decentralize DariusWood into factions, in an effort to manage resources more efficiently? Perhaps he should cede the South, as peaceful as a bag of cats, and relocate to the Northern Territories? He'd been approached by various factions, from the Classical Massachusetts Merchants to the Sylvanians to the Maninites.

In the North, they were experimenting with steam power and electrical current. In the South, they were still eating horses.

Walking back to his desk, he scowled at the stacks of intelligence briefings, finely lettered by strong hands on reclaimed paper. None of the missives held good tidings; he could tell without opening them up.

"Agh!" he cried, sweeping them off his desk. He wanted to tear them to shreds. He threw himself on his feather bed, pulling a pillow over his head.

What had Xerxes muttered when he was aggrieved?

When sorrows come, they come not single spies. But in battalions!

He stood up, angry, restless.

Darius paced his chamber, the doors shut and windows locked. He'd tripled the guards, as he'd heard rumors, caught sidelong-glances, imagined things.

More than anything, he thought, *I'd like someone to talk to.* It was an embarrassment to admit, even to himself. These were the thoughts of an orphan boy left alone in the world, forced to work amongst the looms, interweaving the weft through the warp, a dozen hours a day until his fingers bled.

I had parents, he imagined. *I must have had them once.*

He pushed aside the curtains to let in the early afternoon sun, opening the windows which looked out onto DariusWood and the converted remains of the old amusement park.

Seeing the sprawling acreage of mountains and vales reassured him. *I own all of this*, he reminded himself. *I am not that little boy anymore, that beaten and discarded wastrel. I own these things and these people.*

Deciding to ignore the troubling news from the fronts, he wandered down to the kitchens, feeling peckish, imagining what culinary delights the cooks were conjuring up in their mystical pots and pans.

His kitchen staff had become used to Darius' comings and goings, as he delighted in ordering his preferences in person. Yet, they were unnerved to have Darius close by, as his moods were especially capricious.

A pastry maker whose meringues had cracked after cooling disappeared from service. Young dishwashers were summoned to his chambers to perform unspeakable acts. A GrillMaster overcooked his beaver steak, so Darius ordered the man's feet prepared in the same manner.

When Darius entered the kitchens, all bowed low. He nodded, encouraging them to continue their food preparations while he strode about—tasting this, stirring that.

Mesmerized, he watched dozens of fat squirrels being prepared for one of his evening courses. Holding a squirrel carcass tightly, the cook slit its throat with a sharp knife, directly under its head. With a quick turn of the wrist, the cook folded the skin over so that the fur did not touch its flesh. In moments, the cook cut the squirrel into bloody chunks, tossing the head into the dog scrap pile, immersing the squirrel meat in cold water.

Darius watched another cook heat a pan over a coal stove, add a measure of thick white lard along with onions and garlic and a measure of flour. Once the concoction browned, the cook added vegetable stock and the squirrel meat, seasoning all liberally with salt.

From another bubbling pot on the wood fire, Darius ladled a portion of a rich soup made from pureed beans, cream, and butter. His mouth watered as he spun around to see another cook pull plaited sweetbreads from the stone ovens, drizzling butter, candied walnuts, plump raisins, and honey on top. Darius grinned, helping himself, tearing off hunks, consuming them in large bites.

I own all of this, he reminded himself, his inner urchin never satisfied. *I own all of this.*

The Medicine Woman had never slept more soundly in her life, awakening in the black velvet night that surrounded her. Her skin had cooled in the cave, making nestling into the quilts all the more luxurious. *It is safe here,* she thought, comforted by the folds of cotton batting.

For the first time in weeks, the Medicine Woman didn't feel harangued by Dreadlocks' constant urging to get moving, pushing North, mile after dreary mile.

Deep in the cavern, she basked in the peace and quiet.

In time, she sat up to get her bearings.

The crone sat in a rocking chair by the embers, looking frail in the low light.

"Did you rest?" The Medicine Woman couldn't help asking. "Did you sleep at all?"

The crone gave a low chuckle. "I'm preparing for my final rest. I will sleep enough when it's time."

The Medicine Woman stood, stretched her limbs, and made her way to the firepit.

"May I sit with you?" she asked softly.

"Please do. These others will rest for several hours more."

The Medicine Woman sat at her feet. From the direction of the cavern's entrance came distant sounds of cries, dreadful screams, terrible oaths.

"The men are fighting," the Medicine Woman commented in her matter-of-fact way.

"It may be a few days until they exhaust one another," the crone stoically replied, rocking slowly, rhythmically. "Then the gleaners will come. Then the Pagans will reclaim their dead. In a week, it will be safe to travel again, after the fever of war breaks."

"War is tedious."

"Life can be tedious, too," the crone agreed, "unless one sees its miracles."

"I can barely see anything in the dark—especially with my one eye," the Medicine Woman complained, adding a few small sticks to the flames.

"How did you lose your other eye?" the crone inquired, rocking steadily in her chair.

"I didn't lose it," the Medicine Woman scowled. "My father gouged it out before I killed him."

The crone waited for her to continue.

The Medicine Woman's words spilled out in a torrent. She gesticulated wildly when recounting her father's injustices, what he had done to her mother, how he had sold her off to terrible men. She talked about meeting Jasper and burying Cat, her very first friend. She told the crone about Jalen and the Goatman of Witt and General Chapman. She recounted the reunion with her mother, and the deaths of her little sister and unborn baby brother. Through tears she talked about Lincoln and the horses. Finally, she told the old woman about her father and the night she lost her eye.

While she talked, the firelight threw the Medicine Woman's elongated shadow against the cavern's walls.

"And then my mother and I rode to find Lincoln," she finished.

The crone waited until she was sure the young woman was done.

"I am sorry for your troubles."

"They are what they are," shrugged the Medicine Woman. "But now my field of vision is narrower and my depth perception fails me at times."

"Who treated your eye after the injury?"

"Lincoln's medics tried their best, but I finished the job. I cleaned out the socket. I sewed it shut."

"Were you able to leave the sclera?"

"The white? No. The damage was too great."

"Have you experienced any residual effects?"

"Besides being blind in one eye?" she huffed. "It's itchy sometimes..."

"And what did you use to prevent infection?"

"Thyme oil, mixed with a little Neo."

"You have Neo?" the crone asked, incredulous.

"A little," the Medicine Woman admitted. "I have a few more tubes in Lincolnshire. After that, I'm not sure where to get any more."

"The thyme oil would have sufficed on its own," she explained. "And be careful with your Neo. It is a precious commodity."

"It is."

"Be glad you are young and healthy. The body itself is a miracle and does most of its repair for us."

"The body is *bizarre*. Sometimes I think I still have my eye. And my partner, Jasper, still feels his leg, the one I amputated after a battle many years ago."

"The brain and spinal cord will always try to direct the body in the way it remembers. The body remembers itself as whole."

The Medicine Woman pondered her words. In the quiet, the distant sounds of war flared up again, wholly dispiriting her. The old crone simply rocked, feeling the warmth of the fire, surrounded by the light snores of old women, Dreadlocks, and the bobcats.

"Why do the men fight?" asked the Medicine Woman, nodding in the direction of the noise from outside the cavern.

"Because they choose to," came the crone's reply, simple and concise.

They sat in silence, listening to the horrors of war above them. They didn't speak again until the others awoke, then all busied themselves with the morning's chores.

After many days, the small group prepared to depart the caverns, blinking into the early morning sun. The old women with their leashed bobcats stood behind the crone who bid farewell to the Medicine Woman and Dreadlocks, giving her final pieces of advice on what areas to avoid and where potable water could be found on their journey to the North.

"Thank you." The Medicine Woman extended her right hand for a handshake, a final expression of gratitude.

When the crone responded in kind, the Medicine Woman palmed her the small tube of Neo, stolen from the priest of Xenios. The crone quietly grasped it, tucking it away in her clothing.

A hint of a smile crossed both of their faces before they turned in opposite directions to leave.

"Thank the gods we are out of that hole," Dreadlocks griped, shouldering her knapsack. "We'll head to the Horse Trading Center on the Two Three. We should be able to ride all the way home to Sylvania."

"I've never been to God's Kingdom of Kentucky," admitted the Medicine Woman.

"Oh, you're in for a treat." Dreadlocks soldiered ahead, walking briskly up the road.

The Medicine Woman turned to bid the crone a final goodbye, but the old woman and her friends had departed around the edge of a rock formation, silently and suddenly out of sight.

*The Medicine Woman sat at her feet. From the direction of the cavern's entrance
came distant sounds of cries, dreadful screams, terrible oaths.*

Chapter 10

Fishtrap Lake, God's Kingdom of Kentucky

Papa Jack's wife had been lovely before the Classical Massachusetts Opium consumed her. His daughter had been, too, but she'd been a marvel since birth, hazel eyes and milky white skin. As a baby, he recalled his little girl smelling of spring, a fresh miracle in a filthy world. He remembered his wife and daughter's hair, matching shades of auburn, long and thick. It was often plaited and coiled into intricate braids by his wife's clever hands.

Papa Jack walked and walked, his footsteps silent on the darkened streets. It seemed even the stars had been too preoccupied to shine, as Papa Jack found his thoughts unruly, jangled, half-formed. Though he tried to reason and sort through the concerns of both his mind and heart, he found himself unable to do so.

Grief never leaves, he decided. *It only changes form.*

Of course, there had been better days than others after the death of his family. He could immerse himself in the CouncilMembers's concerns, but then he'd see a little girl who looked like his daughter or hear a woman's laughter, similar to his wife's. Then dark clouds of grief would swirl, threatening to consume him.

Sometimes grief made Papa Jack angry. At those times, he found himself joining the Opium Brigades on their late night raids on the waterfront's opium dens, bludgeoning opium dealers within a colony-inch of their lives with his ever present cudgel. Striking man or woman, young or old—it didn't matter to him, as his hatred extended to all associated with the drug that stole his happiness by offering a ruinous counterfeit.

Papa Jack particularly liked killing the Den Masters, those who directly trafficked with Classical Massachusetts, bringing the scourge to Sylvania in ways that Papa Jack couldn't control or predict. Thus, he took great pleasure in breaking Den Masters' bones, one at a time, hearing their cries until they stopped short.

More often, the depth of his grief made Papa Jack numb, unable to find the desire to eat, to sleep, to bathe. On those days, he wouldn't meet Sounder at the Westin's gym for morning exercise. He'd leave the CouncilMembers's meetings early or failed to attend at all. Those particular days provided excellent fodder for the gossip which ran rampant through Sylvania. It encouraged those with grander ambitions to consider other leadership possibilities.

Papa Jack's attendants worried most when he simply lay in bed, dead eyed and apathetic. In the mornings, they'd bring in hot doughnuts and steamy beechnut coffee, but both delicacies remained untouched. In the evenings, they'd bring in mutton or beef ribs, slathered in spices and savory sauces. But Papa Jack would toss his dinners out the window, feeding the stray dogs that ran through the downtown streets.

A few times his attendants sent in young, comely serving girls, trained in the ways of temporary wives. But their flirtations fell flat. They were politely rebuffed, as Papa Jack couldn't stand anyone to touch him.

On occasion, Papa Jack would grow so despondent, he'd walk all night, his attendants forbidden to follow him. He'd walk to Point State Park, its notable fountain silent, remembered only by the oldest Sylvanian. The near-empty park was now populated with well fed vermin too odious to eat. During these times, Papa Jack looked out on the Three Rivers and wondered which one would be best to drown himself in: the Ohio, Monongahela, or Allegheny.

Why'd you leave me, he asked his wife, peering into the dark night. *Surely she could hear him. Surely she wasn't entirely lost, even though he'd built her funeral pyre himself.* Both she and their daughter had smoked themselves to skeletons, as opium became their preferred sustenance in the end.

Their corpses had been consumed by flames in an instant, the crackling sounds a dagger to his ears. The smell of their charred flesh made him retch at its memory.

His wife and daughter's addiction had come on so suddenly, so unexpectedly, that he scarcely knew the depth of it until there was nothing to be done but mourn their passing.

Why'd you leave me?

Angry, Papa Jack looked skyward for a scapegoat and cursed all the gods back to the Titans.

She, above all, had been his best counselor. *She* had known him intuitively, the decades they'd shared, the pleasure and pain they'd endured. It was *she* who had warned him who to watch and what to believe. *Oh, his wife had been prescient with her understanding of people and their motives.*

Until last year. Until opium came to Sylvania.

Papa Jack stopped his existential railings, hearing her soft reply, as clearly as if she stood behind him, over his right shoulder.

Why not find a little happiness in the world, Jack?

Happiness, indeed.

I should try to find happiness, he decided, looking out on the quiet city. Were there pleasures in the world still to be had?

Perhaps he would jettison his warlordship and wander the world doing good? He liked the idea of himself, a lone man, anonymously mending a fence or milking a farmer's cow—like a benevolent folk hero in the tales his father spun. Or he could spend his remaining years living in debauchery, indulging in all the pleasures of the flesh.

Or he could do both, he ruminated, satisfied with neither option. Both required interacting with people, and his desire for solitude superseded all others.

The early morning air grew heavy as dew condensed on the leaves and grass all about him. He lay on his back, contemplating the world like an old man.

Papa Jack smiled ruefully to himself. *He was an old man, becoming as morose as his father.*

He sat and watched the city wake up.

A few fires flickered on the riverbanks, warming homes and hovels. Boats and skiffs sailed blithely past him, silent on the murky river. Boisterous voices carried from the docks and waterfront shops.

Exhausted by the existence of others, Papa Jack felt the familiar strain of leadership creep into the base of his neck, making his shoulders ache.

He was tired of pretending he knew how to rule the Sylvanians. He was tired of doe-eyed mothers wanting him to save their children's futures and slack-jawed fathers wanting him to remedy the past.

Lead us, guide us, decide for us.

It was all so disheartening.

The Council and I make choices to serve you the best we can, he had explained to them, as if they were children. *You must make choices for yourself and be prepared for the consequences.*

Except that his own wife had made an exceptionally selfish choice, one that embittered him, one that took his little girl away. His wife's choice to escape into oblivion had brought him crippling consequences, ones he did not deserve. At the thought of his wife asking their daughter to accompany her into the opium dens, Papa Jack hardened his heart against her.

"I hate you," he mumbled aloud, standing precariously at the edge of the riverbank. "I hate you for leaving me. I hate you for taking her. I will never forgive you in this life or the next."

With that, he fell to his knees and retched, over and over, until dry heaves left him laying in his own filth.

I am empty, he thought.

When he was able, he stood on the riverbank, thinking back to what Sounder had suggested—an offer he initially took as impertinence, if not outright sedition.

In the morning's light, Sounder's proposal seemed favorable, if not preferable, as it was clear Sounder was smart enough to see Papa Jack's end before he did.

"We have a proposition for you," Sounder had said after the last CouncilMember meeting. He'd been with his girl, Jalen, a sharp-eyed blonde who curled under Sounder's arm.

Between the two, Papa Jack remembered, *she seemed far more capable and far more dangerous.*

He would meet with them both before making an official

announcement.

"Admit it," the Medicine Woman snapped at Dreadlocks. "You're lost."

"I am not lost, goddammit. We're going to take the One One Nine, cross over the Kanawha River, then pick up the Seven Nine all the way to Sylvania. We'll be home in a week."

"*You'll* be home in a week. I'll still be your bitch."

"Well, assuming you behave yourself, you'll be my *living* bitch—along with your friends and family," Dreadlocks added malevolently.

They resumed not speaking.

Dreadlocks resigned herself to the fact that they would have to walk the rest of the way. Her plan to buy horses in God's Kingdom of Kentucky had been a bust.

If she had known procuring horses would have been this problematic, she would have ignored the old women and their damnable bobcats.

The Horse Trading Center had shuttered after the Illuminati Pagans commandeered the herds for their battalions headed to the East, as the Carolingians once again proved their irascible nature.

Although Darius preferred to leave regional commerce to its own devices, knowing well that free markets helped a region feel autonomous, those areas under his aegis understood that Pagan protectorship came at a price. Anything—and anyone for that matter—could be nationalized, especially when the Pagan Empire was under threat.

But Darius had been pleased that horse breeding had become a leading industry after the fall of the United Authority. He'd found ingenious ways to use the beasts in battle, making the Pagans even more efficient in expanding their domain and keeping order.

Trade grew in proportion to the herds. Side industries sprung up, with the need for farriers, veterinarians, breeders, and grooms. LeatherMen earned small fortunes supplying their products to the artisans making horse tack, boots, and saddles. The art of blacksmithing surged into a lucrative profession, as bits, stirrup irons, and horseshoes were needed in record numbers.

As horse breeding became widespread, travel and trade increased, since the Pagans ensured greater safety and security on the trade routes. Dotting the roadways, hostelries and boarding houses sprung up overnight, along with dining establishments, entertainment venues, and CatHouses—in a wide variety of quality and repute.

Darius had seen the heavy handed mistakes the United Authority had made while working his way up the bureaucratic governmental system, so he refrained from excessively taxing and regulating industry. As a result, the economy thrived.

But the pox had curtailed both travel and trade, dragging his citizenry back to isolationism and paranoia. With it, came financial uncertainty, hunger, instability, unrest, and worst of all, fear. A fearful populace was capable of anything, and that kept Darius up at night. These dark concerns sent him into the kitchens, as overindulgence became one of Darius' last remaining comforts.

He was old enough to know fear would end, and things would eventually return to normal. In the meantime, Darius took proactive measures to continue his empire's growth. There were small insurrections to be quelled, crops to be planted, and animals to be bred.

In the times of the pox, horses were so valued that HorseThieves proliferated, even under the threat of public quartering. Darius enjoyed watching four horses pull a man's limbs in opposite directions, an especially unpleasant death. But it proved a strong discouragement to Southerners who'd cultivated a predilection for eating horsemeat.

"Out of curiosity, what road do you think we're on?" the Medicine Woman asked, testily.

"The Two Three."

The Medicine Woman walked over to a rusted road sign, its black numbers faint, eroded by the elements. She wiped the grime off, shook her head in disgust, and pointed to it.

"One Nine Four! We're heading west, you idiot."

Dreadlocks walked faster.

"Stop, okay? We need water. The goatskins are dry."

"We don't have time for your water breaks!" Dreadlocks yelled. "We're already weeks behind schedule. We can rest in a few hours when we've put more miles behind us."

"We will both be severely dehydrated by then," the Medicine Woman replied, walking towards her. She held up Dreadlocks' left hand, pinching the skin on top. "See how slowly it snaps back? Your body needs water... and you are dizzy."

"I'm not dizzy."

"Yes, you are. Look at your footprints," the Medicine Woman nodded back over her shoulder.

Dreadlocks turned to see clear evidence of her footfalls, rocking side to side on the roadway.

"Fine. We'll stop."

The entrance to Fishtrap Lake State Park still looked inviting, though it was clear the man-made lake had suffered much when the dam collapsed. Still, the remaining pond would prove sufficient for the both of them to drink their fill.

As usual, the Medicine Woman chopped kindling for a small fire. Dreadlocks collected water in a small pot, her legs swarmed by mosquitos at the water's edge.

Wordlessly, Dreadlocks returned, placing the pot on the fire. They both watched while it came to a roiling boil. Covering the pot with a cloth, the Medicine Woman took it off the coals to let the purified water cool. Then the two women set off to scavenge for their makeshift meal. Along the way, the Medicine Woman plucked dandelions, munching them whole.

"Can we eat violets, too?" Dreadlocks asked, spying a small patch of purple flowers.

"Eat the leaves. Let the roots be," the Medicine Woman advised.

"How about acorns?"

"No."

"Why not?"

"We don't have time to leach the tannins out. If we did, I'd roast them whole or grind them into flour. But it's a process. Everything takes time."

Above all, be patient, the Medicine Woman's mother had taught her.

Dreadlocks looked at the few nuts in her hand. Disappointed, she threw them down, then spied a strange patch of pale green fruit.

"Hey. Come here," she called out to the Medicine Woman, who was cautiously inspecting a cluster of mushrooms.

"I'm busy."

"Come on. Look at these things. What are they, rotten potatoes?"

The Medicine Woman's eyes grew wide. "Those are pawpaws!" She quickly joined Dreadlocks in gathering the fruit, smiling wider each time she plucked one from the bush. Retrieving the knife at her ankle, the Medicine Woman cut the pawpaw in half across the middle, then squeezed the flesh from the skin into her mouth. Dreadlocks watched as she spit the seeds out, one by one.

"That's delicious," the Medicine Woman sighed with pleasure, immediately preparing another one of the strange fruits for herself.

Dreadlocks followed her lead, hesitantly putting the fruit into her mouth. The first taste was distinctly citrus, but hinted at something else, something much more complex and rich.

It was exquisite.

"Don't eat the skin or the seeds," the Medicine Woman cautioned.

"I've never had anything like this!" Juice dripped from the corners of Dreadlocks' mouth. "I've had an orange before, but this is something else."

"Think of it as if a banana and a mango had a baby," the Medicine Woman laughed.

"I don't know what those are either," replied Dreadlocks. "But I do like these pawpaws."

The Medicine Woman took a break from her feast to lecture Dreadlocks on southern fruits. Though her mother taught her about nutrition, the Medicine Woman recalled the importance of Vitamin C from the high school textbooks from her days in Saltville.

"Where do NorthMen get their Vitamin C? You all must have bleeding gums and scurvy."

"We have greenhouses," Dreadlocks countered. "And cabbages and limes keep us healthy enough, along with liverwurst. Organ meat has plenty of Vitamin C. How do you think the Inuit lived?"

"I don't know who the Inuit are."

It was Dreadlocks' turn to look smug while they consumed the remaining fruit on the way back to their encampment.

The Medicine Woman caught a few grouse for their dinner, adding to their mutual feeling of goodwill and contentment.

"We will stay here for the night," Dreadlocks announced, but the Medicine Woman had already laid out her bedroll.

"If you say so," she agreed, reclining leisurely on the thin bedding.

Dreadlocks positioned herself near their fire to keep the insects away rather than needing its warmth.

Soon the night sky became festooned with dazzling stars, the constellations competing with one another to tell the best story. The Medicine Woman tried to remember all that her mother had told her about Orion's Belt and Pegasus, but all she could clearly recall were the stories of the Big Dipper and the Little Dipper.

"Polaris," she whispered, pointing. "The North Star."

"It is an ever-fixed mark / That looks on tempests and is never shaken; / It is the star to every wand'ring bark," Dreadlocks quoted.

"What does that mean?"

"I don't know," Dreadlocks admitted. "But my father would say it to my mother while she lived, and it pleased her. It might be from the Christian Bible."

"I think it's from Shakespeare," the Medicine Woman suggested. "He wrote poems."

Both women lay down, weariness finally catching up with them. The Medicine Woman put her pack under her feet to elevate them, as her mother had instructed. *After long walks, practice inversion. Lift your legs. Let the blood circulate back into your body, Medicine Girl.*

"How long has Jasper been your man?"

The Medicine Woman was taken aback by Dreadlocks' pointed question. She didn't respond.

"I said, how long has Jasper been your man?"

"It's been a while."

"Does he love you?"

"Of course," the Medicine Woman shot back, a bit defensively.

Dreadlocks laughed at her. "What do you mean, 'of course.' You're such a cold piece of fish, I can't imagine any man warming up next to you."

"Think whatever you wish." The Medicine Woman crossed her arms over her chest. She consoled herself with memories of Jasper, recounting the first time she saw him, a mortally wounded boy on a scrapping field. Later, she'd found him in dire straits outside of Richmond with an abandoned group of people.

She unfolded the memory of their first kiss by the chicken coop, slowly and carefully, remembering the touch of his rough hand on her cheek. That particular kiss ignited other days and nights of touching. One day Jasper simply showed up at the apothecary with all of his things in a tidy bundle. Until Dreadlocks had stolen her away, Jasper's face was the first face she saw in the morning and the last face she saw at night.

A wave of homesickness washed over the Medicine Woman, and it was all she could do not to push Dreadlocks' face into the coals.

She folded her arms again and indulged in self-pity.

Jasper, my Polaris, she prayed, silently mouthing an orison to him. *Don't forget me. I'll be home as soon as I can.*

"I have a man," Dreadlocks interrupted the Medicine Woman's

reverie.

"What?"

"A man," she repeated. "I have a man."

"Did you have to drug him to be with you? Like you drugged me?"

"Of course not."

"You're such a cold piece of fish, I can't imagine any man wanting to warm up next to you." The Medicine Woman mimicked Dreadlocks' Sylvanian accent.

"Oh, he's warmed up to me quite well." Dreadlocks blushed at a lurid memory. "He loves me. More than anyone ever has."

The Medicine Woman heard Dreadlocks smile in the night. "Well, good for you, Lillibet. Now let me get some sleep."

"When did you know your man loved you?"

"Who, Jasper?" the Medicine Woman asked. It was a question she hadn't considered before. "I don't know. Maybe when we first met. It's hard to say."

"My man told me he loved me before I headed South. We spent the week together before I left, and he told me he loved me. More than anyone."

"So who's this lucky man?"

"Sounder," Dreadlocks said. "His name is Sounder."

The Medicine Woman and Dreadlocks started walking North on the One Nine Four several hours before dawn.

As they neared the Kimper outpost, they found the road blocked with detritus. Leaning precariously against the refuse pile was an old door with something written in ash paint in big block lettering.

"Hand me your binoculars," the Medicine Woman asked Dreadlocks. Affixing them to her one good eye, she squinted to read the door's inscription.

Pox—Keep out!

The Medicine Woman heavily exhaled.

Dreadlocks took the binoculars from her to read the sign for herself.

"The whole town is poxy. Oof. That's bad. We'll be delayed, but we can go the long way around," Dreadlocks remarked, turning around.

"No," the Medicine Woman countered. "We're going in."

"Go in?" Dreadlocks stopped short. "Do you have a death wish? There's no way we're going in."

"How else do you think we're going to get enough pox scabs for our lesion powder?"

Retrieving the knife at her ankle, the Medicine Woman cut the pawpaw in half across the middle, then squeezed the flesh from the skin into her mouth.

Chapter 11

Kimper, God's Kingdom of Kentucky

The men around the table clasped each other's hands, arms criss crossed in front of them.

"CouncilMembers of Sylvania," Papa Jack intoned.

"CouncilMembers are here!" the CouncilMembers dutifully repeated.

"We meet as one," Papa Jack continued.

"We meet as one."

"To decide for all."

"To decide for all," came the crisp reply. All released their hands.

Sounder kept his eyes on the papers in front of him.

Papa Jack stood, his trousers hanging loosely about his frame, dark circles ringing his eyes. He took frequent sips from a cup he kept close at hand. While he gathered his thoughts, a few CouncilMembers shifted uncomfortably in the silence. Finally, he spoke.

"CouncilMembers..." Papa Jack paused, considering each man carefully. "I have known you all my life. We've played in these streets. We've scavenged this city to survive. Hell, we've even dated each others' sisters."

"Like Michael's sister Teresa!" someone called out from the far end of the table. Whistles and catcalls followed.

"Who does her latest kid look like?"

"He's not ugly enough to be yours," another CouncilMember good-naturedly shot back. His seatmate burst out into braying laughter. Almost immediately, the room reverberated with verbal parries and thrusts.

Papa Jack smiled indulgently, waiting until their banter ceased. He sipped steadily from his cup. It had been full of clear corn whisky, his newfound panacea that anesthetized him quite well.

He cleared his throat, and the CouncilMembers settled down.

"We've sat at this table hundreds of times, making critical decisions for Sylvanians. All of us have inherited our council seat from our fathers, trying to live up to those good men who formed Sylvania from the ashes of Old Pittsburgh."

He paused, letting the solemnity of the moment fill the room.

"Our fathers survived truly terrible times, establishing an outpost after the wars, after the Great Battle of the Allegheny. Our Council has had its *own* battles."

A few of the CouncilMembers mumbled knowingly. Papa Jack grinned at them, remembering their brawls in the Westin's conference room, both verbally and physically. A few holes in the drywall marked their more contentious disagreements.

He grew wistful, sipping at his cup more frequently.

"I have led the Council for 18 years—in the footsteps of my father. Seeing I have no son to leave my seat to when I die—" Papa Jack's voice caught.

The men looked at one another in concern.

"Long live Papa Jack!" one called out.

"Long live Papa Jack!" the others shouted in return with various degrees of enthusiasm. At this, Sounder turned his gaze directly out the window of the Westin's conference room.

Papa Jack composed himself, noting all that transpired in the room before placing two hands on the table in front of him.

"CouncilMembers, Sylvania is growing at an unprecedented rate. Where our fathers had problems with survival, we face the problems of growth and expansion. We have waves of immigrants flooding into every section, bringing a host of problems with them. But with these problems can be opportunities. What are your initial thoughts on the immigration matter?" Papa Jack polled the room.

"The NewComers will take any job for any pay. My section is thriving with new workers. I vote yea to increase the immigrant allotment," one CouncilMember stated.

"I vote nay. Keep immigrants out. They've ruined wherever they've come from. Why bring their problems here? We need to take care of ourselves. Keep Sylvania for Sylvanians."

"No one wants to live in your section of the city," another man snidely remarked. "Every CouncilMember should have autonomy over his region. Let each member decide for himself!"

The conversation grew more contentious. Observing, watching every facial expression and hearing voice inflection, Papa Jack let the conversation run its course. Only as it diminished did he speak.

"You have valid points about autonomy," he curtailed the heated banter. "And that is why I propose something particularly radical."

He had the men's attention.

"We need *streamlined* leadership. We need structure. Our provincial council is not as nimble in responding to problems as a hierarchy could be. I suggest we create a functional or divisional government. Let's rethink what we've outgrown."

The room went silent. *What did he mean?*

"Papa Jack, what's wrong with how we do things now?"

"It's not as effective as the times require," he replied. "Take our response to the pox. It's ravaging the Carolinas where there's a rumored 30% mortality rate. However, the Carolingians have always been weak people."

"I thought you made contingency plans," a man off to his left commented. "Is each section going to be responsible for pox containment, or are we going to work together?"

"You've made my point," Papa Jack remarked. "Sounder and I have made arrangements for training medical personnel. But we need an entire section of Sylvania behind the provision of health and wellness of our citizens. We need a dedicated sector that specializes in medical treatment and preventative health measures. We need a systematic plan, not one simply for the pox. And not one cobbled together by old men."

"So no more unified decision making? No more CouncilMember meetings?"

"Like I said, we need a more efficient governmental structure if we're going to continue to thrive—or survive, for that matter."

Another CouncilMember leaned forward, nodding. "It makes sense. Take our reaction to the opium epidemic. It varied considerably from section to section. We need one response. Universal since some of your sections seem to welcome the Old Massachusetts trade." He shot a malevolent look across the table.

"Don't look at me. My section is clean," the man snapped back. "We don't traffic in poison."

"Who are you kidding? The Opium Brigades nabbed two of your section leaders," the other quipped. "I wonder who else is getting kickbacks from the opium dens?" He eyed others around the table.

"If you want to accuse me of something, then do it." The man glared back at him, hands curling into fists.

"Enough!" Papa Jack slapped the table. "Your squabbling makes the need for structure all the more urgent."

He stood up and walked the length of the table, silently chastising the CouncilMembers.

"We seem to agree on the need for specialization and using the strengths of each section of Sylvania for our mutual goals. We should be in charge of whatever we can do best." He motioned around the room. "The MetalWorkers. The CatHousers. The MilitiaMen. And soon to be, the MedicMen."

"But Papa Jack, some of the sections don't pull their weight as it is," the oldest CouncilMember muttered. "Am I going to trust my section's water supply to another section? What if there is another drought?"

Papa Jack chose his words carefully, speaking plaintively to the men who'd been his brothers. "If we are to survive, we need to trust each other. If we don't trust each other, then we won't last another generation. Now think about what your section could excel at. Think about the *most* we can do for each other, not the least."

Silence hung as heavy in the room as the Westin's old damask drapes.

"I have the docks," offered a CouncilMember who rarely spoke. "If I didn't have to worry about boiling water for my section, I think we could expand the port. I could focus on some other things. Like farming fish. Like trade..."

"Like security or sanitation or lumbering," Papa Jack replied, encouragingly. "Like the steam engine project the Blacksmiths are working on. Look. We need to progress. We can only do that if we specialize. Establishing a governmental hierarchy is the first step towards that."

A few nods. A few stony faces. A few whispers.

Sidetalk was always dangerous, Sounder thought, making a note of those CouncilMembers in obvious disagreement.

Black eyes inscrutable as always, Papa Jack looked at Sounder. "And since we're here, I've asked Sounder to make some initial comments on the matter. Sounder, would you please?"

All eyes fell to Sounder.

Sounder stood, papers in hand, inked with his spidery scrawl. As the mantle of power appeared to shift from Papa Jack to his successor, an uneasiness crept into the room. *Hadn't Sounder always been too ambitious?*

"Wait a second," a CouncilMember interrupted. "Papa Jack, you'll still be chief, right? Chief CouncilMember? That's your job for life, yes?"

"No," Papa Jack answered him quietly. "I don't think any of us should have our jobs for life. That will make us lazy and complacent in the long term."

Shouts of protest erupted before he quelled them, pounding his fists on the table.

"Sometimes an organization needs restructuring. We need new ideas and new people for new times," Papa Jack explained.

The CouncilMembers looked at one another, unsettled by the abrupt change to their paradigm. *New people?*

"But Papa Jack," someone else interrupted. "If you're not our leader, who is? And what'll you do?"

Papa Jack picked up his empty cup, preparing to exit through the side door to his chambers, leaving Sounder in charge.

Nervous glances were exchanged as Sounder moved to the head of the table.

"What'll I do?" he offered a wry grin. "Well, as of now, I'll be up in the greenhouse, cultivating my garden."

The Medicine Woman and Dreadlocks walked past the makeshift barricade in the roadway, hastily cobbled together to warn outsiders. Someone had drawn a skull in the dust on a broken door painted with the word: *Pox*.

"You are insane," Dreadlocks complained, covering her mouth and nose with a broad strip of cloth. The stench of the dead wafted over the berm. "Why are we walking into certain death? Is that your plan, to kill us both?"

The Medicine Woman ignored her. She ripped four colony-inches from the bottom of her shirt and used it to cover her lower face.

"Don't touch anything," she warned Dreadlocks. "Don't rub your eyes or scratch your nose."

"Fantastic. Now that is all I want to do," Dreadlocks grumbled, shoving her hands deep inside her trouser pockets.

They trudged closer to the residential area, passing the desiccated remains of fields, rusted propane tanks and silos, burnt remnants of buildings.

Near a stream lay dozens of mobile homes in various states of disrepair, lined up in curious patterns. Some of the homes had markings on the sides of them.

All seemed deserted.

"Can we go now? No one is home." Dreadlocks whined, looking over her shoulder. "There's nothing here for us. Nothing to scavenge. Let's go."

"Dreadlocks, if your people need my help, we'll need to find pox survivors. We need their scabs."

"Scabs," Dreadlocks repeated dully. "Disgusting."

"Yes, scabs. Fresh ones."

"I think you'd better explain this process to me again."

The Medicine Woman sighed in annoyance. "People with the pox get blisters filled with pus, starting on their foreheads. After that, the pustules begin to spread to their faces, then their chests, then their arms and legs. The sores are round and look like peas under the skin."

"Got it. Peas under the skin. Not disgusting at all."

"If the person survives the first week or so, the pustules will crust over and form into scabs."

"Aren't they contagious, though? Can't we get the pox from being around them at that point?"

"Yes, of course we can."

"I hate you," Dreadlocks muttered, putting her belongings down and sitting under a shade tree. Undeterred, the Medicine Woman continued her explanation.

"According to the crone, it takes about a month for all of the scabs to fall off. When that happens, the survivors are free from the pox and likely won't get it again. Their bodies have learned to fight it off. The scabs have the antidote in them!"

"So we are going into this pox-ridden area hoping to find *sick* people who are hopefully getting better, but who are still contagious."

"Exactly."

"You *are* insane," Dreadlocks said again, throwing her arms up in the air. "It makes no sense! This is suicide."

"Listen to me. The people whose bodies have figured out how to cure themselves are invaluable. I'll find them, scrape off their scabs, dry them out, and make a powder. Then we'll blow it up the noses of your Sylvanians. After that? I can go home."

"You want to blow scab powder up people's noses?"

The Medicine Woman grinned.

"Why are you looking at me like that?"

"Because that's what the old crone did to you."

"Did what?"

"Blew scab powder up your nose."

"You're lying."

"I do not lie," the Medicine Woman snapped, turning to walk to the trailers.

"When did this happen? In the caves? That old hag drugged me while I was passed out?" Dreadlocks cried, frantically running after her. "Do I have the pox? Am I going to get scabs all over my body?"

The Medicine Woman continued walking to the nearest trailer without a word.

The first few trailers were empty, fetid, and stinking of unwashed linen and fecal matter. Flies buzzed around pools of body fluids and other detritus on the flooring.

In what appeared to be a common area, the Medicine Woman noted the attempts to ameliorate an afflicted person's symptoms. *A tin of water to cool fevers. Wadded bedding to relieve back pain. A plastic bucket to catch vomitus.*

There appeared to be precious little food, but an armful of flowers lay on one rickety outdoor table.

"Daisies?" Dreadlocks asked, seeing the Medicine Woman scrutinize them.

"*Feverfew.* Good for pain relief." She pocketed a few of the blooms.

Dreadlocks inspected the remnants of fires, smaller ones for boiling water or making pottage near larger ones for burning bodies. The remnants of rendered fat lay on the ground.

The Medicine Woman walked between the silent housing, looking for signs of life. The vinyl sidings of the mobile homes were covered in dirt and algae, making the homestead look even more desolate than it was.

There was no joy in this place, the Medicine Woman decided. *Not even before the pox.*

Dreadlocks whistled. The Medicine Woman looked up to see her point to one of the mobile homes situated by the shallow creek. As the Medicine Woman approached the hulking wreckage of a home, a small face appeared at the window, one peppered with pustules.

The Medicine Woman tried the door to the home, but it was secured.

She thrust her shoulder against it, but the metal hinges held. She looked over to Dreadlocks who shrugged.

Unhelpful as always. The Medicine Woman scowled at her. She turned to the window, hoping to get another glimpse of the child.

"Hello?" she called out, knocking loudly on the door. "Hello?"

"Hello," answered a child's tiny voice.

"I'm here to help you. Please open the door," the Medicine Woman asked in earnest. "Will you open the door for me?"

"Are you a gremlin?"

"Yes, she is," Dreadlocks replied, nodding at the child.

The Medicine Woman shot her a deadly look, then returned to the child. "No, I am not a gremlin. I am a woman. I can help you. Are you alone?"

"I'm with granny. We're all here."

"Can you have your granny open the door?"

"No. She's sad."

"Then let me come in, and I'll bring her some flowers," the Medicine Woman replied, pulling out the FeverFews from her pocket. She pushed them through a crack under the door. "Your granny likes flowers. I can bring her some more."

"Okay." The sound of several small feet were heard, pattering, pushing heavy objects away from the entrance.

When the door opened, the stench nearly knocked the Medicine Woman off her feet. In the gloom, numerous pairs of eyes blinked back at her. As her vision adjusted, she saw children clustered together on matted bedding, all laying haphazardly on the ramshackle floor.

A rain cistern had been cleverly set up inside the larger room, PVC piping disappearing into the ceiling. Baskets of squirrel jerky and raw pole beans and persimmons and mulberries lay on a table.

Spying an older woman whom she took to be the children's grandmother laying on a thin mattress, the Medicine Woman noted the corpse's eyes were fixed and dilated.

"Granny shit herself," another child chimed in.

That happens when you die, the Medicine Woman wanted to say. *The muscles in your bowels and bladder relax for a final time. We all soil ourselves in the end.*

"Your grandmother has passed away," the Medicine Woman told the children. "If you feel up to it, you can help me bury her."

Dreadlocks built a large fire to boil water while the Medicine Woman brought the children out of the trailer.

The Medicine Woman inspected each of them, most covered in pustules, but they had low-grade fevers and encouraging vital signs. *These children would live,* she decided.

With her sharp knives, the Medicine Woman sheared off their greasy hair, lock by lock, beginning at the crowns of their heads and shaving in downward strokes. When the fleeing lice crawled up her arms, she brushed them off into the fire, satisfied to hear them pop.

The Medicine Woman ordered the six children to find clothing in the abandoned trailers for her approval. When they returned, she asked them to disrobe and rinse off in the creek while Dreadlocks finished pouring clean, hot water into the animal trough for their baths.

The children scampered away, laughing like children do, ignorant of the perils around them. The Medicine Woman noted the hundreds of pustules that covered their bodies from head to toe, most of them scabbed over on their way to healing. *It would be quite a harvest.*

While the children scrubbed themselves in the troughs with lye soap, the Medicine Woman burned their flea-infested garments. She gave them linen to dry themselves and fitted clean clothing to their thin frames as best she could. Some of the children drowned in the larger apparel, looking like little ghosts in the woods. But Dreadlocks was handy with manipulating fabric with her knife, quickly fashioning sashes and belts.

"Now let's clean our teeth," the Medicine Woman instructed. She demonstrated how to do so by using a witch hazel twig. She offered the children mint leaves from her bundle, and they chewed on them with great pleasure.

"Hey!" Dreadlocks called out, a few rows away from the firepit where they'd gathered. "There's a chicken coop back here."

"Any chickens?"

"A few."

"Grab two of them," the Medicine Woman answered back.

"We can't eat Samuel's chickens," one of the children warned, his eyes rounded in horror. "If we do, he'll kill us all. Those are his birds."

"Is Samuel a man?"

"Samuel is a *big* man," another child added, equally concerned.

The Medicine Woman smiled and held the child's face in her hands like her mother did when imparting truth.

"This big man left a nice old woman alone with six children. He doesn't seem very big to me. He seems like a gremlin. Now I need to see to your scabs," she said, taking out her glass jar and the smallest of her knives.

Dreadlocks had her failings, but she did make good chicken stew, the Medicine Woman thought.

As dusk came, both the women and children sat well-fed, clean, and comfortable by the glowing embers of the fire. Dreadlocks had the littlest boy on her lap, rocking him side to side.

"What is your name?"

"Manasseh," the tyke replied, hiding a shy smile.

"Well, Manasseh. I had a little hobby-horse, and it was dapple gray," she started to sing, galloping the boy on her knees. "Its head was made of straw and its tail was made of hay. I sold it to an old woman for a copper groat, and I'll not sing my song again without a brand new coat!"

The boy dissolved into giggles as Dreadlocks laughed along with him.

But Manasseh's laughter halted abruptly when he heard heavy footfalls come from behind one of the mobile homes.

The Medicine Woman stood, as the oldest child in the group whispered one word.

"Samuel."

But Manasseh's laughter halted abruptly when he heard heavy footfalls come from behind one of the mobile homes.

Chapter 12

Unincorporated Area of Sylvania

Even in the night, Samuel was clearly the largest man the Medicine Woman had ever seen—and probably the angriest.

Dressed in a pair of dungarees, the shirtless man bellowed, causing the children to run to Dreadlocks for protection. Seeing the large stewpot and the remains of his chickens on the ground, the giant of a man broke into a lumbering run, charging directly towards the small group.

Before the last syllable of his indecipherable howl was issued, the Medicine Woman had pulled two long knives from her boot sheaths. She whirled around in time to watch Samuel kick the stewpot from the fire, splashing pottage in a wide arc, splattering those who stood nearby. Scalded children shrieked in pain, while Dreadlocks grabbed the smallest ones in her arms, urgently shepherding the children around the backside of a mobile home.

Meanwhile, the Medicine Woman sprinted towards the behemoth.

Samuel's attention had diverted from the children a bit too late, as the Medicine Woman, nimble on her feet, leapt up to drive her knife deeply into the man's upper shoulder. The forward momentum caused her to roll to the edge of the woods, where she crouched like a cat, pulling a smaller knife from its sheath on her belt.

Samuel looked at the knife in his shoulder, then back in the Medicine Woman's general direction. She found his silence more terrifying than his imposing frame or screams. Bleeding heavily from the wound, Samuel staggered for footing, breathing heavily. He grabbed the knife sticking out of his arm by the hilt, extricating it in a few panicked pulls. The man considered the weapon before flinging it over his other shoulder. Cursing his attacker, Samuel bent down, grabbed a handful of moss and packed it into the gaping wound.

His eyes never left the Medicine Woman's face.

In the meantime, Dreadlocks managed to get the children out of the immediate area, their cries growing more distant in the night. The Medicine Woman needed to keep Samuel distracted as she sensed the small group moving between the rows of mobile homes.

Samuel paused to determine which direction he should proceed. *Would it be better to hurt the black-haired stranger or the blonde one first?*

"Your chickens were delicious," the Medicine Woman interrupted him, goading him, circling the firepit to draw him away from the children. "We're going to fry the rest of them for breakfast. Every last one of them. Then we'll throw the chicken guts into the creek so the fish can eat, too. Then we'll eat the fish."

Samuel faced her, his lips mouthing all of the horrible things he would do to her.

"Let's go, ChickenLover. I know what Kentuckians do with animals. Who'd we kill tonight? Your girlfriend?"

The Medicine Woman took a defensive posture, knees slightly bent. She held her left hand in front of her cheek and the other hand in front of her temple.

"Who are you?" Samuel demanded.

"I'm the person who killed you tonight."

The man responded by throwing a large rock, clipping her on the left side of the face, knocking her to her knees. She kept a grip on her knives as blood streamed from an open gash on her cheekbone, rivulets of red running into her mouth. She spat, clearing her mouth of its coppery taste.

In a fight, protect the eyes, throat, stomach, and groin, her mother had instructed. *Deflect hits to the shoulder or upper torso.*

She threw a knife which lodged in Samuel's lower thigh, causing him to holler more in anger than in pain. He responded by picking up a larger rock to lob at her with surprising accuracy.

"I let all your chickens go," she taunted him wildly. "They'll be a feast for the wolves!"

Samuel then made three unfortunate mistakes.

First, blinded by unchecked rage, he ran straight towards her, ignoring the gray coals under his feet. By the time he registered the burning in his extremities, he had stood in the embers of the fire for several moments. She took full advantage of his befuddlement. Running towards him, she jumped up, twisted slightly midair, and kicked him in the chest with the soles of both her feet. Samuel fell backwards, bottom landing deep in ash.

As he roared, Samuel made a second mistake. Instead of rolling out of the firepit, he put his hands down to steady himself, wanting to rise up and pummel his tall, thin tormentor. Instead, he burned both hands as well, giving the Medicine Woman enough time to drop kick him again, singeing the man's hair and neck and back as they hit the hottest part of the coals.

Thirdly, when he lunged for her, looking all the more like a gremlin covered in ash, dirt, and blood, he grabbed her thin frame, attempting to wrap his arms about her waist. His plan was to butt her with his gigantic head, but the Medicine Woman had been around angry men her whole life. She knew how to wriggle out of desperate arms. She also knew where to land a knife in close proximity when one has but one strike.

The Medicine Woman slid her knife into the base of Samuel's skull, neatly severing the spinal cord from the brain stem. The man's eyes rolled back in his head, and the two fell together in a heap.

Having secured the children, Dreadlocks reappeared, carrying a farming implement, brandishing it like a sword.

"What are you going to do with that," the Medicine Woman asked, breathlessly. "Weed the garden?" She shoved Samuel's heavy frame off of her, the man no longer screaming, no longer moving, no longer breathing.

"Are you all right?" Dreadlocks asked, scanning her from head to foot in the dim light.

"No, I'm not all right," the Medicine Woman complained, delicately touching her wounded cheek. "Next time, I'll hide with the children while you fight Goliath."

"Holy shit," Dreadlocks said, kicking the man over to get a better look at him. "That's a lot of dead guy. He's enormous. He's also cooked medium well. I smelled him from two rows back."

"We need to dispose of the body. The children don't need to see it."

"They don't need to see you bleeding either." Dreadlocks inspected the Medicine Woman's facial wounds with a look of concern. She tore off a colony-inch of her own tunic and mashed it hard against the other woman's cheekbone.

"Stop," the Medicine Woman whined. "You're hurting me."

"You need stitches."

"I'll sew it up myself."

"You'll make a botch of it. Let me get some water and rinse the gash. Then I'll sew you up. My stitches are far more fine and even than yours. Are you still bleeding?"

"Yeah, I need moss. Sphagnum moss."

"Does that help?"

"Ask that guy," the Medicine Woman nodded at Samuel. "It stopped his shoulder wound from bleeding out."

Sounder watched Jalen bathe.

With long rhythmic strokes, she shaved her legs with his straight razor, sharpened daily on a whetstone by one of their many attendants.

"Where is Papa Jack's dinner tonight?"

"Point State Park at sunset. I've reserved a PedalCar so you can wear your heels. Wear the pink ones. The patent leather stilettos."

She grinned at him, knowing his tastes quite well. The shoes were decades old, their tiny rhinestones long dulled. Still, they made her legs look long and arched her back. The pretty shoes had always been his favorite.

"So finish telling me about this morning's meeting. What were your esteemed colleagues arguing about now?"

"Steam engines. Turbines. Electric wire. Potable water. Sanitation. No one knows what direction to proceed in first. They bicker over everything, turning it into a standstill. What to work on individually or collectively? Who will pay and who will benefit? Who has the expertise and who gets in the way?"

"Papa Jack was right," Jalen replied. "Sylvania needs a hierarchy, not a council. It's the only way forward."

"Some of the sections do *nothing* well, except create problems for the rest of us."

"Are some sections coalescing around you? Do they understand you are Papa Jack's de facto leader?"

"The CouncilMembers don't understand Papa Jack's vision of retirement. They think he's going on vacation or taking a sabbatical for a couple weeks. Hopefully tonight's dinner will cement the fact that he is stepping down. He's done."

"But doesn't he still want the final say on Council matters?" Jalen asked.

"Papa Jack wants to sign off on everything."

"That doesn't make sense."

Sounder nodded. "Papa Jack wants the power and prestige of leading Sylvania, but none of the headaches. He's left them all to me."

"You mean he's left them all to us," Jalen said, staring at him. Her head rested on the back edge of the tub while her body continued to soak in tepid water.

"To us," he smiled at her, tucking a wet strand of hair behind her ear. He nibbled on her ear.

"Are the CouncilMembers open to you fully stepping into his role? Maybe you should add a few new members to the Council? Ones who are entirely loyal to you." Jalen leaned out of the claw footed tub to reach for a hand towel. Seeing her body, Sounder was momentarily distracted.

"The Council views my position as temporary until Papa Jack finishes grieving in the greenhouses. They keep thinking he'll resume things as they were once he gets over his loss. But things will never be like they were."

Jalen furrowed her brow, deep in thought.

"Who would support your taking over the Council, restructuring the government in a more hierarchical fashion?"

"Probably most of them. CouncilMembers have their own problems and concerns managing their own sections. Some are content. Others think this is a good time to expand their territory. A few want change. A few want to line their own pockets. Most want more tax revenue to spend how they please."

"Sounder," Jalen said firmly, "you'll have to make internal alliances if you want to shore up support for yourself, for us."

He nodded.

"You have to know who to trust."

"I know who to trust," he said, one finger outlining Jalen's body.

"Point out wives and mistresses and girlfriends to me tonight. Let me work on the CouncilMembers' soft underbellies and get what intel we need to secure our position."

"All right," he concurred. "You are very good at extracting information from people."

I should be, Jalen thought. *I didn't spend all those years on my back at Comfort Stations for nothing.*

"Sounder, have you considered an external alliance?"

"I have not replied to the Ohioans or the emissaries from Old Massachusetts."

"What about the Illuminati Pagans?"

"I've considered their proposal."

"The Pagan's Scout made a credible offer. They are the largest faction spreading North. You might want to bring it up to Papa Jack. Get his blessing. Darius has a solid reputation for supporting his protectorates."

"The Pagan Scout could be a double agent from one of the CouncilMembers to test my loyalty."

"Perhaps," Jalen said. "But we're going to have to trust someone outside our quarters. Throwing in with them makes the most sense for the Sylvanians. The Pagans would ensure peace. If things were more peaceful, and if we spent less time worrying about our borders, we could improve trade, technology, and our general way of life. We could rebuild hospitals and schools, Sounder. There is so much potential."

At this, Sounder took the razor out of her hand and laid it down. He plunged his hands into the water and picked her up, half soapy, all slithery, wrangling her back to bed.

Jalen laughed, as he almost dropped her along the way.

When they fell together in bed, he covered her with his own body.

"Yes, I know who to trust. No one. Not the CouncilMembers. Not Old Massachusetts, not the Ohioans, not the New Yorkers. Not the Pagans or any of the ratty Southern warlords or their militias. I trust only you," he whispered, kissing her neck.

While his hands traveled her body, Jalen's thoughts were elsewhere, looking at the ceiling, making her plans.

Papa Jack had been drinking steadily for most of the day.

At sunset, torches illuminated the CouncilMembers' arrival. Up the walkway, they ferried their wives, girlfriends or both on their arms. All were dressed in their best refurbished apparel or new clothing tailored from the Carolingian textile mills. Serving attendants handed out delicacies from tarnished silver platters. By the river's edge, a few musicians strummed instruments in various states of disrepair.

The end of an era, Papa Jack thought. *A wake for a living corpse, celebrated by childhood friends.* When he looked at them, gathering at the park he'd once taken his daughter to, he felt nothing. The longer he stood, watching the CouncilMembers joke and gibe with each other, the more withdrawn he became. He finally retreated to the edge of the gathering, annoyed by the braying laughter of the men and shrill voices of the women.

He turned to the river's edge, past the musicians.

Papa Jack wished he knew why grief had hollowed him out to such an extent, where simply breathing seemed laborious. His attempts to reconnect with others after the deaths of his family resulted in his feeling even more empty and disconnected.

I don't belong anywhere.

"Papa Jack?"

"I'm here, Sounder," he said, watching Sounder and Jalen walk from the main gathering to where Papa Jack stood. Papa Jack placed a hand on Sounder's shoulder. He recognized the astute blonde who stood by him from the other night, noticing her eyes missed nothing.

"Thanks for inviting us." Jalen leaned over to kiss Papa Jack on the cheek. She smelled like lilacs.

"You know," Papa Jack said, "Our families fished these rivers before the end of electricity before the Great Die-Off. No fish for years! Then a drought, where the water levels were a third of what they are now. But, now look. Now there is life." He attempted a smile that failed to reach his eyes.

"The fish are good to eat again, Papa Jack."

"Maybe not the catfish," Papa Jack laughed. "I'd stick to the carp and drum fish."

"Are you well?" Sounder asked.

"Well enough," Papa Jack replied. "I was in the greenhouses earlier. The attendants are getting quite good at mass production. The new aquaponics and hydroponic techniques are a success. Even my orchids are coming along, but they are pretty only for a season."

He looked at Jalen with his concluding remark, catching her off guard. He saw her eyes recalculate a bit, the smile never leaving her face.

Papa Jack turned to Sounder. "How about you get Jalen and I some corn whisky? I'll keep her company in the meantime."

Jalen smiled at Sounder, who nodded and hurried off. He turned to see Jalen place her hand on Papa Jack's back, talking to him, motioning to the stars overhead.

He heard Papa Jack laugh and smiled to himself.

Jalen could charm anyone.

Sounder returned with the drinks.

"They're going to be serving dinner soon," Sounder announced. "Would you like to join our table, Papa Jack?"

"Yes, of course. I'll be there shortly," Papa Jack waved him off, looking somber. "I'm going to go look at the water for a bit."

"We'll save a seat for you," Sounder added, as Jalen threaded her arm through his.

Papa Jack watched as Sounder and Jalen rejoined the group, his heart growing heavier with their every retreating footfall.

Et tu, Brute?

The Illuminati Pagan's Scout had been commissioned by Papa Jack, initiating a fictitious offer that Sounder seemed to entertain, knowing well that Papa Jack would have never agreed to outside interference in Sylvanian matters.

Before Jalen, Sounder would never have done something the least bit subversive.

Yet now?

Sounder had found himself wrapped around that little girl's finger, a pawn in her beautiful hands.

But the girl had a point, Papa Jack sadly thought. For a long moment, Papa Jack considered if he cared. He walked precariously close to the water's edge, the park high above the choppy currents of the Three Rivers.

Why not find a little happiness in the world, Jack?

There isn't any, he wanted to tell his wife. You packed whatever happiness was left in the world into your opium pipe and smoked it.

You did love fishing, Jack.

I did, he remembered. It was so hard to remember things these days.

Come fishing.

Papa Jack sat on the embankment and took off his black boots and socks.

Then as his childhood friends roared with laughter, drinking toasts to Papa Jack's many years of service to Sylvania, he slipped silently into the dark brown water and under the current.

On the outskirts of Sylvania, the Beth El Congregation of South Hills still stood, a beige brick building with its stained glass windows mostly intact. An elderly rabbi and his wife oversaw the orphanage, a well-run facility that accepted very few charges.

A hodgepodge of gardens surrounded the facility. Nearby was the synagogue's water purification system. The Medicine Woman had been drawn to a large cistern, intrigued by its design. She peppered the attendants with questions about the use of activated charcoal.

"Rabbi Raskin, there are only six of them," Dreadlocks begged. "Please reconsider. When I came to you, there were eight of us. We were as needy—just as willing to work."

"And you were the only one who remained here," the old man reminded her. "The others stole what they could, precious little that there was, and joined up with the New Yorkers."

"But—"

"I'm sorry. We can't take in anyone. We cannot accommodate more than we already have."

"These are good kids, Rabbi, I promise. Look at them. Everyone they know is dead. I was like them. If you hadn't taken me in, I don't know where I'd be."

"Lillibet."

"And they've survived the pox! They aren't carriers. In fact, they're going to help protect Sylvania with their scabs."

"What?"

"I can explain."

The Medicine Woman looked on, unsurprised at the difficulty Dreadlocks was having placing their wards. *Who wanted six more mouths to feed?*

"They are hard workers," Dreadlocks continued. "This one can prepare a chicken from coop to table in no time. This girl can sew clothing and work at a loom. The boys are young, but they are polite and strong. They all work extremely hard. I swear to you, Rabbi, you won't regret it."

"I regret it now," he eyed her.

"Then would you at least watch them until I get settled with Papa Jack and Sounder?"

"I will give you two weeks, Lillibet."

She kissed his check.

Dreadlocks sat on the ground with the Kimper children for a serious talk before leaving for the city.

"You will need to stay here for a bit. The Rabbi and his wife are very strict, but kind. You must do more than they say. Don't cry. Don't complain. Offer to help them at all times and in all things. Take any punishment they give you and learn from it."

"Will you come back?" a six-year-old girl said, her hazel eyes curious. She would have accepted the truth either way as life had already disappointed her.

"I will come back for you. I will come back for you, I promise, and we will all resettle in Sylvania. It's a good place where you will find work."

"What kind of work?"

"You could choose to work on a farm or a dairy. There are fishing boats and dockwork. There are deliveries to make and houses to clean. You could sew clothing for the shops, clean the looms, or work with the BlackSmiths or LeatherMen. You might make matches or muck out horse stalls."

"Are there bad people like Samuel?" the oldest girl asked in a very small voice.

"There are bad people everywhere," Dreadlocks conceded. "But there are good people, too. The secret is to figure out who is who. You know, there is even a Sylvanian School. Maybe you could learn to write and add numbers."

The children were quiet, hanging on to Dreadlocks' every word.

"Don't fret. I'll be back," she promised in earnest, getting up to leave. She had known what it felt like to be left behind.

The Medicine Woman had already left, heading down Roessler Road, anxious to get her work done to earn her freedom. She hoped to head South before the late autumn.

She sorely missed the warmth of Lincolnshire and ached to see Jasper again.

She kept a grip on her knives as blood streamed from an open gash on her cheekbone, rivulets of red running into her mouth.

Chapter 13

The City-State of Sylvania

Papa Jack's body had been found face down in the water, distal extremities abraded from being dragged along the shoreline's rocks and brush. Mud and debris had sloughed off most of the skin from his hands and feet. Putrefaction had ravaged his once ruggedly handsome face, now a waxy yellowish-brown, the water rendering him unrecognizable.

But Sounder knew the man from a distance.

One of the DockTrollops had discovered his remains in the early morning, calling out for a small group of MilitiaMen to fish him out. Eventually, the Council had been alerted, and Sounder had sprinted to the scene.

"No!" Sounder had cried out from the embankment, seeing Papa Jack's body fully exposed to a growing crowd of onlookers. Sounder took off his long coat and covered Papa Jack's face. "Get these people out of here," he muttered to one of the MilitiaMen, trying to preserve Papa Jack's dignity as best he could.

The news of Papa Jack's drowning ricocheted through Sylvania. CouncilMembers gathered by the Riverside, grim faced, somber, crestfallen. Though Papa Jack had been missing for a few days, no one assumed the river had taken him. He had often disappeared of late, usually resurfacing at Council meetings or the greenhouses, a cup full of corn whisky in hand.

Sounder remembered a side remark Jalen had made to him at the retirement party, before the guest of honor had gone missing. She had noticed an emptiness in Papa Jack's eyes, reminiscent of despondent men she'd known, the ones who gave up the things they cherished most, becoming more detached as they found the resolve to end their pain.

Sounder had known that Papa Jack had been inconsolable over the deaths of his wife and daughter. *Could that have been the sole reason for such a desperate act?*

Sounder considered how he would feel at Jalen's death. *What if he lost her in the same way?* His breath constricted. He forced himself to breathe slowly, attempting to control his thoughts and slow the rapid beating of his heart. Now visibly upset, a darker thought intruded as Sounder looked at the men around him: *Worse than her death, what if Jalen left him for another man?*

The mere thought of her infidelity brought angry tears to his eyes. He wiped them away with the backs of his hands, then balled his hands into fists.

"Sounder?"

"Yeah," he murmured. The young MilitiaMan looked unsure of himself.

"What should we do now?"

Sounder exhaled, collected his thoughts.

"Send for the Coroner at the MilitiaMen station. Tell him to bring a bolt of shroud linen. Send for the DeathCart."

"Anything else?"

"Tell the town criers to meet us here—immediately—to discuss how we will disseminate the news," he continued. "And send a PassengerCart to pick up Jalen at the Westin. I need her with me here."

Business settled, he knelt by the corpse, the others stepping away to let Sounder pay his respects in relative peace.

Seeing him up close, Sounder was overcome by Papa Jack's gruesome condition. He fell to his knees, pulled at his hair, and wept.

Spectators on the pier witnessed Sounder's grief, touched by his unfeigned sorrow. Alongside the gossip of Papa Jack's death, news spread of Sounder's fealty and how deeply he'd taken Papa Jack's passing.

Sounder, the whispers echoed. *Sounder was the CouncilMember who should assume Papa Jack's position, leading Sylvanians like a shepherd to better days ahead.* Sylvanians openly confided to one another in the streets, nodding, discussing the only CouncilMember to be seriously considered to fill Papa Jack's shoes.

The funeral was quickly arranged.

Jalen and Sounder wore their best dark wool clothing, held hands, standing close to each other in the night.

As was the custom, Papa Jack's funeral was held at Point State Park, a pyre illuminating the place where the Three Rivers met.

The most prominent CouncilMembers were dressed in heavy fabrics, deftly thwarting the evening's chill, as a late September moon sanctified the proceedings. The less affluent huddled in the back, peering over shoulders to get a better view, blankets and shawls and rags draped around their shoulders.

The MilitiaMen prepared themselves to hoist Papa Jack's corpse onto the flames. They nodded to Sounder who walked towards the pyre. The only sounds were of his footsteps and of the red flames licking the White Oak logs. The popping and crackling of the fire was loud enough for the silent masses to hear in the back.

"Citizens of Sylvania," Sounder called out, voice loud and strong.

"Citizens are here!" came the reply.

"We meet as one," he continued.

"We meet as one."

His eyes watered in the brisk night air. Sounder paused, swallowed hard, cleared his throat. He looked towards Jalen, who nodded at him, offering him her indefatigable strength with a gentle smile.

"We meet as one to honor Papa Jack, leader of the Sylvanian Council, a position handed down to him by his father and his father's father from the days before the end of electricity."

He paused, looking over the crowd, gathering his thoughts.

"I loved Papa Jack. I loved him from the day we were orphaned, both of our fathers dying at the Battle of Three Rivers. We all lost loved ones in those awful days when the New Yorkers came from the East. Then as now, we united, bravely fighting off people who meant us harm, who meant to take away our way of life. But Papa Jack knew Sylvanians would protect their own. He knew that Sylvanians were hard working, devoted, united, and true!"

"Long live Papa Jack!" a call came from the back.

"Long live Papa Jack!" repeated others in the crowd. Their voices carried throughout the park, startling the birds of prey who had roosted nearby.

Sounder waited until all was silent again.

"We've labored together over the decades to secure our borders and provide an orderly community for our families. As we pay homage to Papa Jack, know that our state is strong. The Council is strong. The leadership of Sylvania is well in hand, and all is well!"

"Long live Sounder!" cried a female voice from the far back of the throng.

"Long live Sounder!" A crescendo of voices moved like a wave, until even the other CouncilMembers joined in, some more sincerely than others. Jalen surreptitiously glanced around the proceedings to see whose eyes betrayed their mouths, as cheers for the deceased continued.

Sounder nodded to the MilitiaMen who respectfully placed Papa Jack's remains on top of the burning heap, the fire greedily consuming his shroud in minutes. The body itself would take hours to burn, but no one would leave until the pyre had burnt itself out, with only a few charred remnants lying in the soot.

Sounder returned to stand by Jalen's side. She took his hand and held it as the ashes turned gray.

At the next Council meeting, Sounder sat in Papa Jack's chair at the head of the table. He and Jalen had moved into Papa Jack's living quarters. No one loudly objected, as the CouncilMembers, too, looked for someone to follow, someone to lead, and more importantly, someone to blame if things went awry.

However, Jalen's presence at the meetings was new, taking the CouncilMembers by surprise at their first assembly after Papa Jack's funeral. But her beauty made her presence palatable, and she quietly listened and took notes in the far corner of the Westin's conference room.

In time, the CouncilMembers overlooked her. But Jalen, having long trafficked with men who underestimated her, offered Sounder her shrewd observations afterwards in bed, letting him know who would be useful to their plans and who would pose a problem.

Approaching the city, Dreadlocks and the Medicine Woman ignored the rusted remnants from the days before the end of electricity. Broken chain link fences were clogged with plastic scraps and other waste paper, deposited by intermittent flooding. The ubiquitous husks of cars and trucks lined the gutters, long ago stripped of anything useful. Rebar, electrical wires, and traffic signs hung precariously overhead. Large areas were scorched black, chemical fires that rendered the ground barren.

Decades of blistering summer heat had triggered droughts and flash floods, the residual silt covering a wide swath of pastureland. Because of the warmer weather, Southern plant parasites and insects had expanded Northwards. The corn flea beetle had been especially vexing, crippling even genetically modified crops.

"So there are *three* waterways surrounding Sylvania?" the Medicine Woman asked.

"Yes," Dreadlocks replied as they walked North on the Seven Nine. The Ohio, the Allegheny, the Monongahela. The Monongahela is the brown one. And it flows Northwest—away from the city."

"Does it really flow Northwest?" The Medicine Woman was incredulous. "And different colors? How can that be?"

"Brown and blue. All the way up until they blend into Ohio."

"Huh," the Medicine Woman replied, pondering how any of what she said was possible. "How are we getting across, anyway?"

"We're gonna take the Fort Pitt Tunnel. It leads to the only bridge that wasn't blown up during the Battle of Three Rivers."

"Are there any other options?" the Medicine Woman inquired.

"You want to swim?"

"Of course not. I don't like bridges."

"We're going through the tunnel, then over a bridge. Deal with it."

The Medicine Woman fretted. She had heard too many of her mother's accounts about the country's failing infrastructure, a problem even before the fall of the United Authority. Extreme weather patterns and ground tremors did little to stabilize hundred-year-old roads, bridges, and tunnels. Though StoneMasons in more stable regions had dabbled in making cement, there wasn't a sufficient amount in production to shore up the larger structures.

"We could commission one of the FerryMen to take us across. But this way is much faster. Our arrival is overdue as it is. Papa Jack is going to wonder where we are. C'mon now," Dreadlocks grinned, unusually cheery. "Fortune favors the bold."

"Fortune favors pylons that aren't going to collapse from metal fatigue," the Medicine Woman retorted. She frowned, looking at the tunnel's imposing entrance. "Are you sure we're going to make it to the other side?"

"No. Not at all," Dreadlocks laughed. "But who wants to live forever?"

The Medicine Woman ignored her.

Live forever, indeed.

Sylvanian MilitiaMen guarded the entrance to the Fort Pitt Tunnel. Like Dreadlocks, eight of them carried short-handled cudgels, capable of transmitting enough kinetic energy from the base to its knobby end to severely bludgeon a person.

The largest man in the group stood up as the two women approached the checkpoint in the late morning. He affixed a facial covering as he came near them, but not too near, in order to determine what they wanted and that they were not infected with the pox.

Dreadlocks held up her hands in the formal style of the Sylvanian official greeting. The MilitiaMan did not return the gesture. Too many refugees and migrants knew the Sylvanian signs for her greeting to mean anything.

"You are entering the City-State of Sylvania. This is a pox-free zone. No asylum seekers or unauthorized persons are permitted to enter Sylvanian territory at this time. Turn around and depart or face severe repercussions. This will be your only warning."

The women continued walking towards the entrance of the tunnel.

The MilitiaMan repeated his speech in his terse monotone, as if he had said as much to the hundreds who had come before them.

"I am Lillibet, a covert agent of the Council, sanctioned by Papa Jack for a special assignment in the South."

The men looked at each other.

"Papa Jack is—" The man didn't finish his thought. "Tell us who you are again," he demanded, looking at her suspiciously.

The Medicine Woman sensed something amiss, while Dreadlocks grew outraged.

"Where is your commander?" she demanded.

"Take it easy, girl."

"*Girl?* When Papa Jack is done with you, you'll be on the Eastern front fighting the Amish Warriors. Let us pass."

"Where are your credentials?"

"I lost them."

"You *lost* them."

"Yeah," Dreadlocks walked forward, toe to toe with the biggest one. "I lost them when I had to pick up this Witch Doctor from the Florida Penal Colony. Now stand aside."

"*Witch Doctor?*" the Medicine Woman repeated, scowling.

"And who are *you?*" The largest of the men turned to the Medicine Woman.

"I'm the person who is going to blow powdered pox scabs up your nose in order to save your life."

"Come again?" the man squinted at her, trying to make sense out of what she had said. Dreadlocks ignored him entirely, walking past him and the other men with impunity. The Medicine Woman pushed past him, too.

Dreadlocks turned to triumphantly flip both of her middle fingers at the men.

The largest of the MilitiaMan looked at his compatriots, seven men who looked entirely nonplussed. "She's a Sylvanian , no doubt," he remarked confidently. "Hey!" he yelled after the two women. "You'll need a couple of torches. It's dark inside."

A few curious rats scurried in front of them, as Dreadlocks and the Medicine Woman walked the half colony-mile through the gray concrete.

The torches illuminated ancient graffiti, political slogans, and profane suggestions. There were colorful proclamations about the "End of the World," next to a boldly drawn rendition of the Four Horsemen of the Apocalypse. Instead of War, Death, Disease and Famine, someone had labeled the Horsemen Electricity, Internet, Cellphones, and Social Media. The women ignored the silent rantings of another society long since past.

As Dreadlocks and the Medicine Woman exited the damp tunnel, both extinguished their torches into buckets of sand, situated between the tunnel and the bridge for the very purpose.

As they began walking through the tunnel and into the light, the Medicine Woman watched the entirety of the city unfold itself.

Sylvania was breathtaking.

The bridge curved into the downtown area, framed by the rivers and decorated with early fall foliage, radiant in the midday sun. Oranges, yellows, and reds gave the hills an otherworldly feel. The structures and buildings appeared largely to be intact, not blighted like most of the Southern cities she'd seen.

As they approached the downtown area, a general feel of industriousness permeated the air.

"What's that?" the Medicine Woman pointed to an open warehouse near the river. Men were hauling wheelbarrows of rocks and emptying bags of sand into large containers. The containers were being fed buckets of water by a pulley system leading out to the river.

"That's a water purification center."

"How does it work?"

"River water is purified by dripping through a series of layers. See the rocks? That's followed by sand and charcoal. We use cotton batting at the very end. The water runs the gauntlet. Gravity does the work, and it's much easier than boiling."

"Huh," the Medicine Woman said again, taking in the whole operation. "Could I see it up close?"

"Sure," Dreadlocks agreed. "But we need to get to the Westin and see Papa Jack. I need to make a quick stop though. There's someone I need to see."

"You're going to see your man?"

Dreadlocks nodded. *She couldn't wait to be in Sounder's arms.*

Dreadlocks turned to triumphantly flip both of her middle fingers at the men.

Chapter 14

The Westin Hotel in the City-State of Sylvania

Darius felt relieved when the women finally left. It had been Hector's plan to install a hereditary monarchy, to ensure Darius' bloodline carried on while the Illuminati Pagans ruled. But to Darius, having a legacy or a son meant precious little. *When he was dead, he'd be dead,* Darius reasoned. *The rest of the world could burn for all he cared.*

Finding himself restless, Darius contemplated the North while mindlessly munching on fried potatoes and drinking short beer. He wiped his hands on table linens, burped loudly, then motioned for an attendant to remove the remnants of his midafternoon feast.

Darius had commissioned a new map, one he could take down from the wall to mull over, one he could lay across, envisioning a Pagan realm stretching west of the Mississippi Riverbed.

Darius pulled down the map, gazing at it long into the night. Alone with his thoughts, he strategized his military moves, nudging assorted tokens and charms across the folds of leather. The various-sized pieces represented organizational elements of MilitiaMen. *Platoon. Company. Brigade.* He used long plastic strips to mark supply lines, calculating where they would operate and surmised any possible weak spots. He peppered the map with plastic pieces from Monopoly games, visualizing Illuminati Pagan strongholds, making adjustments as suited his strategy. Darius spent hours shuffling the green and red plastic tokens in his hands, considering the myriad of possibilities.

Above all, Darius needed to be careful. He'd learned from Xerxes not to expand too quickly, not to exhaust his treasury, and, most importantly, not to trust others.

However, when Darius assembled his tacticians and advisors and battled-hardened officers, most agreed that taking the North was possible. *Controlling the Northeastern region wouldn't be hard after it was won,* thought Darius. It would come down to subsuming three key city-states: Classical Massachusetts, Montreal in New Virginia, and Sylvania. If those cities were taken, the rest of the East Coast would fall in line as neatly as the South had.

The thought of ruling the North excited him. Darius thrilled himself with the idea of uniting all of the inhabitable parts of the North American continent. He'd regulate agriculture, open schools, codify law, establish hospitals, train engineers, and erect statues of himself in city squares.

But how to start his Pagan Renaissance?

First, Darius would build printing presses. He'd restock libraries, reprinting all of the information lying fallow from ages past, moldering in books which had survived the wars, knowledge that managed to exist after the end of electricity.

Xerxes had shown Darius how books contained answers to perplexing mysteries. Certainly there were repositories to be found. Volumes to be rediscovered, read, digested, shared. Darius reminded himself to tell Hector about his idea of forming special MilitiaMen teams for that very purpose. *Knowledge RetrievalMen.*

With the availability of horses, the past few years had opened up new trading posts and commercial markets throughout the South. More importantly, the advent of reliable transportation allowed for information to be orally shared, as one community's ideas crossbred with others.

Yes, Darius nodded. *It was time to record and distribute collective knowledge; it was time to usher in a new Age of Enlightenment.*

Darius thought of the fields he saw, ones with endless rows of shiny mirrors facing the sun, connected to wires that snaked into boxes, rusted and stripped of anything valuable. *Did those mirrors make machines move? Were they religious structures, a tribute to a god whose name was lost to history?*

There were endless questions he had whenever he walked through the labyrinth of darkened office buildings, as well as when he viewed the rusted hulks of large machinery. His advisors could not fathom most of their purposes, but there were others who could. *If only the pox hadn't struck when it did, just as new ideas were flourishing,* he mused.

But poxes ended.

Darius walked over to a bowl of honey candy, grabbing a fistful.

Mulling over his plans, Darius sighed. *What was the point?* He could simply rest on his laurels if he wanted to. He had done enough and would live quite comfortably until the end of his days. *But he'd be bored.* The *Pax Darius* had proven monotonous, as protectorate regions faithfully paid their taxes and his MilitiaMen grew stronger. Due to the spread of the pox, rogue groups dissipated, reforming only to be beaten again.

The people under his rule were better fed and safer than any time he remembered during his lifetime. Crops grew in the fields, and the lull of continual bloodshed across the land allowed for people to consider solving their problems instead of merely subsisting.

Metal was scavenged, melted down, and refashioned into tools. Food was becoming more plentiful and fed more bellies. If the pox were contained, there would be little for Darius to worry about as relative prosperity spread across the South. The loyalty of his citizenry increased while the Illuminati Pagan Empire became an efficient bureaucracy.

Yes, Darius thought to himself. *It was time to expand. It was time to make bold moves.*

Darius would discuss the timetable of the move to the North with Hector when they met again. Certainly DariusWood would hold, but he preferred a headquarters farther North. He would ask Hector to recommend a location, as Darius relied on Hector entirely. Hector had proven as meticulous and uncompromising as Darius had been when he attended Xerxes. Back in his younger days. *Back when everything was exciting.* Of late, Darius looked for other distractions to ignore the fact that he was getting older, growing fatter.

The move to the North intrigued him, he thought, shuffling the red and green plastic pieces from hand to hand. *It had his full attention.*

Darius and Hector often dined alone together. Female attendants brought in skewers of marinated beef, flatbreads, sauces and vegetable spreads. Darius steadily ate all, while Hector picked at his meal, updating Darius on the Carolinas.

Darius ignored most of what he reported, as Carolingians were too violent to worry about. They much preferred killing each other in feuds, carrying on long-held grudges stemming from the First Civil War.

"I am decided on it. I want a new DariusWood in the North."

Hector nodded. "Plans are underway as we speak. Several Scouting divisions are making their way to Sylvania to get the lay of the land. After their reports, we will set up a basecamp nearby, organize our forces to liberate the Sylvanian populace, then take the city at an auspicious time. Once DariusWood North is established in Sylvania, we'll plan other Northern incursions. We'll take the lot, bit by bit."

"And you are positive this Jalen woman can be trusted?"

"Yes. More importantly, Sounder trusts her," Hector replied. "All of our Scouts have confirmed that he does nothing without her consent."

"What of the other CouncilMembers?"

"They support Sounder to a point. They are more keen on keeping power over their own sections than propping up Sounder's regime. Since Papa Jack's death, disunity has crept in. Scouts have noted fewer and fewer meetings of the CouncilMembers. Sounder appears to rule by edict alone."

"Excellent," Darius smiled. "A house divided."

"Jalen has proved masterful at creating chaos, planting the right bit of gossip in the wrong person's ear. With each of our shipments of Classical Massachusetts Opium into the city, the CouncilMembers grow increasingly paranoid. They don't know how to stop drugs from flooding their streets, and it's gutting their population more than the pox ever could."

"Perfect."

"Jalen's quite a talent. She'll be a good addition to our councilors," Hector suggested. "There is always a need for people of her considerable talents. Make sure she is safe afterwards."

"Hector," Darius said. "Once we take Sylvania, Jalen will not be useful. Once a Comfort Station attendant, always a Comfort Station attendant."

"Of course, Darius," Hector agreed. "It's a shame, though. Her beauty is renowned."

"Oh?" Darius mused. "Well, when we're done with her and her services to the Illuminati Pagans, bring Jalen to me. I would like to see her for myself."

"You reek," the Medicine Woman muttered to Dreadlocks.

The Medicine Woman surveyed the city, noting how similar it was to Richmond before the United Authority fell. Sylvanians bustled among the ruins, reconstructed to serve a variety of purposes. *A Blacksmith shop. Plastic bottle refilling stations. An open air market with oatcakes and flatbreads.*

Some buildings fared far better than others through the difficult years. During cold Sylvanian winters and hot summers, fissures appeared in some of the reinforced concrete. At more frequent intervals, the Medicine Woman saw pathetic figures slumped into allies and curled into fetal positions, wallowing in filth.

"Who are they?" she asked Dreadlocks as they passed. "They don't show any signs of the pox. I could boil some tea from—"

"No!" Dreadlocks snapped at her. "Those people are no longer Sylvanians. No one who smokes Classical Massachusetts Opium is. They are outcasts and will die in the streets. Their bodies will be thrown into the rivers for the fish."

"But I could—"

"We don't have time for you to cure people who don't care for themselves. Hurry along and quit gawking. You'll be helping the truly sick soon enough."

The Medicine Woman was silenced, but angrily shook her head. *Alleviate suffering,* her mother had taught her, ever since her youth.

When she passed the opium addicts who lay stricken, her hands clenched into fists.

They had walked at a brisk pace ever since leaving the tunnel. Dreadlocks was determined to see Sounder at once, especially when she saw the Westin Hotel's distinctive architecture, visible from blocks away.

"Ugh! I'm walking downwind from you," remarked the Medicine

Woman. "You smell rank."

"I don't care about that. Now hurry up," Dreadlocks urged her on, pushing through throngs of pedestrians.

"You stink!" the Medicine Woman shouted.

"I stink? Well, you're a bitch," Dreadlocks said dismissively, continuing to lengthen her stride. She stood at the bottom of an exterior staircase, the handrails long since looted.

"You *literally* smell like a dead goat, Lillibet. Or a decaying deer carcass in a cesspool. I'd advise you to wash up before you see your man."

"Sounder told me to come straight to him when I returned. He told me that he'd wash me himself."

Walking up to her travel companion, the Medicine Woman stared at her, straight in the face. She noticed a rare flicker of self-doubt in Dreadlocks' eyes.

"Men say a lot of things," the Medicine Woman said evenly. "And you need to bathe."

"What do you know?" Dreadlocks shot back. "Your man is 900 colony-miles away. You're a months-walk away from anyone wanting to touch you."

"Where are your quarters? We should both wash up. The way we look and smell isn't going to go over well with anyone. You need your man. I need to do my job and return home as soon as possible."

Dreadlocks frowned. "C'mon," she relented. Dreadlocks took the Medicine Woman up a back staircase, past the guards, and into the Westin. "I'm on the sixth floor."

The hotel was quite dark in the interior hallways, and it took a moment for the Medicine Woman's vision to adjust. Every so often, an entire hotel room had been removed, allowing for the sunlight to spill out into the central areas.

Greasy oil lamps hung from the walls, offering a pale light in the corridor.

"I'm in 603."

The Medicine Woman followed close behind, holding onto Dreadlocks' shoulder as they rounded a corner.

"Here we are," Dreadlocks announced. She bent down to pick up a wedge that secured the door from swinging out. Other than that, there was no lock from the outside.

The Medicine Woman looked up and down the hallway, locating the exits, scanning the area for possible weapons to use.

"We're safe here," Dreadlocks assured her. "MilitiaMen and attendants monitor every level. Papa Jack made this place into a fortress."

When they entered Dreadlocks' quarters, the Medicine Woman noticed that two hotel rooms had been converted into one unit, one side of the enlarged room facing out onto the street. A series of windows provided a view of the setting sun in the west, illuminating the ripples on the Allegheny River.

A straw tick bed and a few items of clothing were shoved into the corner of the room. Other than that, there was nothing but a few plastic water barrels and assorted tools.

"Help me fill the tub."

The Medicine Woman assisted Dreadlocks in hoisting one of the 55-colony-gallon containers up to pour a good portion of room temperature water into the tiled bathtub, yellowed with age.

In her bathroom were a few bars of ash soap, rustic and unperfumed. Dreadlocks stripped herself bare, tossing her clothing into a chipped plastic bin.

"The attendants will see to your clothing," she said. "They come around twice a week to gather the laundry."

"They might be better off burning it."

"You don't mind going second?"

"Do I have to use your bathwater?"

"There's plenty of clean water here," Dreadlocks said. "We aren't barbarians like you penal colonists."

The Medicine Woman ignored the barb, deciding instead to walk around the room while Dreadlocks scrubbed herself and gushed about

Sounder.

"Papa Jack didn't approve of our seeing each other at first, but he will get used to my being with him."

The Medicine Woman didn't reply, inspecting her own body for cuts and abrasions and parasites from their travels. "I fell in love with Sounder long before he knew who I was. He was with another girl for a long time. Eloise. She was a baker in the main kitchen."

"Mm-hmm," the Medicine Woman replied, turning to the room, rifling through Dreadlocks' personal effects. There was precious little to go through. No mementos or books, no herbs or jars of cosmetics. Only clothing, leather boots, cotton tunics and a few sundries were to be found. She'd learned nothing more about Dreadlocks by rooting through her things.

"Are you done spying on me?"

The Medicine Woman looked up to see Dreadlocks wrapped in a ragged towel.

"You have nothing here. You couldn't be any more boring," the Medicine Woman replied.

"Hurry and take your bath. We'll go meet Papa Jack and Sounder together."

Dressed in Dreadlocks' clothing, both women took the stairs, climbing down two steps at a time. Both women's hair was still wet, but they felt ebullient, clean, having washed off the dirt, vermin, and filth from the road.

"Which floor?"

"3rd. Go down three levels. Dinner is served at sunset in the main hall. Papa Jack's room is connected to the Council Chamber on the other side. They should be finishing up their daily meeting." Dreadlocks was breathless, her voice giddy.

I did it, she grinned. She had succeeded in bringing the Medicine Woman back, surviving the trek home with someone who could teach the Sylvanians how to protect themselves from the pox. *Papa Jack would be proud of her. And Sounder would love her all the more!*

The Medicine Woman managed to keep up with her pace, as Dreadlocks flew down the stairs. She marched after Dreadlocks, striding down a long corridor with faded plush carpeting. Odd rust colored splotches seem to indicate a battle had been waged inside the hotel at some point.

"They are through here," Dreadlocks called out, walking into the CouncilMembers' chamber.

Odd, Dreadlocks thought. *It was empty.*

An attendant walked by and greeted her by name.

"Where is everyone? Is the meeting over?" Dreadlocks' smile faded. *Papa Jack was known for his long meetings, ensuring all had their say, questioning each CouncilMember until he understood their concerns and grievances well.*

"Oh," the attendant replied. "The Council meets infrequently these days. Hardly at all since Papa Jack's death—"

Dreadlocks' hands covered her mouth.

"Death? Papa Jack is *dead?*"

The idea seemed unfathomable.

The Medicine Woman's hands instinctively curled around the knives she had secreted on her person. She glanced up and down the hallways, considering the rust colored splotches.

"Papa Jack drowned, Dreadlocks," the attendant explained. "It was a terrible accident. His funeral pyre was held weeks ago."

"I didn't know. I just returned from the South," she mumbled, tears streaming down her face.

"The CouncilMembers wondered if you'd ever return. It has been so long—"

"Where's Sounder?" Dreadlocks asked in a small raspy voice.

"Preparing for dinner," the attendant responded. "In his room."

"I'll go see him there."

The attendant nodded and disappeared into the back rooms.

"C'mon, Witch Doctor."

"Dreadlocks, we should go back to your room," the Medicine Woman replied in an ominous tone.

"Sounder will tell us what's going on."

"Where is he?"

"Eight floors up."

The eleventh floor was empty of all the fine things Sounder had previously decorated his housing with. Dreadlocks looked for the couches they'd made love on, the fine linens and antique mirrors, but the walls were bare and the current furniture was sparse.

"Sounder?" cried Dreadlocks. Her voice reverberated. The Medicine Woman again felt for her knives, a silent observer in the drama that was unspooling itself.

"*Dreadlocks?* Is that you?" called out an older man, casually sitting in a patched overstuffed chair. He was whittling shafts for arrows while a thin old woman mended a frock from roughspun thread.

"Tommy Ray, why are you in Sounder's quarters? Why aren't the CouncilMembers meeting tonight?"

"Oh, little girl. A lot has changed since you left."

"Papa Jack died!"

"Yes. A tragedy. And we miss him. Terribly! Especially since—" Tommy Ray shut his mouth. *He'd learned long ago not to say too much.*

"Dinner is still at sunset, yes?" Dreadlocks asked hopefully. *Dining together after CouncilMembers' meetings bonded the group. Breaking bread after debating policy kept the unity, Papa Jack had once explained to her.*

"We don't eat together much anymore. There's been a restructuring," Tommy Ray tried to explain. His wife looked at him with concern.

"Where's Sounder? Does he still live in the Westin?" Dreadlocks added a bitter laugh. She raised her hands in a futile gesture. "This is all so strange!"

Tommy Ray looked pointedly at her.

"Sounder is still here, Dready. He's in charge of things now." The old man kept his voice as neutral as possible.

"Then where is he?" Dreadlocks demanded in frustration. "Why isn't Sounder here?"

"He's here. He's still here, running things. But they've moved into Papa Jack's suite."

"They?" Dreadlocks looked incredulous. "Who are *they*?"

"Sounder and Jalen."

Hearing Jalen's name, the Medicine Woman returned to the stairwell, faintly hearing Dreadlocks' angry reply through her gritted teeth.

"Who's Jalen?!"

Are you done spying on me?

Chapter 15

The University of Pitt in the City-State of Sylvania

Jalen sat at her vanity table, leisurely applying face powder to cover the bruises under her left eye and the fingerprints around her neck. The cosmetics Sounder had imported from New Virginia were quite good at hiding the evidence of his frustrations with her. The little jar in her hand contained refined cornstarch mixed with a little cinnamon for color. A few drops of geranium oil kept it the right consistency. It smelled nice on her skin.

The lacerations on her back and buttocks were hidden under cotton lingerie, prettily edged with lace. The finery had been purchased from local merchants, supplied by the textile mills in Classical Massachusetts.

Sounder would expect her to wear his most recent gift. She'd forgive him, of course. She always forgave Sounder, but her eyes narrowed a little bit more each time.

When Darius' Scouts first approached Jalen, they had told her the truth. They'd been hired by Papa Jack to test Sounder's loyalty—a test he would ultimately fail, thanks to Jalen's complicity.

Papa Jack's restructuring of Sylvania had been a concern to Darius, as he preferred unraveling a less unified government. Fortunately for the Illuminati Pagans, Papa Jack's untimely death provided the leadership vacuum they'd hoped for. The CouncilMembers on the Illuminati Pagans' payroll encouraged Sounder's temporary ascension of power.

Sounder's obsession with Jalen made him all the more susceptible to their manipulation. The Scouts had encouraged Jalen to feed Sounder half truths, confirming what information Darius' Scouts routinely planted in the populace. When a harsh reality discredited what Jalen had told him was true, Sounder felt desperate and panicky, feelings mitigated by his physical violence.

The Scouts' intent was to prop Sounder up in a position of power before destabilizing Sylvania. Already Sounder's erratic behavior had made the Sylvanians grumble in the street. They'd had high expectations, Papa Jack's right hand man now flailing at every turn.

The only things coming out of the Westin Hotel were demands for new taxes, new curfews, and new restrictions. MilitiaMen were found more frequently in the streets. Dissidents who voiced objections were taken away for questioning.

As carefully as lining up a row of dominos, Darius' Scouts infiltrated meetings of concerned citizens, artfully planting rumors of worse things to come. Surely under Sounder's leadership there would be food shortages, internecine trade wars, and more opium flooding the streets.

When the time was right, Darius would create a cataclysmic event to topple the dominos, each one taking out the other. Chaos would ensue, allowing the Illuminati Pagans to sweep in as peacekeepers—welcomed saviors—as things fell apart. Sylvanians would heartily welcome an external force, as a scared and hungry populace cared little for personal freedom.

The plan wasn't anything new, Darius grinned. It had certainly worked in many of the communities where the Illuminati Pagans had wrested control.

Through well-placed comments and sidelong glances, Jalen continued to make Sounder paranoid. After Sounder officially took command, she made him feel unsure about the CouncilMembers' loyalty and the Sylvanians' support. This caused Sounder to marginalize former faithful friends, who in turn formed new alliances, both whispering behind his back.

For her part, Jalen played Sounder masterfully, impressing even the jaded Pagan Scouts who were used to working with a fifth column inside city-states.

How quickly things decline, Jalen considered, applying more concealer before dinner. She thought of how much she'd loved Sounder from the start. Aging more rapidly than she'd expected, Jalen had realized Sounder turned her head by showering her with gifts and saying all the sweet-nothings she hadn't heard in years.

Her biggest regret was discarding Mama Mitzi so casually. *Now what did she have?* Jalen looked around the lavish living quarters, the racks of dresses, glittery trinkets, and loads of refurbished high heels.

She shared a bed with a petty tyrant, a petulant, mean-spirited man who lashed out with his tongue and hands whenever he felt threatened. Sounder blamed Jalen while asking her what he should do in the very same breath. *What had she ever seen in him?* His weakness disgusted her.

Darius' Scouts pushed her harder of late, growing bolder, coming directly into the Westin to meet with her whenever Sounder was occupied. Jalen dutifully passed on whatever misinformation they wanted to plant, taking great satisfaction in how it enmeshed Sounder further into the political quagmire he'd started. He had pitted himself against his own CouncilMembers.

She couldn't wait until the tipping point, when it would all come crashing down.

Since Papa Jack's death, Sounder hadn't had a peaceful night's rest. He sat at the head of a conference room table, now used at his personal dining table. Attendants stood at attention, waiting for Jalen to arrive. Though he'd been early himself, Sounder brooded, impatiently waiting for her.

The silverware was mismatched, but the china and stemware had been preserved from the time before the end of electricity. Large beeswax candles dripped on stained linens. Serving attendants held platters of food waiting to be uncovered.

Sounder still had evening meetings to attend, expected to run late into the night. A few CouncilMembers he trusted were urging him to form a Star Chamber of sorts. They wanted reassurances, wanted to discuss things now that they felt the power shift. Sounder needed Jalen to advise him at dinner before the matter.

Rubbing his eyes, he remembered the numerous times he'd watched Papa Jack in this room, always so steady, so strong. He could understand a situation at a glance, knowing a man's heart in an instance. Papa Jack had what Sounder never would: vision and clarity.

He'd made a botch of things, Sounder sulked. He could feel the knives were out for him, and he didn't know which way to turn.

Even worse, Jalen was late for dinner.

❖❖❖

Wearing a green dress that Sounder particularly liked, Jalen left the living quarters. As she turned into the long hallway, a tall, thin woman with long black hair ran towards her. *She looked very familiar.*

"Eve?" Jalen squinted as the Medicine Woman came into view. "Eve!" Jalen took a few quick steps towards her before they embraced. "What are you doing here? How did you get to Sylvania? How's Jasper and Lincoln and Fortinbras—"

"We need to go," the Medicine Woman said in a low voice, pulling back from their embrace.

"What's the matter?"

"Jalen, we need to leave."

"It's so good to see you!" Jalen exclaimed, hugging her again. "Come eat with us. I'm with the Sylvanian leader now. I'm sure he won't mind if you—"

"Jalen, Sounder's lover is here. She's dangerous, and she's coming to find you. While Sounder sorts things out with her, we have to go." The Medicine Woman took hold of Jalen's forearm, shepherding her to the nearest stairwell.

Jalen dug in her heels, wresting her arm from the Medicine Woman's grasp.

"What are you talking about?" Jalen replied. "Sounder doesn't have another woman."

"Sounder has a nasty girlfriend, and she's on her way. You know how these things go, Jalen. Stay out of it."

"Ridiculous," Jalen laughed. "You don't know Sounder. And if you think I'm going to run, you don't know me. Did someone put you up to this? Are you working with one of the CouncilMembers? The White Crosses?"

The Medicine Woman looked back at her in disbelief.

"Goddammit, Jalen. It's me. *Am I working with someone?* How long have we known each other? Now let's go."

"Don't worry about me. I can handle one of Sounder's former lovers—" Jalen continued down the hallway.

"Jalen," the Medicine Woman pleaded.

"You're going soft in your old age," Jalen said breezily, smiling her dazzling smile. "The young Medicine Girl would have preferred to watch a catfight. She would have placed a wager on the winner. How about you go down to the docks? Buy yourself some fish tacos. Meet me back here later and we'll catch up. I want to hear all the news from Lincolnshire."

"You need to go somewhere safe until this is sorted. Send word to Sounder that you're sick." The Medicine Woman attempted to take Jalen's arm again, but Jalen winced in pain at her touch.

The Medicine Woman gave her a knowing look, peering at her face more closely, seeing Jalen's uneven skin tone through the carefully applied cosmetics.

"He's beating you."

"You don't understand," Jalen attempted to explain.

"I understand you are being beaten by a man who's come to power under suspicious circumstances. One who has promised several women all sorts of things."

"Fuck off," Jalen spat, walking past her. Her high heels clacked down the old parquet flooring, patched over the years with various degrees of success.

Hands down by her sides, the Medicine Woman watched Jalen walk midway down the corridor, when a dining attendant greeted her, opening the door to a banquet room off the main area.

Jalen didn't look back to see if the Medicine Woman followed.

"You are late," Sounder muttered.

"I ran into a friend," Jalen smiled, leaning down for a kiss. She bent low enough for him to see that she was wearing his most recent purchase. He ran his hand up her leg.

"Friend? Which friend?"

"No one you know. Someone from my days in Lincolnshire. I'll catch up with her later." Jalen forced a broader smile, seating herself on Sounder's left side.

Attendants poured her a tumbler full of mead, serving the first course of leafy greens accompanied by an assortment of vegetables grown on the top floors of the Westin.

"Your friend is from Tallahassee?"

"Tallahassee is called Lincolnshire now," Jalen remarked, eating a forkful of carrots and peppers. "My friend Eve's stepfather captured the city-state after the Warlord of Tallahassee was stabbed to death. Few people know that it was Eve who did it. She rescued her mother and killed her father. It's quite a story."

"Where is Eve now?"

"I invited her to join us, but—"

"Is Lillibet with her?" Sounder asked, carefully articulating each word.

"Who's Lillibet?"

The question had left Jalen's lips before the door flung open, slamming into the wall, startling everyone in the room.

Dreadlocks stood in the door jamb, quickly assessing who was present. She shot a murderous glare at the blonde clutching Sounder's arm.

Trained to protect Sounder, the attendants dropped their platters, pushing Jalen to the floor while brandishing concealed weapons. Within moments, they flanked Sounder on all sides.

Dreadlocks walking in, seething, breathing in great gulps of air, and exhaling loudly. She'd run through most of the Westin to find the new dining facilities, her eyes wild, glittering from hurt and anger.

"Lillibet!" Sounder exclaimed, standing, straightening his jacket while waving the attendants away. "You've come home at last."

"Who is this whore, Sounder?" Dreadlocks yelled, pointing at the figure lying supine on the carpet. Dazed by the turn of events, Jalen's hair had become disheveled, her dress ripped in the melee.

When Sounder looked from Dreadlocks at Jalen, his eyes grew cold.

"She only kept my bed warm while you were gone."

Jalen bit her lip, hard enough to taste blood. She calculated the few moves she had left.

As Sounder walked towards Dreadlocks, Jalen kicked off her impractical shoes, scuttling to the service door that led into the kitchen.

Safe from a distance, Jalen looked up to see Dreadlocks' jaw clenched. Her knees bent, Dreadlocks had turned her body to face Sounder, twisting to generate enough torque for a resounding punch to his face. Dreadlocks' middle knuckle squarely hit Sounder's nose, resulting in a gurgling crunch. Blood gushed as she withdrew her fist. For good measure, she followed up with a few jabs and a hook until Sounder's knees gave way.

Sounder staggered towards Dreadlocks, steadying himself by grabbing Dreadlocks by the hair. When Dreadlocks screeched in pain, the attendants turned to intervene.

"Get out!" Sounder roared.

The attendants fled in a thick scrum, each one anxious to leave the room as quickly as possible.

"She's back," muttered one of the attendants to another, pushing past Jalen.

Jalen's face was now a mess of makeup and tears and phlegm. Frozen, she could not move, silently watching Sounder and Dreadlocks verbally and physically assault one another. A dish of meatballs exploded directly over Jalen's head. Other items from the aborted dinner were thrown, one right after another, including cutlery. *Including knives.*

Jalen scrambled to her feet, scurrying into the kitchen after the attendants. There, she found the staff calmly putting away foodstuffs and preparing to clean up once the fracas ended.

"Are they—are they always like this?" Jalen asked, immediately cognizant of her lowered status.

The attendants didn't respond; instead, they went about their duties of making cinnamon rolls, salting pork, trimming beans and peppers. Three began the arduous task of boiling water for cleaning the dishes which remained intact after Dreadlocks and Sounder's latest imbroglio.

Standing blithely by the meat counter, the Medicine Woman calmly ate what appeared to be the main course from Jalen's meal, a freshly caught fish, lightly fried in a cornmeal batter. The Medicine Woman wiped her mouth on the back of her hand. *It was delicious.*

"You ready to go now?" the Medicine Woman asked Jalen between bites.

From the moment Mama Mitzi opened the door, there was no question of her taking Jalen in.

"Draw a bath," Mama Mitzi ordered an attendant. "Use the tub in my quarters. Find the best towels and soap in the CatHouse and bring them here."

Still sobbing, Jalen was led away.

"You've done well," the Medicine Woman noted, observing the CatHouse's parlor. It was full of MilitiaMen, DockWorkers, and TradesMen.

"Business is good. And I've streamlined things. We've done away with the paperwork of taking temporary wives," Mama Mitzi explained. "That patriarchal system was typical of the United Authority's hypocrisy. Our women are now called CatHouse Workers. They are free to come and go as they wish. It works out better for all of us."

The Medicine Woman nodded.

"Do you need a room, too?"

"Only for the night. I'm going back to the Westin after things settle down," the Medicine Woman replied. "The pox is coming North. I've been brought here to train the Sylvanians how to prevent its spread."

"Is it possible? Some of the horror stories coming out of the South—"

"There's no stopping the pox coming North. But there are preventative measures. Inoculations. Increased public hygiene. Possible quarantines."

"I'm glad you're here, Eve. The Sylvanians are good people. A little rough around the edges, but generally hardworking and fair."

"I didn't have a choice, Mitzi. They threatened my family."

Mama Mitzi frowned, putting a hand on the Medicine Woman's shoulder. "People do stupid things when they are afraid."

"People do stupid things even when they aren't afraid."

"Agreed," Mama Mitzi laughed.

"You'll help Jalen?" the Medicine Woman asked.

"Jalen will always have a home with me," Mama Mitzi replied. She turned away before the Medicine Woman could see her wipe her eyes.

The next morning, the Medicine Woman appeared at the entrance of the Westin, now guarded by numerous MilitiaMen.

"State your business."

"I'm here to save Sylvania," the Medicine Woman said.

"Excuse me?"

"I'm here to see Lillibet or Sounder, assuming either one is still alive."

"Are you the Witch Doctor from Tallahassee?"

"Allegedly."

"Dreadlocks said to send you directly to Pitt."

"I'm going into a *pit*?"

"The University of Pitt. Dr. Mort is expecting you. These men will take you there."

"That's all well and good, but I'm starving. Tell Lillibet I need to be fed if I'm going to stop the pox."

"Come again?"

"There are some cinnamon rolls in the main kitchen," the Medicine Woman added. "I'll take a half colony-dozen of them before I go."

It had taken a colony-decade, but Dr. Mort finally convinced the

Sylvanian farmers to rotate their crops.

"Grow lentils first, then wheat. This should be followed by root crops, primarily for the animals. Only then should we grow barley!"

Of course the farmers wanted to plant barley every year, as Sylvanian beer was renowned throughout the region. It was their most profitable export. They'd almost lynched Dr. Mort when he suggested they plow under the alfalfa crop. However, it did successfully replenish the soil. The amount of grain grown in the next cycle yielded enough for Sylvanians to live on for two years.

"We're going to collect fecal matter," he had informed Papa Jack in the years Sylvania was stable enough to grow crops.

Papa Jack was puzzled at first, but trusted Dr. Mort and his knowledge of agriculture. He seemed to be the only person in the city-state who knew how a dibber, sickle, and flail were properly used.

In time, Sylvanians grew corn, oats, potatoes, and sorghum. Tall sunflowers grew by the roadways, their seeds collected to make into cooking oil. Sweet potatoes were a favorite of Dr. Mort's. He could often be seen in the fields snacking on one like an apple.

Dr. Mort had raided local museums for antique harrows and seed drills. He instructed the Blacksmiths how to forge adequate plows and StoneMasons to create functioning millstones.

Next to Papa Jack, Dr. Mort had ensured Sylvanians survived the brutal winters with warm homes and full bellies.

"Eating well relies on chemistry," he told Papa Jack on a visit to his facilities at Pitt. "Behold yeast!"

He offered Papa Jack a container of a sourdough culture that had fermented particularly well. Soon, Sylvanian bakeries and breweries had enough microbes to produce bread and beer in sufficient quantities for use and export.

The attendants to Dr. Mort usually had to search the entire campus for him. If he wasn't in the agricultural wing, he was in the medical training building or the blast furnace room. They finally found him in the experimental warehouse, filled with assorted plastic buckets containing animal and human excrement. It smelled like a cesspit.

"Doctor Mort?"

"Yes?"

"The Witch Doctor is here."

"Send her down here, please. I don't want to walk all the way back to my office," he said, not looking up from the methane gas storage tank he'd been inspecting.

It was working. By blocking the oxygen from the fecal matter's decomposition, the anaerobic bacteria thrived. *He could pipe the gas into a container for civilian use!* He foresaw gas powered lights, stoves—and possibly cars.

Sylvania would become a shining city on the hill! A beacon for like-minded communities who wanted to leave the prehistoric world behind.

As the colony-minutes passed, Dr. Mort had forgotten that the Medicine Woman was coming.

"Sir?" a voice came.

"What?" he snapped. Irritated, Dr. Mort turned to see a tall Native American woman looking down at him. Her eyes were watering from the stench that he'd grown used to.

"I was sent to see you."

"Well, what do you want?"

"I want to go home to Lincolnshire and not have my family slaughtered by Sylvanian Scouts."

Dr. Mort sighed.

"Let's start at the beginning. I'm Doctor Mort, the chancellor of Pitt. Come into the shithouse and sit down."

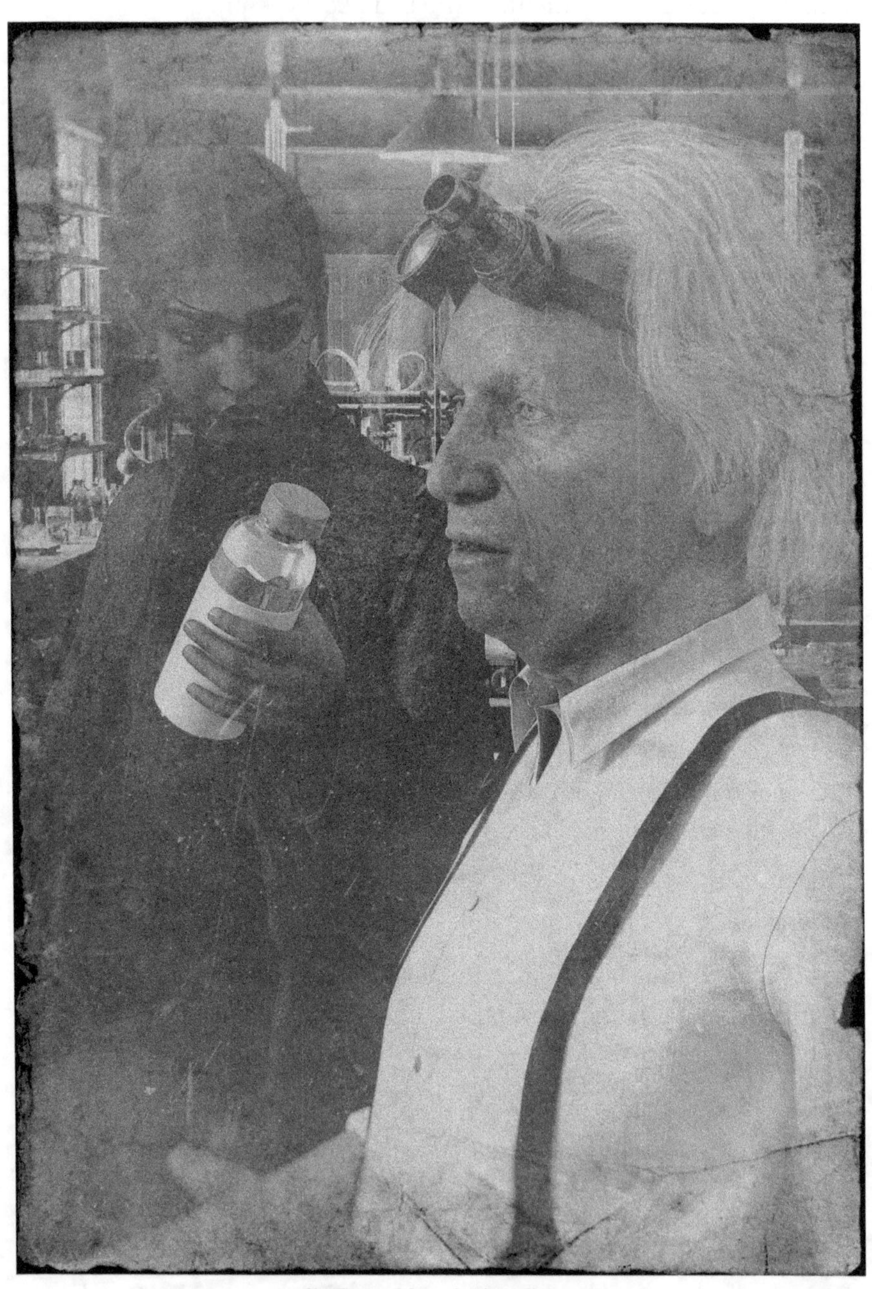

I'm Doctor Mort, the chancellor of Pitt.

Chapter 16

Observatory Hill in Riverview Park in the City-State of Sylvania

Before dawn, Sounder woke up to see Dreadlocks standing over him. He quickly checked her hands for weapons, knowing that if she'd wanted him dead, he would have already been dispatched. But after last night, he doubted her murderous intentions.

"Her things are gone," Dreadlocks said.

"Did you send them to—"

"Her things have been burned," Dreadlocks replied, daring him to object. "I don't want to hear another word about her."

Sounder reached up to take Dreadlocks' wrist, but she pulled her hand away.

"Lillibet, I will tell you again. I didn't know you were alive," he said softly.

"You could have mourned me a little longer. You could have sent out Scouts to make sure my heart had quit beating before you broke it."

"Lillibet."

"You could have sent out Scouts, looking for us. Looking for me. You don't know what I had to do—"

"We did send out Scouts. Your trail had gone cold." Sounder put his head in his hands like a little boy. "We knew you'd made it to Lincolnshire. We knew you had picked up the package. After that...nothing."

"The package is now with Dr. Mort, and you were right to send for her. She's going to be very useful to Sylvania," Dreadlocks murmured. She walked over and let him hold her.

Breakfast had been delivered to their room. She slathered raspberry preserves on a warm piece of fried dough and handed it to him. Sounder took the doughnut from her hand, popping it into his mouth.

"You can dispose of the Medicine Woman when Dr. Mort is done with her," he said as he finished chewing.

Dreadlocks turned and glared at him.

"What? Say that again…"

"When Dr. Mort has extracted everything we need from the Medicine Woman, dispatch her. Maybe into one of the rivers…"

"No, Sounder. I won't." She was defiant and appalled. "Is that where you are now—with your governance? Simply kill off whomever isn't *useful* at the moment?"

"Of course not," he snapped.

"What happens when I'm not useful or even attractive to you anymore? Am I going to be run off to the CatHouses like Jalen?" Sounder wilted under her words. "It's no wonder you replaced me so quickly. Or maybe Jalen was waiting on the side until I left? How long have you been with her, anyway?"

"She means nothing to me. I would have remained faithful if I had known you were alive."

"I didn't know you were so fickle," she muttered, finishing her breakfast. "When Dr. Mort is done with the Medicine Woman, I will take her home. My promises actually mean something."

"You aren't going anywhere. I almost lost you, and I don't have the manpower to take the Medicine Woman down South—things are *complicated* these days."

"Sounder, I'm taking her back to Lincolnshire."

He didn't respond.

"The Medicine Woman has a lot to teach us," Dreadlocks continued. "I watched her treat wounds that should have been amputations. After her treatment, injuries healed overnight. She can pick a berry or a piece of tree bark and make a tea that cures everything from headaches to diarrhea. We have a lot to share with her, too. What's wrong with making allies in the South? At some point, we're going to have to deal with other city-states. Diplomacy has always beat warfare."

He looked at his hands, as if mulling things over.

"Will the Medicine Woman fully cooperate with Dr. Mort?"

"Of course she will," Dreadlocks replied. "She understands what we need from her. She knows we can offer her people new technologies to improve their community as well. From the very start, I reasoned with her to come."

Sounder laughed. "You threatened her."

"Well, she's here now, isn't she?" Dreadlocks sat next to him on his side of the bed. He put his arm around her.

"I love you," he said, nuzzling her forehead.

"Why wouldn't you? I'm amazing." She let him kiss her again.

"Where are you going?" Sounder asked, pulling up his trousers.

"I'm heading to Pitt," Dreadlocks replied, washing her hands in a plastic basin. "I want to see how Dr. Mort and the Medicine Woman are progressing. He's setting up conferences with the MedicMen later this week to disseminate information on pox inoculations."

"The pox is coming out from the East in record numbers. Lime pits have been set up to deal with bodies on the Sylvanian perimeter. Quarantining migrants isn't working as well as we'd hoped. We're going to close the borders this week. No one comes in. No one goes out."

"How long do you expect to quarantine?"

"Dr. Mort suggested sometime in late spring. He figures the pox should burn itself out by then. We're going to take a hit on trade."

"You plan on keeping the Medicine Woman here until spring?" Dreadlocks shook her head. "She'll want to know as soon as possible. She'll need to get in touch with her family. I should be the one to tell her—"

"Goddammit, Lillibet! I heard you. Take her home when the time comes. But we will keep her here as long as we need to."

"I understand," Dreadlocks replied, momentarily shocked at his outburst.

"Don't worry about her family. We have Scouts on the Lincolnshire perimeter, observing conditions there generally and Fortinbras specifically. You know we have Scouts on the inside. Even now they are planting rumors of the Medicine Woman's death, blaming the Snake

Handlers for it. She won't be missed for long."

Dreadlocks looked at him pointedly. "When she's done here, Sounder, I'm taking her home."

"You will probably die on the way." Sounder shrugged his shoulders. "We'll see what happens."

"I gave her my word. I told her nothing would happen to her family."

"Fine," Sounder relented. "Nothing will happen to the Medicine Woman or her family. Now leave me be. I have matters to attend to."

He got up and washed his face in the basin, still warm from his dutiful attendants' labors. Dreadlocks noticed he was wearing some of Papa Jack's clothing. *And jewelry.*

"What are your plans for today?" she asked, having caught a note in his voice that invited suspicion.

"First, I'm going to meet with the heads of the MilitiaMen from each sector. Then there's the pox to deal with. Some migrant groups are claiming asylum. The sewer project has major cost overruns. And a dozen other headaches that you don't need to worry about."

"I do worry about Sylvania, Sounder. And I worry about you," she added. "What's your biggest concern?"

"It changes from day to day, but the Classical Massachusetts Opium continues to pour in unabated. Nobody seems to know how to stop it. We need to take more severe measures," he frowned.

"We should stop the demand to control the supply," she suggested. "Why don't you try to educate Sylvanians on opium abuse? The Medicine Woman said that—"

"Hah! You've gone soft," Sounder chided her. "We'll talk about these things later." He walked over and lifted her chin for another kiss.

"Sounder, the Medicine Woman said—"

"Frankly, I don't care what she says. She needs to work with Dr. Mort and get our MedicMen up to speed on the pox. Then we'll send her home."

"Fine," Dreadlocks said, her face indicating that nothing about his dismissive comments was fine at all.

"Good." Sounder grinned, tucking a long strand of her hair behind her ear. "Dr. Mort is coming this evening to report on the implementation of pox procedures. Join us for dinner. Maybe wear that red outfit."

"Will the CouncilMembers be there?" Dreadlocks inquired, watching his expression closely.

"We don't find the need to meet as frequently," Sounder replied, meeting her eyes. "But the CouncilMembers will be advised how we are going to proceed."

"Fine," she replied, unsatisfied.

"Now tell me about Papa Jack."

"He died."

"I'm aware of that," she replied, irritated by something she couldn't place. "But what happened? I left months ago and he was fine. The CouncilMembers and he worked seamlessly to fix things. When I got back, there was a strange woman in my bed. I heard rumors about insider opium rings and political conspiracies. And now you're sending out MilitiaMen into the streets. What's really going on?"

Sounder sighed. "You don't need to know the granular details, Lillibet. Papa Jack? After his wife and daughter died, Papa Jack got sick. Sick in both body and mind. He couldn't fulfill his obligations, so he put me in charge of the government and streamlined all the civic operations. Then he drowned himself in the Three Rivers. That's all there is."

"Sounder, no. That's not all there is," Dreadlocks whispered, eyes brimming with tears. "We loved that man. He was like a father to both of us!"

She watched Sounder swallow hard. "Lillibet, Papa Jack is dead. That's all there is."

The cold finality of his remarks sent a sickness crawling into her gut. He finished dressing in silence, as she covered her face with her hands.

"Oh, Sounder," she muttered. "Don't you miss him at all?"

He chose not to hear her.

Observatory Hill in Riverview Park was the highest point in Sylvania, offering a beautiful view of the sunrise. Its perimeter was generally patrolled by Sylvanian MilitiaMen at all hours of the day and night. But the Pagan Scouts were as stealthy as they were deadly, especially the ones who formed vanguards, clearing the way for Darius' regiments to move in.

A brotherhood of their own, the Scouts had their own training programs, cobbled together from remnants of the United Authority's elite military units. Instead of names, they sported numbers, inked in blue on the sides of their necks.

"Go for Liberation Day." 80577 read the missive signed by Darius himself to his platoon. After those four words were read, dozens of Scouts fanned out through Sylvania while the few Sylvanian MilitiaMen were dispatched on Observation Hill.

Now, thought 80577, *there was the wait for several thousand Illuminati Pagan Militiamen to arrive from the outskirts.* In the meantime, there was still work to do.

For weeks, the Scouts slandered Sounder's reputation, engaging in a whispering campaign, primarily about his inept leadership. However, sowing discord became easier with the gossip surrounding Sounder's lurid personal life. When public support shifted after Jalen's abrupt departure, Sounder was lampooned in the streets. He forbade streetplays and cartoons drawn about him, his former CatHouse lover, and his estranged girlfriend. Clamping down on public entertainment to show a semblance of order won him no favors with the Sylvanians. Even longtime loyalists had started to grumble.

Now that Liberation Day had commenced, within the hour most CouncilMembers in Sylvania would be dispatched, their bodies strung up with their families outside their private residences to incite terror. The Scouts would leave a few CouncilMembers badly tortured, still breathing, to broadcast "Sounder's crimes."

Toppling a government was easier in times of uncertainty, the Scouts were taught. Destabilizing the general populace by false flags helped prod the public's predilection for finding scapegoats. All the Scouts had to do was to identify one or two.

Additionally, it proved useful to take out governmental and community leaders, removing anyone in authority who could rally the populace or anyone else who could give people hope: government officials, military personnel, religious leaders, intellectuals, or MedicMen.

Darius' Scouts had done this many times before, and they were particularly good at it.

"Dr. Mort?" the Medicine Woman called out. "The attendants brought breakfast to the lab. Are you eating this morning?"

Dr. Mort often forgot to eat, usually preoccupied with discovering something new under his microscope or reading an old medical textbook that the Medicine Woman drew his attention towards.

"Pardon me?"

She spoke louder, as Dr. Mort often practiced selective hearing, shutting out distractions while he worked.

"I said it's time to eat!"

As expected, he ignored her.

She helped herself to the lavish spread. There were biscuits and herb butters served alongside several soft boiled eggs. She spooned freshly picked berries and cracked nuts into a crock of yogurt.

The Medicine Woman was keen to get back to work. They'd harvested lesions from the migrants in the detention compound and were drying the scabs using a new process to condense their inoculation's efficacy. Purple pitcher plant had been discovered in the surrounding territories. She had planned to demonstrate its medicinal properties to the MedicMen at a conference later that week.

A loud noise came from off in the distance. It was followed by several more.

The Medicine Woman stopped mid-bite of a pastry, her forehead furrowing at the commotion. She chewed and swallowed hastily.

The old scientist scurried across the room, looked out from one of the university's bay windows, and peered into the distance.

"Help me with this," he ordered, fumbling with a refurbished telescope from a cluttered coat closet. the Medicine Woman and he struggled to carry the unwieldy optical instrument to the window, fixating the lens on a plume of thick, black smoke less than ten colony-miles away.

"Dr. Mort, what is it?"

"It looks like—it looks like the port is burning!"

"Oh my god," Dr. Mort muttered. His normal enthusiasm was muted, as he scanned the horizon, hoping to glean more information.

"Medicine Woman, call for the attendants."

Without hesitation, the Medicine Woman hastily ran to the laboratory's entrance corridor.

Dr. Mort was not a man of high passions, normally as unflappable as they come. The edge in his voice caused the Medicine Woman to palm two of the medical scalpels from a tray, carefully putting them in her side pants pockets.

"Assistance! Assistance!" the Medicine Woman called down the hallway. From a glance, she saw doors ajar, papers and detritus on the floor. Soon she heard the running of feet, slamming of doors, arguing of harried voices.

"Long live Sounder!" a male voice screamed from the courtyard. The Medicine Woman peeked over the balcony.

It was a ruse!

She could see the man's tattooed numerals on his neck, right before the man slit the throat of Dr. Mort's best surgeon.

Pagan Scouts were on the campus. Mayhem erupted from all directions.

The Medicine Woman looked down at the dead surgeon and her anger raged. Torn between scaling down the trellis to take care of the Pagan Scout herself or protecting Dr. Mort, she chose the latter. She returned to his quarters, out of breath, frantic, holding a scalpel in each hand.

"Dr. Mort, we need to go. The Pagans are here. They'll kill anyone in command—"

Dr. Mort waved her off.

"I've seen enough warfare these past decades. Let them come." Dr. Mort busied himself with pulling out an old bottle of bourbon from the bottom of a filing cabinet.

"Dr. Mort—our work! There is so much here that is useful!" The Medicine Woman gathered pox scabs into a plastic bin, while the sounds of men and women retching and screaming increased with the sounds of flesh beaten and bones snapping.

"Oh come here, girl." Dr. Mort purposefully moved behind his desk, pushing aside a faded tapestry. Fumbling with a set of metal keys, he found the one he wanted, holding it up in delight.

Along with the scabs, the Medicine Woman grabbed a bottle of purple pitcher plant tincture before following Dr. Mort to a thick metal door. He opened a series of deadbolts as the sounds of glass shattering down the hallway made her hair stand on end.

"What is this?" she whispered, entering through the hidden door.

"This is where I keep all the things that matter," he calmly replied. "And for the moment, that includes you and me."

Along with the scabs, the Medicine Woman grabbed a bottle of purple pitcher plant tincture before following Dr. Mort to a thick metal door.

Chapter 17

South Hills in the City-State of Sylvania

"Quickly!" Dr. Mort motioned to the Medicine Woman to follow him. "Bar the door."

She momentarily hesitated, hearing anguished cries from outside the lab. *Gentle scholars and academics were being brutalized.* She considered running towards the cries, but Dr. Mort called to her again.

"Bar the door!"

Her heart was as heavy as the walnut plank. She grunted with its weight, affixing it into thick metal brackets. Catching her breath, she rested her palms on the wall.

Why would violence come here?

Dr. Mort's safe rooms were far bigger than the Medicine Woman had first imagined. Striking a flint, he lit a thick tallow candle for each of them, illuminating the main room enough for her to see long wooden shelves from floor to ceiling. The shelves were chockablock, stuffed with plastic bins, thick books with moldy covers, metallic gadgets, electrical cords, faded pictures, schematic drawings, blueprints, assorted wires, and bottles of various colored liquid. A staircase at the end of the corridor led downwards. The safe room had no windows. She had no way of seeing what was happening, but she could hazard a guess. *An unprovoked attack.*

The only questions remaining were who instigated the siege and when would the bloodshed be over. Regardless, both Dr. Mort and the Medicine Woman knew what would greet them when they exited the calm of their temporary shelter.

They stayed silent for a colony-hour or so, collecting their thoughts, breathing slowly, acclimating to the low light, accepting the new normal.

Dr. Mort's office was being destroyed.

"We were long overdue," Dr. Mort mumbled to himself, rubbing his eyes. "We'd been too successful. We'd been prosperous for far too long! Peace made us complacent. 'All your strongholds are fig trees with ripened fruit; if they are shaken, they will fall into the mouth of the eater.'"

As usual, the Medicine Woman had no idea what Dr. Mort's biblical allusions meant. She had quit trying to untangle the figurative language of his scriptural passages. She generally ignored him when he lamented the world, gray head in hands. *The OldOnes tended to quickly fall into despair.*

After securing the door, the Medicine Woman searched the rooms, one after another, looking for weaponry, checking the exits. There were thin strips of metal and hand tools in a forgotten bin. She picked up a pair of pliers and a wrench from a small toolbox, felt their heft, pocketed them alongside the scalpels.

"Is there water and food?"

Dr. Mort nodded tersely, looking at her as if she thought he were stupid.

"We have sufficient supplies for several weeks."

"This is a good place to hide," she remarked, pacifying him. "Until the first wave of attacks are over, we will be safe here." Mulling their options over, she fell deeply in thought.

Dr. Mort walked to the farthest corner of the main room, uninterested in her opinions. He focused on what he was going to salvage, what he could pass on to future generations, momentarily regretting those things he didn't rescue from his office.

"Is this a civil war?" the Medicine Woman asked.

"Hmm?" Dr. Mort muttered absent-mindedly, as he sorted through photographs filed haphazardly in a crumbling banker's box.

"A civil war, Dr. Mort," she repeated. "Do you think one of the CouncilMembers started an insurrection?"

"It's possible, but not probable. I can't imagine which of them would dare. Sounder is not popular, but he is not hated. Sylvanians see him as having the mantle of Papa Jack's authority. It's not hard to see why. When Sounder parades around town, he walks like Papa Jack and wears his jewelry like a son. Clothes do not make the man."

"A military coup, then? Some rogue general wresting control?"

"Sylvanian MilitiaMen aren't inclined to revolt. They have been peacekeepers over the decades, not aggressors. Besides, their strength is divided. They may be more loyal to their own CouncilMember than to the state. Regardless, Pitt would have never been attacked from inside. No true Sylvanian would jeopardize what we have done here. The loss of Pitt—of what we do here—will destabilize the region."

"Perhaps that is why Pitt has been targeted," she suggested.

Dr. Mort shrugged his shoulders, wholly demoralized, sitting among the remnants of his life's work. "Let the dead bury the dead," he murmured to himself.

"We will wait here until the worst is over," she decided, reassuring herself more than her companion.

"You and I both know the worst comes after the battles are fought, my dear. Afterward, there is disorder and disease and death. Even in your short lifespan, you have seen these types of things come and go."

She looked down, reluctant to respond.

"It's painfully predictable," Dr. Mort mused. "Someone will eventually claim victory, then we will have a new taskmaster to serve. All we can hope for is that our new overlord will be reasonable in his gluttony, and that he will appreciate the need for knowledge of any kind..."

"I've seen books and libraries burned," the Medicine Woman confessed.

"I've seen professors and scientists burned," Dr. Mort added somberly.

Again, they fell silent.

Dr. Mort looked at his beakers and test tubes. *I could make carbon monoxide,* he thought. *We could sleep forever.*

"Why must men be this way, Dr. Mort?"

"Hmm?"

"Why do men have to conquer other men?"

"Because human resources are finite. This leads to fear, and fear causes man to be inhumane. It has been this way since Adam and Eve left the Garden of Eden—or when blue-green algae first converted carbon dioxide into oxygen. Pick your creation myth." He smiled a little to himself.

"We aren't going to die here," she said, mouth set firm.

"Does it matter if we do?" he asked, philosophically.

"Yes, Dr. Mort. It does. I am going to return to Lincolnshire. There are things I need to do there," her voice trailed off.

"Like what?" Dr. Mort asked, genuinely curious.

"Like alleviate people's suffering." The Medicine Woman jutted out her chin.

"Oh, there is always more suffering. I don't think you can extinguish that. Do whatever you think is useful. Do whatever brings meaning to your life. Thinking you can find life's purpose is the main reason we OldOnes envy you young people," he sat, rubbing his knees. "Well, that and the fact that your bodies haven't betrayed you—yet."

He walked over in the half-light with his candle, finding the receptacles of purified water. He filled two plastic cups and returned.

The two sat for a long while, listening, sipping water in silence, drifting off in a fitful sleep.

Awakening later, the Medicine Woman stood, stretched, milled about. She investigated a variety of objects in the room, picking them up to inspect them more closely, trying to divine their use.

She returned to find Dr. Mort organizing textbooks on a lower shelf.

"I need you to explain things to me, Dr. Mort," she said, sitting down beside him. She'd found a nub of a pencil and a swatch of reclaimed paper. With both items in her hands, she looked at him expectantly, poised to write down whatever he said. "I have seen the things you've implemented to improve Sylvanians' lives. Significant improvements. But what else has been forgotten that lives amongst these shelves? What knowledge can you bring back from the dead?"

"Little girl, it took 2000 years for modern generations to understand how the Romans made their underwater concrete harden. Turns out it was just a mixture of basic oxides and volcanic ash, a concoction that strengthened in seawater. The Romans were geniuses! They understood chemical reactions. Although Romans borrowed most of their knowledge from the Greeks—they significantly improved upon it!"

The Medicine Woman scribbled down notes.

"Volcanic ash?" She looked up.

Dr. Mort sighed. "I could tell you about the technology we had when I was your age, but you would not believe me." He grinned wistfully. "We Sylvanians were well on our way to reclaiming some of that way of life. But now this!" He made a helpless, futile gesture towards the barred door.

The clamoring noise of war had come and gone throughout the afternoon and into evening, first disturbingly loud and then eerily quiet.

"Those are the sounds of ignorance and brutality," replied the Medicine Woman dismissively, her mouth pursed in disgust. "There is no progress in times of war. But when I return home, there will be peace. I need to know specifically what to do to make things better for Lincolnshire. I've seen Sylvania's water filtration systems and sewage treatment plants. I've seen how you make charcoal. Your work at Pitt on composting human waste into methane gas will make cooking and heating infinitely easier. But since we're here for the foreseeable future, tell me what else I can do to help my people."

The old man gazed around his storehouse of intellectual treasures, looking for a moment like a lost child.

"Where to begin!"

"It doesn't matter where, Dr. Mort. Just tell me something."

He nodded. "All right. We need to talk about lime."

"My mother told me about limes and lemons. I know all about vitamin C and scurvy."

"No, no. Not limes. Lime. Calcium carbonate."

"Oh."

"In the former penal colony, there is coral and seashells aplenty! Both are pure sources of lime, but you will eventually need to quarry limestone."

"What is lime used for?"

"A thousand different things. Growing crops. Sanitation. Making glass."

"Lime," she said, scribbling down his descriptions. "What else is important?"

"It's all important," Dr. Mort gestured to the shelves. "But we should talk about wood pyrolysis."

"Wood pie? Rolls? I'm sorry, what?"

"P. Y. R. O. L. Y. S. I. S."

"I don't know what that is," she said quietly.

"When you make charcoal from wood, capture the gas while it's burning to make crude tar. From that, you can easily convert the tar into creosote and pitch for building new houses and patching old ones."

"How do I capture the gas?"

"I have a schematic somewhere," he said. "You can also trap the fumes to create acetic acid for preserving foods and making acetone. Acetone is very useful."

"Acetone?"

"And wait until we talk about acids! Start with acetic acid and work your way up to sulfuric and hydrochloric..."

The Medicine Woman looked overwhelmed. She put the pencil nub down.

Dr. Mort offered her a conciliatory smile.

"I'm sorry, my dear. I got ahead of myself. Let's start with the basic principles of agriculture and work our way forward."

About thirty colony-minutes after Dreadlocks left the Westin to walk to Pitt, the first of three fertilizer bombs went off.

The initial blast knocked her off her feet at the corner of Centre Avenue and Dinwiddie. She fell face forward into the street, nearly trampled by a team of horses, who whinnied wild-eyed. Their astute wagonmaster pulled back on the reins with all his strength.

Dreadlocks rolled quickly out of the street, her elbows and forearms bleeding, her right cheek bloodied.

She turned towards the Sylvanian skyline in time to see the western portion of the Westin Hotel listing, glass panes bowing and breaking. The side of the old hotel had been sheared off, leaving a smoking, creaking crevasse.

About her, Dreadlocks heard the sounds of men shouting and women screaming. As she arose, she noticed passersby hanging on to one another, searching the streets and skies for an unseen assailant.

"Is it an earthquake?" a middle aged woman asked.

One person wordlessly howled, pointing towards the black plumes of smoke.

"We need to evacuate the governmental buildings!" a MilitiaMan called to another.

A second blast silenced them all. With a great rumble that followed, larger black clouds billowed from the building's wreckage and flames. What remained of the Westin was on fire.

The final blast took down the eastern portion, to the horror and dismay of the Sylvanians. It seemed interminable, but the building folded in on itself like a wave.

Now, the entire populace seemed to be in the streets, a few trudging their way downtown, some stopping others to inquire what had happened, most concerned with their own safety.

What if there were more explosions?

Dreadlocks didn't realize she was weeping until she couldn't see, blinded by her tears.

She turned to face the black smoke, plowed forward, ignoring the people moving in various directions. *Only one thing mattered now*, she thought as she broke into a run.

Sounder.

Several blocks from the Westin, Dreadlocks saw soldiers and MilitaMen in all manner of military dress. Some detained Sylvanians, harshly interrogating them, dragging them into wagons. Other soldiers shared cigarettes and gossiped with pedestrians gawking at the Westin's wreckage.

"Snake Handlers are in the city!" one of the men cried aloud.

"They've teamed up with the White Crosses. No place is safe!" confirmed another.

"The Armaggedonists have reconvened and are ushering in the End of Times!" This time, a Sylvanian man joined in.

Dreadlocks clenched her teeth, walking past them at a brisk pace. She stole a look at the men's necks.

Of course.

The tell-tale blue numbered tattoos revealed Darius' false flag operation. *Illuminati Pagans!* She spat. *Oh, they were good.* Sylvanians were already seeking refuge from the men in unmarked uniforms.

She felt for her cudgel, ignoring everything but the most direct way to get to the Westin's entrance.

But there was no entrance to the Westin.

Instead, in front of the mountain of rebar and detritus, a long gallows had been hastily erected.

As Dreadlocks approached, she squinted, trying to make out what was hung from the frame.

Michael. Vincent. Buraty.

A few of the CouncilMembers' bodies were displayed, arranged to show their torture and multilations in full array. . What remained of the men dangled from ropes.

A sign was painted, neatly propped up near the dead men's feet: *Long live Sounder.*

"We should leave," The Medicine Woman suggested to Dr. Mort.

There had been no sounds for days. Dr. Mort's water supplies were running low. Living in almost perpetual darkness had made her restless.

"And where would we go, my dear?" Dr. Mort inquired.

"Out of the safe rooms." She walked towards the staircase. "I will go out first."

"Medicine Woman," Dr. Mort said quietly, stopping her. "I'm not leaving these rooms."

She looked at him, trying to divine his meaning.

"Let's finish our discussions on overshot water wheels and self-orienting turret windmills. Lincolnshire must master both thermal and mechanical energy."

The Medicine Woman put her hands on her hips. He ignored her petulance.

"So," he continued. "I've shown you the diagram for a piston-based heat engine and how to construct a simple battery. Try to master the electrochemical cell as soon as possible. Do that, and harnessing the power of electricity on a wider scale won't be too far behind!"

"Dr. Mort," she interrupted. "We have previously discussed those things. I'm going outside to assess our situation."

"Go, then. As you wish." He slumped in his chair.

"I'll be back shortly."

He watched her go, her candlelight flickering as she made her way down the staircase.

"I'm not leaving these rooms," he repeated to himself.

The staircase led to the university's laundry facilities and exited behind one of its large vats. The Medicine Woman moved quietly, but her surroundings were unnaturally quiet.

More disturbing to her was that the room was *orderly*. She grew bolder, walking down a few corridors, glancing into vacant offices and empty laboratories. All were spotless.

It was clear there had been damage, but it had been repaired and scrubbed clean. There were no blood sprays or evidence of carnage. *There was nothing.* She turned the corner, smelling fresh paint in the hallway, making the Medicine Woman feel more unsettled.

Walking through most of the campus, she felt it had been abandoned. She was alone not only in Dr. Mort's building, but apparently the entire campus.

Where had people been evacuated?

She exited through a side door into what had previously been a parking lot, blinking in the late afternoon sun.

She breathed in and out, slowly, wondering which direction to head.

Several hours later, the Medicine Woman returned to the safe rooms, arms full of the supplies she had salvaged. *Beef jerky from the cafeteria. Rope from the empty stables. A wheel of cheese from the MilitiaMen's vacant outpost.*

In her exploits around Pitt, she had seen no one. At the base of the stairs, she had left her flint and steel. Using both now, she lit a thick beeswax candle.

"Dr. Mort!" she called out, taking the stairs up from the laundry, two at a time. "Dr. Mort! Pitt still stands, but everyone has gone!"

There was no response. The former sanctuary of the safe rooms felt ludicrous in light of the abandoned campus.

Walking to the old scientist's desk, she knew he was dead before she felt his wrists, both deeply cut, slick with coppery blood.

"Oh, you old fool," she muttered angrily.

Along with Dr. Mort's death went untold knowledge and intelligence. She would have taken him South—she had told him as much! Dr. Mort would have been beloved in Lincolnshire, valued for his contributions. Now, he was as useful as the rusted electronics forgotten on the dusty shelves.

She retreated back down the staircase, through the laundry's exit, disappearing into the dark woods.

On the outskirts of Sylvania, the Medicine Woman cautiously

approached the Beth El Congregation of South Hills in the early hours at dawn.

It was a longshot, she thought while fleeing Sylvania. *But if anyone could provide her clarity on her present situation, it would be Rabbi Raskin.* She needed to know if the fighting was localized or widespread.

As she walked closer to the synagogue, it was apparent the darkened temple had been looted. As she stepped through the doorless entrance, she saw the remnants of thoughtless thieves, who had torn up whatever they had no use for.

Her heart heavy, she stepped over mouldering corpses, both old and young. Making her way to the sanctuary, she found it ravaged as well— with only a few pews still standing.

Feeling utterly spent, the Medicine Woman staggered to sit, if only for a little while.

The sun's rays poured through the remaining stained glass windows, creating a kaleidoscope of colorful patterns on the floor in front of her. The sheer beauty of the lights stunned her, and she began to weep.

"Why are you sad?" a small voice asked.

The Medicine Woman stood at once, both scalpels in her hands.

"Are you going to hurt us?" another voice queried, not in fear, but out of curiosity.

"Oh," the Medicine Woman collected herself. "You are the children from Kimper." She remembered their faces and pocketed the knives. Two little boys stood in front of her, no more than seven years old. "I'm the Medicine Woman. What are your names?"

"The Rabbi and his wife called us Ephraim and Manasseh," the older of the two said. "I'm Ephraim."

"Where are the other children?"

The child replied with a shrug, as if he'd been asked where a frog had jumped.

"Where is the Rabbi? Where is his wife?"

"They died." Ephraim said matter-of-factly. Manasseh nodded.

"Are there any other grownups here?"

Ephraim nodded, eyes unblinking.

"Where, Ephraim?"

"I'll show you!" the boy replied, taking the Medicine Woman by the hand. Manasseh took her other.

Barefoot, the boys dodged shards of glass and hopped over pools of congealed blood on the flooring. They exited the sanctuary, walking towards one of the outbuildings, near an oversized garden that had been stripped of its plenty.

"The lady is in here," Ephraim announced. "She doesn't talk much."

Manasseh entered first and stood by the figure, splayed out, supine, on a dark rug.

The Medicine Woman approached the woman covered in filth, apparently unconscious, faintly breathing. She reached down to remove a tattered prayer shawl, one which had covered her head and part of her face.

Dreadlocks.

About thirty colony-minutes after Dreadlocks left the Westin to walk to Pitt, the first of three fertilizer bombs went off.

Chapter 18

Albany, Classical Massachusetts

"Boys," the Medicine Woman said in a low voice, kneeling down to talk to them. "I am going to help Dreadlocks, but I'll need your help."

Hollow-eyed and pale, Ephraim and Manasseh stood near both women, unsure of what to do.

The Medicine Woman spoke calmly, quietly. "The first thing I need you to do is to eat something."

"We don't have any food," Ephraim replied, apologetically. "The men took everything away. Even the rabbits."

The Medicine Woman opened up her rucksack and dug deep. Curious, the boys came nearer.

"It's a good thing I have plenty in here. Let me see…" She pretended to rummage, making silly faces as she fumbled.

The boys laughed.

"Do you like walnuts?"

Their eyes went wide.

"How about some meat sticks?"

The boys' mouths watered seeing thick strips of beef jerky and wedges of hard cheese—even a jar of sweet-pickled vegetables.

Grinning, the famished boys ate hand over fist.

"Go slowly," the Medicine Woman advised. "I don't want you to throw it all up."

"Okay!" Manasseh's dark blue eyes were alight.

Thank you!"

"Yes, thank you," Ephraim added soberly. "The Rabbi told us to always be grateful. He's dead, though."

She watched them eat for a bit, keeping an eye on Dreadlocks.

"Now, boys," the Medicine Woman said, putting her hands on their thin shoulders. "Can you bring me water from the cistern?"

Ephraim shook his head while thoughtfully chewing a rye cracker. "The cistern is broke. The men smashed it up."

Wasteful bastards, the Medicine Woman frowned. *What could have been the men's purpose in looting and pillaging a house of worship?*

"No matter. I'll make a fire," she said. "When you're done eating, get me some wood from the covered porch. Then fetch me buckets of pond water and one of the large cooking pots from the kitchen."

As the boys finished their first meal in days, the Medicine Woman turned her full attention to Dreadlocks. The woman's breathing was almost as shallow as her pulse. But, gratefully, her inhalations and exhalations were steady. *No rasping, no gurgling, no whistling.*

Carefully, the Medicine Woman examined the crown of Dreadlocks' head, then her face—eyes, mouth, nose. Although covered from head to toe in grime, Dreadlock appeared in better shape than she'd thought. Her skin color was a bit ashen, but it was hard to tell the full extent of her condition until she was bathed.

Removing Dreadlocks' clothing in the morning chill, the Medicine Woman looked for deep cuts and contusions, carefully feeling her bones for unnatural bumps and fissures. Once done, the Medicine Woman covered Dreadlocks up in an equally dirty blanket. *There must be some clothing in the synagogue. The rabbi's kittel would be better than Dreadlocks' rags.* She would send the boys to search the living quarters for suitable apparel for both of them when they returned.

Dreadlocks' eyes fluttered.

"Lillibet," the Medicine Woman said in a loud, firm voice. "Lillibet, you are in the synagogue. You are safe."

Dreadlocks gave a low moan, rolled over on her side, and retched.

The Medicine Woman rubbed her back, helping Dreadlocks to a seated position.

"Are you in any pain or discomfort?"

Dreadlocks shook her head, wincing at the effort.

"I'm going to need you to take some very deep breaths."

Dreadlocks attempted to comply, breathing in, coughing, breathing out, while the Medicine Woman felt her abdomen.

"Now, shrug your shoulders. Okay, good." The Medicine Woman's deft hands felt her clavicle. "Move your fingers. All ten. Now your hands. Ball your hands into fists. Good, good. Can you lift your arms overhead?"

"Leave me alone." Dreadlocks lay back down, resuming the fetal position. "Let me rest."

"Drink this." The Medicine Woman handed her a flask of herbal tea. The tea was cold, but it was clear from her perfunctory examination that Dreadlocks needed fluids more than anything else.

She wanted to call after the boys, to make them hurry with the wood and water.

"Lillibet. Don't sleep until I see if you have a concussion. There is a large bruise on the side of your face."

"Don't worry about it," Dreadlocks spat. "The man who hit me is dead, and I'll kill you, too, if you wake me up again."

They sat in silence for a bit, hearing the two boys call out and laugh near the pond.

"What happened in Sylvania?" the Medicine Woman asked.

"Not now." Dreadlocks waved her off. "Later. I'll tell you everything later."

"Drink this. Please."

"I just need sleep."

"Drink, dammit! You need fluids. Drink all of it."

Dreadlocks grudgingly complied, sitting up, gulping the liquid too quickly, coughing and spluttering. When she could breathe normally, she started to cry, pulling the prayer shawl over her face.

In due time, the boys returned to the hovel with containers of pond water, most of it sloshing from the buckets they carried, splashing onto the cement flooring.

"Well done, boys. Now let me show you how to build a fire for boiling water."

With her knives, the Medicine Woman skewered a few fat squirrels scrambling up the walls of the ruined temple. As the boiled water cooled, she prepared the meat for a spit.

Manasseh proved useful in turning the meat over the fire, allowing it to cook equally on all sides. Ephraim gathered clothing and blankets from the main building, still cluttered with the remnants of a one-sided battle.

We will bury the dead, she had told them, but the boys seemed unconcerned. They had full bellies and the late winter day was mild. They busied themselves in the early afternoon by climbing trees.

The Medicine Woman checked on Dreadlocks, who slept fitfully, lost in subconsciousness, calling out nonsense in her sleep.

Content that her patient was more sick at heart than in body, the Medicine Woman left the small group to comb through the wreckage of the synagogue and appropriate that which could be useful.

The dead were scattered throughout, some taken in hiding, others apparently having fought before being cut down. She covered her nose and mouth with a thick cloth to guard against the stench of cadaverine before tightly securing the bodies in bedsheets.

On assessing the total number of corpses and the ruination of the building, the Medicine Woman determined how to best dispose of the dead. *Before we head South,* she decided, *we will set fire to this place.*

The thought of finally returning home—of heading South—made the Medicine Woman homesick, more than ever before. She closed her eyes and leaned against a doorway. Cold, tired, lonely, and overwhelmed, she wanted Jasper's arms around her.

If she could have conjured him to be with her at that moment, she would have gladly sold her soul to whichever god or demon wanted it.

She wanted only Jasper and his calm, reassuring voice.

Instead? There was a sick woman to care for and two little boys who needed far more than she was able to give. At that point, all she could think of was the hundreds of colony-miles that separated her from anyone she loved.

She sat down, removed her eye patch, and rubbed the empty eye socket. It always itched when she cried.

"I hate squirrels."

"That's all we have to eat right now."

Dreadlocks frowned at the stew, but ate it steadily nonetheless.

"Where's Dr. Mort?" she asked between mouthfuls. "Did he make it out of Pitt?"

The Medicine Woman shook her head, her expression blank.

"Illuminati Pagans got him, I bet." Dreadlocks wiped her mouth on the back of her hand. "They like to go after the educated first."

"He was killed by the enemy," the Medicine Woman lied, protective of Dr. Mort and his fatal decision. With all he had taught her during the two weeks in the safe room, she felt she owed him that much.

"That man was brilliant."

"He was."

"Tragic. It's all so goddamned tragic." Dreadlocks voice faded as she continued to eat.

They finished their meager dinner.

The two boys had long eaten their fill and now were challenging each other to smash what remained of the synagogue's stained glass windows. They made a game out of throwing rocks, finishing what the looters had started. When the glass shattered, neither of the women had the heart to tell them to stop. *The place had long been desecrated.*

"We will need to burn this place when we leave," the Medicine Woman stated flatly. "There has been too much evil here. Too many bodies."

"Agreed," Dreadlocks mumbled. "I once felt safe here. I loved the Rabbi and his wife. The attendants. The other children—" she broke off. "I arrived too late. Only Ephraim and Manasseh were left."

"Did they tell you what happened here?"

"No. They won't talk about it, and I don't really want to know anymore than I do."

"We'll take the boys South," the Medicine Woman decided.

"South? We can't go South. All roads are blocked heading South. The Pagans have curfews in effect throughout Sylvania. Anyone out of their homes without written permission is being summarily executed."

"How long will the curfew stand?" the Medicine Woman asked.

"Probably until Darius shores up his new headquarters in the North."

"*Darius?*"

"It's not a surprise. Papa Jack had been warning us for years about that ambitious prick expanding his empire. That's what despots do."

"I'm going to kill Darius," the Medicine Woman said. "I should have killed him when I had the chance."

"Hold up. You had the chance to kill Darius? *Darius* Darius? You versus the Leader of the Illuminati Pagans?"

"It was a long time ago," the Medicine Woman pursed her lips. "When he worked for Xerxes."

Dreadlocks looked skeptical, but impressed. "You're going to have to fill me in on more of your exploits before I kidnapped you."

The Medicine Woman leaned over and punched her in the shoulder. Hard.

"What the hell!" Dreadlocks cursed at her under her breath.

"You deserved that."

"For what?"

"You should have left me alone. I should be in Lincolnshire instead of freezing in the North."

"We've been over this. Sylvania needed your expertise with the pox. You wouldn't have come otherwise."

"You threatened my family!"

"Well, now all of Sylvania is an Illuminati Pagan shithole," Dreadlocks replied snidely. "So karma took care of your little vendetta. So *quit hitting me!*"

"I should poison your next bowl of stew and take the boys South myself."

"Poison might taste better," Dreadlocks grinned, but her smile faded. "What do you want me to say, that I'm sorry I tried to help my people?"

"You tried to help your people at the expense of my people. My people needed me, too." The Medicine Woman punched her again for good measure, then brooded.

"Look, I'll get you home. I promise." The words rang hollow, making Dreadlocks feel foolish. She knew she couldn't promise the Medicine Woman anything.

"Lillibet, when did you see Sounder last?"

Dreadlocks looked out the window and shrugged.

"Do you know where he is?"

"I don't know. Under a tree. Under the Westin. Under another woman. People claimed he was working with the Illuminati Pagans. Others said he was hanged. One of CouncilMember's wives said he escaped into New Virginia. No one seems to know."

Dreadlocks swiped at the unwanted tears that streamed down her face. The Medicine Woman moved to sit closer to her, putting an arm around her thin frame. Dreadlocks buried her face into the Medicine Woman's shoulder and wept.

"Where are we going?" Ephraim asked.

"North. North to a place called Albany." Dreadlocks replied. "We'll be there for a little while."

"Maybe the Northern roads are closed as well?" the Medicine Woman interjected. "Are you sure we won't be arrested on site in Classical Massachusetts? Sylvanians aren't welcomed in that part of the North."

"My brother is the Chief Attendant to the Albanian Warlord. He'll take us in."

"Your brother likes you?"

"My brother hates me," Dreadlocks murmured. "But we're all that we have left. As much as he hates me, he hates Darius more, especially when he finds out what happened here. He loved this place when we were little. We showed up on the Rabbi's doorstep, starving, like a pack of spring kittens."

Dreadlocks continued to prepare the synagogue. She helped the boys pour solvents and cooking oil while arranging flammable materials throughout the remaining structure. The boys had heartily enjoyed ripping up the remaining carpet and making kindling out of the broken up pews and furniture.

Dreadlocks and the Medicine Woman carried out the bodies, wrapped in bedding, and laid them reverently next to one another in the prayer room.

"Can I say something before the fire?" Ephraim looked up, his eyes shining in the torchlight.

"Please do," Dreadlocks replied.

Ephraim bowed his head to the corpses. Manasseh held his brother's hand.

"May God bless you and protect you. May God show you kindness and grant you peace."

"Thank you, Ephraim," Dreadlocks said, kneeling down to hug him.

"The Rabbi said those words to us every night before we went to bed," he explained. "Maybe God will listen this time."

The Medicine Woman looked pointedly at Dreadlocks, then handed Ephraim a match.

The weather had grown colder as they headed to the North, yet neither of the boys complained. They enjoyed throwing snowballs at each other and catching delicate white flakes on their tongues. But the Medicine Woman complained incessantly.

"I cannot feel my feet. I'm going to have to amputate both of them, and you'll have to drag me around on my stumps!" she cried. She had shoved reclaimed paper in the bottom of her leather boots, dampened by the heavy snow.

"I can carry you!" Manasseh offered, taking one of her legs. He tried to lift her up, but only succeeded in knocking them both over.

The Medicine Woman landed bottom up in a snowdrift. There was nothing to do but laugh.

Dreadlocks helped her up.

After leaving the synagogue, Dreadlocks led the small band due east around Sylvania, steering clear of Pagan checkpoints. She avoided the main trade routes and the thoroughfares, taking the snowy hunting trails and deserted byways that paralleled the more heavily traveled roads.

They hadn't seen anyone in days.

"It's not much farther to Albany," Dreadlocks said, trying to cheer her up. "Another week or so. But let's camp here for the night."

She motioned to a dilapidated farmhouse that looked promising. Its windows were intact, there were two chimneys, and it appeared vacant.

"I'll build the fire this time!" Ephraim called, racing to the side door.

"I'm going to have to teach him how to find deciduous trees," the Medicine Woman murmured to Dreadlocks. "He keeps using lichen and bark to make a smoky mess."

"Well, show him again. I doubt you got it right on your first try."

"Actually, I did," the Medicine Woman replied, defensively. "I have always picked things up quickly."

"Then your mother must have been an excellent teacher," Dreadlocks replied. "How she managed to get anything through your thick head is beyond me."

Days later, they inched their way to the North, walking out of sight, off the Eight Seven. Hearing an odd clatter, the Medicine Woman squinted into the distance.

A hulk of metal on wheels moved towards them at a glacial speed. There was an exhaust pipe that bellowed thick white clouds.

"What is that?" Manasseh whispered, pointing at the jalopy, which creaked and grumbled the closer it came.

Dreadlocks grinned, pulling out her long knives from her side sheaths. She nodded at the Medicine Woman for her to do the same.

"What is *that?*" Manasseh asked again.

All four of them looked at the sputtering contraption, making its way gingerly down the uneven pavement.

"That's a SteamCar," Dreadlocks smiled. "And it will get us to Albany much faster than walking.

Dreadlocks buried her face into the Medicine Woman's shoulder and wept.

Chapter 19

Springfield, Classical Massachusetts

The Albanian dispatch carrier had been sent without his companion for a delivery to Kingston. Though dispatch carriers usually traveled in pairs, there had been far too many communiqués precluding that particular luxury. Besides, with the use of a SteamCar, he'd arrive at his destination in under 11 colony-hours.

The dispatch carrier felt for his pistol, set within arm's reach, placed under the dash. Three bullets were left in the chamber after an altercation in New France, but the Acadians had always been territorial. Unless he encountered a band of rogue MilitiaMen, three bullets would suffice to defend himself. If not, he'd destroy what information he carried and use the last bullet on himself.

For the past month, he'd done little except courier missives from one warlord to another, in an attempt to forge some unity against the growing threat from the South. But worrying over politics was beyond his pay grade. His job was to deliver government directives, in envelopes and packages, both large and small.

The SteamCar made his job much more efficient than in the days of the dispatch runners. Hours before, the dispatch carrier had checked the water level in the boiler, primed and lit the heat source, and waited patiently until the pressure was high enough to allow the engine to turn the wheels.

The newly fallen snow made gathering water to keep the boiler running an easier task than in the summer months. He had several jugs of fuel in the back to keep the machinery functioning, as Albany had manufactured kerosene for years, using wood from the Helderberg Mountain.

With his sack lunch in hand, the dispatch carrier felt at peace driving through the deserted landscape. Few people braved midwinter's frigid air, but he thrived on the cold weather and the solitude.

The miles sped by uneventfully until he squinted to see a distraught mother standing on the right side of the road. Her young son lay on the ground, motionless.

Although the woman waved frantically at him to stop, the protocol was to continue on and ignore civilian concerns. If he had stopped at the sight of every desperate soul, he'd have been waylaid by brigands a dozen times.

He looked up again, seeing the woman's dark face framed by a thick dark scarf. Though she wore an eyepatch, her beauty was unmistakable.

She picked up the small, lifeless child in her arms, his wan features eliciting sympathy. He slowed the SteamCar, preparing only to throw the mother and son some food before heading on his way. As he approached them, he heard a thud on the carriage's rooftop before two booted feet kicked him in the side of the face. At once, a woman with blonde dreadlocks entered the cab, pressing her right knee into the small of the dispatch carrier's back. She leaned hard on his neck, her full weight on her right forearm, pinning him across the front seat.

"Don't move or I'll shove my knife into your temple as far as it can go."

The dispatch carrier eyed his gun but didn't move, as the tip of the blonde woman's knife poked insistently at his skull. In a moment, the woman he'd seen alongside the roadway appeared with *two* boys, one of whom opened the back door as they all climbed into the SteamCar.

"Oh, it's much warmer here," the tall woman with long black hair said, shuddering with relief. "I didn't think the North could get any colder." She rubbed her hands together, then began making herself and the boys comfortable in the confined space.

The boys busied themselves by touching everything, asking one question after another. The dark haired woman fussed over them, answering the questions as best she could.

"Ephraim, you have eaten nothing today. Eat some walnuts."

The dispatch carrier heard the boy protest before the inevitable sounds of him dutifully munching.

The blonde spoke to him again.

"Okay, this is how it's going to go. After I pat you down, I'm going to tie your hands in front of you. You'll drive us to Albany, we'll get out of your car, and you'll continue on your way."

"Lady, I don't know who you are, but I have a delivery in Kingston for the Warlord of Albany. He won't like the delay."

"The Warlord of Albany is an ass, and I'll gladly tell him that to his face."

The dispatch carrier fell silent.

"Do you want some cheese, Manasseh?" the woman in the backseat asked.

"Yes, please."

"It's no trouble getting you to eat. That's a good lad. Dreadlocks, do you want—"

Dreadlocks shifted her weight long enough for the dispatch carrier to make his move. Rolling the woman off his back, the dispatch carrier reached for the gun with his right hand while grabbing Dreadlock's throat with the other.

Seeing the gun raised by the man in the front seat, her dark haired companion moved to cover the boys, her hands striking a quick blow. His first bullet went wide, shattering the back window. The dispatch carrier turned to fire point-blank into Dreadlocks' face, but she ducked as the bullet missed by a colony-inch. He took aim again, lowering his gaze towards Dreadlocks' chest, his shaky finger on the trigger.

"Hey!" Dreadlocks yelled, holding up her hands. "I'm the Chief Attendant's sister! You know what the Albanian Warlord will do to you if you harm anything that Davin loves?"

The dispatch carrier peered at her carefully. *The resemblance to Davin was unmistakable.*

"All right, Davin's sister. I need to take this letter to Kingston," he stated. "It's urgent."

"Fine. Kingston first, then Albany. But you're taking us with you."

"Put the knife away."

"Put the gun away," she countered. "Better yet, give me the gun, and

I'll forget about what almost happened here."

"What happened here is that you attacked an Albanian dispatch carrier. That's a high crime."

"Give it a rest, will you? Both you and I are still breathing." Dreadlocks exited the car and walked around to the passenger's side.

"What are you doing?" he asked, gun still in hand, still aimed at her chest.

"Either use that thing or put it away," she griped.

The dispatch carrier lowered the gun. He secured it under the dash while she opened the passenger side door. Dreadlocks leaned in to give him an exasperated look.

"Move over," she said. Once she settled in, she looked over her shoulder.

Her three blithe companions had nestled under a thick woolen blanket, waiting for the SteamCar to go.

During the riots after the end of electricity, the New York State Capitol building had been seized by New Yorkers, then pillaged by various MilitiaMen who used it for housing before the First Treaty.

When the city museums were looted, docents found ways to secure some of the artwork and antiquities, storing them alongside governmental records at the State University of New York's main campus near the Hudson River, west of the Seven Eight Seven. After the Second Treaty, the SUNY campus became the de facto capital of the City-State of Albany, its territory stretching as far North as Poughkeepsie.

The dispatch carrier said little to the women on the return trip; however, he did answer the boys' queries.

"How fast can the SteamCar go?" Manasseh asked.

"Over seven colony-miles in a colony-hour."

The boys gasped in astonishment.

"Do the wheels go round by themselves?" Ephraim asked, impatiently waiting his turn, wanting to know everything he could. His little hands had felt all the nooks and crannies inside the carriage, trying to divine their purposes.

"The wheels don't turn by themselves," the man replied. "The engine turns the axle. The axle turns the wheels."

"How does the engine work?"

"There are four cylinders that take up steam from the boiler. The steam moves the piston rods and crossheads and cranks. I'll show you when we stop to refill the boiler."

"So it runs on water?"

"Not just water. The boiler needs kerosene to heat the water to make steam. That's what makes the pistons move."

The Medicine Woman listened carefully as the boys quizzed the man in depth about the mechanics. She was pleased at their inquisitive nature and general curiosity about the world.

Her mother would have loved them. They would have sat patiently at her feet, watching Mika show them how to make remedies from natural sources. She'd have shown them how to extract the essence from plants and flowers. Of course, she knew how to make poisons, as well. Destructive forces traveled alongside creative ones, and her mother imparted the wisdom to know which one to use and when.

The Medicine Woman considered if her mother would have liked the North. *There was so much knowledge to be had!* Her heart ached, thinking how her mother suffered under ignorant men like her father—*the epitome of stupidity and violence!* Then again, she found those two personality traits generally went hand in hand.

As the SteamCar traveled farther, the Medicine Woman turned her thoughts to more useful things. *Lincolnshire could use SteamCars in so many ways,* she smiled. She could show her people how to build them, how to extract kerosene from wood, and how to improve transportation for the betterment of all.

She instinctively knew how much Jasper would love one for himself. That thought alone brought her immense pleasure.

It was noon the following day when the SteamCar creaked onto

Broadway, light snow flurries dusting the roads and quieting the city. Few people were outside, as the bitter winds blew South from New Virginia.

"Here it is," the dispatch carrier announced, stopping the SteamCar in front of the former university quad. They were flanked on all sides by buildings in various states of disrepair.

Dreadlocks hopped out of the car and stretched. Sitting for so long had made her anxious.

"Which building does Davin work in?"

"The same one as the Warlord of Albany." The dispatch courier nodded to a fairly intact structure to his right.

The Medicine Woman helped the two boys out of the back. As soon as they emerged, they touched everything they could on the outside of the SteamCar. Manasseh seemed fascinated by the tires, while Ephraim looked underneath the carriage to see how it all was assembled.

"See the chimney?" Ephraim said in awe. Manasseh reached for it, touching the hot metal before the Medicine Woman warned him not to.

"Ouch!" he cried, sticking his burned fingers into his mouth.

She walked over to him. "Show me your hand."

Manasseh shook his head.

"Show me," the Medicine Woman demanded.

Angry blisters were already forming.

"Put snow on it!" Ephraim yelled.

"No," the Medicine Woman said, pulling out her container of drinking water. "Snow and ice are too cold for burns. They constrict blood vessels and make the hurt worse. Let's put some cool water on your hand, all right?"

Manasseh nodded.

She poured water onto his injury, and he managed a weak smile while tears streamed down his face.

"I'm sorry you hurt yourself, Manasseh, but you won't hurt yourself this way again. Today you've learned something important. In the future, keep in mind that you can learn things two ways—by observation or by experience. Observing or taking someone else's advice is a good way to learn, but personal experience is a much better teacher."

"Okay," Manasseh mumbled. "My hand still hurts."

"It will hurt for a little while, but leave it alone. Let your body heal itself. Don't pick or pop any blisters or scratch at the sores. Let your body do what it needs to do to get better."

Walking into the main atrium, Dreadlocks walked next to the Medicine Woman, the two boys following directly behind them. Ephraim looked up and around, taking in the sights of the city, while Manasseh kept checking his burned hand.

"Is someone expecting you?" Two grim-faced MilitiaMen stood at an imposing desk. Others stood nearby, guarding the entrances and exits to other parts of the spacious building. Kerosene lamps were lit throughout the numerous hallways, fireplaces roared to fight back the pervasive chill.

"I'm here to see Davin," Dreadlocks stated flatly. "Tell him his sister is here."

"You may stay in the atrium after being checked for weapons."

"Wait. I'm Lillibet. You don't need to—"

Several MilitiaMen patted Dreadlocks down, taking every cudgel and knife she'd secreted on her person.

Wordlessly, the Medicine Woman walked over to join her. She deposited her knives, spread her arms, and moved her legs apart for the MilitiaMen to search. Then she walked back to the boys to look at the paintings and sculptures adorning the walls.

"What are those?" Ephraim asked, reaching out to touch a marble statue.

"Boys, touch nothing that isn't yours. All of these things are artworks." She motioned to items saved from the looting of the local museums. "There are different types of art like there are different types of fish or leaves. This is called a statue."

"Why are the lady's arms missing?"

"Because some statues are old. Thousands of years old. Sometimes things break if they aren't taken care of properly. Sometimes people ruin things because they are envious of people who create them. The point of art is to enjoy what beauty you can find."

"She's pretty."

"She is."

Lillibet sat alone on a bench near the MilitiaMen, waiting long into the afternoon.

The boys had been taken to the outhouse and fed the remaining scraps of food the Medicine Woman had in her knapsack.

When the third hour passed, the Medicine Woman took off her long coat and covered up the sleepy boys with it, their heads pillowed by her thighs.

Dreadlocks wandered miserably over to sit next to them on the floor.

"You sure your brother still works here, Lillibet? Are you sure he wants to see you?"

"No," Dreadlocks mumbled, peevishly. "I'm not sure about anything except that you are incredibly annoying."

"Say the word and I'm gone. I should have headed South without you weeks ago."

"You wouldn't have made it."

"Sitting in a foreign capital with no money and no contacts isn't exactly *making it.*"

"You want to leave? Leave. You've done your duty to Sylvania." She bowed. "We appreciate your service in helping Sylvanians survive the pox. Too bad you couldn't prevent a war while you were at it."

The boys snored lightly.

"You want to take your petulance down a notch? None of this is my fault. I belong about a thousand colony-miles South from here. It's about time I leave this godforsaken iceberg."

Dreadlocks fumed. She got up and returned to the men at the front desk.

"Where's Davin?"

"Miss, we've told you previously. Davin is in conferences all day. He will send word when he can meet with you."

"I'm Davin's sister."

"So you've said."

"I would like a private room for my companion and our children."

The men looked at each other.

"We have been instructed to have you wait here until Davin arrives."

Dreadlocks glared at them, but it was clear they were at an impasse.

There was nothing to do but wait.

At sunset, Davin appeared, walking into the foyer with a retinue of advisors and armed attendants. He was dressed in fine woolens, his blonde hair the same shade as Dreadlocks. He had the same angular facial features, same color eyes, same scowl.

Dreadlocks stood as he walked towards her.

"It's about damn time—" she said.

Before she could finish her complaint, Davin slapped her across the face so hard she fell to the ground.

He held out his hand to help her up.

"So I guess you're not over it yet," she muttered.

"I'm working on it," Davin replied. "Get your friends and come with me."

Dreadlocks started walking immediately.

The Medicine Woman quickly stood up, waking the boys and gathering their few possessions.

"Where are we going now?" Ephraim asked.

"I don't know," the Medicine Woman replied truthfully. "But we will be all right. Stay close to me and keep your hands by your sides. Now we need to be very quiet. Okay?"

"Okay," Manasseh whispered.

"Lillibet, you and your guests may refresh yourself in this room. I'll send in an attendant to see what else you require. I need to take care of a few more matters before we can sit down and talk."

"Fine. I look forward to it," Dreadlocks replied, entering the room he gestured to. The Medicine Woman and the boys filed in after her.

Near the entrance of the long room were steaming basins of hot water, freshly laundered towels, lotions, soaps, tooth powder, combs, and toothbrushes. In a chifforobe lay an assortment of clothing for both women and the little boys, including woolen socks and new leather boots.

A dining table boasted cold roast turkey and smoked ham, peas and potatoes, warm scones and apple butter, plates of sugared cranberry cookies and dried apricots. A stack of toys, puzzles and picture books lay on the far side of the room.

"Is this heaven?" Manasseh asked, grinning from ear to ear. His eyes shone with contentment.

"Probably not," stated the Medicine Woman. "Before you eat and play, let's get you washed up."

For the first time in weeks, the boys were dressed in clean, warm clothes. They busied themselves setting up metal toy soldiers and wooden animals in the corner of the room.

"How long has it been since you've seen Davin?" asked the Medicine Woman, combing out her wet black hair in long strokes.

Dreadlocks exhaled. "God, let me think. Four or five years, at least."

"I wasn't sure if the Albanians were erecting gallows for us. And when your brother hit you—"

"Ah, don't worry about that. I had it coming."

"Dreadlocks, are we in any danger here? You and I can take care of ourselves, but—" The Medicine Woman nodded to Manasseh and Ephraim.

"No, no. We're good. Trust me."

"You're a kidnapper and a psychopath. I don't trust you."

"You don't have a choice. You're going to have to."

The Medicine Woman glared at her, disgusted at having to be reliant on anyone.

"Your brother wields a lot of power for an attendant—even for a Chief Attendant."

"If you must know, he's the Warlord of Albany's lover."

"Ah," the Medicine Woman nodded. "Understood."

After they had eaten their fill, the door at the back of the room opened, and Davin walked in, alone.

"I hope you are making yourselves comfortable," he said, quietly.

"We're good, Davin. Thanks for the hospitality."

While the two siblings awkwardly embraced, the Medicine Woman was struck again at how similar they looked.

"I'd worried about you when I heard about Sylvania," Davin said. "The stories coming out of the West are horrific."

"You know I can handle myself," Dreadlocks replied.

"I do," Davin said quietly. "And I'm glad you are safe. I'm glad you are here."

"Thanks for taking us in."

The Medicine Woman was taken aback at hearing her traveling companion's gratitude. She'd never heard Dreadlocks so sincere.

"Lillibet," Davin continued. "We're going to need to know what you know. About Sylvania. About the Pagans. About Sounder."

"For all I know, Sounder is dead." Dreadlocks looked down at her feet.

"That's not what I hear."

Lillibet turned quickly. "You think Sounder is alive?"

"I think Sounder is working with Darius."

"No. Not a chance," she murmured. "He couldn't be. That's impossible."

Davin gauged her response, as if weighing her words against the intelligence he'd received from Albanian Scouts.

"There's an emergency meeting of the Northern Warlords in Springfield. We're leaving tomorrow by SteamCar. I'll need you to come with me."

Near the entrance of the long room were steaming basins of hot water, freshly laundered towels, lotions and soaps and tooth powder, combs, and toothbrushes.

Chapter 20

Westover Military Base - Neutral Territory

"Welcome to Westover," an attendant said, opening the door to Davin's SteamCar. He wore a heavy woolen overcoat, oversized hat with ear flaps, and thick leather gloves to protect himself against the inclement weather.

Albanian MilitiaMen had arrived en masse moments before Davin's entourage. Other warlords had come throughout the day, some by handcart, some on horseback, others in SteamCars or pedal cabs.

As an advance team lead, Davin was entrusted to inspect the venue, sending word to the Warlord of Albany if everything checked out. The former military air base had long been fortified with triple strands of barbed wire, the remains of cargo planes strategically positioned around the hangars on the crumbling tarmac.

Davin exited the SteamCar first, briefly looking over the security detail that Classical Massachusetts had provided. Behind Davin, Dreadlocks emerged, followed by Ephraim and Manasseh, who pointed at the hulking aircraft. The Medicine Woman exited the car last, looking over the main area with a skillful eye.

Organizing a gathering of Northern Warlords on such short notice was no small feat. Security logistics had been the first priority. Now, personnel and luggage had to be sorted into the dormitories. Makeshift kitchens were blazing in full force, preparing food and beverages for the hundreds of attendees. SteamCars were numbered and parked. Wagons were unhitched. Horses were led to newly constructed barns, where sweet hay and HorseMen awaited to care for the exhausted animals.

Davin's group followed the attendants into one of the closest hangars, flanked by MilitiaMen on all sides. Several bonfires blazed inside the metal cavern to thwart the intemperate chill, their smoky plumes wafting through holes cut in the ceiling.

Through the gaps, the Medicine Woman could see the flat-based cloud formations, lower in altitude than normal. Instead of the gentle snowfall in Sylvania, icy snow pellets had rained down on them all the way east, pinging their metal cab like a steel drum. She'd watched the purplish-blue flashes of lightning streak across the gray horizon.

A wide array of MilitiaMen stood alongside their peers in companionable silence. Albanians had established a strong rapport with Classical Massachusetts from the days of cyberterrorism and dirty bombs, ever since the erratic weather patterns had emptied out Northeastern cities.

Boston had retreated as far west as Worcester, as nor'easters made living on the Atlantic seaboard untenable. Rising sea levels caused New Yorkers to migrate farther North, though Manhattan had been charred and barren after the Decade of Terror. Stubborn New Yorkers who remained on the island spent their days fending off remnants of the former Trenton Penal Colony. Philly Gangs had attempted to increase their territory, pushed back by the Baltimorians who met savagery with their own.

From year to year, most warlords found their regions expanding or contracting. Lines remained indistinct. But with life after the end of electricity, there were few fixed boundaries to be had anywhere.

The Medicine Woman remembered sifting through an assortment of maps in General Chapman's archives. She had unrolled one in particular that showed the dominions from the Penal Colony of Florida to New Virginia.

What are these? She had asked, pestering the General with endless questions.

Chapman had waved her off with a tired smile. *Those are Northern cities. Most of them have ceased to exist. NorthMen often join together and break apart as often as it suits them.*

Just like the South?

Just like the South, but the Southerners are erratic and violent. They often fight against their own self-interest.

Are NorthMen more peaceful?

No, General Chapman had replied, rubbing his temples. *But their wars are more diplomatic. They will send an edict before their MilitiaMen arrive. But just like the South, the outcome is the same. Violence. Chaos. Death.*

Suffering, she replied. *The outcome is always suffering.*

Yes, Medicine Girl. But it's usually the women and children who suffer the most. Men simply die.

While Dreadlocks, the Medicine Woman, and the children waited, Davin stalked the perimeter of the former military base, inspecting it from every angle. He questioned MilitiaMen, patting them on the shoulders and nodding at their appropriate responses. *All appeared as it should be.*

In time, he returned, pleased with the arrangements for the conference.

"Now what?" Dreadlocks asked him. "When do the other warlords arrive?"

"This afternoon," Davin replied crisply. "The conference begins this evening during dinner."

"Where should we take our things?"

"You'll be quartered in the airport hangar to the east." He motioned to one of the structures.

"The boys are hungry," the Medicine Woman said. The boys were always hungry.

"The dining hall should be open. Second hangar in the back. Take them there and get yourselves situated. I'll visit you later this afternoon to prepare for the warlords' questions."

"Davin," Dreadlocks pulled at his sleeve. "What's going on in Sylvania? Where's Sounder? What have you heard?"

"Later, Lillibet. We'll talk much later." He gave her a thin smile. Davin turned to an attaché. "Percy, tell the Warlord of Albany that it's clear to proceed."

Without another word, Davin walked off towards a gathering of senior attendants.

"Hey," the Medicine Woman said, interrupting Dreadlocks' thoughts. "I'm going to need you to fill me in on a few things."

"Like what?"

"Start with the basics. Who are these warlords and where are their territories? Who is in league with whom? Who do they disfavor? Who do they hate? What do their territories produce, what do they need, what bonds their populace together..."

"It's complicated," Dreadlocks said softly, rubbing her hands for warmth near one of the fires.

"People are complicated," the Medicine Woman replied.

Ephraim pulled on the Medicine Woman's coat. "I'm so hungry I could eat firewood."

"All right boys," the Medicine Woman said, taking hold of their hands. "Let's go eat. Dreadlocks will tell us stories."

"Absolutely!" Dreadlocks grinned, pointing at a cargo plane. "Once upon a time before the end of electricity, these things flew in the sky."

"No!" Manasseh said. "I don't believe you!"

"It's true," she assured him.

"It's magic," Manasseh whispered to Ephraim.

"The planes were built in another country called Texas. It's called the Lone Star."

"Why?" Ephraim asked.

"Well, I don't know why. But at that time—the whole land was ruled by one warlord."

The boys' eyes grew wide.

The Medicine Woman listened intently, while Manasseh and Ephraim interrupted Dreadlocks with far too many questions. She watched with pride as the boys carried their bags over their thin shoulders, enraptured by every word, asking thoughtful questions.

They also laughed and caught droplets of icy sleet on their tongues. So did she.

With full bellies, the boys were more than happy to retire to their cots for the evening. The boys were the only children on the base. As such, their bedding was placed the farthest away from the conference areas to keep them out of mischief and out from under foot.

Dreadlocks used a basin of warm water to clean the boys' faces while they jabbered about the wonders of the day. The Medicine Woman instructed them, once again, on how to clean their teeth with purple nutsedge.

"It tastes like dirt," complained Manasseh.

"Don't listen to your tongue—listen to your body," the Medicine Woman advised. "Your teeth will feel happier when you finish."

Dutifully, the boys continued without complaint.

After tucking them into quilted bedding, the Medicine Woman handed each one a stuffed animal that Davin had procured. Ephraim and Manasseh hugged the little bears to their chests.

"Dreadlocks and I have to go to a meeting. You must stay here. Do not wander about. The privy is behind that screen. Only get up if you need to use it."

"But I don't have to use it," Manasseh whispered, stricken by the thought he might fail her in some way.

"Then don't get up," she replied, smiling to ease his worry. "Tomorrow we will take you to look at the planes and see the horses—but promise me you will stay right here. Under no circumstances should you leave this area."

"What is the meeting about?"

"Keeping us safe," Dreadlocks replied, handing Manasseh a plastic cup of boiled water.

"Will you tell us what they say?" Ephraim asked. He sipped the water before handing it to his brother.

"I will tell you what you need to know," the Medicine Woman promised, ruffling his hair. "But promise me to stay here. No matter what."

"Okay," Ephraim said, throwing both of his arms around the

Medicine Woman's waist.

For a moment she was taken aback. She sat down on the edge of his cot and held him for a bit, then moved to Manasseh and hugged him as well.

"You all right, Manny?" she asked.

"Yep," he said, his eyes half closed. *Tonight he had consumed more than most of the MilitiaMen,* she thought. She delighted in Manasseh's accomplishment of eating an entire roast chicken himself.

Davin walked in the side entrance of the airport hangar, alone, motioning for both women to follow him.

Dreadlocks kissed Ephraim and Manasseh on their foreheads.

"Goodnight, boys. We'll see you in the morning."

As they left the warmth of the domestic quarters to follow Davin to another airport hangar, the bitter winds seemed to blow right through the Medicine Woman.

"How was the North ever settled?" she wondered aloud, grumbling against the chill.

"The cold makes people strong and resilient," Dreadlocks replied. "How boring it would be to just pick fruit off a tree or catch a fish in a lake any time of year. In the North, we have to think, we have to plan. You Southerners could use a bit more thoughtful reasoning."

The Medicine Woman quit listening to her as they entered a heavily-guarded structure. Inside, areas were cordoned off. Small fires burned in metal stoves to ensure private gatherings were comfortable.

The Medicine Woman scanned the area which housed higher level attendants, noting the positioning of the MilitiaMen. The layout was precise, thoughtfully laid out for maximum efficiency. *One entrance. One exit. Water station. Food table. Privy. Organized weaponry. Supplies.*

Davin directed them to a small table, draped with a heavy tablecloth, and a flickering beeswax candle. A bottle of mead, jug of spring water, and three glasses awaited them.

"Ah, you remembered!" Dreadlocks said, pouring herself a large glass. She took a long drink of mead before sitting down, sighing with pleasure. "I've needed this for months."

Davin sat, joining them, but he poured himself a half measure of mead. The Medicine Woman declined when he offered to fill her glass, opting for water instead.

"You don't drink?" Dreadlocks asked incredulously.

"I don't need to," the Medicine Woman replied. Davin laughed, seeing his little sister bested by the tall dark-haired woman.

"So you might be wondering who this is," Dreadlocks said, pointing to the Medicine Woman.

"We know who she is," Davin replied. "Her father was the Warlord of Tallahassee. He sold her mother to Lincoln in Old Virginia. She is unallied in the North."

"Does *unallied* mean kidnapped? Because I've fulfilled my duty. I've established pox protocols for a nation-state that has ceased to exist. It's past time for me to return South. May I leave?" the Medicine Woman said.

Davin turned to her. "I wouldn't advise it. Darius has claimed everything south of the Mason-Dixon Line and westward to the Sovereign State of Texas. You would be killed before you reached the border. The Pagans have pushed North, farther and faster than any of us suspected."

"How?" Dreadlocks asked, pouring herself a second glass of mead. "How didn't anyone see this coming? Your Scouts have been surveilling Darius since he was a toady for Xerxes."

Davin shrugged. "No one thought Darius would be as aggressive or as successful. The warlords in the North have always regarded him as a clown, painted in cosmetics, fat as a pig, wallowing in his retrofitted amusement park. No one took him seriously. His crucifying Southerners for sport. His praying to dark gods from antiquity..."

"But his successes in the South—"

"The South is backward and brutal. No warlord here cares about their poisoned rivers and blighted fields and inbred populace. The South can go straight to hell for all the North cares."

"And now he's here fresh from hell to burn down the North," the Medicine Woman interjected.

"He is," Davin agreed, his face grim. "And the Southern MilitiaMen have united behind him. He's almost a deity in certain parts, giving his citizens what they want most: peace. But Southerners have always been willing to give up their freedom for the promise of prosperity, even if it's bought with their own blood."

"So he has the numbers," Dreadlocks mumbled. "He has the Southern MilitiaMen."

"And weapons, Lillibet. Darius has amassed an incredible arsenal and munitions. After the Sylvanian Massacre, we've learned he produces an enormous quantity of black powder."

"No," Dreadlocks cried aloud. "It can't be true!"

"Once Darius took control of the sulfur mines in the Carolinas, it was all but certain he'd go into black powder production. He already had all the saltpeter he needed from the Arkansippi caves."

"Is black powder that easy to make?"

"Saltpeter, sulfur, charcoal," the Medicine Woman murmured, looking at her hands. "That's all you need."

For a moment, the Medicine Woman despaired, remembering what Dr. Mort had said about black powder: *The real use of it is to make all men tall.*

Dreadlocks continued to fret over Darius' advancements.

"The Pagans have functionable artillery and rockets. The North's firearms cannot compete on that level." Davin finished his drink, then poured himself another.

"Sylvania was his main target?" Dreadlocks asked.

"Sylvania was Darius's opening salvo. He made it an example. He hopes to take over other city-states without firing a shot. There are many who would like to avoid bloodshed."

"Has he met with the Northern Warlords?" Dreadlocks asked.

"Darius prefers to deal directly with the people, mainly through propaganda. He takes out the leadership. Publicly. Brutally. It's easier to establish a Pagan power structure that way."

"Oh Sounder," Dreadlocks whispered to herself, tears spilling down her face.

"Save your sympathy for someone who deserves it," Davin replied. "Sounder was working with Darius to overthrow Sylvania."

"You lie!"

"Why would I lie to my own sister?"

"Sounder would have told me. He said he was going to carry on the legacy of Papa Jack—"

"Sounder and his mistress were plotting with Darius long before Papa Jack died. Sounder sold out Sylvania while you were kidnapping people." Davin nodded to her companion.

"But he's—he's gone, isn't he? Sounder is dead?"

"Sounder is safely ensconced in DariusWood. He's now one of Darius's CouncilMembers."

"Oh my god," Dreadlocks said. "I'm going to be sick!" She stood up, face flushed with the alcohol. She staggered to the indoor privy, retching.

The other two watched her leave, Davin shaking his head. Again, the Medicine Woman was struck by how much they looked alike, then brooded over Davin's disturbing revelations.

"Why did you slap Lillibet when we first arrived?" the Medicine Woman asked frankly.

Davin looked hard at her. After brief consideration, he shrugged to himself, deciding to answer her question.

"When we moved to Sylvania, Lillibet and I joined the Sylvanian MilitiaMen—mainly to have someplace to sleep and a little food to eat. Both of us had acquired skills—skills that brought us to Papa Jack's attention. Lillibet trained to be a Scout, Papa Jack's favorite. He nicknamed her Dreadlocks—Dready for short." Davin had a wistful smile on his face, remembering simpler times.

"So she became an assassin for him," the Medicine Woman surmised.

"Lillibet is a very good *Scout,*" he said. "As for me? She told Papa Jack that I would make him an excellent bodyguard, and that I would give my life to protect him." Davin's eyes grew distant. The smile faded.

"What's wrong with that?" the Medicine Woman asked.

"She told Papa Jack that I would protect him because I was in love with him. Me. A young man with nothing, smitten by one of the wealthiest warlords."

"You hit her for lying—all those years ago?" the Medicine Woman asked.

"No," he replied. "I hit her for telling the truth."

Candles lit the proceedings, held in the hangar farthest away from the main entrance.

"Call to order the evening session of the Emergency Winter Council of the Northern Warlords. Warlord of Albany?"

"Here."

"Warlord of Amishland?"

"Aye."

"Warlord of Classical Massachusetts?"

"Here."

"Warlord of Columbia?"

"In attendance, sir."

"Warlord of Vermont?"

"Present and accounted for."

"Warlord of New Virginia?"

"Aye."

The Medicine Woman watched the men around the rectangular table as they scribbled notes and whispered to their attendants while roll was taken.

Davin stood directly behind the Warlord of Albany's chair. The

Medicine Woman and Dreadlocks sat with other attendants at small tables near the kitchen.

The Medicine Woman was struck at the orderly nature of the meeting, compared to what she'd seen at the Southern warlord gatherings during her father's time.

Instead of taking the matters of state seriously, Southern warlords preferred speechifying, grandstanding, showing off their temporary wives and concubines, imbibing too much, and making unwarranted and childish threats against one another.

"Let the record reflect that all Northern Warlords are in attendance. The Warlord of Springfield will lead this session. In four weeks time, we will reconvene in Amishland. Location will be delivered by dispatch courier at the appropriate time. Please read the minutes from last month's convocation."

"Trade routes have been renegotiated favorably to the Ohio border. Regarding the production of opium by Classical Massachusetts—"

Hours passed as the warlords discussed various sundry matters.

Dreadlocks yawned. "Oh, this is dreary," she complained to the Medicine Woman. She poured herself another glass of mead. "Darius consolidates his power by the colony-minute and these men are quibbling over taxes and trade."

"When are we to be questioned? When are they going to talk about Sylvania?"

"At the end."

"You would think they'd be more concerned with the Pagans on their doorstep," the Medicine Woman whispered.

"Davin said they are more worried about ensuring their citizens can work and feed themselves this winter. Sylvania is an abstract concept at this point."

"Then they are fools. Darius won't quit until the Pagans reclaim everything from here to New Virginia."

Davin glared at the women, silencing them with a frown.

"At this time," the officiant held his gavel aloft. "We will recess for the evening meal."

He banged the gavel as the warlords disbursed.

Attendants clustered around them in a scrum, holding trays ladened with roasted meats and root vegetables on skewers. Hot breads from the oven were served with dill butter. A dessert table was overfilled with cakes and pies of every kind.

No one noticed anything was amiss until the first lead ball caught the Warlord of Vermont in the neck.

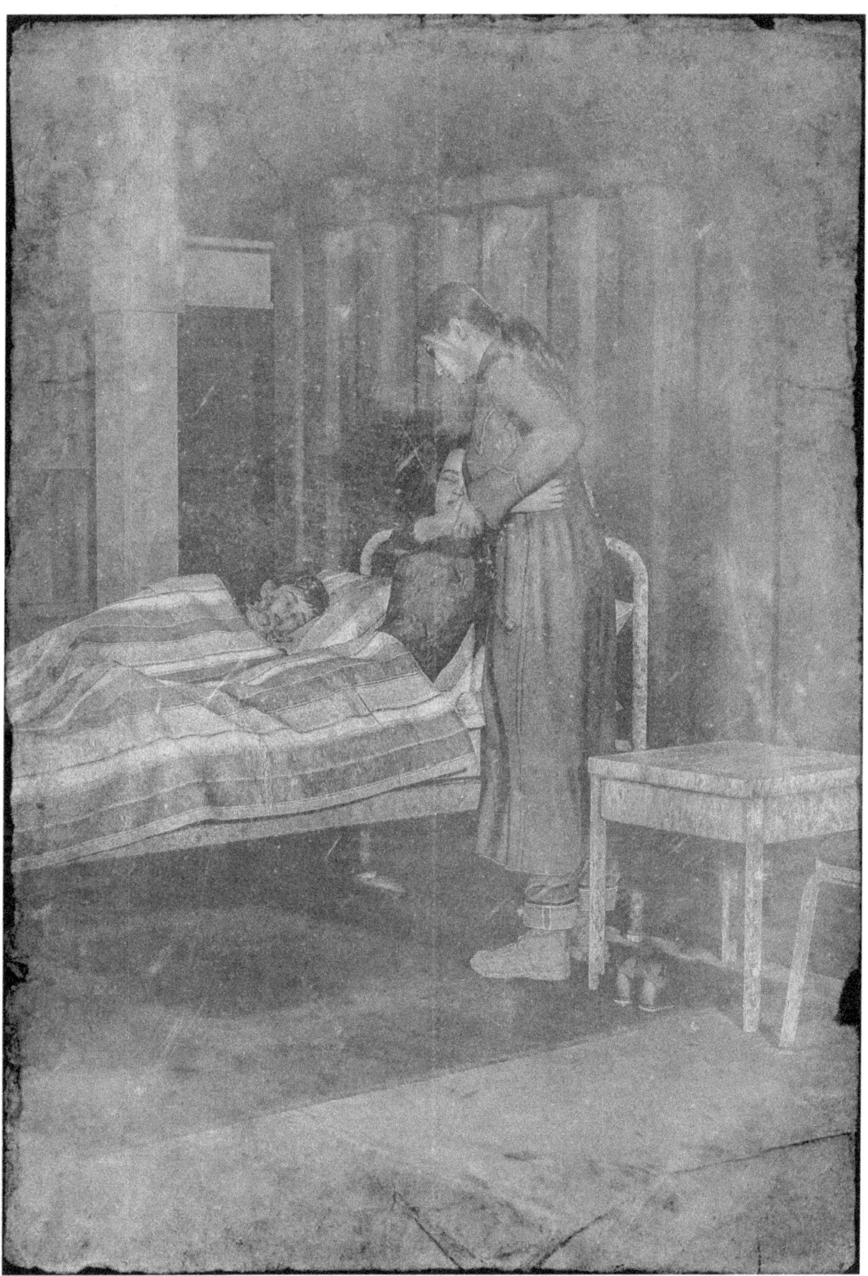

"Okay," Ephriam said, throwing both of his arms around the Medicine Woman's waist.

Chapter 21

Westover Military Base - Neutral Territory

The Medicine Woman turned in time to see the Warlord of Vermont's neck explode in a red shower of gore. She dropped to the floor as the popping sounds increased. MilitiaMen flooded in through each of the main hangar's entrances.

From her limited peripheral vision, she saw Dreadlocks sprint towards her brother. Davin appeared to be in shock, face fixed and emotionless, as he held the remains of the Warlord of Albany in his arms.

The Medicine Woman slid underneath the small table, feeling for her knives while pulling the floor length tablecloth over herself. Fending off fear and panic, she forced herself to remember the closest exits.

The boys, she thought. *She needed to get to the boys. She needed to get out. Staying where she was meant death.*

But how?

The Medicine Woman knew she had little time. From her precarious vantage point, she lifted the tablecloth to see what she was up against.

Unidentified MilitiaMen, faces covered, continued to stream into the hangar, sweeping throughout the space, threatening, shouting, waving PVC carbines. Dressed in heavy gray wool, the men's uniforms carried no insignia or identifying marks.

They were ghosts, deadly phantoms coming in from the icy chill on a dark night. Glinting in the candlelight, bayonets had been affixed to their guns' white muzzles, the men clearly prepared for close-quarters combat.

Though attendants had been trained to defend their warlords, they were caught unaware, valiantly using swords, arrows, cudgels, and cutlery from the table. All proved useless against the interlopers' newly constructed firearms, bullets, and black powder.

As lead balls slammed into flesh and bone, the Medicine Woman despaired at the carnage. She resisted the urge to triage wounds, tie off tourniquets, and help dying men breathe again. As much as she felt for the men's suffering, she had two boys who needed her more.

There will be no better time to run than now, she told herself.

From underneath the table, the Medicine Woman reached up to knock over Dreadlocks' glass of mead, spilling the entire bottle of alcohol for good measure. Retreating to the safety below, she gathered both ends of the tablecloth, violently pulling them back and forth until the candle toppled over from its base. Once the tablecloth burst into flames, she hoisted the small table in front of her, firmly holding on to the ends. Using the table as a blazing shield, she madly dashed through the closest door.

Assorted MilitiaMen scattered to get away from the fire, giving the Medicine Woman enough time to barrel through the doorway. As the men regrouped, she lobbed the small table at them, hearing their curses as it scorched a few of them before harmlessly smashing to the cold, hard ground.

She didn't wait to gauge any further reaction. Instead, she broke into a run, long strides taking her far afield, the arctic air burning her lungs, making her one good eye water.

She heard weapons discharge and felt projectiles pass by her, but the thick lead balls sunk into trees and metal siding. She steeled herself, waiting to be hit, but sprinted faster into the dark.

The gunfire directed towards her eventually decreased. The men had more important game to hunt. Still, she ran the length of the base to get to the boys as if she were being pursued, faster than she'd ever run before.

Clouds hid the moon and stars.

She tripped over roots and stumbled over broken shards of pavement, but moved forward, single-mindedly in her purpose.

Ducking behind a PedalCar, she felt safe for the moment. She reoriented herself, double checking her pathway forward, ignoring the shrieks and cries from the far end of the military base. She noted both the gunfire and screams grew louder, spreading, following her across the length of the military base.

As she approached the hangar where the boys were lodged, people streamed out, carrying makeshift weapons, shoving and pushing, moaning and weeping. Any orderly movement was shattered as base self-preservation took over. The Medicine Woman knew what this meant for the weak and the slow. *Violence. Chaos. Death.*

As the doorways were jammed with people fleeing, she felt her way along the far end, where the hangar butted up against barbed wire fencing. Large pine tree branches scraped across her face and neck as she searched for an opening, a fissure, a breach in the metal husk.

Where the attendants had set up an exterior kitchen, two windows had flanked a doorway. All appeared to be nailed shut, with new sheets of plywood covering the openings.

She looked out across the field to see the warlords' hangar alight in an explosion of fire. MilitiaMen fanned out to the other hangars like a dark tide.

Oh my god, she realized. She had much less time than she thought.

Unchecked fear choked her while she pulled out her thickest knife. *A serrated beast of a knife.* Hacking at the plywood, she used her hands and fingernails to pry the thin boards from the windows. Thick splinters sunk deep into her fingers and hands, spurring her on. The pain was irrelevant, as she sought to get inside the facility, gather two little boys to her chest, and find a way out of the North.

Removing a larger section of plywood gave her enough room to slither through and drop down to the floor. She left bloody handprints as she went.

Finally inside the dormitory, her vision adjusted, the enclosure darker than the starless night.

The clamor of frantic men made the darkness feel claustrophobic. She continued to move where she believed she had left the boys only hours earlier, stumbling on broken furniture and glass, stepping over things forgotten in the chaotic exodus.

Hearing a delicate crunch underfoot, she bent down to pick up a small object. *Not an object. A toy bear.*

Her throat constricted. Swallowing hard, she ignored the pounding of her heart.

"Ephraim! Mannasseh!" she called out, her voice hardly registering above the din.

Popping gunshots rang out, and she dropped to her knees. She crawled across the flooring, ignoring the various puddles of fluids she preferred not to think about.

"Boys!" she called out again. Her voice quavered. "Manny! Effy!"

Her hands blindly felt for their cots. Expecting both of the beds to be empty, she was startled to feel two little feet at the end of one bed, swaddled in blankets.

She grabbed ahold of the feet, expecting them to feel lifeless, heavy, cold. *But they were warm.* A wave of relief threatened to undo her.

"Meddy?" a little voice asked.

"Yes, Manny. It's Medicine Woman," she replied. "Hold on to me, all right?"

"Can I come, too?" asked Ephraim, sticking his head out from underneath Manasseh's cot.

Without a word, the Medicine Woman pulled Ephraim out and slung him onto her back. In her arms, she cradled Manny, still wrapped in a thick blanket.

In moments, the three scurried through the plywood hole, finding a respite on the other side of the hangar's walls.

The boys stood before her, both huddled under the blanket in the frigid night air.

"Are you alright?" she asked, looking at their eyes and checking for any wounds. She felt their pulses, racing a little faster than her own.

"We stayed where you put us," Manasseh replied, managing a crooked smile before bursting into tears.

Ephraim put a protective arm around his brother.

"You did very well, and I'm proud of you," the Medicine Woman whispered. "But I'm going to ask you to do some very hard things." She stood up and took the blanket off of them.

"It's cold," Manasseh remarked.

"I know, and I'm sorry." Taking their hands, the Medicine Woman placed them on either side of her waistband. "Hold on to my belt and run directly behind me. Don't look around. Don't look up or down. Keep running. Stop when I stop. Go when I go. Keep your eyes straight ahead, no matter what you hear."

"Okay," Ephraim replied solemnly. "We will."

Manasseh used his shirt to wipe his tears, then gripped the Medicine Woman's pants. "I'm ready," he said, voice full of resolve.

"Then let's go." the Medicine Woman murmured, ensuring their little hands were holding on tight.

As she turned into the night, she put one of her hands on each of the boys' heads, hugging them to her sides.

"You are good boys."

With that, she started to pace around the far perimeter of the military base, at a speed which two little boys could keep up.

There was only one place to go.

The horse paddock.

While the MilitiaMen continued streaming into the main hangar, Dreadlocks had to pry the corpse from Davin's hands. Frozen in grief, her brother wept into the Warlord of Albany's neck.

"Davin!" she screamed. "He's gone. He's gone." She pulled Davin down to the floor to avoid the lead balls, deadly arrows, and other projectiles that were cutting down warlords, attendants, and MilitiaMen alike.

Looking up with glazed eyes, Davin seemed not to recognize her, utter hopelessness apparent in his eyes. He was covered in his lover's gore, shards of the warlord's bones speckling Davin's clothing.

"We need to get out of here, Davin."

He gave no indication that he'd heard her.

Dreadlocks frantically considered her options. All were bad.

"There she is!" one of the unmarked MilitiaMen called out, pointing to Dreadlocks. Three of the men advanced towards her, holstering their weapons at their sides.

Dreadlocks pulled out her cudgel, planted her feet, prepared to die. If she were to be killed, at least she would take one of the MilitiaMen out with her. *Possibly two.*

Davin remained on the ground, supine, oblivious to everything about him.

"You sure this is the girl?" One of the men asked their leader. "This is the one Darius wants?"

"Sounder wants this one. Darius wants the tall dark girl with one eye."

Dreadlocks froze upon hearing Sounder's name, long enough for a MilitiaMan to disarm her. Another came from behind and pulled her into a chokehold.

"What about him?" The MilitiaMan nodded to the figure splayed out on the hangar's floor.

"Davin, the brother. The Albanian's attendant. Take him, too, for now. He might prove useful."

"We have orders to kill those not on the list."

The other man shrugged. "Ask the Colonel first. Take them to the impoundment."

"Ouch! You bitch!" screamed the MilitiaMen who held Dreadlocks in his grip. She had sunk her teeth into his forearm.

He threw her to the floor, took the weapon out of her hand, and hit her with her own cudgel.

"Don't kill her," the leader suggested, "if you can help it."

The man hit her again for good measure.

"We could claim it was collateral damage. You know how these things go." The man kneeled down to check the wound on the side of Dreadlocks' face. "Aw, she'll be alright. Nothing like a concussion to take the wind out your sails, right darlin'?" He slapped her cheek, then scowled at the bite marks on his arm.

"Impoundment now. Expedite them via OxCart transport." The leader barked commands over his shoulder before stalking out.

"Who knows what can happen on the way to Sylvania?" The man who'd been bitten leered at Dreadlocks.

When the MilitiaMen picked up the boys like sacks of cabbage, Dreadlocks opened her eyes to a slit. Without making a move, she carefully looked at each MilititaMan's face—especially the one who had hit her.

She couldn't wait to kill them all.

"Why did we stop?" Ephraim breathlessly whispered, crouching down behind a hollowed out tree trunk. Manasseh snuggled in tightly between the two, burrowing into the Medicine Woman's chest.

"I'm cold," Manasseh said, teeth chattering.

Ephraim wrapped his thin arms around his brother. The Medicine Woman enveloped them both, taking off her long coat to cover their thin frames.

"Are we gonna find a horse?" Manasseh said, wiping his nose on the sleeve of her jacket.

"Yes," she said. "But not yet."

"Can you ride a horse?"

"I can," she said.

"Then what are we waiting for?" Ephraim wondered. "We could ride to a warm place."

The Medicine Woman smiled, holding them closely under her coat.

"We will take a horse when it's safe. Then I will take you South," she decided. "It's always warm in the South."

"I would like that," Manasseh said, shivering.

The sleet decidedly turned into heavy snowflakes.

The Illuminati Pagans had cordoned off the impoundment near the main entrance of the military base to hold persons of interest. OxCarts were lined up, prepared to take prisoners and the warlords' belongings back to Sylvania. Maps, treatises, notes, and memorandum were carried out of the conference rooms in heavy wooden crates.

Darius was getting a treasure trove of intelligence, Dreadlocks thought ruefully. *He would soon know everything about the North, its strengths and its weaknesses.*

They sat behind cartons of ammunition and bottles of fire accelerant. Other terrified prisoners in the impoundment kept to themselves or crowded the opening, a few pleading with the MilitiaMen to save their own lives.

Her brother was awake, but quiet, introspective.

"It's my fault," he said, shaking his head. "It was my job to protect him, to see the things he couldn't see."

"Don't do this now, Davin."

"And as for the loyal MilitiaMen of the North?" Davin gave a bitter laugh. "Half of them had been colluding with the Pagans. Like Sounder."

"You don't know that," Dreadlocks countered.

"But I do. And you know it, too. Sounder was always too ambitious for his own good."

It was her turn to be silent.

"They took my cudgel," she pouted.

"They took your knives, too." Davin added. "And they took the love of my life. I watched as his eyes dimmed." Davin put his head down and wept.

Dreadlocks reached over to hold her brother's hand. He eventually swallowed hard and turned to face her.

"You're bleeding," he said.

"It'll stop," she waved him off.

"Lillibet, you need to go South."

"We both need to go South, Davin. I—"

Davin reached out to put his hand across her mouth. "Listen."

"I—"

"Shut. Up."

She sighed.

"In two weeks, MilitiaMen from the North's city-states—from Old Virginia to New Brunswick—will meet in Harrisburg."

"Amishland?"

Davin nodded. "Deep in the heart of Amishland. The Albanians were planning to lead the United Front against Darius."

"Even after this?" Dreadlocks asked.

"Especially after this," Davin whispered. "If I learned one thing over the years, little sister, it is that everyone is replaceable. New warlords are undoubtedly taking the helm of their territories as we speak. And the Pagans can't keep something like this quiet. If I'm not mistaken, the counterattack against Darius will be moved up, not abandoned."

"But how—"

"Because NorthMen hate tyrants, and freedom isn't a privilege, Lillibet. It's the only thing worth fighting for. Now take off your clothes."

"What?"

"Take off your cloak, scarf, hat and give them all to me. You need to put on my attendant's tunic."

She did as he asked, luxuriating in the quality of the governmental garb. "Damn, this is warm. Goatskin? I like it."

"Now put on the cap. Tuck your stupid hair into it, or I'll pull out each one of your dreadlocks myself."

"Fine." Dreadlocks fumbled with her hair. "Now what?"

"Now wait. In a little while, there will be a diversion. It's meant for me to escape with one of the Amishlanders. Their Scouts have been on the southern perimeter since our arrival. Someone will come for me. Go in my stead. When you get to Harrisburg, tell them who you are. Ask to speak to the major general."

"Who is the major general?"

"Whoever is left alive," Davin muttered. "Darius' incursion into the North will be checked hard. The North will not fall prey to that particular idiot."

"Why send me? You should go."

"No, I shouldn't."

"Davin. This is crazy. We both should go. What are you planning to do?"

"I am going to lay here until our ruse is discovered. Then one of the Pagan MilitiaMen will kill me."

"Davin!"

"Dready, I'm dead already," he smiled, eyes brimming with unshed tears. "My reason for living is currently burning to ash in that airport hangar."

"But—"

"I'm done, Lillibet."

"Davin, please." Dreadlocks clenched her teeth to keep from screaming, but her brother's face was calm, at peace with his decision.

"I have done everything I've wanted," he said. "You, my dear sister, have other things to do. Find Sounder. Find some answers."

Across the gravel walkway, a MilitiaMan wearing a nondescript uniform led two horses, packed with supplies, in plain sight of the other Pagan MilitiaMen. Among the disorder after the invasion, no one noticed that man was about to lead a prisoner off in plain sight.

The man made eye contact with Davin, flashing a hand gesture that Dreadlocks couldn't quite make out. Davin gave him a slight nod.

"That's your ticket to Harrisburg."

"Davin—"

"You make a handsome man, Dreadlocks." He finished tucking in her hair, then gave his sister a quick embrace. Davin swirled her scarf around his own head, covering his nose and mouth. "And I'm sure you'll agree that I'm quite fetching myself."

Dreadlocks laughed in spite of herself.

A fireball erupted near the horse paddock, alarming the Pagans. Shrill voices called out orders, shifting personnel towards the fracas, thinning out the MilitiaMen who guarded the impoundment.

The man with the horses gestured again.

"It's time to go."

"Okay," she murmured. "I'll see you, Davin."

"And I'll see you, Lillibet. I'll see you on the other side."

*Ephraim wrapped his thin arms around his brother. The Medicine Woman
enveloped them both.*

Chapter 22

Harrisburg, Amishland

"Meddy has been gone for a long time," Manasseh fretted, wrapping himself in the Medicine Woman's coat more tightly. "Should we go find her?"

The Medicine Woman had run the boys to the southwestern quadrant of the base, past the treeline, near the clearing, by the frozen reservoir. Snow flurries had fallen unabated, accumulating in colony-inches on the ground, on their shoulders, on their eyelashes.

"Meddy said to wait here, so we're not going anywhere until she comes back," Ephraim replied. They nestled up against a pile of cinder blocks.

Hearing muted explosions, both boys flinched, staring in the general direction where the Medicine Woman had gone. Thin columns of black and gray smoke poured skyward, mixing with the thick low clouds.

"If she doesn't ever come back, where will we go?" Manasseh wondered. "The Rabbi is dead. Kimper is far away."

"Meddy will come back for us."

"What if she's hurt?"

"I don't think she gets hurt."

"Everybody gets hurt."

"Meddy is different."

"Maybe she'll find Dreadlocks."

"Dreadlocks probably went to Sylvania," Ephraim replied. "Her boyfriend lives there."

"I think Meddy is dead."

"Meddy isn't dead!" Annoyed by his brother, Ephraim decided to ignore him, brushing off the snow collecting on his boots.

"Everyone we know is dead," Manasseh sulked. "I think Meddy's dead, too."

"Take that back." Ephraim punched him in the shoulder.

"Don't hit!" Manasseh yelled.

"Say Meddy isn't dead!" Ephraim punched him again for good measure.

"Okay! Okay! Meddy isn't dead," he relented, putting his hands up to fend off his brother's blows.

"Meddy will be back! You'll see," Ephraim said. "She's getting horses to take us South, where it's warm. She's going to show us how to eat the heart of a palm, just like she promised!"

"Okay," Manasseh grumbled, shifting under the shared coat. "But I hope she comes soon. I don't like MilitiaMen."

"MilitiaMen brought us here."

"Not those kind. I hate the kind with guns. The ones killing everybody like at the Rabbi's house."

"Those weren't MilitiaMen at the Rabbi's house. Those were bad guys. They didn't have guns," Ephraim corrected his brother.

"It would have been better for the rabbi if they did."

Dawn approached, but the leaden skies kept the sunlight at bay. The Medicine Woman shivered, cursing the North again for its wretched weather, then she fell to her knees in despair.

The horse paddock had been emptied.

A few caracasses littered the snowy field, horses shot in the crossfire, along with a score of MilitiaMen. The fencing around the enclosure had been compromised in the chaos. Several PedalCars and a SteamCar had been purposely crashed into the barbed wire, causing breaches. *Perhaps the majority of horses escaped into the surrounding area*, she hoped.

She walked over to the cars, getting a good look at the machinery. *A good horse could easily outrun either of these ridiculous contraptions*, the Medicine Woman thought bitterly.

With the paddock abandoned, she was out of easy options.

The Medicine Woman leaned against the cold trunk of an icy tree for a moment, catching her breath, recalibrating her plans. *She couldn't leave the boys alone for too long, but they needed shelter. They needed a safe place to warm themselves, water to drink, food to eat.*

Anger and frustration knotted in her stomach. To calm herself, she checked her knives, slowed her breathing, and remembered her mother's words: *Above all, be patient.*

But patient for what?

The Medicine Woman walked over to the remains of a stallion with gaping wounds in the neck. Fortunately, whoever had shot it had left the saddle. She knelt down to unbuckle it, retrieved the thick saddle blanket underneath, and slid it over her shoulders. She welcomed the blanket's warmth as she contemplated her next move.

Maybe there are no options, she mused. *Maybe she should lay down in a snowbank and quietly freeze to death?*

Before she could ruminate further, she heard a couple of men laughing, talking loudly as they made their way towards the ruins of the paddock.

"They want us to check," the larger one of the two said. "Unless we find a person's name on the list, we exterminate with extreme prejudice."

"Even the horses?"

"Not the horses, you idiot! They'd hang us both for even suggesting such a ridiculous thing."

"So who are we looking for?"

His colleague consulted the names scrawled on reclaimed paper. "The Vermont cook. The Warlord's Attendant from New Brunswick. A tall one-eyed lady doctor. Three Ohioan temporary wives. Anyone who is a farrier. Darius wants all the hoof specialists he can get. They're assembling calvaries in DariusWood."

"Well, I think Darius is out of luck here. There's nothing but dead men and dying animals," the other MilitiaMan replied. He kicked at one of the horses on the ground, looking over the field with bodies of men and beasts intermingled. Footprints peppered the snow, their patterns showing evidence of panic and disorder.

One of the men gave a low whistle. "Whoever the son of a bitch is who shot these horses is going to pay a hefty price."

They walked in tandem towards the main breach in the paddock.

"Should we salvage the SteamCar?"

"That's too heavy for the both of us. Let's start with the PedalCar. It's only tangled in barbed wire."

The men began rocking the hulk of metal from side to side, finally dislodging it. The PedalCar rolled backward into a trench, fully clogged with ice and snow.

"Dammit to hell!"

"Let's go around the front. We'll push it up the embankment onto the roadway."

Both men stood thigh deep in the mucky trench. Cursing and grunting, they finally extricated the PedalCar with one final push. The PedalCar slowly rolled forward, tires finding purchase on the roadway. With their hands on their hips, the men celebrated, preparing to slog through the deep ditch's slush and snow to get to higher ground.

From its depths, the Medicine Woman arose behind them, an icy phoenix from the snowbank. Before either man could cry out, she simultaneously plunged two of her longest knives into the sides of their heads, piercing their skulls straight through their temples.

The Medicine Woman folded the corpses, headfirst, into the snow before the blood seeped on to their uniforms. As their bodies cooled, she stripped off their clothing, feeling especially grateful for the dead men's thick gloves and woolen socks. Gods

Grabbing both men's PVC carbines and supply packs, she scrambled up the embankment, opened the driver's side door of the PedalCar, then threw everything except the horse blanket into the backseat.

Sitting in the driver's seat with the blanket around her shoulders, she placed her feet on the pedals, using what little remained of her strength to power the car forward. As she pumped her legs, laboring to motor the car uphill, she turned the stiff steering wheel towards the boys' direction, praying to nameless gods that they were still safe.

The sky above her now blued, the sun finally deciding to show its face.

The Illuminati Pagan Command had arrived at the military base after the warfare had ended. MilitiaMen on the ground moved into high gear, organizing personnel, managing high level prisoners, executing expendable ones.

The cleanup started as well. MilitiaMen began to build pyres to dispose of the corpses. Attendants boiled water to clean the floors of bodily fluids. Other attendants salvaged foodstuffs from the dormitory hangar to feed the victors and pilfered the laundries to appropriate cold weather gear for the incoming MilitiaMen.

The AmishMan said very little to Dreadlocks, helping her up on her horse. As a show for the impoundment attendants, he bound Dreadlocks' hands behind her back while she perched awkwardly on her saddle. Davin's heavy tunic and coat hid her frame quite well, his cap fully covering her telltale hair.

"Where are you heading?" barked a fraught attendant with a clipboard, lost amidst the bustling men near the impoundment.

"I have orders to transport the Albanian Chief Attendant."

"From whom?"

"It's classified," the AmishMan said stoically, handing him a sealed document. "But here are the general orders from Pagan Command."

The attendant unceremoniously opened the envelope, peering at the scrawl. "These papers are unsigned! Who are you exactly and where are you taking him?"

"That's classified, too. If you want to waste the Illuminati Pagans' time, that's on you. Lives are at stake. There are people who need to question this man, sooner rather than later."

The attendant tapped his fingers on the clipboard, irritated, unsure of what to do. "Go. Just go," he decided rashly, waving him off.

The AmishMan mounted his horse, while holding tightly onto the reins of Dreadlocks' horse. He spurred his horse forward, riding side by side with Dreadlocks, giving a wide berth to the SteamCars, transports, and other mounts in the roadway.

After a few minutes, the crowds thinned as they headed for the main thoroughfare.

"You going to untie me now?"

"Not yet."

Dreadlocks heard the AmishMan exhale sharply once the military base was out of sight. They rode a bit further down the Nine Zero, as a convoy of MilitiaMen streamed into the military base on foot, on horse, by wagon, by PedalCar, by SteamCar.

The AmishMan and Dreadlocks kept to the far right of the road, seemingly oblivious to the waves of MilitiaMen and their commanders. Carts of captured men and women stoically rolled past.

"Looks like we got out of that one pretty easy, huh?" Dreadlocks remarked, watching supply trucks and medical personnel pass by in the opposite direction. "How about we get off the main road and you untie me?"

"Not yet," the AmishMan said, risking a look back.

"I'm going to need you to untie my hands. Seriously. And why are we traveling in full view? I think we should—"

She quit speaking as the AmishMan turned from her.

"Buddy, I'm not comfortable on a horse," she tried again. "I certainly am not comfortable with my hands tied behind my back while I'm riding on a horse. So let's dip into the woods for a colony-second. Pretend you need to take a piss or something. No one is watching us. No one will care."

The AmishMan looked back one more time before the side of his face exploded in a coppery cloud.

In horror, Dreadlocks closed her eyes and opened her mouth, screaming from shock as the horses reared up from the sounds of gunfire. A colony-dozen lead balls sunk into trees around them. Several MilitiaMen screamed at her as the AmishMan fell from his horse, his lifeless hands releasing both reins.

As the subsequent yelling continued, the two horses arched their backs, showing the whites of their eyes before bolting in a zigzag pattern into the dense brush. Dreadlocks pinned her legs to her horse's body, praying he wouldn't buck harder than he already had. She leaned forward, clenching down on the horse's mane with her teeth in an attempt to remain upright in the saddle.

The horses galloped at a breakneck pace alongside each other, slowing as they plowed deeper into the snowy woods.

Once away from the commotion, the horses began to trot, then to walk, their labored breath making white clouds in the brisk air. Dreadlocks wiggled her wrists, attempting to free her hands, but the AmishMan's knots were secure.

The AmishMan had failed. Dreadlocks began to wonder if the United Front would flounder as badly in the coming weeks. *But she had survived for now.* She felt a brief wave of relief wash over her before she noted that the horses were moving purposefully.

"No, no, no," she realized, clamping down harder in the stirrups, but her horse seemed to know she was powerless. Ignoring their solo rider, the horses inexorably tramped through the muddy snow.

Hungry, tired, and scared, the horses sought a place of refuge, a place they knew could provide care and comfort.

Oh my god, Dreadlocks realized. *They're going back to the horse paddock.*

After her return from the paddock, the Medicine Woman had pushed the PedalCar off the roadway by the reservoir and deep into the thicket, covering it with brambles and brush.

The boys were frigid, showing early signs of frostbite, as she huddled them into the car. She dressed them in the MilitiaMen's woolen socks, jackets, gloves, and hats. For herself, she'd put on both of the men's pants, cinching them tightly at her waist with one of the men's belts. Though stiff from the layers of clothing, she and the boys warmed.

"Can we go South now?" asked Manasseh.

"No, Manny. We need to wait until the sun goes down," explained the Medicine Woman for the third time.

Manasseh had the horse blanket wrapped around his shoulders, kicking at the pedals, wanting badly to push them around and around to make the car go.

"Can I hold the gun?" Ephraim wondered, his eyes hopeful.

"You may not."

"Oh, c'mon." His disappointment was palpable. *He sounded like Dreadlocks.*

"I'm still hungry," Manasseh complained.

"Another piece of jerky, coming up!" Ephraim said in a silly voice to his brother, making one of the men's oversized gloves into a puppet.

"Thank you, Glovey," Manasseh said, taking the dried squirrel from Ephraim and popping it whole into his mouth.

"What's that, Glovey? Manny's ticklish? You don't say." Ephraim lunged at his brother, making "Glovey" tickle his brother's ribs, causing both of them to laugh.

"Boys," the Medicine Woman said in a very low voice. "We need to be as quiet as mice."

"Can anyone see us?" asked Ephraim.

"Are bad guys coming?" cried Manasseh, mouth still full of jerky.

"No, but we should rest now. We'll have to pedal all night, and I will need your help. Please, try to close your eyes and sleep."

"I like the horse blanket," Manasseh grinned. "It's warm."

"Good," the Medicine Woman said, gathering him up in her arms. "Now kiss Glovey goodnight and let's close our eyes."

Dutifully, Manasseh leaned over and kissed the glove on Ephraim's hand.

With nearly full bellies and ensconced in the coziness of the PedalCar, the small group grew very sleepy. As the boys drifted off, they looked at each other, listening to the Medicine Woman snore, which caused them no end of amusement.

"Meddy, where did you get the horses?" asked Ephraim.

"W-What?" The Medicine Woman snapped awake, bolting upright.

"The horses," Ephraim repeated.

"What horses?"

"Those."

The Medicine Woman peered out of the frosted windshield, seeing two horses in the clearing, only one with a rider. The horses noisily lapped up the icy water, drinking from the thawed edges of the reservoir.

"Stay here," the Medicine Woman said, rummaging through the MilitiaMen's packs, pocketing a few dried apples and carrots. She pulled out her thickest knife, holding it in her right hand.

After she shut the car door, the boys crawled up to the front seat to watch the Medicine Woman silently approach the rider from behind.

Clearly exhausted, its rider had slumped forward on the horse, hands tied from behind like a criminal.

The Medicine Woman did a double take at the riderless horse that stood nearby. She stared at its dark hooves and legs, blue eyes, and white markings alongside the body and neck. *The horse looked strikingly similar to Patches, the first horse she'd ever ridden.*

Lost in her recollections, the Medicine Woman turned back to the rider, ducking in time to avoid being kicked in the face. The rider kicked again at the Medicine Woman before losing momentum, sprawling backwards, sliding off the horse's rear end.

In the struggle to stand up, the rider's cap came off.

"Dreadlocks?" the Medicine Woman yelled, with her knife poised high overhead, ready to strike.

"Medicine Woman? Is that you? Oh shit," Dreadlocks replied, sheepishly. "Stab me later. Right now, will you please cut off these goddamned ropes?"

As the Medicine Woman and Dreadlocks led the horses to the

PedalCar, Ephraim and Manasseh jumped out, running into Dreadlocks' arms.

"You're here!" Manasseh cried, burying his face into her shoulder. Ephraim joined in the reunion as Dreadlocks hugged him within an inch of his life.

"I'm so glad to see you two," Dreadlocks said, tousling their hair.

"Boys, take these apples and carrots and feed them to the horses. Lay them on the flat on your hands, like this." The Medicine Woman demonstrated. "Make sure you approach them from the side. Talk nicely to them. Pet their necks and shoulders—and don't stand behind them or you'll get kicked!"

Ephraim and Manasseh didn't need much encouragement, as the boys were delighted to see the horses close up, giggling as the horses' lips tickled their hands. Now tied to the PedalCar's rear bumper, the horses greedily ate the boys' offerings.

"Well, now what?" the Medicine Woman muttered to Dreadlocks, once the boys were out of earshot.

"We need to get to Harrisburg," Dreadlocks replied.

"Harrisburg?"

"The United Front is assembling there to push the Pagans out of the North, out of Sylvania—and hopefully all the way back to Tennessee."

"What's the time frame?"

"Davin said the initial strike on Sylvania would take place in a couple of weeks. All of Darius's incursions in the North are now being coordinated from there, including the one we have managed to survive, so far."

"How far away is Harrisburg?"

"Roughly 500 colony-miles. The roadways are clogged with Pagans, MilitiaMen, refugees—it's lawless out there. We're going to have to take the horses and travel off road. Especially with the boys."

"Especially with the boys," the Medicine Woman repeated soberly, nodding in agreement. "It'll take us nine or ten days, Dreadlocks. We'll need to move out as soon as possible. This is not a safe place."

"Agreed."

The boys ran over to the women, grinning from ear to ear.

"Do we have any more apples? They love them!" Manasseh said.

"The horses are probably full by now. But we're going to get packed up and go on a long horse ride. Would you like that?" the Medicine Woman asked.

"Yes! Yes! Yes!" the two brothers replied, jumping up and down.

Over their heads, Dreadlocks gave the Medicine Woman a thin smile.

They were captured by the United Front eight days later at Lacey Spring, an outpost on the border of Harrisburg.

"Who are they?" The captain of the platoon asked his attendant.

"No one seems to know. We're bringing them in now, sir."

The Medicine Woman walked ahead of Dreadlocks, the two boys silent at her side.

"I wanted to personally thank you for your medical services, ma'am." The captain stood and shook the Medicine Woman's hand. "They tell me Corporal Samuels would have died from blood poisoning if you hadn't acted as quickly as you did. We're woefully short staffed and unused to treating gunshot wounds. There's been no time to train adequate medical personnel during the build up."

"There are ways to expedite that," the Medicine Woman replied. "I've done that kind of work before under United Authority Command."

"We could use your expertise. Harrisburg is sending—"

"I need to see whoever the major general is," Dreadlocks interrupted. "I have Pagan intel straight from the Chief Attendant himself."

"Is it credible?" The captain looked at Dreadlocks with one eyebrow arched.

"The Albanian Chief Attendant is her brother," the Medicine Woman replied, vouching for her.

"I'll see what can be arranged." The captain nodded to his attendant.

By midafternoon, a fleet of armored SteamCars arrived at the Lacey Spring outpost to pick up the women and children, driving them the short distance back to the United Front headquarters in Harrisburg, situated in the former National Civil War Museum.

"It's warmer in the South," Manasseh said, looking out the car window. The sky was blue, warm zephyrs effectively melting the remnants of frost and snow.

"And it'll get warmer and warmer the farther South we go," the Medicine Woman explained. "Sometimes it's too warm. Sometimes it gets very hot."

"I like hot," Manasseh replied.

Pulling into Reservoir Park, the boys fell silent at seeing thousands of MilitiaMen in all sorts of uniforms—from New Brunswick to the Carolinas—assembling on the field.

"Good god," Dreadlocks said. "There are so many of them."

Pulling up to the repurposed museum, the Medicine Woman felt as if she were back with General Chapman in Richmond again.

In the lobby, two older female attendants took Ephraim and Manasseh, promising the boys a visit to see the SteamTransports and new SteamTanks in the armory, as well as a visit to the canteen for snow-cream.

Dreadlocks and the Medicine Woman were ferried to the main conference room. A phalanx of attendants and MilitiaMen of assorted ranks sat at tables, arguing over strategies, drawing out plans for the reclaiming of Sylvania.

"These aren't to scale," Dreadlocks complained, walking up to one of the maps. "The Westin stood here, not over there." To the attendants' chagrin, she picked up an oil pencil to redraw the map more accurately.

"I'm sure you have a lot to teach us, Lillibet," called out a feminine voice from the far end of the conference table.

"I do," Dreadlocks replied. "You seem to know me. Who the hell are you?"

"I'm Major General Christina Roberts of the United Front. Welcome to Amishland."

The boys ran over to the women, grinning from ear to ear.

Chapter 23

Harrisburg, Amishland

"You're a woman," Dreadlocks remarked, taking her in. Roberts approached, hand outstretched in greeting. She was an older woman, taller than most, sporting a close crop of gray hair.

Roberts' flinty gaze scanned Dreadlocks in return, the General's hazel eyes nearly matching her dark khaki uniform. "Indeed, I am a woman. Are you always such a keen observer?" the General replied good-naturedly.

The other military personnel surrounding them chuckled.

"In Sylvania—"

"Forgive me for saying so, but even at its height, Sylvania wasn't exactly a bastion for feminism—or anything else for that matter." Several of her attendants made unflattering remarks about Sylvanians under their breath.

Dreadlocks face reddened. "I didn't—"

Roberts held up a hand. "Whatever you did or didn't do is unimportant. What's important now is that you are here to help us better understand the Sylvania situation on the ground. You are here to help the United Front in its prime directive: expelling Pagans from the North."

General Roberts pulled out a chair at the conference table, indicating with a nod that Dreadlocks should sit.

"My brother—"

"Your brother was the Chief Attendant to the Albanian Warlord," the General brusquely said. "The Albanian Warlord is dead. Many of the Northern Warlords are dead."

"Davin—"

"Lillibet," the General said quietly, "I think you know quite well that Davin is dead." General Roberts stood up and began to pace. "It was my father who taught me the truth of *horror vacui*. Nature abhors a vacuum. Unfilled space goes against the laws of nature. Don't shed any tears for warlords. Replacements have already been appointed to perform their civic duties."

"Davin thought that—"

"Davin was our man on the inside, Lillibet. Some of the warlords encouraged Darius, working with him on Pagan expansion deep into the North. It's well known that Darius will stop at nothing to ensure that the Illuminati Pagans rule *from sea to shining sea*," she added sarcastically.

"The Warlord of Albany—"

"The Warlord of Albany was a traitor to the North, Lillibet. He sold out every Albanian—even Davin."

Gritting her teeth from saying anything, Dreadlocks sat down hard, folding hands in front of her.

"I want you to know Davin didn't suffer," the General added. "While the MilitiaMen prepared him for torture, one of our best Scouts dispatched him before the Pagans did their worst. Regrettably, our Scout ended up taking Davin's place."

Dreadlocks remained stoic but managed a curt nod.

"I'm going to leave you with the brigadiers who are working up our invasion plans. The intent is to drive Pagans right back to hell where they belong."

"Hell or Tennessee, whichever is hotter!" called out one of the brigadiers, coming to sit next to Dreadlocks. He carried newly drawn maps, as territorial lines had collapsed into one another in the weeks after the Pagan takeover of the Westover military base.

"As long as Darius is out of the North, that's all I care about," General Roberts replied, then turned to the Medicine Woman. "As for you, come with me and we'll get something to eat. Frank? Tell the chief officers to report to my office immediately after lunch. Ask the MedicMen, the pharmacology team, the sanitation engineers, and the agriculture specialists to join as well. We have a special guest for them to meet."

Walking through the former National Civil War Museum's rotunda,

General Roberts led the Medicine Woman through various corridors into the canteen. Higher ranking officers from a dozen territories ate their meals at mismatched tables, tucking into plates full of boiled root vegetables, potato and leek soup, wedges of cheese, and small loaves of oatmeal bread. NewComers picked up large plastic trays to carry their fare through the makeshift lunchline. The trays were relics from the cafeteria-style eateries, so common before the end of electricity.

"I hope you have New Brunswick Stew. It's my favorite," General Roberts called out to a kitchen attendant while handing the Medicine Woman a wooden bowl.

"Not today, Ma'am," the kitchen attendant laughed. "It's venison."

"How many goddamned deer are around here anyway? You'd think we'd have killed them all off by now." General Roberts grumbled. "Well, give me an extra slice of cornbread and we'll call it even."

"Yes, Ma'am." The kitchen attendant added a few more cookies to her tray.

"Ooo. Maple gingersnaps. My favorite." The General nibbled on one as they progressed through the line.

The Medicine Woman carried her tray, following closely behind the General, threading through quiet clusters of somber Albanians, New Virginians, and Mainenites. The Old Virginians and Carolingians loudly bickered about politics, disagreeing on almost every point. Their banter was punctuated by scathing remarks made by the personnel from Classical Massachusetts who had long grown weary of the MidAtlantic's posturing.

"Where do the others eat?" the Medicine Woman asked.

"Non-coms and enlisted personnel eat outside in the tents. They're used to the elements. We tried to invite them inside, but they prefer it that way. *To each his own*, my father used to say."

The Medicine Woman nodded, noting the canteen's sanitation measures. There were hand washing stations with scraps of clean towels, compost bins for the few leftovers, tubs of hot sudsy water for soaking dishes and silverware. *All was efficiently organized. Useful.*

"How many times has the pox passed through this region?" the

Medicine Woman asked.

"Twice," General Roberts replied. "Both times accompanied by an influx of refugees. For the most part, we've been spared during the winter, but the cold weather is breaking. We're hoping you'll help us prepare for a resurgence in the spring."

"I can do that."

"Spring comes earlier and earlier each year, but they've been saying that since I was a little girl," General Roberts remarked, silently acknowledging a few key people in the room. Both women found their way to a nondescript table in the far corner of the canteen, next to the door leading out to the staging grounds.

For a moment, the General stood, looking out of the paneless window at the throngs of MilitiaMen, disparately dressed in a variety of uniforms, drilling together in tight formation. She turned to the Medicine Woman, smiled, and sat down.

"I like to be near the exit," the General confided.

"I like to count the exits," the Medicine Woman replied, much to the General's delight.

Several attendants joined them at different intervals, intermittently asking the General a series of wide-ranging questions—everything from approving increased charcoal production to funding another SteamTransport to punishing kitchen thieves.

"We cannot tolerate theft on any level, lieutenant. Do with thieves what we do to Pagan Scouts. Quickly and publicly."

"That severe?" the lieutenant replied.

General Roberts gently put her fork down and lowered her voice. "Yes, lieutenant. Would you like me to repeat my decision or demonstrate it for you?"

The table went silent at the General's icy glare. Several beats too late, he collected himself.

"No, Ma'am. We will do as you order. Thank you." He quickly gathered his things and departed.

"Cookie?" the General said, offering the plate to the Medicine

Woman.

"Meddy! Meddy!"

The Medicine Woman turned to see Ephraim and Manasseh scurrying towards her.

"We went to the munitions warehouse!" Ephraim recounted breathlessly, as Manasseh hugged the Medicine Woman, throwing his thin arms around her middle.

"What did you see?" she asked.

"Lots of stuff! Bombs and shells and round bullet balls. Muskets and gunpowder—just like Pagans!" Manasseh was breathless.

"I got to go inside a SteamTank. They let us climb on the main gun and everything," Ephraim added.

Both of the boys held waffle cones filled with a cold, gooey confection.

"What are you eating?" the Medicine Woman asked.

"It's snow-cream! It's really good." Manasseh gave his cone a hearty lick. "Mine is strawberry."

"They took us to the kitchen, and they showed us how to make flat pancakes and wrap them into this." Ephraim pointed at the cone. "Then they take ice and snow and mix it with stuff. Fruit and maple syrup from New Virginia. Do you want to try it?"

"I do," the Medicine Woman fondly remembered, leaning over to take a small bite. *It was heavenly.*

"Are these your children?" General Roberts asked offhandedly, while reading through a document on reclaimed paper. She crossed out whole sections, scrawling her initials on others.

The boys looked at her, expectantly.

"Yes," the Medicine Woman smiled. "Those are my boys." She attempted to use her napkin to clean the boys' faces and hands.

Hearing the Medicine Woman's response, both Ephraim and Manasseh grinned from ear to ear. Their faces were still covered in snow-cream, resistant to the Medicine Woman's best efforts.

"Well, hello boys," the General greeted them cheerily, looking up for a fraction of a second before handing the papers to an attendant.

"Will that be all?" the attendant asked.

"Tell Frank we'll convene in T-3 colony-minutes."

"Yes, Ma'am."

"And have an attendant take the boys to the commissary for new clothes and boots—assuming we have their size. If not, ask one of the tailors or seamstresses to modify what's in stock. We have an order of uniforms coming from the Carolingian textile mills later in the week."

"Yes, Ma'am."

"I'll see you later," the Medicine Woman said, patting the boys' shoulders affectionately. "I have to go to a meeting."

"Like Dready?"

"Just like Dready."

"You gonna teach them how to do stuff?" Manasseh asked.

"Yep. There's always lots to teach and lots to learn. Keep your eyes open, all right? That's the best way to learn. Observe things for yourself."

She gave them a quick hug before they trotted off with another attendant.

Manasseh turned around and kissed his hand, then pantomimed throwing the kiss toward her. The Medicine Woman pretended to catch his kiss, then placed her hands over her heart.

He rewarded her with a dazzling smile, rimmed with strawberry snow-cream.

Yes, she thought. *Those are my boys.*

It was past midnight when the Medicine Woman's meetings concluded. She followed an attendant out of the repurposed museum into the cool night air where a sea of tents had been set up.

MilitiaMen milled about the campfires, talking quietly as the Medicine Woman passed by. She noticed the soldiers ranged widely in age. There were talkative boys, slightly older than Ephraim, splitting firewood alongside whitebeards with stooped shoulders who silently cleaned their muskets.

"Your quarters are positioned near the officers' tents," the attendant said, adjusting the kerosene lamp to illuminate the muddy pathway. Straw had been laid out to make walking the grounds easier.

"Latrines and bathhouses are located due east. There are armed patrols throughout the night. This particular quadrant is heavily monitored, especially after the Westover incident. Ah, here we are."

The Medicine Woman entered through the door flaps of the canvas tent. It smelled of mildew and smoke.

"Your first meeting tomorrow will be at 0700 hours. WaterBoys will bring hot water and towels by 0600. The canteen opens at 0530."

"Thank you," the Medicine Woman replied wearily, sitting on her cot.

"An attendant will take the boys to the ChildrenSchool on the grounds at 0630. Many of the officers have their families on site for safekeeping. The children will have six colony-hours of basic arithmetic, reading, writing, and history. They'll also have instruction in medical first aid and outdoorsmanship."

"Ephraim and Manasseh could probably teach those last two classes," she replied, tucking in the thin quilts to fully cover the boys, nestled side by side in one of the cots. She took a toy from one of their hands and laid it at the foot of the bedding.

"Is Dreadlocks lodging with us?"

The attendant consulted a clipboard, scanning down a long list of names. "Let me see. Tent 374-F. Yes. Four cots total."

"They are used to taking care of each other."

"I think we Northerners are learning to do that as well," the attendant remarked somberly. "Will that be all?"

"Yes, thank you."

When the tent flaps closed behind him, the Medicine Woman busied herself getting their things situated. The boys had upended their rucksacks, scattering toys and clothes and socks throughout the small space.

After sorting out Ephraim's and Manasseh's belongings, she pulled out the dozen knives she kept secreted on her person. Laying them out in an array, she cleaned them one by one, sharpening the ones in need.

Eventually, she heard the tent flaps rustle. With a large serrated knife in her hand, she looked up to see Dreadlocks entering the tent looking entirely spent.

"Holy shit," Dreadlocks complained. "I would rather fight every pox-ridden Pagan in DariusWood than sit in one more meeting."

"When are they planning to move on Sylvania?"

"In a couple of colony-weeks."

"Are you going to go with them?" the Medicine Woman asked, pointedly.

"Hell yes, I'm going—and I'm going to find Sounder, too," she said. "Assuming he's still alive."

"You think he's still alive?"

"If I find him alive, he'll be dead." She gave a bitter laugh. "There are mixed reports of his whereabouts. None of the Scouts have solid intel. It's like Sounder never existed, and it feels that way, too."

The Medicine Woman remained silent.

"So what about you?" Dreadlocks asked. "How are the support services coming along?"

"They're solid. General Roberts knows what she's doing. From start to finish. We talked about assembling cholera units after the war. I showed her MedicMen how to make salted sugar water. Rehydration is the only real remedy..."

"Hard to have a war without cholera," sighed Dreadlocks, sitting down. She shrugged off her knapsack before taking out two bottles of amber liquid. "You want to get drunk?"

"No," the Medicine Woman replied. "Not even a little bit. Did you steal someone's booze?"

"I *appropriated* a few bottles from the canteen for services rendered and all that. We should be paid for our expertise in one way or another."

The Medicine Woman ignored her and prepared for bed.

Dreadlocks opened up a bottle with one of the Medicine Woman's knives before taking a long satisfying swig. "Well, that's not entirely awful."

"I tried to show the MedicMen how to use willow bark for pain relief, but they are hopelessly tethered to using Classical Massachusetts Opium. They're making tinctures with it," the Medicine Woman said quietly.

"Tinctures?"

"A reduction. A concentration. As if opium needed to be concentrated. Now they're dissolving powdered opium into alcohol for combat use."

"Sounds great to me," Dreadlocks replied, taking another drink.

"They're going to have a laudanum epidemic when the smoke clears," the Medicine Woman mumbled. "Those who take it may survive the war, but not the addiction."

"Hey, if I got a lead ball lodged in my chest, I'll take my chances with addiction," Dreadlocks remarked.

"You say that now, but opium withdrawal might change your mind. Be that as it may, Roberts definitely plans ahead. She has a team of MedicMen working on fermenting mold juice in small glass jars."

"*Mold juice?*"

The Medicine Woman chuckled. "They called it *penicillium* before the end of electricity. It's an antibiotic like honey, but much more powerful."

"Is it addictive?"

"I don't think so," the Medicine Woman replied.

"Do they have it ready to use?"

"Not yet. They need to work on extraction and purification. They've tested a few batches on captured Pagan Scouts. All died from what they call anaphylactic shock."

"Good. The only good Pagan is a dead one."

"Is that what you talked about in the war room all night? Killing Pagans?"

"Well, that, and how to subvert and intimidate the enemy. How to exhaust and frustrate the enemy. And finally, how to maim and kill the enemy. Glorious stuff." Dreadlocks took another pull of the half-emptied bottle.

"You're working on killing people while I'm working on saving them."

"That's the way of the world, Meddy. Life and death. Light and dark. Bitter and sweet. Dualism is older than any other religion or philosophy that man has dreamed up."

"You're drunk," the Medicine Woman grumbled, rolling over on her cot, already half asleep.

"I'm not drunk, yet," Dreadlocks replied. "But I'm working on it."

"I'm not drunk yet," Dreadlocks replied. "But I'm working on it."

Chapter 24

An Overpass by the Conodoguinet Creek

In the weeks leading up to the United Front's assault on Sylvania, MilitiaMen, attendants, and other personnel fell into well-ordered routines, chiefly due to General Robert's expectations.

After another long day of instructional meetings, the Medicine Woman slept fitfully, rolling over in a vain attempt to find a comfortable spot. She woke intermittently throughout the night, cursing the uncomfortable cot.

Staring at the ceiling, she became aggravated by Dreadlocks' guttural snoring. In a fit of pique, the Medicine Woman threw a plastic cup at Dreadlocks, hitting her squarely in the forehead. Dreadlocks muttered a few choice profanities before pulling the quilt over her head and rolling over.

Satisfied, the Medicine Woman returned to her own thoughts, conjuring up Jasper, remembering his face, his blue eyes, his kind smile. She remembered every detail of the apothecary shop and bumbling Megs, but the pressing matters at hand eventually intruded on more peaceful thoughts.

Finally, sheer exhaustion drove her deep into an inky black, dreamless slumber. She awoke in the early morning, well before she needed to get the boys moving.

Assuming there was sufficient hot water, she needed to get them bathed and dressed for ChildrenSchool. This was no small feat, as the boys much preferred running through camp than sitting in a classroom.

General Roberts wanted her to address the supply line personnel about cross-contamination and food safety. The Medicine Woman hadn't prepared for the meeting and frowned at the stinking pile of laundry which had accumulated into a mound in their quarters. As attendants were short-handed, the Medicine Woman would most likely be boiling the bugs and filth out of their clothing later in the afternoon.

At least the day would be fair. Spring had come in earnest to the region, warming up the rich loam and sparking the tree branches to sprout small buds of green. The boys quickly jettisoned their layers of heavy clothing and became fixtures throughout the camp, friendly with MilitiaMen and attendants alike. Even General Roberts cracked a rare smile when they enthusiastically waved at her, using both hands and calling out her name until she responded.

The Medicine Woman lay in the dark of the tent, enjoying a few quiet moments before the day's hectic schedule. *Breathe in and hold,* her mother had instructed her. *Let your breath travel through your mind, enlivening it. Breathe in and hold to calm your blood.*

As usual, the things her mother had told her proved useful. But all too soon, the time she had alone to herself was gone.

"Ephraim. Manasseh," she called out. "It's time to wake up."

Instead of the boys' normal protesting, there was nothing. Not one sound.

"Boys," the Medicine Woman repeated, more loudly. "Don't play possum with me. We need to get ready for the day. I know you don't like sitting in ChildrenSchool. You should try sitting in conferences all day, showing MilitiaMen how to make a proper tourniquet."

The Medicine Woman stood up, gingerly making her way to the boys' cots, situated on the farthest side of the tent.

"Boys," she said crossly, reaching down to feel for their feet.

There was nothing.

Fumbling in the near darkness, the Medicine Woman felt the length of both cots before dropping to her knees.

"Ephraim? Manasseh!" She reached out in all directions, digging through clothing and books and toys.

"Meddy, what in the hell—"

"The boys are gone," the Medicine Woman shouted in disbelief.

Dreadlocks sat up, rubbing her eyes. "Calm down. They're probably in the latrines taking a piss."

As the Medicine Woman searched around the cots, she felt cool air on the back of her heels. Tracing the canvas walls to find where the draft originated, her fingers felt the opening of frayed fabric. *The canvas had been slit.*

As horror washed over her, the Medicine Woman pushed on the flap of a neatly cut square panel. *Large enough for a Scout to reach in. Large enough to pull two little boys through.*

"The boys are gone," the Medicine Woman whispered, her voice an agony.

"Stay here," Dreadlocks commanded, running to alert the morning attendants.

Dreadlocks' order proved unnecessary, as the Medicine Woman fell prone. In the darkness that threatened to undo her, she only heard her mother's voice, gently repeating the same words, over and over.

Breathe in, Medicine Girl. Breathe in and hold to calm your mind. Breathe out to soothe your blood.

"When did you see them last?"

Dreadlocks and the Medicine Woman had been ushered into General Robert's office the moment the attendants learned what happened.

"Last night," Dreadlocks reported, pacing in front of General Roberts and her Chief Attendants. "After dinner, we went back to the tent. The boys worked on their slates. Doing math. Times tables."

"Division," the Medicine Woman corrected her. "They were doing long division." The Medicine Woman sat stoically in a chair, her face blank, her one gray eye darkened in the early morning hours.

"Would the boys cut through the tent and run off?" General Roberts inquired.

"Absolutely not," the Medicine Woman snapped. Dreadlocks nodded in agreement.

"The camp is being searched from stem to stern. If they are here, we'll find them."

"And if they're not?" asked the Medicine Woman.

"We've sent out all the Scouts we can spare," the General replied. "But we're moving west in 48 colony-hours. I don't know how many resources we can spare—"

"Thank you, General Roberts," the Medicine Woman said, standing up to leave.

"We're doing everything we can," the General added, apologetically.

"And so will I."

There was a small commotion outside the door. Instinctively, the Medicine Woman reached for her knives, as Dreadlocks pulled out her cudgel from her waistband. They looked over to see General Roberts holding a revolver, cocked and aimed at the door.

"General!" an attendant entered without knocking. "There's news on the boys."

"Let him in," the General said, sliding her weapon into her shoulder holster.

The attendant entered, pale and breathless.

"One of Darius' Scouts was left for dead in the woods near the latrines. They'd come on foot. He'd fallen, broken his ankle. Another Pagan Scout must have stabbed him in the chest, but the wound wasn't fatal. He could talk...with a little encouragement," reported the attendant.

"Where is the Scout now?"

"We promised him a quick death."

"And?" General Roberts asked. "Did his information merit one?"

"It was imminent regardless. But we learned that Sounder ordered the boys to be taken to Sylvania."

"For what purpose?"

"For us," the Medicine Woman interjected. "Darius wants Dreadlocks and me to trail them back to Sylvania. The boys are bait."

The General looked skeptical. "Why would the leader of the Illuminati Pagans trouble himself with the likes of you two?"

"We have unfinished business," the Medicine Woman replied soberly. "Darius knows that I've been working with the Sylvanians and the United Front." She sat down, leaning forward on her elbows. "I should have killed Darius when I had the chance."

Restless, Dreadlocks began to pace. "And Sounder appears to be Darius' Chief Attendant. I should have killed him when *I* had the chance."

Speechless, General Roberts considered both women for a moment.

"We are going to war. I need you to help me drive the Pagans out of the North," she stood, walking towards them. "I need Dreadlocks on the ground in Sylvania. I need Medicine Woman in Field Support. I know all that matters to you right now is finding two little boys, but we have tens of thousands of lives at stake. The freedom of the North is at stake."

Both Dreadlocks and the Medicine Woman stood up, preparing to depart.

"Twelve colony-hours," the Medicine Woman said. "Give us half a day to find them. If we can't track down the boys by then, they're lost to us anyway."

The General considered her offer.

"Attendant," General Roberts said, scribbling down orders on a pad of reclaimed paper. "Take these two to get provisioned. Give them two of our fastest horses."

"Yes, Ma'am."

"Dreadlocks. Medicine Woman. I will see you in twelve colony-hours, hopefully with the boys." General Roberts said, holding out her hand, giving them each a firm handshake. "Good luck."

By mid-morning, they'd ridden in a modified grid pattern, looking for any signs of the Pagan Scouts on foot.

"Nothing," Dreadlocks spat, shaking her head.

As war was in the air, few travelers were on the Eight One. The Medicine Woman peered in all directions, praying for guidance to the silent gods her mother had told her about.

If there were a time to make yourself known, she thought, *now would be good.*

"What do you think?" Dreadlocks asked, sliding off her mount. She led her horse to a patch of new spring grass to feed.

The Medicine Woman dismounted as well, helping herself to the water container. "I don't think they're on the road," she murmured. She drank deeply, wiped her mouth.

"You think they're holed up somewhere?"

"No, they're on the move. Darius is too impatient to wait for something he wants."

"So?" Dreadlocks asked impatiently. "Where are they?"

The Medicine Woman looked down at the container in her hand.

"Water," the Medicine Woman said. "They're on the water."

The Susquehanna River had been choked to death by algae blooms before the end of electricity as farm runoff neatly asphyxiated what lay below the surface. In time, the river had cleared. New flora and fauna appeared on the margins, genetically altered by the pollutants of the previous generations. Nothing was safe to eat, but at least the water no longer burned the skin on contact.

The winding Conodoguinet Creek was a tributary to the Susquehanna, curling west out of the Harrisburg area. The waterway was the perfect place for those who did not want to be found.

Dreadlocks and the Medicine Woman rode hard, North on the Five Eight One, until they came to a wide turn in the creek. As the Pagan Scouts would have to paddle against the current in the meandering waterway, the Medicine Woman roughly calculated the distance needed to intercept the boys' kidnappers. Dreadlocks stood watch while the Medicine Woman stacked rocks and twigs at intervals by the water.

Afterwards, silently, they tied up the horses and settled in to wait at an overpass.

"You sure about this?" Dreadlocks asked.

"I'm not sure about *any* of this," the Medicine Woman admitted, her face grim. She silently inventoried her knives, repositioning them, one by one, as she set them back into their sheathes.

"We don't have a second shot, Meddy. I hope whatever you are figuring out in that silent skull of yours—"

The Medicine Woman's hand shot out to grab Dreadlocks by the throat.

"You're telling me there's no room for error here? You don't think I know that?" Her voice cracked as she released her grip.

Dreadlocks coughed and pushed her away. "You murderous bitch, why'd you—"

The Medicine Woman moved closer to her, their faces inches apart. "Ephraim and Manasseh are probably dead already. The Pagan Scouts should have headed North or South. Anywhere but the West. They've already screwed up by leaving one of their own behind. Darius will kill them for that."

"Look, I—"

"Dreadlocks, if you have a better plan, then let me know. But if I were these Scouts, I'd steer clear of all roads leading towards the biggest military build up since Richmond's fall."

"I want you to be sure," Dreadlocks said, chastened a bit, rubbing her neck.

"And I want you to tell me what anyone can be sure of," the Medicine Woman muttered. She threw one of her daggers with such force that it sunk into a rotten Black Gum tree up to its hilt.

Ephraim saw the markings on the trees first. He tapped his brother with his foot, the only part of him that could move freely on the flatboat. When Manasseh turned his battered face towards him, Ephraim tilted his head. Manasseh looked in the direction his brother indicated, seeing three rocks piled on top of one another in decreasing size at the base of a tree.

Meddy.

The Pagan Scouts were oblivious, focused on getting the two packages to Darius in a timely manner. Already, they had been delayed when their companion—one of the newer Scouts—had tripped on a gopher hole and broken his ankle. Debating whether to cut his neck or stop his heart, the leader had opted for the latter. There was little time for second-guessing, but the fallen Scout left a pall over the successful extraction. Few Scouts could have pulled off a double abduction in the heart of the United Front.

The creek was tranquil, lulling the three Scouts into standing down. The boys, which had been hellions from the start, had ceased thrashing and biting. They'd been bound like sarcophagi and gagged like dogs.

"You're behaving now—aren't you?" one of the men said. "Don't worry. There'll be a place for you in New DariusWood. You'll like it there. It's the Home of the Three Rivers."

The two brothers didn't move, keeping their eyes focused on the shoreline for any more signs from Meddy. As time passed, Ephraim despaired that he'd miss some other sign along the river. But implanted on the creek's bank, he noted a small forked branch holding up a longer stick with four leaves.

He turned to Manasseh and blinked four times. Manasseh returned the blinks, an acknowledgment of his understanding.

On the next turn of the creek, both boys spied another forked branch holding a stick with three leaves. They blinked at each other in tandem, growing very still, silently loosening their bindings.

Another turn, another branch, a stick with two leaves.

Then one.

As the three Pagan Scouts continued to paddle the flatboat at a moderate pace, Ephraim nodded at his brother.

It was time.

The two trussed up little boys simply rolled off the end of the flatboat. It took a minute for their splashes to resonate with the Scouts.

"Wait—no!" one of the men yelled. He pointed at the boys, immobilized, sinking down into the muddy creekwater.

A woman with blonde dreadlocks dove from the water's edge, neatly reaching the boys in a few strokes. Tucking them under her arms, she held their heads above water while scissor-kicking her way back to shore.

In moments, a Scout pulled out a round ball pistol from his pack. Steadily, he took aim and fired, just as Dreadlocks eyed him, dunking herself and the boys underwater. The first shot went wide. He loaded powder and ball again, taking aim at the figures, ignoring the overpass ahead.

The Medicine Woman threw the first of several boulders from off the bridge in rapid succession. The first rock took out the man with the round ball pistol, his head exploding like an overripe melon. As his two companions screamed, covered in gore, the Medicine Woman lobbed large pieces of asphalt to puncture holes in everything below.

As the listing flatboat passed underneath, the Medicine Woman leapt over the other side of the overpass, down onto the vessel, her unsheathed Bowie knives in her hands.

One of the Scouts lay supine, a chunk of rock lodged in his chest. But as he was a Pagan Scout and not to be trusted, she slit his throat for good measure.

"Stop, stop!" the last man called out, holding up one of his hands. His other arm had been immobilized, the shoulder crushed by one of her more accurate throws.

"What is it you would like me to stop?" the Medicine Woman replied evenly. The flatboat tilted to one side, lazily turning around in the wide creek to float back towards the Susquehanna.

"What do you want?" the man cried. "I know things. I can help you."

"You can't even help yourself," she said softly, as he fell to his knees, slipping on his own blood, his vision blackening.

The man looked at her, wincing at the Medicine Woman's stoic countenance—one without a shred of mercy. Feeling a sick coldness envelop him, he tried again. "Anything. I'll give you anything. Troop movements. Battle plans. What do you want?"

"The name of your mother," the Medicine Woman replied.

They looked over to see General Roberts holding a revolver, cocked and aimed at the door.

Chapter 25

Darius Wood

The Medicine Woman rode back to Harrisburg with Manasseh's arms encircling her waist. She lashed him to her back with a length of rope as he appeared unsteady from the night's terrors.

"We're almost to camp," she called over her shoulder. She patted his cold hands that clutched her tight. "You'll be back in your own bed. Back to your toys."

"It's not safe there," he mumbled. "It's not safe anywhere…"

The Medicine Woman thought how to comfort him, but no gentle words came to her mind. Instead, she held his hands in one of hers to assure him that she was there. That was all she could promise him.

Out of the corner of her eye, she saw Ephraim riding tandem with Dreadlocks, holding the reins alongside her as Dreadlocks instructed him what to do. Far from being traumatized, Ephraim let out a war cry, triumphantly whooping on their breakneck ride back to camp.

The moment the women had freed the boys, Ephraim was giddy, pleased with himself for divining the wilderness signals that the Medicine Woman had left for them.

"You remembered," the Medicine Woman had said, smiling.

"Of course I did," Ephraim replied. "I remember everything you've taught us!"

The Medicine Woman's heart swelled with pride, delighted with Ephraim's performance under very difficult circumstances. At the same time, her heart ached for Manasseh who appeared withdrawn.

Perhaps it was his age?

The Medicine Woman could only imagine what her mother would say to her. *Don't judge the boy too harshly. You were once little, too, and I have seen the Medicine Girl weep over dead butterflies.*

General Roberts greeted them in the mess hall with freshly made griddle cakes drizzled with hot strawberry syrup.

While Dreadlocks washed the muck from the boys' faces and hands, the Medicine Woman watched the attendants whisk the horses away to the paddock.

The camp was bustling, crackling with organized chaos. SteamTanks clanked into formation, lining up in precise rows. Newly minted guns were checked and rechecked, cleaned and loaded into wooden packing crates for SteamTransports. PedalCars were outfitted with racks of provisions for onsite Field Support Centers.

"Welcome back," General Roberts said, shoving a forkful of fluffy griddle cakes into her mouth. She chewed with pleasure.

"Good to be back." Dreadlocks grinned and shook the General's hand.

"Any information from the Scouts?"

"They died poorly," the Medicine Woman remarked. "I remember a time when Scouts died with dignity, not begging for their lives."

"Loyalty is hard to come by these days. Darius is finding that out with his subpar Scouts. He may have greater numbers than we do, but his men serve him because they are compelled to."

Dreadlocks agreed. "It's far easier to lead people who are fighting for their homes and their families."

"You'd think colonizers would learn that," the General mused. She continued to eat steadily. "Our timetable has changed. We're moving out tomorrow."

"Is the United Front ready to move out?" the Medicine Woman asked, feeling the general anxiety in the mess hall.

General Roberts paused for a second longer than normal. "We're as ready as we're going to get, and we need to move now. The Pagan build up on the South Side of Sylvania has been surprisingly robust. We've cut their Tennessee supply lines, but more lines spring up like heads on the Hydra."

"What about the other NorthMen? The plan was to stage here. Are they diverting to the West?" asked Dreadlocks. "Are we not going in together?"

"Allegedly, several brigades from the North are expected to join us onsite. Final staging will take place outside of Sylvania."

"*Allegedly?*" Dreadlocks repeated, in both shock and disgust. "NorthMen are *allegedly* joining us?"

"Several warlords have decided to wait. They want to see the unified United Front before committing to the coalition."

"But they *are* coming?" Dreadlocks asked.

"They are hedging their bets." The General looked soberly at Dreadlocks and the Medicine Woman. "We've made contingency plans. In my experience, NorthMen unite when it suits them. Generally, they are inclined to be left alone and fend for themselves."

"But the United Front has assembled a substantial army!" Dreadlocks protested, pointing to the staging grounds where throngs of MilitiaMen drilled. "Surely this is enough to take out the Pagan occupation in Sylvania? Trust me, General. Sylvanians will rise up in the streets. They are waiting for the opportunity to kill the first Pagan they can!"

The General pursed her lips before replying.

"Dreadlocks, our Scouts have reported that Sounder is leading an effective campaign. He has managed to convince a number of influential Sylvanians that the Pagans are liberators."

"That can't be," Dreadlocks replied.

"Sounder's message to Sylvanians is that Darius ended their opium crisis and prevented the pox. Market shelves are full, crime is nonexistent, and clean water is abundant and free. As a political stunt, Darius sent in teams of Tennessee MedicMen to treat the citizenry, free of charge."

"Is that all true?"

"It's more true than not," replied the General. "But it's not sustainable. The Sylvanians will eventually be crippled by Pagan tribute. Nothing's sure in life but death and taxes."

"Don't the NorthMen want to drive the Pagans out?"

"Most do," the General speculated. "A few warlords are waiting for the bulk of the United Front to arrive. They've made their own alliances though. It's hard to know where anyone's loyalty lies these days." General Roberts seemed to speak more to herself than to her guests.

"You're worried that Darius has offered the NorthMen something better than the United Front can," the Medicine Woman said.

"What could that be? What's better than freedom?" Dreadlocks asked.

"Peace," the Medicine Woman said.

The General nodded, her eyes hollow.

Dreadlocks muttered to herself while her eyes filled with tears.

"It's understandable. No one wants endless war," the General said, helping herself to three more griddle cakes. "Think about it from a NorthMen's perspective. If we oust the Pagans from Sylvania, there will most likely be a civil war in the region. Or maybe the Pagans return with an even larger force? You can't blame them for thinking it would be easier to send diplomats to Tennessee to redraw the maps."

"Is that what you want?" the Medicine Woman asked.

"I don't want anything. My job is to serve the NorthMen's coalition. For as long as it lasts..." General Roberts gave them both a weary smile, one that turned steely when she turned to face her attendants. Two chief attendants leaned in to speak to her in low voices. She dabbed her mouth with a napkin and placed her empty plate on one of the mess hall's tables.

"If you'll excuse me, I need to see to a few things," General Roberts said, her voice firm. "I trust you both will be ready to move out at first light tomorrow. Thank you for your service to the North."

Dreadlocks nodded. The Medicine Woman remained still.

"Goodbye, General Roberts!" Ephraim called out from a table away.

"Goodbye General Ephraim and General Manasseh!" General Roberts replied, favoring them with a genuine smile. "Keep an eye out for Pagans!"

"Ma'am, yes, ma'am!" Ephraim stood up tall and saluted.

Manasseh took the opportunity to spear Ephraim's remaining griddle cake with his fork and ate it.

Spring had arrived in the MidAtlantic in its full array, warm zephyrs making the two-week trek from Harrisburg to Sylvania more agreeable than expected.

The vanguard of the United Front's Brigade arrived as expected, quickly cordoning off the Pittsburgh Botanical Gardens for a staging ground. Tents were erected, water was boiled, game was hunted as the MilitiaMen fell into preparations for war.

Dreadlocks followed General Roberts around like a whipped puppy, devouring the latest intelligence from the Scouts. She explained the best way to attack the Pagan headquarters, set up at the former University of Pitt.

Throughout the days, small squads and platoons arrived from northern districts, adding to the United Front's numbers, though in smaller increments than expected. Dispatches came and went from Command, but General Robert's staff was even more tight-lipped than usual.

Surely more men are on their way, Dreadlocks thought to herself. She considered bringing up her concerns to the General, but General Roberts was in no mood for Cassandras. Pagan skirmishes on the Sylvanian border began far earlier than anyone had anticipated, and too many of her Scouts were being sent back to them, piece by piece.

The MedicMen and the Medicine Woman set up Field Support operations at the former Nevillewood Country Club, four colony-miles southeast of the United Front's headquarters at the Botanical Gardens.

"We can send the boys with the other children to the countryside until the worst is over," an attendant suggested.

"The boys stay with me," the Medicine Woman said flatly. "At all times."

Manasseh stopped rolling bandages, but resumed when the Medicine Woman looked sternly at him. Ephraim prepared tool kits for the MedicMen, including sterilized extractors, scalpels, and forceps. He carefully measured out vinegar for cleaning wounds and opium for pain relief into small jars with cork stoppers.

"Please tell the MedicMen we'll meet together after dinner," the Medicine Woman asked an attendant. "We need to go over how to properly administer diethyl ether again."

Late into the evening, the Medicine Woman walked the two boys to their makeshift quarters, a refurbished office from the Country Club's better days.

Foodstuffs and medical supplies lined the walls, stacked in rows alongside their cots. The boys started a guessing game as to what was in each bin or crate.

"Apples?"

"Nope. This one has honey. Is honey a food or medicine?" Manasseh asked.

"Both," the Medicine Woman replied.

The evening had chilled a bit, and she had wrapped rough-spun blankets around each boy, tucking them in for a short night's sleep.

"Ephraim. Manasseh." She addressed them seriously, and they gave her their full attention. "Thank you for helping the United Front get the Field Hospital ready."

"You're welcome," Ephraim said. "One of the MedicMen said I would be a good doctor."

"You would," the Medicine Woman agreed. "But I need to warn you about what is to come. When the United Front crosses over the Pitt Bridge to Sylvania, a lot of people will get hurt."

"MilitiaMen?"

"Yes, but civilians, too. Women and children. There will be many people who will need our help. So I want you to prepare yourselves. You will need to be strong in your body and your mind. I know you've seen terrible things—unspeakable things—but I need you to understand that war itself is a terrible thing."

"So why are we here?" Manasseh wondered.

"I am here to do what my mother has taught me to do. *Alleviate suffering.* And you are here to help me."

"The other children were sent away."

"I know," the Medicine Woman nodded. "But you are here so I can keep you safe. You are safe with me."

"I can keep us safe," said Ephraim. "I can get a gun from one of these crates."

"Leave the guns to the MilitiaMen," the Medicine Woman said. "If things get too frightening here, let me know and we will leave."

"Where we gonna go?" Ephraim asked.

"South. We will go to the South," she replied.

"Okay," Manasseh agreed.

"And when our patients start to come in, remain in my eyesight at all times."

The first casualties arrived at the Field Hospital in a fleet of PedalCars, painted white with red crosses on the side.

As attendants unstrapped wounded MilitiaMen from gurneys, the Medicine Woman directed triage. With fistfuls of cotton batting, she packed wounds to stop patients hemorrhaging from gunshot and stab wounds.

"Level 1 - Urgent. Take this one into surgery now."

Attendants hustled the patient into a surgical tent where MedicMen attempted to stop his bleeding, using tourniquets neatly stacked by each bedside.

Ephraim and Manasseh threaded their way in between tables, replacing supplies as needed, bringing clean water, taking out bloody refuse bins full of unspeakable gore.

"Level 3 - this one can wait." She motioned for the MilitiaMan to move the patient off to the side. The man left holding a bloody rag to his mouth.

"Level 0." The Medicine Woman muttered, nodding to the attendants to take the deceased to the burnpile. "That one should have never taken up space on the transport!" she said angrily.

By midafternoon, a river of blood covered the floor of the Country Club.

Days passed in a blur, with the Medicine Woman in constant motion, occasionally falling asleep on her feet.

"You've been up for eighteen hours straight, Meddy. Find a cot and get some rest," one of the attendants advised.

"In a bit," she said, pushing back a greasy strand of her hair. She worked to remove an arrowhead lodged precariously near a MilitiaMan's brachial artery.

"Go to bed! If not for you, then for the boys. They won't rest until you do."

She glanced over to see the brothers leaning against one another, struggling to stand up straight.

"Fine," the Medicine Woman said, as another fleet of PedalCars arrived. "How's it going in Sylvania?" she murmured to an attendant.

"There hasn't been a dispatch today," the attendant replied, shaking his head. "And we can't keep up with the burnpile."

"Can we sleep next to you?" Ephraim asked.

The Medicine Woman had just lain down, luxuriating in the feeling of being clean and off her feet. After bathing the boys, she had soaked in a wash basin full of warm water and lye soap, scrubbing off all manner of bloody viscera with one of the few clean towels.

Attendants were too busy to boil water for laundry. Other than dried fruit and hardtack and a bit of cheese, meals were infrequent, as the wounded arrived at an inexhaustible clip.

"Can we sleep next to you, *please?*" Ephraim asked again. His eyes were ringed with dark circles. Manasseh stared at her, too, his eyes red-rimmed and bloodshot.

"Of course," the Medicine Woman said, moving over to allow them to nestle alongside her.

"I saw a MilitiaMan cry today," Manasseh said. "He was so sad."

"Are you sad, too?" asked the Medicine Woman.

"No," said Manasseh. "I'm elevating suffering."

"*Alleviating* suffering," the Medicine Woman corrected him. "That means you are making things better."

"The man died," Manasseh added. "Which I guess is better. He was hurt really bad."

"I'm glad you tried your best to help him."

Ephraim reached for the Medicine Woman's hand.

"I heard some of the PedalCar drivers talk. They say that General Roberts couldn't even get across the bridge. The fighting is outside the city," he said.

The Medicine Woman remained silent.

"How can they beat the Pagans if they can't get to them?"

"I don't know," the Medicine Woman said. "We'll have to wait and see."

"Where's Dreadlocks?" Manasseh asked.

"Dreadlocks is fighting with her people. I wouldn't worry about her. She can handle herself. She always finds a way," the Medicine Woman chuckled to herself. *God help whoever tries to hurt Lillibet.*

"Do we have a plan?" Ephraim asked.

"We do. For now, stay by me. I'll make sure we're always safe, all right? Now let's get some rest."

She kissed the tops of their heads, tucked both under her arms. In moments, both boys were breathing deep and rhythmically.

The Medicine Woman lay still, her mind working through possible scenarios, untangling a puzzle that refused to be solved. *How could she keep these two safe?*

She listened to the sounds of the Field Hospital long into the night.

At first light, she jolted awake, both boys at her side. It was clear that exhaustion still ravaged her body and mind or she would have noticed what was amiss.

The complete silence should have been her first warning.

There was no clamor of the PedalCar arrivals, no calling out for triage attendants, no screaming of dying men.

Only silence.

But the silence only lasted until the door burst open. Pagan MilitiaMen filed in, with guns drawn.

"Meddy," came a small voice. "Meddy, are these good guys or bad guys?"

She looked down to see tears streaming down Manasseh's face. Ephraim sported a murderous scowl, itching to rip a weapon out of one of the men's hands and use it on the lot of them.

"Stay with me," she kissed the tops of their heads. "Stay close by me."

While the boys were caged in the back of a transport, the MilitiaMen took the Medicine Woman's knives and tied her hands in front of her. She stood helplessly behind the cart, frantically looking around the wreckage of the Field Hospital.

The tents were down. The PedalCars were gone. Pagan MilitiaMen were breaking open supply crates and looting storage bins. The bodies in the burnpile seemed to have quadrupled overnight.

"Where are the MedicMen?" she demanded, addressing the leader.

"Well, the helpful ones are on their way to Sylvania to assist in the Pagan cause," he replied. "The Pagans expect you to be useful, too."

"You expect me to walk all the way to Sylvania?"

"*Sylvania?*" The leader laughed. "Oh Darlin'—Darius doesn't want you in Sylvania. You're a troublemaker. Darius likes to deal with troublemakers himself."

"You don't mean—"

"Yes, I do. Get yourself ready for a very long walk. We're heading home to Tennessee."

"Why? What does Darius want with me?" the Medicine Woman asked.

"I don't know what Darius wants to do with you specifically, but you can ask him yourself in a month or so. My job was to come get you and bring you back. But we can talk about whatever else is on your mind. Tennessee is a long way from here. We'll have lots of time to chat. Hee-ya!" he cried, whipping the lumbering ox which moved at a glacial pace.

The boys pressed their faces against the wooden slats, eyes peering out of the cart towards the Medicine Woman. She took one hesitant step after another, offering the boys a faint smile.

"It's okay—it's okay," she whispered, treading barefoot in the soft spring mud.

Ephraim nodded back as if he believed her.

Manasseh reached out his spindly arms in an effort to reach her, to assure himself that she was still there.

Manasseh reached out his spindly arms in an effort to reach her, to assure himself that she was there.

Chapter 26

Scout County, Old Virginia

"Tell me where the boys are," the Medicine Woman demanded.

The Pagan attendant sighed, putting down her jug of boiled water. She turned to the tall, thin detainee with silvery gray hair, shorn to the scalp. The woman hadn't affixed her eye patch yet, and the sight of the pink mucosal tissue in her empty eye socket gave the attendant pause.

"The boys," the Medicine Woman repeated. "Where are they?"

"You've been asking the same question for years," the attendant replied. She set out her breakfast tray. "Who knows? Surely they are young men now, living their own lives."

"Assuming they still live. Do they live? I was told if I stayed—if I cooperated—the boys would live."

"What makes you think anyone tells me anything," the attendant grumbled, setting out wedges of flatbread and apple butter alongside a slab of mutton. She poured the woman an extra large mug of goat milk since she seemed especially agitated. She was particularly fond of the stuff.

The Medicine Woman took the earthen mug from the table, walked over to the barred window, and sipped the milk moodily. She watched another pink dawn crawl over the blue mountains that encircled DariusWood.

Late spring was heartbreakingly beautiful in Tennessee, even though the black walnut trees had succumbed to the Thousand Cankers fungus. With the warmth of the season, though, came memories of the Medicine Woman's separation from her boys.

Ephraim. Manasseh.

They'd been parted immediately after their arrival in DariusWood. With her feet callused and bloody, her scabby wrists bruised and abraded, the Medicine Woman had stood helpless behind the OxCart as Pagan

MilitiaMen carried the boys away. The look of anguish on Manasseh's face seared itself into her memory.

"I'm going to kill you! I'm going to kill *all* of you!" Ephraim had yelled, lashing out at the hands who held him firm. He was silenced by a few rough slaps across his face.

Manasseh hid his face in his dirty hands.

The attendant continued to mutter to herself while changing the Medicine Woman's bed linens. "I don't know anything about anything," she grumbled. "I'm only here to help you do your job."

To hell with my job, the Medicine Woman thought bitterly. *I alleviate suffering for Pagans so they can take over the North and the South.* For the hundredth time, she wondered if she should throw herself into a timber rattlesnake nest and be done with it.

"How many patients are waiting for me this morning?" the Medicine Woman asked between bites of mutton.

"Twelve. All men. No one appears to be in distress."

"From the recent arrival of temporary wives from the Carolinas, I'm guessing most of them have syphilis."

The attendant couldn't help but snicker under her breath.

The former amusement park's Palace Theater had been converted into an elite health care facility for the Pagan leadership. Monitored at all times, the Medicine Woman was kept inside and on call at all hours. From her comfortable cage, she helped scores of Pagans fully recover or painlessly pass away.

As weeks and months passed into years, the Medicine Woman learned how to traffic in hearsay, gossiping with her patients, hoping for useful news, always looking for the means and ability to escape. She mainly caught snippets of conflicting reports, as if the Pagan leadership had no more idea what they were doing than she did.

"What are your symptoms?" she asked an older man who strode into the cordoned off area on the main stage. The Medicine Woman looked out into the audience to see how many more patients were waiting.

Before the end of electricity, she had heard that people had faced the stage, singing and clapping along with musical performers. Now a somber waiting room, the rows of theater seats were sectioned off. The most dire cases were settled into the front rows, now vacant for the time being.

"I'm achy. All over," her patient replied. "I feel sick to my stomach, and I can't take a shit."

The Medicine Woman felt his forehead. "You have a high fever."

The man took in the small examination space, sitting on a low bed. Jars of colored ointments and vials of tinctures littered a back table, next to rolls of cotton bandages. Anything sharp was kept under guard since the Medicine Woman had dispatched a few orderlies in the past in a misguided attempt to escape.

"What other symptoms have you experienced?" The Medicine Woman asked, stifling a yawn. She'd been on her feet for hours.

"I got sores," the man admitted, looking sheepishly. "Lots of them."

"Where?"

"All over," he mumbled.

"Have you recently served in the North?" she asked.

"Is that relevant to my condition?"

"I need to know where you were stationed to know which strain of venereal disease we're dealing with," she said evenly. Her look of disdain was barely concealed.

"I fought against the NorthMen for two years," he said. "I led the final raid on Pitt."

"I see," she replied, flipping through some reclaimed papers, making notations. She walked to an apothecary cabinet and pulled out a beaker and a flask.

"Did you serve in the Sylvania region?"

"I did."

"Did the temporary wives encourage you to smoke opium?"

"I—what? Opium? I don't smoke opium!"

"You have nausea. Constipation. You have dried mucous membranes. You've been licking your lips since you've come in. Dry mouth, right? All signs of opium addiction."

The man looked at his boots. "Well, I've tried it a couple times."

"In Sylvania?"

"Yes, but—"

"Is the Sylvanian Civil War over?"

"No," he replied. "No, it is not, and neither is the fight for the South."

"How far South?" The Medicine Woman forced herself to sound indifferent.

"All the way South," he replied. "Florida."

"What's Darius want with that sandtrap?" she said.

"It is a hellhole down there, no doubt."

The Medicine Woman continued to examine her patient, then casually asked, "So what trouble is the former penal colony in now?"

"They're resisting Darius' offer to join the Pagan Empire. *Ridiculous!* Floridians couldn't be more backward. They live off coconuts and lizards. You think they'd want to evolve and join us in the 22nd century."

"Floridians are a fierce lot. Stubborn to a man."

"Darius will change their minds."

"Has he sent troops down to encourage their compliance?"

"Not yet, but Darius doesn't need to send many MilitiaMen. Those savages use nothing but knives and sticks to defend themselves." The older man laughed. "Besides, the only settlement worth taking is Lincolnshire."

"So I hear," the Medicine Woman replied, suddenly busying herself by scraping out a beaker of fermented penicillin.

"What are you going to do with that stuff?" the man asked suspiciously.

"I'm going to strain out the chunks and use the penicillin liquid to cure your sexually transmitted diseases. Then I'll give you a few vials so you can apply it to the affected areas over the next week. In the future, please use sheep or goat intestines for protection. Come back in a week."

As the man dressed, she kept her face averted while her heart sank.

Lincolnshire.

More than ever before, she was determined to leave DariusWood and return home, by any means necessary.

Wearily, the Medicine Woman walked back to her lodgings with two armed MilitiaMen flanking her sides. In order to avoid her becoming too friendly with the guards, the Pagans rotated the men who escorted her.

A year prior, she'd convinced two MilitiaMen to let her freely walk the grounds after an exceptionally long shift. She'd been caught almost immediately, and the MilitiaMen's heads were displayed in their barracks as a warning to others about fraternization.

The Medicine Woman was pleased her room was empty, no overly helpful attendant bringing her late night fare or watching her fall asleep. The bars on the windows depressed her, the sight of them causing her throat to constrict.

Her mother had almost died in a cage.

With Ephraim, Manasseh, Jasper, and Lincolnshire heavy on her mind, the Medicine Woman lay on the straw tick mattress, covered by a thin quilt. Once her head lay on the duck down pillow, she felt a wave of fatigue wash over her.

Everything hurt.

Physically, mentally, and spiritually spent, the Medicine Woman felt more bereft than ever. The darkness of her room was a shroud.

I won't alleviate any more Pagan suffering—not tomorrow. Not ever, she vowed. *Let them kill me. I wish they would.*

"You look old," came a voice in the night.

The Medicine Woman sat up in her bed, reaching for knives that had been taken long ago.

"W-who's there?" she demanded.

A beam of light clicked off, leaving them both alone in the dark.

"Will you shut up," the voice replied. "Goddamn, you are still so *annoying.*"

"Dreadlocks?"

"Grandma?" Dreadlocks replied, ruffling the Medicine Woman's short silver hair.

"Where are the boys? Where are Ephraim and Manasseh?" the Medicine Woman asked, grasping for Dreadlocks' hands, pleading for answers.

Dreadlocks face fell. "I was going to ask you the same questions."

The Medicine Woman responded by throwing her arms around Dreadlocks, then weeping into her shoulder.

"Hey, hey, c'mon now," Dreadlocks whispered, patting the Medicine Woman's back. "We'll find them. I promise you. We *will* find them." She stood with the Medicine Woman and walked to the window.

"We will," the Medicine Woman murmured. She dried her eyes and blew her nose. "It's good to see you, Dready. How'd you get in?"

"Better not to ask," Dreadlocks replied, trying the strength of the window's bars. "Damn. These things are not going to budge, are they?"

"What was that light you shined on me?"

"Oh, this?' Dreadlocks flicked a switch on a small cylinder. A faint light appeared. "It's called a flashlight. The Mainenites figured out how to make batteries. It's pretty cool." Dreadlocks handed the flashlight to the Medicine Woman who clicked it on and off a few times, a grin curling the corners of her mouth. *Useful.*

"I'm going to keep this," the Medicine Woman said, tucking it into her underclothes.

Discordant sounds came from the courtyard. Men's voices. Angry. A few guard dogs barked.

"We're going to have to leave," Dreadlocks said.

"Did you kill anybody getting in here?"

"I tried not to." Dreadlocks looked apologetic. "Grab whatever you need. I'm taking you back to Lincolnshire—just like I promised."

"You're a few years overdue. Can we kill Darius on the way out?"

"I'd love to, but he's not in DariusWood, Meddy. He's in Sylvania."

"So Sylvania is—"

"Lost. For now." Dreadlocks had a malevolent glint in her eye.

The commotion in the courtyard grew louder.

"*What* did you do?" asked the Medicine Woman.

"I'll tell you later. If we don't get out of here now, we'll be lost, too."

Heading south, Dreadlocks and the Medicine Woman walked parallel to the Two Seven all the way to Lincolnshire. On the way, Pagan MilitiaMen came by in waves, driving SteamTanks and PedalCars, armed for occupation.

The two women were adept at raiding supply lines, through flattery or subterfuge. Dreadlocks chewed on the Pagan's rations. "Oh my god, this fig and peanut bar is ridiculously good. Say what you will about the Pagans, but they feed their soldiers quite well."

"Tell me about Sounder."

Dreadlocks shook her head. "There's not much to tell. No one has seen him since the Westin bombing."

"What about the rumors of him fighting with the Sylvanian resistance? That's all my patients have talked about for years."

"Rumors, lies, gossip," Dreadlocks said. "Sounder is a specter that Darius encourages."

"For what purpose?"

"To serve as a boogeyman. The Pagans need a reason to kill Sylvanians. It's hard to shoot women and children without a noble cause. The *evil* Sounder who lurks in the shadows and threatens the new Sylvanian way of life makes a compelling narrative."

"Oh my god," the Medicine Woman whispered under her breath.

"Having Sounder alive works in manipulating Sylvanians, too. Pagan Scouts are master propagandists. They've distributed leaflets containing directives allegedly written by Sounder. I can't tell you how many times our resistance fighters have walked into Pagan shooting galleries because of 'Sounder's orders.' It's really quite brilliant to have one man responsible for all of Sylvania's ills."

"So where *is* Sounder?"

"If I were guessing," Dreadlocks said, "I'd say he's underneath a few colony-tons of rubble. I don't think he made it out of the Westin alive."

The last day.

As the Medicine Woman awoke, her blistered feet and aching legs were rejuvenated with a newfound energy. *One more day and she would be home!* The warm, humid air was welcoming, a familiar friend.

"Get up!" she jostled Dreadlocks, who was unwilling to leave the mossy embankment.

"I'm still sleeping."

"I'm almost home. I will remind you that you drugged and kidnapped me, so get the hell up."

"All for a good cause," Dreadlocks mumbled, rolling over.

"Let's go!" She kicked Dreadlocks into moving, albeit slowly.

Dreadlocks groaned.

"We are going to sprint the rest of the way," the Medicine Woman said gleefully, pulling Dreadlocks to her feet.

"Ugh," Dreadlocks replied. "I hate you so much."

In the late afternoon, the women approached Lincolnshire in a circuitous route, keeping an eye out for both Lincolnshire and Pagan Scouts. Scouts were notorious for killing first, asking questions later, no matter whose side they were on.

Lincolnshire had grown exponentially in the years the Medicine Woman had been North. From the outskirts, she could see the expansion of settlements.

"Faster!" she cried, leaving Dreadlocks far behind. Trotting like one of her horses, the Medicine Woman passed by a string of new construction—a water purification facility, a MetalSmith shop, horse paddocks, and an open air market.

Dreadlocks labored to keep pace with her as the Medicine Woman ran faster, getting winded the closer she approached. At the end of the lane would be her apothecary. Her and Jasper's home was situated directly behind the shop.

Time seemed to shift, colors and hues amplified, as the Medicine Woman approached the familiar streets, trees, stones. She felt as if her heart would burst from pure joy.

"Jasper!" the Medicine Woman called out as she threw open the front door. She entered the unattended apothecary, stocked with herbs and tree bark and flower petals. *Megs had been diligent while she was away*, the Medicine Woman smiled, pleased with the thought.

"Jasper!" she called out again, peeking expectantly in each room, exiting through the courtyard. She walked across the yard, opened the front door to her home. Things had been somewhat rearranged, different in a way she couldn't place.

It was empty, too.

Dreadlocks found the Medicine Woman standing in the doorway.

"No one's here," the Medicine Woman said in disbelief.

"I—I think they're in the garden," Dreadlocks said. "Meddy, you might want to—"

The Medicine Woman scrambled to the top of the hill, finding the path that curved towards the garden.

There the Medicine Woman saw Jasper and Megs, his hand lightly on the small of her back. Jasper held a little boy on his hip, singing a snippet of a song that made the boy laugh. Megs held a younger child's hands, one who appeared to have recently learned to walk. When Megs turned in profile, it was clear that another child was on the way.

Dreadlocks pulled the Medicine Woman behind a large tree.

"Look at me," Dreadlocks whispered, staring into the Medicine

Woman's one good eye. "I know what you want to do, but there's nothing here for you anymore."

"But Jasper—"

"Let him be, Meddy."

The Medicine Woman took one last look at the little family, blissful in the early afternoon sun.

Without another word, she turned to follow Dreadlocks.

As they prepared to leave through the apothecary's back door, the Medicine Woman noticed a large wooden marker by the far side of the building. She walked towards it, engraved with a few words and pictures of baby goats.

Here lies our Beloved Goatman.

The Medicine Woman fell to her knees, kissed the placard, weeping, until Dreadlocks spirited her away.

They spoke little until they reached The Kingdom of Georgia. According to the sign, the Honey Tavern outside of Thomasville served the strongest mead in the deep South.

"We'd like two of your biggest tankards," Dreadlocks said, ordering from the barkeep. He nodded and disappeared into the back.

"I don't drink," the Medicine Woman replied sharply, perched on a stool.

"You need to get drunk, Meddy. You also need to eat a slab of kidney pie and half a honey cake. See the menu? It's their specialty."

"We have no money. We're ordering neither pie nor cake."

"Maybe you don't have any money, but I do." Dreadlocks pulled out a fine leather wallet, stuffed with Pagan currency.

The barkeep returned with two overflowing tankards of mead. Dreadlocks paid, leaving an exorbitant tip.

"When did you pickpocket that?"

"I'm not sure. Last checkpoint?" Dreadlocks pulled out four more wallets and sorted through them all. "We've got plenty here to keep us both drunk for a month. Ooo. Look at this! A tiny family portrait. A fare rendering, too. This looks exactly like the man I stole it from. And he's got quite a brood—seven kids!"

The Medicine Woman pursed her lips and raised one eyebrow.

"Oh, right." Dreadlocks grimaced. "Too soon?"

Without replying, the Medicine Woman took her tankard and finished it off in one draught.

With Dreadlocks' ill-gotten gain, they boarded a room for the night. After ordering several more tankards, walking anywhere else seemed improbable.

"The bed seems good. I don't think there's any bugs, but we'll see in the morning if we're covered in bites!" Dreadlocks said, checking the mattress again before hopping in. "It'll be nice not sleeping rough for a night or two. A hot bath in the morning will set us both right." She hiccuped loudly.

The Medicine Woman laid down next to her on the bed, exhaling as if it were her last. "What now," she said.

"Is that a question?"

"Not really," the Medicine Woman replied. "I was wondering what will happen tomorrow, after the bath, after I throw up all this mead. And the pie—"

"I don't know, Meddy. I'm heading back to Sylvania. Now that I've fulfilled my duty to you, I can join the resistance. Death to Pagans!" Dreadlocks held up her fist.

"I thought you said the Sylvanian resistance movement was a lost cause?"

"It is," Dreadlocks said. "Is there anything more noble that isn't a lost cause?"

"I suppose everyone needs a purpose, and yours appears to be an ignominious death at the hands of Pagan torturers. I wish you well."

"Thank you," Dreadlocks replied, offering her a slight bow. "So, how about you? What will you do now that Lincolnshire isn't in need of another apothecary?"

The Medicine Woman propped herself on one elbow. "Well, Dready, there are three things I want to do before I die."

"Is getting drunk one of them?"

"No, but I enjoyed that more than I thought I would."

"I'm pleased," Dreadlocks smiled. "So tell me the three things left in this world for you."

"First, I'm going to find our boys."

"Good. Let's find the boys."

"Second, I'm going to hunt down Darius and hack him into bite-size pieces. Then I'll feed those pieces to his guard dogs."

"Absolutely. Darius will be dog food. Count me in."

"But before all of that, I'm going to need someone to tell me the truth."

"Who?"

"Someone smart. Someone significantly older and wiser than I am. I'm having a hard time making sense of things these days."

"Meddy, Goatman is dead," Dreadlocks said softly. "Your general is dead, too. And my Rabbi and his wife. Who else is there to learn from? No one. No one cares whether you and I live or die."

"The crones," the Medicine Woman replied. "The crones will have some answers for me. Let's go back to Old Virginia. I need to start there."

"You think they'd give me a bobcat? I'd like a bobcat."

"You'd probably kill it," the Medicine Woman mumbled, turning over to sleep.

From their bed, Dreadlocks peered out the boarding room's window overlooking the main street. As dusk settled in, the major thoroughfares of Thomasville lit up with a few strings of lights.

"Come and see, Medicine Woman!"

"Come and see what?—"

"Come and see!"

The Medicine Woman sat up, leaned in near her friend to look out onto an illuminated street.

"Oh," the Medicine Woman murmured. "It's here."

"What's here?" Dreadlocks asked.

"The beginning." The Medicine Woman grinned. "The beginning of electricity."

"The beginning." the Medicine Woman grinned. "The beginning of electricity."

334

The Medicine Girl Saga
The Medicine Crone

Book Three in the Series

After the Illuminati Pagans wrest control from regional warlords, an era of relative peace and prosperity ensues, allowing both old and new technologies to thrive. However, as greater wealth flows into fewer hands, the nation's citizenry becomes restless, chafing under the regime's arbitrary and capricious brutality.

Now older and a fugitive on the run, the Medicine Crone rejoins Dreadlocks to settle old scores. With daily survival still a Herculean task, the women continue their search for two orphan boys lost into servitude while planning to mete out justice to the two most powerful men in the Pagan Empire.

Ten years have taken their toll on the Medicine Crone, who will have to battle her personal demons before fighting them incarnate. Will she remember her mother's dictate to "alleviate suffering" or be consumed by the darkness that surrounds her?

Scheduled for publication in 2024

Please Check

www.deidrawhittlovegren.com

for updates.